6

"I want you to say it, Isabella."

The devouring note in his voice and the look in his eyes had her heart ramming against her ribs as if unable to bear the confinement.

"I want you to say you've craved reclaiming what we had. That every time you closed your eyes, I was there, in your mind, on your tongue, all over you and inside you, giving you everything only I could ever give you."

Every word he said, soaked in hunger, seething with demand, brought a wave of wet heat surging in her core, her body readying itself for its master doing all the things she'd yearned for, as he'd said, for years, during every moment she had to herself.

Yet she still had to resist. Because what he'd done to her in the past. Ab

is part of T   astle series:
    Only   ats could lead these
         men to the light of true love.

CLAIMING HIS SECRET SON

BY
OLIVIA GATES

MILLS
BOON

Published in Great Britain 2015
by Mills & Boon, an imprint of Harlequin (UK) Limited,
Eton House, 18-24 Paradise Road, Richmond, Surrey, TW9 1SR

© 2015 Olivia Gates

ISBN: 978-0-263-25268-2

51-0715

Harlequin (UK) Limited's policy is to use papers that are natural, renewable and recyclable products and made from wood grown in sustainable forests. The logging and manufacturing processes conform to the legal environmental regulations of the country of origin.

Printed and bound in Spain
by CPI, Barcelona

Olivia Gates has always pursued creative passions such as singing and handicrafts. She still does, but only one of her passions grew gratifying enough, consuming enough, to become an ongoing career—writing.

She is most fulfilled when she is creating worlds and conflicts for her characters, then exploring and untangling them bit by bit, sharing her protagonists' every heart-wrenching heartache and hope, their every heart-pounding doubt and trial, until she leads them to an indisputably earned and gloriously satisfying happy ending.

When she's not writing, she is a doctor, a wife to her own alpha male, and a mother to one brilliant girl and one demanding Angora cat. Visit Olivia at www.oliviagates.com.

To the romance writing community—
editors, authors, reviewers and readers—who
helped me realize not one but two major life goals.
This one is for you. Love you all.

One

Richard Graves adjusted his electric recliner, sipped a mouthful of straight bourbon and hit Pause.

The image on the hundred-plus-inch TV screen stilled, eliminating the unsteadiness of the recording. Murdock, his second-in-command, had taken the footage while following his quarry on foot. The quality was expectedly unsatisfactory, but the frame he'd paused was clear enough to bring a smile to his lips.

The only time a smile touched his lips, or he experienced emotions of any sort, was when he looked at her. At that graceful figure and energetic step, that animated face and streaming raven hair. At least, he guessed they were emotions. He had no frame of reference. Not in the past quarter of a century.

What he remembered feeling in his youth was so distant, it was as if he'd heard about it from someone else. Which was accurate. The boy he'd been before he'd joined The Organization—the criminal cartel that abducted and imprisoned children and turned them into unstoppable mercenaries—though as tough as nails, still held no resemblance to the invulnerable bastard everyone believed him—rightfully so—to be.

From what he remembered before his metamorphosis, and even after it, the most he'd felt had been allegiance, protectiveness, responsibility. For his best-friend-turned-nemesis Numair, for his disciple-turned-ally Rafael and to varying degrees for the Black Castle blokes—his reluctant partners in their globe-spanning business empire, Black Castle Enterprises—and their own. But that was where he drew the line in noble sentiments. What came naturally to him were dark, extreme, vicious ones. Power lust, vengeance, mercilessness.

So it never failed to stun him when beholding her provoked something he'd believed himself incapable of feeling. What he could only diagnose as…tenderness. He'd been feeling it regularly since he'd upgraded his daily ritual of reading surveillance reports on her to watching footage of what Murdock thought were relevant parts of her day.

Anyone, starting with her, would be horrified to learn he'd been keeping her under a microscope for years. And interfering in her life however he saw fit, undetectably changing the dynamics of the world she inhabited. He broke a dozen laws on a daily basis, from breach of privacy to coercion to…far worse, in his ongoing mission of being her guardian demon. Not that this was even a concern. The law existed for him to either break…or wield as a weapon.

But he *was* concerned she'd ever sense his surveillance or suspect his interference. Even if she never suspected it was him behind it all.

After all, she didn't even know he was alive.

As far as she knew he'd been lost since she was six. He doubted she even remembered him. Even if she did, it was best for her to continue thinking him gone, too.

Like the rest of their family.

So he only watched over her. As he had since she was born. At least, he'd tried to. There'd been years when he'd been powerless to protect her. But the moment he could, he'd given her a second chance for a safe and normal existence.

He sighed as he froze another image. He vividly remembered the day his parents had brought her home. Such a tiny, helpless creature. He'd been the one to give her her name. His little Rose.

She wasn't little now and certainly not helpless, but a surgeon, a wife, a mother and a social activist. He might help her here and there, but her achievements had all been ones of merit. He just made sure she got what she worked so hard for and abundantly deserved.

Now she had a successful career, a vocation and a husband who adored her—one he'd thoroughly vetted before letting him near her—and two children. Her family was picture-perfect, and not only on the outside.

Unfreezing the video, he huffed and tossed back the last of the bourbon. If only the Black Castle lads knew that he, aka Cobra, the most lethal operative The Organization had ever known and who was now responsible for their collective security, spent his evenings watching the sister they didn't know existed, who didn't know *he* existed, go about her very normal life. He'd never hear the end of it.

Suddenly he frowned, realizing something.

This footage didn't make sense. Rose was entering her and her husband's new private practice in Lower Manhattan. Murdock always only included new developments, emergencies or anything else that was out of the ordinary.

So watching Rose *was* his only source of enjoyment. But when he'd told Murdock to provide samples of Rose's normal activities, he'd stared emptily at him then continued to provide him only with what he considered worth seeing.

Had Murdock now decided to heed him and start giving him snippets of Rose walking down the street or shopping or picking her children up from school?

He snorted. That Vulcan would never do anything he didn't consider logical or pertinent. Even if he obeyed him blindly otherwise, Murdock wouldn't fulfill a demand he considered to be fueled by pointless sentiment and a waste of both their time.

This meant there was more to what he was watching than Rose entering her workplace.

What was he missing here?

Suddenly his heart seemed to hit Pause itself. Everything inside him followed suit, coming to a juddering standstill.

The person who entered the frame, the one Rose turned to talk to in such delight… Though the image was still from the back with only a hint of a profile apparent, he'd know that shape, that…*being*…blindfolded in a crowd of a million. *Her*.

Sitting up, exercising the same caution he'd approached armed bombs with, he reached to the side table, vaguely noting how the glass rattled as he set it down. It wasn't his hand that shook. It was his heart. The heart that never crossed sixty beats per minute even under extreme duress. It now exploded from its momentary cessation in thunderclaps, sending recoil jolting through every artery and nerve.

The once waist-length, golden hair was now a dark, shoulder-length curtain. The body once rife with dangerous curves was svelte and athletic in a prim skirt suit. But there wasn't the slightest doubt in his mind. That *was* her.

Isabella.

The woman he'd once craved with a force that had threatened the fulfillment of his lifelong obsession.

He'd long resolved it according to his meticulous plan. It was *her* issue that hadn't been concluded satisfactorily. Or at all. She'd been his one feebleness, remained his only failure. The only one who'd made him swerve from his course and at times forget all about it. She remained the only woman he'd been unable—*unwilling* to use. But he'd let her use him. After their incendiary fling, when a choice had had to be made, she'd told him he'd never been an option.

Not that the memory of his one lapse was what had set off this detonation of aggression.

It was who she was. *What* she was.

The wife of the man who'd been responsible for the deaths of his family and for orphaning Rose.

He'd gone after her almost nine years ago as her husband's only Achilles' heel. But nothing had gone according to plan.

Her impact had been unprecedented. And it had had nothing to do with her rare beauty. Beauty never turned a hair on his head. Desire was his weapon, never his weakness. He'd been the one The Organization sent when women were involved, to seduce, use, then discard with utmost coldness.

But she'd been an enigma. At once clearly reveling in being the wife of a brute forty years her senior, who doted on her and submerged her in luxuries, while studying to be a doctor and involving herself in many humanitarian activities.

Going in, he'd been convinced her benevolent facade had been designed to launder her husband's image, in which she'd been succeeding, spectacularly.

But after he'd been exposed to her, this twenty-four-year-old who seemed much older than her years, he'd no longer been sure of anything. Seducing her had also proved much harder than he'd anticipated.

Though he'd been certain she'd reciprocated his unstoppable desire, she wouldn't let him near. Thinking she'd been only whetting his appetite until he was ready to do anything for a taste of her, as her husband had been, he'd intensified his pursuit. But it had only been after he'd followed her on a relief mission in Colombia—saving her and her companions during a guerilla attack—that her resistance had finally crumbled. The following four months had been the most delirious experience of his life.

He'd had to force himself to remember who she was to continue his mission. But it had been the hardest thing he'd ever done. When he'd had her in his arms, when he'd been inside her, he'd forgotten who he was.

But he'd finally extracted secrets only she'd known about her husband without her realizing it. Then he'd been ready to make his move. Not that it had been that easy.

Putting his plan into action had meant the end of his mission. The end of them. And he'd been unable to stomach walking away from her. He'd wanted more of her. Limitlessly more.

So he'd done what he'd never thought he'd do. He'd asked her to leave with him.

Though she'd claimed she couldn't think of life without him, her rejection had been instantaneous. And final. She'd never considered leaving her husband for him.

In his fever for a continuation of the affair, he'd convinced himself she'd refused because she feared her husband. So he'd pledged carte blanche of his protection.

But playing the distraught lover seamlessly, she'd still refused, adamant that there was no other way.

It had been only then that the red heat of coveting had hardened into the cold steel of cynicism. And he'd faced the truth.

She'd preferred her protection and luxury from the less-demanding man she'd married when she'd been twenty and had wrapped around her finger. Him, she'd only replace in her bed. There'd never been any reason she'd choose him over her decades-older ogre.

But he was certain she'd long regretted her choice when he'd shortly afterward destroyed her sugar daddy, protractedly, agonizingly, pulverizing her own life of excess with him.

Not that he'd cared what had happened to her. She'd made her bed of thorns thinking it was the lap of eternal luxury. It was only fitting she'd be torn apart lying in it.

But this searing vision from his past looked patently whole. Even in the video's inferior quality, he could sense her sangfroid. None of the hardships she must have suffered had come close to touching her.

Then it was over. The two women entered the building, and the video came to an abrupt end.

He stared at the black screen, questions an erupting geyser.

What was she doing at Rose's practice? This didn't seem to be a first-time meeting. So how had he missed the earlier ones leading to this level of familiarity? How had she come in touch with Rose at all?

This couldn't be a coincidence.

But what else could it be? There was no way she could know of his connection to Rose. His Richard Graves persona—the one he'd adopted after he'd left his Cobra days behind—had been meticulously manufactured. Not even The Organization with its limitless intelligence resources had found a shred of evidence tying him to their vanished agent.

Even if she'd somehow discovered the relationship between him and Rose, their affair had ended in unequivocal finality. No thanks to his own resolve. While he'd sworn he'd never check on her, he'd weakened on another front. He'd left the door ajar for a year afterward, in case she'd wanted to reestablish contact. Which she hadn't. If she'd wanted to do so now, she would have found a way to bring herself to his attention. It didn't make sense she'd target Rose to get to him. Or did it?

He exploded to his feet, snatched his phone out and punched Murdock's speed-dial number.

The moment the line opened, he barked, "Talk to me."

After a moment Murdock's deep voice was at once composed and surprised. "Sir?"

Impatience almost boiled his blood. "The woman with my sister. What was she doing with her?"

"It's all in the report, sir."

"Bloody hell, Murdock, I'm not reading your thirty-page report."

Silence greeted his snarl this time. Murdock must be stunned, since that was exactly what Richard had been doing for the past year. Murdock's documentation of Rose's every breath had been getting more extensive at his own demand. But right now he couldn't focus on a single paragraph.

"Everything I found out about Dr. Anderson's liaison with the woman in question is in the last two pages, sir."

"Did you sustain a serious head injury lately, Murdock? Am I not talking the Queen's English? I'm not reading two damned words. I want your verbal report. *Now*."

At his barrage the man's chagrin almost crackled down the line, reminding him again that Owen Murdock was a relic of a bygone era.

Richard had always thought he'd be more at home in something like King Arthur's round table. He did treat Richard with the fervor of a knight in the service of his liege.

He'd been the first boy Richard had been given to train when he'd first joined The Organization as a handler...six years old to his own sixteen, making Murdock Rafael's age. He'd had him for six more years before Murdock had been taken from him and Rafael given to him instead.

Murdock had refused to accept anyone else's leadership, until Richard had been summoned to straighten him out. Richard had only told him to play along, that one day he'd get him out. Murdock had unquestioningly obeyed him. And believed him.

Richard had fulfilled his pledge, taking him away with him when he'd left, manufacturing a new identity for him, too. But instead of striking out on his own, Murdock had insisted on remaining in his service, claiming his training hadn't been complete. He'd actually been on par with the rest of the Black Castle chaps from day one, could have become a mogul in his own right, too. But Murdock had only wished to repay what he considered his debt to Richard before he could move on. Knowing how vital that had been to him, Richard had let him.

Now, ten years later, Murdock showed no signs of moving on. He'd have to shove him off the ledge soon, no matter if it would be like losing his right arm for real.

Murdock's current silence made Richard regret his outburst more. His number two prided himself on always anticipating his needs and surpassing his expectations. The last thing he wanted was to abuse such loyalty.

Before he made a retraction, Murdock talked, his tone betraying no resentment or mortification.

"Very well. At first, that woman appeared to be just another colleague of Dr. Anderson's. I ran a check on her, as I always do, and found nothing of note. But a development made me dig deeper. I discovered she'd changed her name legally five years ago, just before she made her first entry into the United States after a six-year hiatus. Her name was…"

"Isabella Burton."

Murdock digested the fact that Richard already knew her. He'd told neither him nor Rafael about the intensely personal mission he'd undertaken, or about her.

Murdock continued, "She's now Dr. Isabella Sandoval."

Sandoval. That wasn't either of her maiden names. Coming from Colombia, she'd had two. She must have been trying to become someone else when she'd adopted the new surname, after what had happened to her husband. That would also explain the changes in her appearance. And she *was* a doctor now.

Murdock went on, "But that wasn't what made me wary—what made me single out her meeting with Dr. Anderson to present to you. It's because I found a gaping thirteen-year hole in her history. From the age of twelve to the age of twenty-five, I couldn't find a shred of information on her."

Of course. She'd wiped clean the time she'd been Burton's wife, and for some reason only known to her, years before that. No doubt to hide more incriminating evidence that would prevent her from being accepted by any respect-ful society.

"The information trail starts when she was twenty-six, when she started a four-year surgical residency in Colombia, in affiliation with a pediatric surgery program in Califor-nia. It was a special 'out of the match' residency arrange-ment with the chief of surgery of a major teaching hospital. She obtained her US credentials and board certification last year. Then a week ago, she arrived in the United States and signed a one-year lease on a six-bedroom house in the For-est Hills Gardens section of Queens. She is here at the be-hest of doctors Rose and Jeffrey Anderson to start working in their private practice as a full partner, major shareholder and board member."

After that, Richard didn't know when he ended the call.

He only knew he was replaying that video over and over, Murdock's words a revolving loop in his mind.

Isabella. She was going to be his sister's partner.

Swearing under his breath, he almost cracked the remote in two as he pressed the off button.

Like hell she was.

Four hours later Richard felt as if the driver's seat of his Rolls Royce Phantom was sprouting red-hot needles.

It had been more than two hours since he'd parked across the street from his sister's house. He'd driven here immedi-ately when Murdock had called back saying he'd neglected to tell him Isabella was having dinner there tonight. She had yet to make an exit.

What was taking the bloody woman that long? What kind of dinner lasted more than four hours?

This alone told him things were worse than he'd first thought. Isabella seemed to be a close friend of his sister's, not just a prospective partner. And though Murdock hadn't been able to pinpoint the events leading to this bizarre status quo, Richard was certain this wasn't an innocent friendship.

Not on Isabella's side. She always had an angle. And obtained her objectives through deception and manipulation. Her medical qualifications themselves had probably been obtained through some meticulously constructed fraud.

Yet that was all conjecture. He had nothing solid to explain how Rose and her husband had developed such a deep connection with her that they'd invite her to be their equal partner in their life's crowning achievement. She'd made herself so invisible, her past so untraceable she'd fallen off Murdock's radar until now, when she was about to be fully lodged into their lives.

He'd torn over here once Murdock had informed him they'd finished dinner and coffee, expecting to intercept her soon afterward as she left. That had been—he flicked a glance at his watch—two and a half bloody hours ago.

Every minute of those he'd struggled with the urge to storm inside and drag her out.

He hadn't stayed out of his sister's life only to let that siren infect it with the ugliness of her past, the malice of her intentions and the exploitation in her blood.

Suddenly the front door of Rose's two-level, stucco house opened and two figures walked out. Isabella first, then Rose. His every muscle tensing, he strained to decipher the merriness that carried on the summer night air through his open window. Then they kissed and hugged and Isabella descended the stairs. At the bottom she turned to wave to Rose, urging her to go in, before she turned and crossed the street, heading to her car.

The moment Rose closed her door he got down from his car.

In the dim streetlights, Isabella's figure seemed to glow in a light-colored summer coat unbuttoned over a lighter dress beneath, its supple material undulating with her brisk walk. Her hair was a swathe of dark silk swinging over her face, her eyes downcast as she rummaged through her purse.

Then feet before he intercepted her, he stopped.

"Well, well, if it isn't Isabella Burton."

Her momentum came to a startled halt, her alarm a sharp gasp that echoed in the night's still, humid silence. Then her face jerked up and her eyes slammed into his.

A bolt struck him through the heart.

His sudden appearance seemed to have hit her even harder. If a ghost had stopped her to ask her the time, she wouldn't have looked more shocked...or horrified.

"What...where the hell did you...?"

She stopped. As if she found no words. Or breath with which to say them. He was almost as shocked as she was... at his reaction. He'd thought he'd feel nothing at the sight of her. He didn't know what he did feel now. But it was... enormous.

And it wasn't an overwhelming sense of familiarity. It was her impact as she was now.

She'd changed. Almost beyond recognition. It made it that much stranger he'd recognized her in that video so instantaneously. For this woman had very little in common with the younger one he'd known in total, tempestuous intimacy.

Her face had lost all the plumpness of youth, had been chiseled into a masterpiece of refinement and uncompromising character. If she'd been irresistible before, even with shock still seizing her every feature, the influence she'd exuded had matured into something far more formidable.

But her eyes had changed the most. Those eyes that had haunted him, eyes he'd once thought had opened up into a magical realm, that of her being. They *looked* the same, glowing that unique emerald-topaz chameleon color. But apart from the familiar shape and hue, and beneath the shock, they were bottomless. Whatever lay inside her now was dark and fathomless. And far more hard-hitting for it.

Her lids swept down, severing the two-way hypnosis. Gritting his teeth at losing the contact, his own gaze lowered to sweep her body. Even through the loose clothes, it still had his every sense revving. Just being near her had always made him ache.

Then a puff of breeze had her scent inundating him and his body flooded with molten steel. That was the one thing about her that hadn't changed. This distillation of her essence and femininity that had constantly hovered at the edge of his memory, tormenting him with craving the real thing.

And here it was at last. What he'd once thought an aphrodisiac nature had tailored to his senses. That belief was renewed in full force.

Hard all over, he returned his gaze to hers, eager to read her own response. She poured every bit of height and poise into her statuesque figure, made him feel she was looking him in at eye level when even in three-inch heels, she stood seven inches below his six-foot-six frame.

"Richard." She gave a formal nod as if greeting a virtual stranger. Then she just circumvented him and continued walking to her car.

He let her pass him, one eyebrow rising.

So. His opening strike hadn't been as effective as he'd planned. She'd gotten over her shock at seeing him faster than he had and had decided to dismiss him.

Surely she considered anyone who knew her real identity a threat to her carefully constructed new persona. But if there were levels of danger to blasts from the past, she must think his potential damage equivalent to a ballistic missile. She couldn't end this "chance" meeting fast enough.

Which proved she hadn't tied him to Rose, wasn't here because of anything concerning him. But that changed nothing.

Whatever she was here for, she wasn't getting it.

He stared ahead, listening to the steady staccato of her receding heels, a grim smile twisting his lips.

In the past he'd been the one who'd walked away. But it had been her who'd made the decision. It now entertained him to let her think the choice remained hers. He'd let her strike his presence up to coincidence, think it would cause no repercussions for her. Then he'd disabuse her of the notion.

Last time, he hadn't been able to override her will. This time, he'd make her do what he wanted. And right now, all he wanted was to taste her once more. He'd postpone his real purpose until he satisfied the hunger that had roared to life inside him again at the sight of her.

He'd much prefer it if she struggled, though.

The moment he heard her opening her car, he turned and sauntered toward her.

She lurched as he passed behind her and murmured, "I'll drive ahead. Follow me."

He felt her gaze boring into his back as he reached his car two spaces ahead. Opening his door, he turned around smoothly, just in time to witness her reaction.

"What the hell...?" She stopped, as if it hurt to talk.

He sighed. "My patience has already been expended for the night. Follow me. Now."

Her eyes blazed at him as she found her voice again. Not the velvety caress that had echoed in his head for eight endless years but a sharp blade. "I'll do no such thing."

"My demand was actually a courtesy. I was trying to give you a chance to preserve your dignity."

Her mouth dropped open. His own lips tingled.

Then his tongue stung when hers lashed him. "Gee, thanks. I can preserve it very well on my own. I'll drive away now, and if you follow me, I'll call the police."

Hostility was the last thing he'd predicted her reaction would be, considering the last time he'd seen her she'd wept as he'd walked away as if her heart were being dragged out of her body. But it only made his blood hurtle with vicious exhilaration. She was giving him the struggle he'd hoped for, the opportunity to force her to succumb to him this time. And he would make her satisfy his every whim.

He gave her the patented smile that made monsters quiver. "If you drive away, I won't follow you. I'll knock on your friends' door and tell them whom they're really getting into business with. I don't think the Andersons would relish knowing you were—and maybe still are—the wife of a drug lord, slave trader and international terrorist."

Two

Isabella stared up at the juggernaut that blocked out the world, every synapse in her brain short-circuiting.

When he'd materialized in front of her, like a huge chunk of night taking the form of her most hated entity, her heart had almost ruptured.

But she'd survived so many horrors, had always had so much to protect, her survival mechanisms were perpetually on red alert. After the initial brutal blow, they'd kicked in as she'd made an instinctive escape. That didn't mean she hadn't felt about to crumple to the ground with every breath.

Richard. Here. Out of the depths of the dark, sordid past. The man who'd seduced and used…and almost destroyed her.

That he hadn't succeeded hadn't been because he hadn't given it his best shot. Ever since, she'd been trying to mend the rifts he'd created in the very foundations of her being. She'd only succeeded in painting over the deepest ones. Though she now seemed whole and strong, those cracks had been worsening over time, and she was sure they'd fissured right to her soul.

But she'd just reached what would truly be a new start. Then he'd appeared out of thin air.

It had flabbergasted her even more because she'd just been thinking of him. It had been as if she'd conjured him.

Yet when had she ever stopped thinking of him? Her memory of him had been like a pervasive background noise

that could never be silenced. A clamor that rose to a crescendo periodically before it settled back to a constant, maddening drone.

But there was one explanation for his reappearance. That
it was a fluke. An appalling one, but one nonetheless. What
else could it have been after eight years?

Not that time elapsed was even an issue. It could have
been eight days and she would have thought the same thing.
She'd long realized he'd left her believing he'd never see
her again.

After all, he must have known what he'd done would
most probably get her killed.

Believing their meeting to be a coincidence, she'd run
off, thinking the man who'd once exploited her then left
her to a terrible fate would shrug and continue on his way.

But just as she'd thought she'd escaped, that he'd fade
into the night like some dreadful apparition, he'd followed
her. Before she could deal with the dismay of thinking this
ordeal would be prolonged, he'd made his preposterous demand.

Not that it had felt like one. It had felt like an ultimatum.
Her instinct had been correct.

She hadn't forgiven him, nor would she ever forgive him,
but she'd long rationalized his actions. From what she'd
discovered—long after the fact—he obtained his objectives
over anyone's dead body, figuratively or literally. She, and
everything he'd done to her, had been part of a mission.
She only had theories what that had been or why he'd undertaken it, according to the end result.

But what he was doing now, threatening with such patent
enjoyment what he must know would destroy everything
she'd struggled to build over the past eight years, was for
his own entertainment. That man she'd once loved, with
everything in her scarred psyche and starving soul, had
progressed from a cold-bloodedly pragmatic bastard into
a full-fledged monster.

"Don't look so horrified."

His bottomless baritone swamped her again, another thing about him that had become more hard-hitting. The years had turned the thirty-four-year-old demigod of sensuality she'd known into an outright god, if one of malice. He still exuded sex and exerted a compulsion—both now magnified by increased power and maturity. But it was this new malevolence that now seemed to define him. And it made him more overwhelming than ever.

But that must have been his true nature all along. It was she who'd been blinded and under his control. She hadn't even suspected what he'd been capable of long after he'd gotten everything he'd wanted from her, then tossed her to the wolf.

"I'm not interested in exposing you." His voice had her every hair standing on end. "As long as you comply, your secret can remain intact."

Summoning the opaqueness she'd developed as her greatest weapon against bullies such as him, she cocked her head.

"What makes you think I haven't told them everything?"

"I don't think. I know. You resorted to extreme measures to construct this St. Sandoval image. You'd go as far to preserve it. You'll certainly give in to anything I demand so no one, starting with the Andersons, ever finds out what you really are."

"*What* I am? You make it sound as if I'm some monster."

"You're married to one. It makes you the same species."

"I'm not married to Caleb Burton. I haven't been for eight years."

Something…scary slithered in the depths of his cold steel eyes. But when he spoke, he sounded as offhand as before.

"So it's in the past tense. A past full of crimes."

"I never had a criminal record."

"Your crimes remain the same even if you're not caught."

"What about your crimes? Let's talk about those."

"Let's not. It would take months to talk about those, as

they're countless. But they're also untraceable. But yours could be easily proved. You knew exactly how your husband made his mushrooming fortune and you made no effort to expose him, making you an accessory to his every crime. Not to mention that you helped yourself to millions of his blood money. Those two charges could still get you ten to fifteen years in a snug little cell in a maximum-security prison."

"Are you threatening to turn me in to the law, too?"

"Don't be daft. I don't resort to such mundane measures. I don't let the law take care of my enemies or chastise those who don't fall in line with my wishes. I have my own methods. Not that I have to resort to those in your case. Just a little chat with your upstanding friends and they wouldn't consider getting mixed up with someone with your past."

"Contrary to what you believe, from your own twisted self and life, there are ethical, benevolent people in the world. The Andersons don't hold people's pasts against them."

He gave her back her pitying disdain, raised her his own brand of annihilating taunting. "If you believed that, you wouldn't have gone to such painstaking lengths to give your history, and yourself, a total makeover."

"The makeover was only for protection, as I'm sure you, as the world's foremost mogul of security solutions, are in the best position to appreciate."

His lethal lips tugged. "Then, it won't matter if your partners in progress find out the details of your previous marriage to one of the world's most prominent figures in organized crime. Along with the open buffet of unlawful immorality that marriage entailed and that you buried. Refuse to follow me and we get to put your conviction of *their* convictions to the test."

Feeling the world emptying of the last atom of oxygen, she snapped, "What the hell do you want from me?"

"To catch up."

Her mouth dropped open.

It took effort to draw it back up, to hiss her disbelief. "So you see me walking down the street and decide on the spot to blackmail me because the urge to 'catch up' over-whelmed you?"

His painstakingly chiseled lips twisted, making her guts follow suit. "Don't tell me you thought it even a possibility I happened to be taking a stroll in a limbo of suburban do-mesticity called Pleasantville, of all names?"

"You were following me."

The instant certainty congealed her blood. Realizing his premeditation made it all so much worse. And the possible outcomes unthinkable.

He shrugged. "You took your time in there. I was about to knock on the Andersons' door anyway to see what was taking you so long."

Not putting anything beyond him, she imagined how much worse it would have been if he'd done that. "And you went to all this trouble to 'catch up'?"

"Yes. Among other things."

"What other things?"

"Things you'll find out when you stop wasting time and follow me. I'd tell you to leave your car, but your friend might see it and get all sorts of worrisome ideas."

"None would be as bad as what's really happening."

His expression hardened. She was sure it had brought powerful men to their knees. "Are you afraid of me?"

That possibility clearly hadn't occurred to him before. Now that it did, it seemed to...offend him.

The weirdest part was, though she'd long known he was a merciless terminator, her actual safety wasn't even a con-cern.

It was in every other way that she feared him.

She wasn't about to tell him that. But she did give him an honest answer to his query. "I'm not."

"Good."

His satisfaction chafed her. The urge to wipe it off his cruelly perfect face surged. "I'm not, because I know if you wanted to harm me, I wouldn't have known what hit me. That you're only coercing me indicates I'm not on your hit list."

"It is heartening that you grasp the situation." That soul-searing smile played on his lips again. "Shall we?"

She stood there, her gaze trapped in his, her thoughts tangling.

They both knew he'd cornered her from the first moment. But succumbing to this devil without resistance would have been too pathetic. She'd at least let loose some of her anger and bitterness toward him first. What she'd thought long extinguished.

It was clear they'd only been suppressed under layers of self-delusion so they wouldn't destroy whatever remained of her stability, what everything—and everyone—in her life depended on.

Now that she'd admitted that, it was easier to admit why she'd succumb to his coercion.

The first reason was that she would have, even without his threat. If he'd turned a consummate fiend like Burton into mincemeat so effortlessly when he'd been a younger and less powerful man, she didn't want to know what he was capable of now. She was nowhere in his league. No one was.

The second was harder to face. But what she'd belatedly learned about his truth and that of what they'd shared and what he'd done to her *had* left a gaping hole inside her.

She wanted that hole filled. She wanted closure.

Holding his hypnotic gaze, she finally nodded.

He just turned and walked away. Before he lowered himself into the gleaming black beast that looked as sleek, powerful and ruthless as he did, he tossed her an imperious glance over his acres-wide shoulders.

"Chivvy along."

At his command to hurry up in his native British English, she expelled the breath she'd been holding.

Chivvy along, indeed.

Might as well get this over with as quickly as possible.

In minutes she was following him as ordered as he headed to Manhattan, emotions seething inside her. Fury, frustration, fear—and something else.

That "something else" felt like…excitement.

How sick would that be? To be excited by the man who'd decimated her heart and almost her world, who'd just threatened to complete the job and had her following him like a puppy?

But…maybe not so sick. Excitement could encompass trepidation, anxiety, uncertainty. And everything with Richard had always contained maximum doses of all that. It was why he'd been the only one who'd made her feel…alive. She'd been in suspended animation before she'd met him and since he'd walked away.

For better, or in his case, for worse, it seemed he'd remain the only one who could reanimate her.

"Get it over with. Catch up."

Isabella threw her purse on the black-and-bronze Roberto Cavalli leather couch and looked at Richard across his gigantic, forty-foot-ceilinged, marble-floored reception area.

He only continued preparing their drinks at the bar, his lupine expression deepening.

So. He'd talk when he wished. And he hadn't wished. Yet. Got it.

Good thing she'd called home during the forty-minute drive to say she'd be *very* late.

Pretending to shrug away his disregard, she looked around. And was stunned all over again.

The Fifth Avenue penthouse overlooking the now shrouded in darkness Central Park and Manhattan's glittering Upper East Side drove home to her how staggeringly wealthy he was now. The opulent, technologically futuristic duplex on the sixty-seventh and sixty-eighth floors had to have cost tens of millions.

Among the jaw-dropping features of the fully automatic smart-home was its own elevator, its remote-, voice- and retinal-recognition doors and just about everything else.

It even housed a thirty-by-fifty-foot pool.

As they'd passed the sparkling expanse, he'd told her something she hadn't known about him. That he hated the sun and preferred indoor sports. She'd already worked out that he hated people, too. A pool in his living room at the top of the world away from the nuisance of mere mortals was a no-brainer to someone with his kind of money.

He'd been saying he'd expand the pool to get a decent exercise without having to flip over and over when she'd stopped listening. The image of him shooting through the liquid turquoise like a human torpedo, then rising from the water like an aquatic deity with rivulets weeping down his masterpiece body had tampered with her mental faculties.

Snatching her thoughts away before they slid back into *that* abyss, she examined the L-shaped terrace of at least five-thousand square feet. The city views must be breathtaking from there. They were from every corner in this marvel of a home.

Though *home* sounded so wrong. Anywhere he was could never be a home. This place felt like an ultramodern demon's den.

Avoiding looking at him, she noted the designer furniture and architectural touches that punctuated each zone, couldn't guess at many of the functional features. But it was spectacular how the mezzanine level took advantage of the massive ceiling heights and ingeniously provided extensive library shelves. He'd probably read every book. And archived its contents in that labyrinthine mind of his.

But what made the mezzanine truly unique was its glass floors and balustrade, with the staircase continuing the transparent theme. Looking down wouldn't be for the fainthearted.

But Richard didn't have to worry about that, since he was heartless. A fact this astounding but soulless place clearly underlined.

That he had other residences on the West Coast and in England, as he'd offhandedly informed her as they'd entered this place, no doubt on the same level of luxury and technology, was even more mind-boggling. Burton had been a billionaire and it had been hard to grasp the power such wealth brought. But those had been a fraction of Richard's, who was currently counted among the top one hundred richest men on the planet. The security business was booming, and his empire reigned over that domain.

But money, in his case, was the result of the immense influence of his personality and expertise, not the other way around. And then there were his connections. Black Castle Enterprises, which he'd built from the ground up with six other partners, had a major hand in everything that made the world go round and was one of the most influential businesses in history.

"I just learned of your presence in the country today."

His comment dragged her out of her musings, his deepened voice making the cultured precision of his British accent even more shiver worthy. She'd always thought that killer brogue of his the most evocative music. She used to ask him to speak just so she could revel in listening to him enunciate. It had always aroused the hell out of her, too.

But everything about him always had. During the four months of their affair she'd been in a perpetual fugue of arousal.

She watched him approach like a leisurely tiger stalking his kill, every muscle and sinew flexing and pulling at his fitted black shirt and pants, his stormy sky-hued eyes striking her with a million volts of charisma. The familiar ache she hadn't felt since she'd last seen him, that had been trembling under the suppression of shock, hostility and anxiety since he'd appeared before her, stirred in her deepest recesses.

Time had been criminally indulgent with him, enhancing his every asset—widening his shoulders, hardening his waist and hips, bulking up his torso and thighs. Age had taken a sharper chisel to his face, hewing it to dizzying planes and angles, turning his skin a darker copper, intensifying the luminescence of his eyes. His luxurious raven hair had been brushed with silver at the temples, adding the last touch of allure. He was now the full potential of premium manhood realized.

As he reached for the cocktail glass, his fingertips grazed hers, zapping her with a bolt of exquisite electricity.

Great. His deceit and her ignorance of his true nature and intentions had had nothing to do with his effect on her as she'd long told herself. He'd almost cost her her life, and she knew what he truly was and how she'd been a chess piece he'd played and disposed of…yet it made no difference to her body. It didn't deal in logic, cared nothing about dignity and hadn't learned a thing from the harsh lessons of experience. It only saw and sensed the man who'd once possessed and pleasured it almost beyond endurance.

She sat before he realized he still liquefied her knees… and everything else. When she'd thought she'd irreversibly turned to stone.

But she'd thought that before she'd first met him. It had taken him one glance to get the heart she'd believed long petrified quivering. He remained the one man who could reverse any protective metamorphosis.

Safe on a horizontal surface, she looked way, way up at him as he loomed over her like a mystic knight, or rather a malevolent wizard, from an Arthurian fairy tale.

"So the moment you realized I was on American soil, you decided to track me down and ambush me."

"Precisely."

In a heartbeat he was beside her. She marveled again at the strength and control needed for someone of his height and bulk to move so effortlessly. Even though he didn't come too near, her every nerve fired.

Sipping the amber liquid in his crystal glass, he turned to face her fully. "I've been remembering how we met."

She sipped her drink only to suppress the impulse to hurl it in his face. The moment it slid down her throat she realized how parched she was. And how it hit the spot. Perfect coolness and flavor, light on alcohol, heavy on sweetness.

He remembered. How she took her drinks.

Something suffocating, something similar to regret, swept her.

Suddenly the bitterness that had lain dormant in her depths seethed to the surface again. "We didn't meet, Richard. You tracked me down then, too. And set me up."

Nonchalance tugged a corner of his lips. "True."

She took another sip, channeling her anger into sarcasm. "Thanks for sparing me the aggravation of denial."

His gaze lengthened, becoming more unreadable and disturbing. Then he shrugged. "I don't waste time on pointless pursuits. I already realized you know everything. From the first moment, your hostile attitude made it clear I'm not talking to the woman who cried rivers at my departure."

"Why conclude that was because I *know everything*? That could have been classic feminine bitterness for said departure. Surely you didn't expect even the stupid goose I used to be to throw herself in your arms after eight years?"

"Time is irrelevant." Just what she'd been thinking. "It's what you realized that caused you to change. You clearly worked everything out." His gaze intensified, making her feel he was probing her to her cellular level. "So how did you?"

"You know how."

"I probably do. But I'd still like to know the actual details of how you came to realize the truth."

A mirthless laugh escaped her. "If you're asking so you never repeat whatever clued me in, don't bother. Working it all out wasn't due to any discernment on my side, and I only did over three years after the fact." One formidable eyebrow rose at that particular detail. "Yeah, pathetic, right?"

"Not the adjective I'd use." She waited for him to substitute his own evaluation, but he left her hanging. "I don't want details as a prophylactic measure for future operations. I know I am untraceable. Your deductions couldn't have been backed up by any evidence. Even if they were, I made sure your best interest remained in burying any."

"So you're asking only to marvel at how good you are?"

"I know exactly how good I am." The way he said that… The ache deep inside started to throb. "I don't need validations nor do I indulge in self-congratulations." Eyes narrowing, his focus sliced through her. "Why the reluctance to tell me? We're laying our cards down now that the game is long over."

"You laid down nothing."

"I'll lay down whatever you wish." When she opened her mouth to demand he start, he preempted her. "You first."

Knowing she'd end up giving him what he wanted, she sighed. "When the blows to Burton started coming out of the blue, I just thought he'd slipped in his secrecy measures. One day, when he was finally on his knees, he asserted that the breach hadn't come from his side, that I was the only one who knew everything he did. I thought he was just looking for someone to blame, but that didn't change a thing. I believed he'd soon make up his mind that I betrayed him. So I ran."

Draining his glass, he grimaced, set it down on the coffee table. Then he sat back, his eyes so intense it felt as if he was physically attempting to yank the rest out of her.

Torrents of accusations almost spilled from her. Forcing them down, she skipped over the two worst years of a generally hellish existence, and went on, "I only revisited his accusations *much* later, started to wonder if I'd been some-how indiscreet. That pointed me in the direction of the only one I could have been indiscreet with. You. That led to a reexamination of our time together, and to realizing your ingeniousness in milking me for information."

"And you realized it was I who sent him to hell."

She nodded, mute with the remembered agony of that awareness. She'd felt such utter betrayal, such total loss. Her will to go on, for a while, had been completely spent.

"It dawned on me that you had targeted me only to get my insider info and asked me to leave with you to agonize and humiliate him on every front. Everything made so much sense then I couldn't believe I didn't suspect you for years. Who else but you could have devised such a spectacular downfall for him? It takes a monster to bring down another."

His watchfulness lifted, fiendishness replacing it. "*Monster* wasn't what you screamed all those times in my bed."

"Don't be redundant. I already admitted I was too oblivi-ous to live. But once the fog of my obliviousness cleared, I only wished I could forget ever meeting you."

"Don't hold your breath. Even if our meeting wasn't spontaneous, it wasn't only memorable, it remains indel-ible."

The fateful encounter that had turned her life upside down had been that way for him, too?

His cover story had been arranging security for the hu-manitarian organization she'd been working with. He'd de-manded to meet all volunteers for a dangerous mission in Colombia to judge who should go.

Her first glimpse of him remained branded in her mind.

Nothing and no one had ever overwhelmed her as he had. And not because he'd been the most gorgeous male she'd ever seen. His influence far transcended that. His scrutiny had been denuding, his questions deconstructing. He'd rocked her to her core, making her feel like a swooning moron as she'd sluggishly answered his rapid-fire questions.

After telling her she'd passed his test, she'd exited his office reeling. She hadn't known it possible for a human being to be so beautiful, so overpowering. She hadn't known a man could have her hot and wet just by looking at her across a desk. She hadn't been interested in a man before, so the intensity of her desire for him, for his approval, and her delight at earning it had flung her in chaos. She'd never known such excitement, such joy...

"The changes become you."

She blinked, realized she'd been staring at him all the time. As he'd been staring at her.

"The sculpting of your body and features...the darkening of your hair. An effective disguise, but also an enhancement."

"I wanted to look different for security reasons, but ended up not needing to do anything. Time and what it brought did it all."

"You talk as if you're over the hill."

"I feel it. And that's my real hair color. No longer bleaching my hair was the second best thing I ever did, after getting rid of Burton himself, who insisted I looked better as a blonde."

His lips compressed. "Burton wasn't only a depraved wanker, but a gaudy maggot, too. The feast of caramels and chocolates of your hair pays tribute to your creamy complexion and jeweled eyes far better than any blond shade would, framing them to the best effect possible."

She blinked again. Richard Graves paying her a compliment? And such a flowery one, too?

And he wasn't finished. "Before I approached you, I had photos, knew of your unusual beauty. But when I saw you in the flesh, the total effect punched me in the gut and not just on account of your looks. Time had only scraped away whatever prettiness youth inflicted and brought you profound beauty in its place. I believe it will only keep bestowing more on you. You were stunning, but you've become exquisite. With age, you'll become divine."

She gaped at him. Once, when she'd believed him to be a human being, not a machine that made money and devised plans of annihilation, she'd believed him when he'd praised her beauty. But even then, when he'd been doing everything to keep her under his spell, he'd never done it with such fervor and poetry. That he did so now…offended her beyond words.

Fury tumbled in her blood. "Spare me the nausea. We both know what you really think of me. Is this one of the 'other things' you had in mind? To ply me with preposterous flattery and have some more sick fun at my expense?"

"I was actually trying my hand at sincerity." He turned fully to her. "As for the 'other things' I had in mind, it's… *this*."

And she found herself flat on her back with Richard on top of her, his chest crushing her breasts, his hips between her splayed thighs.

Before her heart could fire the next fractured beat, he rose over her and stopped it.

This was how a devil must look before he took one's soul. Inescapable. Ravenous. Dreadfully beautiful.

"Eight years, Isabella. Eight years without this. Now I'll have it all again. I'll consume every last inch and drop of you. That's why I brought you here. And that's why you really came."

Three

Time congealed as she lay beneath Richard, paralyzed. Even her heart seemed afraid it would rupture if it beat.

Then everything that had been gathering inside her since he'd walked away—all the betrayal and despondence and yearning—broke through the cracks and she started to tremble.

A shudder traversed his great body as if her tremors had electrified him, making him crush her harder beneath him, crash his lips on her wide-open ones.

His tongue thrust deeply and his scent and taste flooded her bloodstream, a hit of a drug she'd gone mad for since she'd been forced to give it up cold turkey. Gulping it down, she rode rapids of mindlessness as he filled her, drank her the way she remembered and craved. Richard didn't kiss. He invaded, ravaged.

He didn't only catapult her into a frenzy, but sent her spiraling into a reenactment of that first kiss that had launched her addiction.

That day he'd materialized like an answer to a prayer, cutting down the guerillas who'd been threatening her team with death…or worse. She'd been so shaken thinking she could have died without having the one thing she'd ever wanted—him—had been so grateful, so awed, she'd gone to offer him what he'd seemed to want so relentlessly. Herself.

He'd let her into his room, his gaze consuming her, letting her see what he'd do to her once she gave him consent.

And she had, melting against him, giving him permission to do anything and everything to her.

He'd taken her mouth for the first time then, with that same thorough devouring, that coiled ferocity. From that moment on her body had learned what heart-stopping pleasure his kiss would lead to, had afterward burst into flames at his merest touch, the fire raging higher with each exposure.

The conflagration was fiercer now, with the fuel of anger and animosity, with the accumulation of pain and craving and repression. This was wrong, insane. And it only made her want it—want *him*—more than her next breath.

His roughness as he teased her turgid nipples, his dominance as he ground against her molten core, made her spread her thighs wider, strain to enfold him, her moans rising, blind arousal fracturing the shackles of hostility and memory, drowning them and her.

Suddenly he severed their meld, wrenching a cry of loss from her as he rose above her.

His gaze scalded her, his lips filled with grim sensuality. "I should have listened to my body—and yours—and done this the moment I got you in here."

His arrogance should have made her buck him off. But lust for this memorized yet unknown entity, so deadly and irresistible, seethed its demand for satisfaction.

"Say this is what you wanted all along. *Say* it, Isabella."

A hard thrust and squeeze of her buttocks accompanied his brusque order, melting her further. But it was the harshness on his face that jogged her heart out of its sluggish surrender.

The world spun with too many emotions, after years of stasis. Years when she'd felt him this way only in dreams that had always turned into nightmares. In those visions, he'd always aroused her to desperation before pushing her away and taking off his mask. The merciless face he'd exposed before walking over her sobbing body had always woken her in tears then plunged her into deeper despondence.

Dreading those nightmares had robbed her of the ability to rest. It was the memory of them now that made her struggle to stop her plummet into the abyss of addiction all over again.

"What if I don't say it?" Her voice shook.

At her challenge, his gaze emptied of intensity. He released her trembling flesh and in one of those impossible moves, he separated their bodies and was on his feet.

To her shame, she'd thought his response to her challenge would be to take his onslaught to the next level. She still expected he'd pick her up and carry her off to bed.

He only sat on the coffee table, clearly deciding to end their encounter. The letdown deepened her paralysis.

His brooding gaze made her acutely aware of how pathetic she looked prostrated as she was, sending chagrin surging through her numb limbs. Feeling she'd turned to jelly, she pulled herself up and her dress down.

Once she'd tidied the dishevelment he'd caused, he drawled, "Now that there's no hint of physical coercion... *say* it."

Her heart skidded at his deceptively calm command. "You mean there's no coercion because you're not on top of me anymore? I'm here *purely* by coercion."

"I submit, this is false. I only gave you an excuse to have your cake and eat it, too, a justification you can placate your dignity with. But it's easy to invalidate your self-exonerating assertion. I'll escort you to the door, activate it for you and you can walk right out."

"And then you'll call my friends."

"There *are* things you could do that would make me do that. None of them include choosing to walk out now." He rose to his feet. "Shall we?"

She scrambled to her feet only when she found him striding away for real and had to almost run in his wake.

"That's it? You go to all this trouble to get me here, interrogate me for a bit, then abruptly shift to what seems to be your real objective, and when I refuse to 'say it' you show me the door?"

"I have to. It won't open unless I tell it to."

His derision, and the fact that he'd shrugged off what had happened when it had turned her inside out had her fury sizzling.

Catching up with his endless strides beside the pool, she snatched at his arm. Her fingers only slipped off his rock-hard muscles. It was he who stopped of his own accord, daring to look as if he had no idea what was eating her, but was resigned to putting up with an inexplicably hysterical female.

"Why do you want me to say it?" she seethed. "Is your ego that distorted? You want me to admit how much I want you when you never wanted me in the first place?"

His winged eyebrow arched more. "I didn't?"

"If we're both certain of one thing, it's that."

"And you've come to that conclusion, how?"

"Like I did all the rest. Seduction is no doubt your weapon of choice with women, and pretending to desire me was only to turn me into your willing thrall. The info I had was my only real use to you."

He inclined his head as if examining a creature he'd never known existed. "You think I spent four months in bed with you and didn't desire you?"

"You're a man, and an overendowed one. I bet you could…perform with any reasonably attractive female, especially one in heat."

"That you were." His reminiscent look made her want to smack him across that smug mouth. "I never thought a woman could always be that hot and ready for me." Before she lashed out, he sighed. "I *would* have seduced you even if you'd been a slime-oozing monstrosity. Stomaching a mark was never a prerequisite in my search-and-seduce missions. But even based on my indiscriminate libido, as you presume, I would have still suffered the minimum of physical contact to keep you on the hook. I wouldn't have gone to lengths you can't imagine to create a rendezvous almost daily, and then to have sex with you as many times as could be squeezed into each encounter. Even with my 'endowments' I couldn't have *performed* that repeatedly or that…vigorously if I wasn't even hotter and readier for you than you were for me. And I was. None of that was an act."

Her heart stuttered as she met the gaze that suddenly felt as if it held no barriers. As if he was telling the truth, probably for the first time.

He'd really wanted her?

But… "If you wanted me as much as you claim, and still used and discarded me like any other woman you didn't want, that makes you an even colder bastard."

His gaze grew inscrutable again. "I didn't discard you. You chose Burton."

"Is that what you call what I did? I had no choice."

"You always have a choice."

"Spare me the human-development slogans."

"A choice doesn't have to be an easy one, but it remains one. Every choice has pros and cons. Once you make one, you put up with its consequences. You don't blame others for those."

"I categorically disagree. I certainly blame others, namely Burton and you, for making it impossible for me to have a choice. Leaving him was out of the question."

"You did end up leaving him."

"I didn't leave, I ran for my life."

"You could have done so with me."

"Could I? And where would I have been if you failed to destroy him, then had enough of me, as I'm sure you would have sooner or later, and discarded me *then*, after I made a mortal enemy of him?"

His glance was haughtiness itself. "There was no pos-

sibility I wouldn't destroy him." His eyes narrowed with...
reproof? "And I promised you protection."

"You dare make it my fault I ended up in mortal danger
when you executed your plan? When I couldn't have known
your promise would amount to anything, when you didn't
tell me anything of your real abilities, let alone purpose?"

"You dare ask why I didn't when you were his accomplice?"

A bitter scoff escaped her. "You promoted me from pas-
sive accessory to active accomplice in under an hour? Wonder what you'd make me by the end of this conversation."

"Whatever *you* call what you did, my desire for you
didn't blind me to the probability you'd run to him if I con-
fided in you. It would have been an opportunity to entrench
yourself further in his favor, adding indebtedness to his already pathological infatuation with you. And I was right."

She closed the mouth that had dropped open at his preposterous interpretations. "Yeah? How so?"

"When a choice was to be made, not knowing my real
'abilities,' you chose the man you thought more powerful.
This indicates what you would have done had you thought I
was a threat to your billion-dollar meal ticket." He shrugged
his massive shoulders. "Not that I blame you. You thought
you made the right choice based on available information.
That you were grossly misinformed and therefore made a
catastrophic mistake doesn't make you a victim."

Protests boiled in her blood. But there was no point in
voicing any. She had no proof, as he'd said.

Even if she did, to whom would she submit it? To him?
The mastermind of her misery?

Her shoulders slumped as the surge of aggression he'd
provoked drained. "You have everything worked out, don't
you?"

"Very much so."

She exhaled in resignation. "So you orchestrated everything, got the result you desired, while even Fate indulged

you and gave you the bonus of a mark to enjoy sexually, huh? That must have made your mission of patiently milking me for all I had more palatable."

His shrug was indifference incarnate. "More or less." His gaze shifted to an expression that seemed to sear her marrow. "With one amendment. It wasn't palatable. It was phenomenal."

"I—it was?"

"Along with a dozen superlative adjectives. Being with you was the only true and absolute pleasure I ever had."

He'd already said he'd wanted her. But the way he'd spelled it out now... His words fell on her like a punch, jogging her brain in her skull.

It had been what had most mutilated her, had left her feeling desecrated. Thinking she'd wanted him with every fiber of her being while he'd only reviled her even as he'd used her in every way. Learning that he'd wanted her had just begun to ameliorate her humiliation. But now his claim that it had been as unprecedented to him... It felt genuine. If it was, then at least their intimacies, which had been so profound to her, among all the lies and exploitation, had been real. She could at least cleanse those intensely intimate memories and have them back.

"And that's why I want you to say it, Isabella."

The hunger in his voice and eyes had her heart ramming against her ribs as if unable to bear their confinement.

"I want you to say you've craved having again what we had all those years ago. That every time you closed your eyes, I was there, in your mind, on your tongue, all over you and inside you, giving you everything only I could ever give you."

Every word he said, soaked in hunger, seething with demand, brought a wave of wet heat surging in her core, her body readying itself for its master doing all the things she'd never stopped yearning for.

She still had to resist. Because of what he'd done to her.

Past and present. Because of what he thought of her. What he was. For every reason that existed, really.

"What if I don't say it?"

Those incredible eyes crinkled, those lips that made her every inch ache with the memory of what they could do to her twisted.

"You want me to force you to take what you're dying to take, so you'd have it, and the moral high ground, too? No, my exquisite siren. If I take you now, it will be because you'll tell me in no uncertain terms that you want me to. That you're *burning* for me to. It's that...or you can go."

And it turned out every reason under the sun to tell him to go to hell was nothing compared to the one reason she had to give him what he wanted.

That he was right.

Giving in, she reached out, wound his tie around her hand and yanked on it with all her strength.

Which didn't say much right now. Her tug was trembling and weak like the rest of her. She was that aroused. He wouldn't have moved if he hadn't wanted to.

But her action was seemingly enough of an appeasement. He let her drag him down so his face was two inches from hers.

His virility-laden, madness-inducing breath flayed her lips, filled her lungs. "Now say it."

Voice as unsteady as her legs, she did. "I want you."

"Say it *all*, Isabella."

That cruel bastard had to extract her very soul, didn't he? Just as he had in the past.

Knowing she'd regret it when her body stopped clamoring, *if* it ever did—but she'd sooner stop her next breath—she gave him the full capitulation he demanded. "I wanted you with every single breath these past eight years."

His satisfaction was so ferocious it seared her as his hand covered the one spastically pulling on his tie, untangling it in such unhurried smoothness. Then, like the serpent he was, he slinked away from her. Heartbeats shook her as she watched him sit on the huge couch facing the pool.

After sprawling back in utmost comfort, he beckoned. "Show me."

Not knowing whom to curse more viciously, him or herself, she walked toward him as if on the end of a hook.

Once her knees bumped his, she lost all coordination and slumped over him under the weight of eight years' worth of craving. Barely slowing her collapse with shaking hands against his unyielding shoulders, her dress rode up thighs that opened to straddle his hips. His eyes burned into hers with gratification up until her lips crashed down on his.

He opened his mouth to her urgency, let her show him how much she needed everything he had as her hands roamed his formidable body, convulsed in his too-short-for-her-liking wealth of hair and her molten core rode the daunting rock of his manhood through their clothes.

"I want you, Richard...I've gone mad wanting you."

At her feverish moan he took over, his lips stopping her uncoordinated efforts to posses them. Sighing raggedly, she luxuriated in his domination, what he'd so maddeningly interrupted before.

His hands roved her, melting clothes off her burning body with the same virtuosity that had always made her breathless. His every move was loaded with the precise ruthlessness of a starving predator unleashed on a prey long kept out of reach.

Breaking the kiss, he drew back, his pupils flaring, blackness engulfing the silvered steel as he spilled her breasts into his palms. His homage was brief but devastating before he swept her around, had her sitting on the couch and kneeled before her. After dragging her panties off in one sweep, he lunged, buried his lips in her flowing readiness. She shrieked at the long-yearned-for feel of his tongue and teeth, her thighs spreading wider to give him fuller access to her intimate flesh, which had always been his.

Hours ago she'd been going about her new life, certain she'd never see him again. Now he was here, pleasuring her as only he had ever done.

Was she dreaming all this?

He nipped her bud, and the slam of pleasure was too jarring to be anything but real. One more sweep or suckle or graze would finish her. And she didn't want release.

She wanted *him*.

"Richard…you…" she gasped. "I need *you*…inside me… *please*…"

Growling, he heaved up, caught her plea in his savage mouth, letting her taste herself on his tongue as he rose, lifting her in his arms. Then the world moved in hurried thuds before it stopped abruptly with her steaming back against cool glass.

The idea that Richard was about to take her against a window overlooking the city almost made her come right then.

Plastering her to the glass with his bulk, he locked her feet around his buttocks, thrilling her with his effortless strength. Then he leaned back, freeing his erection.

The potency that had possessed her during so many long, hard rides had her mouth watering, her core gushing. And that was before the intimidating weight and length of it thudded against her swollen flesh, squeezing another plea from her depths. He only glided his incredible heat and hardness through the molten lips of her core, sending a million arrows of pleasure to her womb, until she writhed.

He didn't penetrate her until she wailed, *"Fill me."*

Only then did he ram inside her.

The savagery and abruptness of his invasion, the unbearable expansion around his too-thick girth, was a shock so acute the world flickered, darkened.

Her senses sparked again to him growling, "Too long… too damned long…" as his teeth sank into her shoulder like a lion tethering his mate for a jarring ride. Then he withdrew.

It felt as if he was dragging her life force out with him. Her arms tightened around his back, her hands clawing it, begging his return. He complied with a harder, deeper plunge, blacking out her senses again with the beyond-limits fullness. After a few thrusts forced her flesh to yield fully to him, he quickened his tempo.

Every withdrawal brought maddening loss, every plunge excruciating ecstasy. Her cries blurred and her muttered name on his lips became a litany, each thrust accentuated by the carnal sounds of their flesh slapping together. The scents of sex and abandon intensified, the glide and burn of his hard flesh inside her stoked her until she felt she'd combust.

She needed...needed... *Please...please*...please...

He'd always known what she needed, when and how hard and fast. He gave it to her now, hammering his hips between her splayed thighs, his erection pounding inside her with the cadence and force to unleash everything inside her, until he breached her womb and shattered the wound-up coil of need.

Her body detonated from where he was buried deepest outward, currents of release crashing through her, squeezing her around him, choking her shrieks.

Roaring her name, he exploded in his own climax, jetting the fuel of his pleasure over hers, filling her to overflowing, sharpening the throes of release until he wrung her of the last spark of sensation her body was capable of.

She felt him pulse the last of his seed into her depths, and a long-forgotten smile of satisfaction curved her lips as her head slumped in contentment over his chest...

A rumble beneath her ear jogged her back to consciousness. "Not enough, Isabella...never enough..."

Feeling boneless, her head spun as he strode away from the window, still buried within her depths. Knowing he'd carry her to his bedroom now, she drifted off again, wanting to rest so she'd be ready for round two...

She jerked out of her sensual stupor as he laid her down.

His scent rose from dark cotton sheets to cloak her in its hot delight, compensating her for his loss as he left her body to rid himself of his clothes. Her clamoring senses needed him back on top of her, inside her. She held out unsteady arms, begged for him again.

This time he didn't let her beg long. He lunged back over her, had her skidding on the sheets with the force of his impact. Spreading her quivering thighs, he pushed her knees up to her chest, hooking his arms behind them, opening her fully. Then, lowering himself over her to thrust his tongue inside her panting mouth, he reentered her in a long, burning plunge.

A shriek tore out of her as he forged inside her swollen flesh, undulating against her, inside her, churning soreness and ecstasy into an excruciating mixture as he took her in even more primal possession than the first time. He translated every liberty he was taking with her body into raw, explicit words that intensified the pleasure of his every move inside her beyond endurance. She climaxed all over him again, then again, eight years of deprivation exploding into torrents of sensation, each fiercer than the previous one.

At her fourth peak, he rammed her harder, faster, till he lodged into the gates of her womb, held himself there, roaring his release. Her body convulsed as she clutched his straining mass to her, her oversensitized flesh milking him for every drop of satisfaction for both of them.

At last, he gave her his full weight, which she'd always begged him for after the storm was over, his heartbeat a slow thunder against her decelerating one, completing his domination.

Always able to judge accurately when his weight would turn from necessity to burden, he rose off her, swept her enervated mass over his rock-solid one, dragging a crisp sheet over their cooling bodies.

She wanted to cling to this moment, to savor the descent with him…but everything slipped away…

* * *

Her mind a silent, empty scape, she tried to open lids that felt glued together. How strange. There'd never been peace after Richard...

Richard!

Her lids tore open, almost literally, and there he was. Illuminated by the dim daylight seeping in from the window of what she now realized was a hangar-size bedroom. He was propped up on one elbow beside her, looking down at her, his gaze one of supreme male triumph as he coated the body he'd savagely pleasured in languid caresses.

She was in his bed. She'd begged him to take her—repeatedly. If she could find her voice, she'd do it again right now.

"I didn't intend to rush your pleasure the first...or subsequent times. I wanted to keep you hovering on the edge of orgasm so long, when I finally gave it to you, I knocked you out on the first try."

"You did knock me out every single time," she croaked.

"No. Knocked out as in nothing could wake you up for hours afterward. I did that the last time only." He pinched and rolled one delightfully sore nipple, glided his hair-roughened leg between hers and pressed his knee to the soaked junction of her legs, dragging a whimper from her depth. "But no harm done. It's time to savor driving you crazy."

Her body clamored for him harder than ever. This addiction hadn't subsided; it had gotten worse.

She caressed his face, his shoulders, his chest, reveling in the longed-for delight of feeling him this way. "Your efforts would be in vain. I'm already crazy for you."

"I know. But I want you desperate."

Before she could protest, his tongue thrust inside her mouth, claiming, conquering. His hands, lips and teeth sought all her secrets, sparked her ever-simmering insanities until he had her writhing, nothing left inside her but the need for him to finish her, annihilate her, leave nothing of her.

Clawing at him, crushing herself against him, she tried to drag him inside her. "Just take me again, Richard."

He held her filling eyes, as if gauging if she was truly at his required level of desperation. Seemingly satisfied, from the grim twist of his lips and the flare of his nostrils, he rose above her, leveling her beneath him.

Locking her arms above her head, his knees spreading her legs wide-open, he was where she needed him most, penetrating her in one forceful thrust.

This time the expansion of her already swollen and sore tissues around his massive erection sharpened into pleasure so fierce, it was almost unbearable. Darkness danced at the periphery of her vision. She gasped, thrashed, voiceless, breathless. His face clenched with something like agony as she clung to him as she would a raft in a tempestuous sea.

She sobbed into his lips. "I wanted this every minute…"

"*Yes*. Every. Single. Minute." His growls filled her lungs even as he refilled her, the head of his shaft sliding against all her internal triggers, setting off a string of discharges that buried her under layers of sensations. It all felt maddeningly familiar, yet totally new.

Then everything compacted into one unendurable moment before detonating outward. She shattered.

Her flesh pulsed around his so forcefully she couldn't breathe for the first dozen excruciating clenches. He rumbled for her to come all over him, to scream her pleasure at the top of her lungs. His encouragement snapped something inside her, flooded air into her. And she screamed. And screamed and screamed as he pumped her to the last twitches of fulfillment.

Then he rose above her, supernatural in beauty, his muscles bulging, his eyes tempestuous. He threw his head back, roared her name as every muscle in his body locked and surrendered to his own explosive orgasm.

Instead of fainting, she remained fully aware this time throughout the stages of the most blissful aftermath she'd ever experienced with him.

Suddenly he spoke. "I wasn't satisfied with how things ended with you in the past. It felt…incomplete. And I must have everything wrapped up to my satisfaction."

For long moments she couldn't breathe, waiting for a qualification to tell her she'd jumped to the worst conclusions of his words.

He only validated her suspicion. "I got you here to close your case. If I may say so, I reached a spectacular conclusion."

Feeling as if he'd dumped her into freezing water, she fought to rise to the surface and from his arms.

Without one more word or glance she dragged the sheet off his body, wrapped herself in it and teetered out of the bedroom, looking for the clothes she hadn't been able to wait for him to tear off her body earlier.

She felt him following her, heading to the open-plan kitchen. Her numbness deepened.

When she was dressed, and as neat as she could get herself after he'd ravaged her, she turned to him.

He raised a mug. "Coffee? Or will you storm out now?"

"You have every right to do this." Her voice was thick and raw as it always had been when he'd made her scream her heart out in repeated ecstasy. It intensified her shame. "I deserve whatever you say or do. After all you've done to me, I disregarded all the injuries you caused me and fell into your arms again."

"And even now, you'd fall there again if I let you. But I'm no longer interested. I'm done."

Gritting her teeth against the pain digging its talons inside her, she said, "Then, I can look forward to never seeing you again for real this time. And no matter what you'd like to tell yourself you can get me to do, *I'm* beyond done."

"Yes, you are. That's the other thing I got you here to do. To tell you that."

She frowned. "What the hell do you mean by that?"

"You're done *here*. You will tell your new partners you've changed your mind about the partnership. You will terminate your lease, pay whatever early termination penalty your contract states, then pack your bags and leave this city, preferably the States. And this time, you will never return."

Four

In her first twenty-four years, Isabella had suffered so many brutal blows, had endured and survived them all, she'd believed nothing would shake her or knock her down again.

Then Richard had happened to her. Every second with him, and because of him, had been a succession of earthquakes and knockouts. After he'd exited her life, it had been a constant struggle not to fall facedown and stay there. But it hadn't been an option to give up. She'd had no choice but to forge on. But she'd thought even if she saw him again, whatever madness he'd induced in her, her own ability to experience towering passions, had been expended.

Then he'd reappeared and just by dangling himself in front of her, he'd made her relinquish all sanity and beg for his destruction.

Now there he stood, barefoot, in only pants, leaning indolently on the counter of his futuristic kitchen, looking like the god of malice that he was. He sipped painfully aromatic coffee in utmost serenity, clearly savoring its taste and her upheaval.

But what else did she think would happen after she'd committed that act of madness? Hadn't she already known she'd regret it? Or had she been that pathetic she'd hoped it wouldn't end horribly? That she'd have the ecstasy she'd hankered for without the agony that she'd learned would come with it? Had she even thought of the consequences as she'd grabbed for the appeasement only he could provide?

But this… What he'd ordered her to do wasn't only horrific, it was…incomprehensible.

The numbness of humiliation and self-abuse splintered under the blow of indignation. "Just who the hell do you think you are? How dare you presume to tell me what to do?"

Almost groaning at how clichéd and cornered she sounded, she watched in dismay as he gave her a glance she was certain had hardened criminals quaking in their shoes.

"Trust me, you don't want to know who I really am."

"Oh, I know enough to extrapolate the absolute worst."

Another tranquil sip. "From your defiant response I actually gather the worst you can imagine is nothing approaching the truth. But your misconception might be the result of my own faux pas. If I gave you the impression that this is a negotiation, I sincerely apologize. I also apologize for previously stating you always have a choice. You never do with me. Of course, there are *always* catastrophic mistakes, still categorized as choices, open to you. In this situation, the wrong choice is to stall. I strongly advise you don't exercise it."

Even now, his delivery of this load of bullying was so sexy and sophisticated his every enunciation reverberated in her reawakened senses like a shock wave.

Loathing her unwilling response, she gave him a baleful glance. "I assure you I won't stall. I will ignore you and your deranged demands altogether."

"In that case *my* only choice is to force you. So you're now down to one catastrophic choice, and it's how hard you decide to make this for yourself."

"Give it your best shot. Hard is my middle name."

As she kicked herself for how lame and how reeking of innuendo that had come out, his lips twitched his enjoyment of her slipup.

Out loud, he only said, "I can assure you, you wouldn't like it if I resorted to extreme measures."

"What extreme measures? Are you threatening to off me?"

His eyes turned to slits opening into thunderclouds. "Don't be daft."

It again seemed to insult him she'd suggest he'd physically harm her. But she wasn't falling yet again into the trap of seeing any measure of light in his darkness.

She twisted the strap of her purse around her hand until her fingers went numb. "I guess you don't off people if you could at all help it. You don't put people out of their misery. You didn't even kill Burton, just consigned him to a worse hell than even I hoped for him."

"Are you *extrapolating* what I did to him?"

"No, I know." His eyebrows rose in astonishment-tinged curiosity, and she hugged herself against a shudder that took her by surprise. "I wasn't a kingpin's trophy wife for four years without cultivating methods and sources to navigate his world and to execute an escape plan when necessary."

Heat entered his gaze again, this time tinged with... admiration? "Indeed. The way you wiped your history was a work of art. We must discuss said methods and sources at length sometime. It could be mutually beneficial to exchange notes on how we execute our deceptions."

She watched his mesmerizing face, wondering how he made anything he said so...appealing to her on her most fundamental levels, logic, self-respect and even survival be damned.

The only explanation was that she was sick. She'd contracted a disease called Richard Graves. And it was either incurable or would have to be cured at the cost of her life.

She huffed in resignation. "Nothing I developed could be of use to you. Next to yours, my abilities are like an ape's IQ to Einstein's. And I use fraud only to survive. It's a fundamental part of your career, of your character. Deceit is a preference to you, a pleasure. But you are right."

He raised an eyebrow. "In my advice not to stall?"

"In supposing I'm extrapolating Burton's fate at your hands. I know where you sent him, what that place is. But what is being done to him there?" She shook her head, the nausea she'd felt since he'd told her he was done intensifying. "Even after all I've seen in my life, my imagination isn't twisted enough to conceive what your warped mind could devise, or what you're capable of."

His gaze fixed on her with a new kind of intensity as he put down his mug, straightened from the counter and prowled closer.

Feeling more exposed now that daylight gave her no place to hide, she forced herself to stand her ground. "If physical threats aren't among your extreme measures, what then? If you think your previous warning of exposing me to Rose and Jeffrey stands, it doesn't. I'm walking out of here and going straight to the practice to tell them everything."

His ridiculing glance told her he didn't believe her capable of doing that. Out loud he only taunted, "I'd still have dozens of ways to make you comply."

"Why are you even asking me to do this?"

"I'm not asking you. I'm telling you."

She rolled her eyes. "Yeah, yeah…I got that already. You're the man who says 'jump' and everyone hops in the air and freezes there until you say down. Quit marveling at your unstoppable powers. It got old after the first dozen times. So give me a straight answer already. It's not as if you care about going easy on me, or about me at all."

"Bloody hell, who am I kidding." Without seeming to move closer, he was all over her. Before she could even gasp, he buried his face in her neck and groaned, "It was I who made a catastrophic mistake, Isabella. I'm not done. I'll never be."

Suffocating under the feel of him, the hard heat and perfection of him, with the mess of reactions he wrenched from her depths, she started struggling. "Let me go. *Now.*"

He only carried her off the ground. She opened her lips to blast him and he closed them with a mind-melting kiss, tasting her as if he couldn't stop.

It was only when she went limp in his arms that he let her lips go, barely setting her back on her feet, pouring one final groan of enjoyment inside her.

"Got that out of your system?" She glared up at him, wishing her hatred could melt his flawless face off his skull.

"I just told you there is no getting you out of my system. So let's not waste more time in posturing and theatrics. Let's get past what I said to you earlier."

"Just like that, huh?"

He squeezed her tighter. "It would be more time efficient. I already admitted to being a pillock and a tosser."

"What?"

His lips spread wider at her croak. It wasn't right. Nature was such a random, unjust system, to endow him with such an array of assets and abundance of charisma. But then, that was what made him such an exemplary fiend.

"That means *massive idiot* and *supreme jerk* in the tongue of my people."

"And you think calling yourself a couple of fancy British insults exonerates you and compensates me? I'm sure in your universe you consider tossing a half-assed apology at someone will wipe away any injury you've dealt them. Not in mine."

His eyes sobered. "I got you here thinking I could get closure and move past you at last. I went through the motions but not only didn't I get said closure, I no longer want it."

Needing to poke out his eyes and wrap her legs around him at once, she pushed at him, bracing against the feel of his silk-sprinkled steel flesh. Just remembering what that chest had done to her as he'd tormented her breasts and pounded his potency inside her...

She gave a strong enough shove that he let her go at last. Because he'd decided to, she was sure.

Regaining her footing, she steadied herself. "So you're not even apologizing. You just realized you've jumped the gun, that you didn't get enough of me and want a few more rounds."

He stroked his hands over his chest, as if tracing the imprint of her hands against it. "I want unlimited rounds. And I never thought it a possibility to have enough of you. I only wanted to be rid of my need for you. I no longer want that. I want to indulge that need, to wallow in it." He reached for her again, slamming her against him, cupping one of the breasts he'd ravaged with pleasure. "And before I made that bloody blunder of following through with my no-longer-viable intention, you wanted nothing more than to binge on me, too."

She pushed his hands away from her quivering flesh. "I'm actually grateful for said bloody blunder. It gave me the closure *I* needed, in the form of a vicious slap that jogged me out of my pathological tendencies where you're concerned."

He grabbed both her hands and dragged them up to his face. "Slap me back as hard as you like. Or better still..." He pulled her hands down, pressed them nails first over his chest. "Take your pound of flesh, Isabella. Claw it out of me."

Trembling with the need to sink her nails and teeth into his chest, not to hurt but to worship him, she fisted her hands against the urge and stepped back. "Thanks, but no thanks."

Circumventing him, the soreness of his possession and the evidence of their intimacies between her legs making her gait awkward, made her curse him and herself all over again.

His voice dipped another octave, penetrating her between the shoulder blades. "I'm rescinding my ultimatum."

That made her turn, that mixture of rage and swooning warring inside her. "You're no longer threatening unimaginable punishments so I'd leave and never return? How kind of you."

He covered the distance she'd put between them, eyes boring into her as if he wanted to hypnotize her. "You only need to end your partnership."

Before she took him up on his offer of slashing her hands open on those razor-sharp cheekbones, or breaking her nails claiming a handful of those steel pectorals, he went on, "Give the Doctors Anderson a personal excuse. If you'd rather not, I will manufacture an airtight one for you and pay the penalty for unilaterally dissolving the partnership. But you don't have to worry about that. I'll arrange a far more prestigious and lucrative partnership for you. Better still, I'll establish your own private practice or even hospital."

Head spinning at the total turnabout he'd made, but more at the sheer nerve of his standing there orchestrating her life for her, the utter insanities he was spouting, she raised her hands. "Stop. Just stop. What the hell is wrong with you? Were you always a madman and I never noticed it?"

"I *am* definitely mad, with wanting you. And you showed me you're as out of your mind for me. So you'll stay and we'll pick up where we left off, without the restrictions of the past. I'll acquire a new residence for you close to me, so you won't waste time commuting. You can have anything else you want or need. You can work with anyone in the world, have access to all the funds and facilities and personnel you wish for. I will accommodate and fulfill your every desire."

He dragged her back to him, hauling her by the buttocks against his hardness, his other hand twisting in her hair, tilting her head back, exposing her neck to the ravaging of his tongue and teeth. His growl spilled into her blood at her pulse point. "Every single one."

Her traitorous body melting inside and out for him, she felt she was drowning again. "Richard...this is insane..."

"We've already established I am, for you." He punctuated every word with a thrust, and her voracious body soaked up the pleasure of every rough grind. "I discovered I have been all these years, but my training, and everything else, held it all in check. I no longer want to hold back. And I won't." He took her mouth in a compulsive kiss that almost made her orgasm there and then. He ended the kiss, transferred his possession to the rest of her face. "If you ever thought Burton indulged you, that was nothing compared to what I'll do for you."

Lurching, feeling as if he'd slapped her, she punched her way out of his arms this time, her voice rising to a strident shout. "I don't want anything from you, just like I never wanted anything from him. So you can take your promises and offers and shove them."

He caressed his body where her blows had landed, licked his lips as if savoring her taste. "I'm telling you everything on offer, for full disclosure's sake. You're free to make use of whatever you choose." He captured her hands again, pressing his lips in her aching palms. "But I am compensating you for the termination of your partnership. That's the one thing that's not negotiable."

She snatched her hands away. "Are you done?"

"I told you I could never be done with you."

"Okay, I've changed my diagnosis. You're not insane, you're delusional. On top of having multiple personality disorder. I'm terminating nothing. And I already told you what you can do with your 'compensations.'"

He tutted, all indulgence now. "I'm not letting you go until we get this settled. So let's get on with it so I can leave you to get on with the rest of your day. You have new partners you have to let down easy after all."

"'This' is already settled. And you're letting me go *now*, Richard."

Turning, she strode the long way back to the door. Though slower, his impossibly long strides kept him a step behind her.

At the door, he pressed himself into her back, plastering her against it, seeking all her triggers. But she was finally angry enough to resist and desperate enough to leave.

"Tell your damn pet door to open sesame, Richard."

Taking a last suckle of her earlobe, sending fireworks all over her nervous system, he sighed. The sound poured right into her brain as he mercifully ended their body meld. But instead of murmuring the door open, he leaned on outstretched arms, bars of virility on both sides of her body, and pressed his hands against it.

So it also had palm-print sensors.

The moment the door opened, she spilled outside as if from a flooding tunnel.

Once she reached the elevator, he called out, "I've laid all my cards on the table. It's your turn."

Looking over her shoulder, she found him standing on his threshold, long legs planted apart, hands in pockets, the embodiment of magnificence and temptation. And knowing it.

She cursed under her breath. "Yeah, my turn. To tell you what I want. I want you to take your cards and go to a hell even you can't imagine, where crazy monsters like you belong."

He threw his head back and laughed.

She'd never heard him laugh before.

Rushing into the elevator to escape the enervating sound, she was still followed by his amusement-soaked question.

"Want me to pick you up from work, or will you finish your vital errand and come back on your own?"

She almost stomped her foot in frustration. The elevator buttons made as much sense as hieroglyphics in her condition.

She smacked every button. "I'll willingly go to hell first."

His dark chuckle drenched her again. "The hell for irresistible sirens is the same one for crazy monsters?"

She glowered at him in fuming silence as the elevator doors finally swished smoothly closed.

The moment she could no longer see him, she slumped against the brushed-steel wall…then shot up straight again.

The damn snake must have cameras in here. She'd dissolved all over him all night, and even just now, she wasn't about to let him see he still messed her up, albeit remotely. She had to hold it together until she was out of his range.

By the time she was in her car, one realization had emerged from the chaos.

She'd never be out of his range. There was no place on earth he couldn't follow her to if he felt like it. And he'd made it clear that he had nothing else on his mind right now.

There was only one way out of this. To change it for him somehow, before he took one step further into her life. And destroyed everything. Irrevocably this time.

How she would do that, she had absolutely no idea.

Richard closed the door, stood staring at it as if he could still see Isabella through it.

He could monitor her for real until she exited the building. But he preferred imagining her in his mind's eye. As she stood there in the elevator, letting go of the act of defiance. As she walked to his private parking area where her car was, every step impeded by the soreness he'd caused her as he'd given her and taken from her unimaginable pleasure. As she drove home in an uproar, furious at him yet reliving their climactic night, her every inch throbbing, needing an encore.

Dropping his forehead against the door he'd sandwiched her against, he could almost feel her every thought and breath mingling with his, melding, tangling, wrestling. Just as her limbs had with his, as her core had yielded to him, and clasped him in a mindless inferno. His body buzzed with exquisite agony as his hardness turned to burning steel.

Pushing away from the door, he discarded his pants as he headed to the pool, his steps picking up speed until he launched himself into the air, arced down to slice into the cool water like a missile.

It was an hour before he'd expended sufficient incendiary energy and centered his thoughts enough to consider the exercise had served its purpose. Pulling himself out of the pool, he sat on its edge, staring through forty-foot-high windows at the sprawling green expanse of Central Park, seeing nothing but Isabella and everything that had happened between them.

So. For the first time in…ever, nothing had gone according to his plan. And he couldn't be more thrilled about it.

Though he'd known she'd been his only kryptonite, he'd believed she wouldn't retain any power over him. Even after he'd realized he still coveted her, he hadn't thought there'd been the slightest danger she'd breach his impenetrable armor.

But every moment with her had been pleasure beyond imagining. Even more indescribable than anything he remembered sharing with her in the past. He now realized his invulnerability had only been the deep freeze he'd plunged into when he'd walked away from her, thinking he'd never have her again. He'd stored everything inside him, starting with his libido, which he'd kept behind barricades of thorns and ice. But mere re-exposure to her had pulverized them as if they were cobwebs, thawed him out as quickly as New York's summer sun melted an ice cube.

He'd tried to fool himself into thinking he could apply brakes to the desire that had overtaken him. But even as he'd told her he was done, the thought of losing her again had made him want to take it back at once. The utter contempt that had dawned on her face had made him willing to do anything to erase it, to restore the contentment his words had wiped away.

And he *had* offered everything. Again. Without trying, she'd snared him again. It was a trap he'd eagerly been caught in. She remained the only person who had his secret access code. The one, in spite of every reason on earth against it, he gladly relinquished power to.

Satisfaction spread like wildfire, pulling at his lips as he jumped to his feet and headed for the shower.

Once beneath the pummeling water, he closed his eyes and relived his nightlong possession of her and her captivation of him. Next time, this was where he'd end their intimacies, soothing and refreshing her before he let her leave him. He certainly wouldn't end another climactic night together by doing his best to alienate her.

After his contradictory behavior, she'd run away screaming *monster. Crazy monster*, to be exact.

She wouldn't come back on her own. No matter how much she craved him. As he was now beyond certain she did.

So he had to pursue her. But he predicted that the harder he did, the more she'd push him away. He had no problem with that. It would only make the hunt that much more intoxicating.

He *would* have her at his mercy and that of the unstoppable passion they shared. This time, he wouldn't let her go before he was glutted. If he couldn't be, then he wasn't letting her go at all.

Exiting the shower, he stood in front of the floor-length mirror, grimacing his displeasure with his too-short hair.

She'd loved it when it had been longer. He'd woken so many times still feeling her clinging to it as he'd ridden her, or combing through it languorously in blissful aftermaths. It had been why he'd kept it razed, thinking it would abort the phantom sensations. Not that it had.

Deciding to grow it out, he took extra care with his grooming, but didn't shave so he wouldn't have a stubble by the time he saw her again. It had driven her out of her mind when his whiskers had burned her during sex. But she'd always complained afterward that he'd sandpapered her. When he hadn't been able to meet her smooth-shaven as he had last night, he'd learned how to handle his facial hair to keep the pro of pleasuring her without the con of scraping her sensitive skin raw. By tonight, when he had her again, his current stubble would be the perfect length to give her the stimulation without the abrasion.

After dressing in clothes she'd love, he called Murdock. As always, he answered on the second ring. "Sir."

"I need to get into Dr. Sandoval's home."

"Sir?"

Annoyed that Murdock's response wasn't a straight "Yes, sir," he frowned. "I want to prepare a surprise for her."

After a beat, Murdock said, "You didn't read my report."

Suddenly, Richard was at the end of his tether. He was unable to bear a hint of obstacle or delay when it came to Isabella. "What is it with you and your fixation on that bloody report, Murdock? Did you even hear what I said?"

"Indeed, sir. But if you'd read my report, you would have known it wouldn't be wise to break into Dr. Sandoval's home."

"Why the bloody hell not?"

"Because her family is in there."

Two hours later Richard was driving through Isabella's neighborhood, a sense of déjà vu overwhelming him.

He hadn't even known such a place existed in New York. But there it was—Forest Hills Gardens, what looked like a quaint English village transplanted into the heart of Queens.

A private, tucked-away community within the Forest Hills neighborhood, it was based on the model of garden communities in England. Its streets were open to the public, but street parking was reserved for the residents of the elegant Tudor and Colonial single-family homes that flaunted towers, spires, fancy brickwork and red-tiled clay roofs. Wrought iron streetlights inspired by Old English lanterns lined the block, while the curving street grid was lined with London plane and white ash trees.

It felt as though he was back where he'd grown up.

Shaking off the oppressive memories, he parked in front of Isabella's leased residence, a magnificently renovated Tudor.

Glaring at the massive edifice, he exhaled. If he'd been in any condition to think last night, he would have deduced the reason why she'd leased such a big house when Murdock had imparted that information. It was understatement to say he'd been unpleasantly surprised to find out she lived with her mother, a sister and three children.

That put a serious crimp in his plans of relocating her to be near him. Now instead of invading her home to execute the seduction he'd had in mind, he'd come to get the lay of the land and to lie in wait for her.

Exiting his car, he strode across the wide pavement and ran up the steps to her front porch. He rang the bell then stood back as the long-forgotten sounds of children rose from inside.

The last time he'd heard sounds like that had been the day he'd left his family home.

He'd stood outside as he did now, listening to Robert and Rose playing. They'd sounded so carefree with the ominous shadow of Burton lifted, if only temporarily.

Little had his brother and sister known that Burton had only been absent because he was finalizing the deal that would make Richard the indentured slave of The Organization. They wouldn't have been so playful if they'd known it would be the last time they'd ever see their older brother.

Gritting his teeth, he reeled back the bilious recollections as feet approached, too fast and too light to be those of an adult.

Splendid. One of the little people in her stable was the one who'd volunteered to open the door. An obnoxious miniature human to vex him more than he already was.

All of a sudden the door rattled with what sounded like a little body crashing into it. That twerp had used the door to abort his momentum, no doubt not considering slowing down instead. Maybe waiting for Isabella in a home infested with abominations-in-progress who might aggravate him into devouring them wasn't a good idea.

But the door was already opening. It was too late to change his plan. Or maybe he'd pretend he'd knocked on the wrong door and—

He blinked at the boy who'd opened the door and was looking at him with enormous eyes, his mind going blank.

His heart crashed to one side inside his chest as the whole world seemed to tilt on its axis.

Then his mind, his very existence, seemed to explode.

Bloody hell...that's...that's...

Robert.

The bolt of realization almost felled him.

There was only one explanation for finding a duplicate of his dead younger brother in Isabella's home.

This boy was his.

Five

"Who're you?"

The melodious question sank through him, detonated like a depth mine. Observations came flooding in at such an intolerable rate, they buried him under an avalanche of details.

The texture of the boy's raven locks, the azure sky of his eyes, the slant of his eyebrows, the bow of his lips. His height and size and posture and every inch of his sturdy, energy-packed body...

But it was the boundless inquisitiveness and unwavering determination on his face that hit Richard so forcefully it threatened to expel whatever he had inside him that passed for a soul. That expression was imprinted in his mind. He'd seen it on his brother's face so many times when he'd been that same age. Before exposure to Burton had put out his fire and spontaneity and hope, everything that had made him a child.

Even had it not been for the almost identical resemblance, that jolt in his blood would have filled him with certainty. That Isabella had had his child.

This was his son.

"Mauri...don't open the door!"

"Already opened it, Abuela!" the boy yelled, never taking his eyes off Richard. Then he asked again, "Who're you?"

Before Richard considered if he could speak any longer, a woman in her fifties came rushing into the foyer.

Her hurried steps faltered as soon as her eyes fell on him,

becoming as wide as the boy's, the anxiety in them dissipating, a genial smile lighting up her face.

"Can I help you, sir?"

Something tugged at his sleeve. The boy—Mauri—pursuing his prior claim to his attention. And insisting on his all-important question. "Who're you?"

Richard stared down at him, literally having trouble remembering the name he'd invented for himself.

The boy held out his hand in great decorum, taking the initiative, as if to help him with his obvious difficulty in answering that elementary question. "I'm Mauricio Sandoval."

In the chaos his mind had become, he noted that Isabella had given the boy her new invented surname. He stared at the small proffered hand, stunned to find his heart booming with apprehension at the idea of touching him.

So he didn't, but finally answered instead, his voice an alien rasp to his own ears. "I'm Richard Graves."

The boy nodded, lowering his hand, then only said, "Yes, but who are you?"

"Mauri!"

At the woman's gentle reprimand, Richard raised his gaze to her, shaking his head, jogging himself out of the trance he'd fallen in. "Mauricio is right. Telling you my name didn't really tell you who I am."

"You talk funny."

"Mauri!"

The boy shrugged at the woman's embarrassment, undeterred. "I don't mean funny ha-ha, I mean not like us. I like it. You sound so…important. Wish I could speak like that." His gaze grew more penetrating, as if he wanted to drag answers from him. "Why do you speak like that?"

"Because I'm British."

"You mean from Britain?" At Richard's nod he persisted, "That's not the same as English, is it?"

The boy knew things most adults didn't. "Not exactly. I do happen to be English, too, or rather, English first, having been born in England. But a lot of people are British—and that means they're citizens of Great Britain—but not English. They could be Scottish, Welsh, or some Irish from Northern Ireland, too. But most of those people hate being called British, rather insisting on calling themselves English or Scottish or Welsh or Irish. I say British because the majority of people from the rest of the world don't know the difference. And most don't care."

"So you say British so they won't ask questions when they don't care about the answers. I ask questions because I like to know stuff."

Richard marveled at the boy's articulate, thorough logic, his insight into what made people tick. He was too well informed and socially developed for his age. Isabella and her family were clearly doing a superlative job raising him.

After digesting the new information, the boy persisted. "You still didn't tell us who you are."

At the woman's groan, Richard felt a smile tug at his lips at the boy's dogged determination. It was clear when he latched on to something, little Mauricio never let go.

That trait was more like him than Robert.

On his next erratic heartbeat his involuntary smile froze. He sensed that there was more to Mauricio's insistence than the drilling curiosity of a young and tenacious mind. Could it be the boy was that sensitive he felt the blood bond between them?

No. Of course not. That was preposterous.

But what was really ridiculous was him standing there like a gigantic oaf, unable to carry his end of an introduction with a curious child and a kindly lady.

Forcing himself out of his near stupor, he cocked his head at the boy, that bolt of recognition striking him all over again. "In my defense, you told me only your name, too."

That perfect little face, so earnest and involved, tilted at him in challenge. "You're visiting us, so you know stuff about us already. We don't know anything about you."

Richard's lips twisted at how absurd the boy's rebuttal made his previous comment. It really hadn't occurred to him to consider that simple fact when he'd made it. His mental faculties had been all but demolished.

While the boy was as sharp and alert as his mother. He got to the point and held his ground. As she always did.

He inhaled a much-needed draft of oxygen. "You're quite right. Knowing your name tells me a lot about you, based on what I already know about your…family, while knowing mine tells you nothing about me. You're also right to insist on knowing who I am. It's the first thing you always need to know about other people, so you can decide what to expect from them. Let me introduce myself better this time."

He held out his hand. The boy didn't give him a chance to brace himself for the contact, eagerly putting his hand in his. And an enervating current zapped through him.

He barely withdrew his hand instead of snatching it away, suppressing the growl that clawed at his throat at the lash of sensations.

"My name is Richard Graves and I'm an old…associate of Dr. Sandoval's."

Mauricio ricocheted a new question. "Are you a doctor?"

"No, I'm not."

"Then, what are you?"

"I'm a security specialist."

"What's that?"

Richard frowned. No one had ever asked him that question. When they probably should have. People assumed they understood what he did when most had no idea. That boy didn't presume. He asked so he'd know exact details, build his knowledge on solid ground. As Robert had.

Realizing his shoulders had slumped under the still-intensifying shock, he straightened. "It's a lot of things, actually, and it's all very important and very much in demand. The world is a dangerous place—and that's why your grandmother was rightfully upset that you opened the door. I'm sure she told you never to do that."

The boy sheepishly looked at the woman who was standing there watching them, her expression arrested. "Yeah, she did. Mamita, too. Sorry, Abuela."

Anxious to drive his point home, make it stick, Richard pressed on. "You must promise never to do that again, to always—*always*—do as your mother and grandmother say. Security is the most important thing in the world. I know, trust me."

The boy only nodded. "I trust you."

The boy's unexpected, earnest response was another blow.

Before he could deal with it, the boy added, "I promise." Then his solemn look was replaced by that burning interest again. "So what do you do?"

"I am the one people come to, to make them safe."

"Are you a bodyguard?"

"I'm the trainer and provider of bodyguards. To banks, companies, individuals, private and public events and transportation, and of course my own business and partners— and many other interests. I also keep people's private lives and businesses safe in other ways, protecting their computers, communications and information against accidental loss or hacking."

With every detail, Mauricio's blue eyes sparkled brighter in the declining sun. "How did you learn to do all that?"

With another groan, the woman intervened again. "Mauri, what did we say about not asking a new question every time someone gives you an answer?" Then she squeezed her dark eyes in mortification. "As if my manners are any better!" She rushed toward him and touched him on the arm. Her smile was exquisite, reminding him so much of Isabella, even though she barely resembled her. "Please come in."

Her gentle invitation agitated him even more. The idea of spending more time with that little boy with the endless questions and enormous eyes that probed his very essence felt as appealing as electrocution. In fact, *that* would have been preferable. He'd suffered it before, and he could say for certain what he was feeling now was worse.

Wishing only to run away, he cleared his throat. "It's all right. I don't want to interrupt your day. I'll connect with Isabella some other time."

The woman's hand tightened on his forearm, aborting his movement away from the threshold. "You wouldn't interrupt anything. I already cooked and updated my website where I do some of my volunteer work. Bella stayed overnight at work, but Saturday is her half day, so she'll be home soon."

So Isabella had explained her night away. But that wasn't the important thing now. The pressing matter was the alien feeling coming over him as he looked into this woman's kind eyes. He could only diagnose it as…helplessness. For the first time in his life he was being exposed to genuine hospitality, and he had no idea how to deal with it.

As if sensing his predicament, she patted his forearm, her eyes and voice gentling. "We'd really love to have you."

Corroborating his grandmother's request, the boy grabbed his other forearm. "Yes, please. You can tell me how you learned everything you do. Your job is as cool as a super-hero!"

The woman looked at her grandson with tender reproof. "Mr. Graves isn't here to entertain you, Mauri."

The boy nodded his acceptance. "I know. He's here to see Mamita." He swerved into negotiation mode seamlessly, fixing Richard with his entreaty. "But you have to do something while we wait for her."

At Richard's hesitation, the boy changed his bargaining tactic on the fly. "If your job is top secret and you can't talk about it, I can show you my drawings."

Richard stared down at the boy. He drew. Like him. Something no one knew about him.

His whole body was going numb with…dread? It was

beyond ludicrous to be feeling this way. But he'd been in shackles, had been tortured within an inch of his sanity, and he'd never felt as trapped and as desperate as he did now with those two transfixing him with gentleness and eagerness.

But there was no escape and he knew it. Those two frail yet overwhelming creatures had him cornered.

Feeling as if he was swallowing red-hot nails, he nodded.

Mauricio's smile blinded him as he whooped his excitement, pulling at Richard. Once he had him over the threshold, he let him go and streaked away, calling over his shoulder, "I'll go get my stuff!"

Watching Mauricio disappear, Richard stepped into Isabella's home as if stepping out from under tons of rubble.

The woman closed the door behind him and guided him inside. "I'm Marta, by the way. Isabella's mother, in case you didn't work that out. I don't know if Bella ever talked about me."

She hadn't. Isabella had never mentioned her family. When he'd tried to investigate them as part of his research into her life, there'd only been basic info until she was thirteen. Anything beyond that age had been blank until she'd married Burton. He now knew she'd later wiped out her years of marriage to him, too. But at the time he hadn't bothered to probe the missing parts, thinking them irrelevant to his mission. But he did remember Marta was her mother's name. She hadn't changed her name, either.

Suddenly something else bothered him. He stopped. Marta stopped, too, her gaze questioning.

"Once your grandson puts that logical mind of his to use, he'll realize you didn't follow your own rule about security. You didn't make sure I know Isabella, or if I do, that we're on the sort of terms that make it safe to let me into your home."

She waved his concern away. "Oh, I'm certain you know her, and well enough. And that it's safe to invite you in."

Warmth spread in his chest at yet another thing he'd never been exposed to. Unquestioning trust. Not even Murdock, Rafael or Isabella had trusted him so completely that quickly.

But such trust was unlikely coming from someone of Marta's age, and one who'd grown up in a country where danger was a part of daily life to so many people.

Was she letting her guard down now that they were in the States and in a secure neighborhood? Or because she judged people by appearances and from his she judged him to be refined and civilized? If she was that trusting with strangers, she could expose them all to untold dangers.

He didn't budge when she urged him onward, needing to make sure she didn't make that mistake again, either. "How did you come by that certainty? Did your daughter ever talk about me?"

"No." She grinned. "And she's going to hear my opinion of that omission later." Her eyes grew serious, but remained the most genial thing he'd ever seen. "But in a long and very eventful life, I've learned to judge people with absolute accuracy. I've yet to be wrong about anyone."

He grimaced. "You think you have an infallible danger radar? That's even worse than having no discretion at all."

She chuckled in response to his groan. "So you first feared I drag in anyone who comes to our door, and now you think I overestimate my judgment?" She tugged at him again, her face alight with merriment. "Don't worry, I'm neither oblivious nor overconfident. I am a happy medium."

He still resisted her, imagining how silly they must look, a slight woman trying to drag a behemoth more than twice her size, with him appearing the one in distress.

"What happy medium? You think I'm harmless."

This made her giggle. "I'd sooner mistake a tiger for a kitten." She sobered, though she continued grinning. "I think you're *extremely* harmful. I know a predator when I see one, and I've never seen anyone I thought as lethal as you. But I'm also sure you don't hunt the innocent or the defenseless. I have a feeling your staple diet is those who prey on them."

His thoughts blipped, stalled. How could this woman who'd just met him read him so accurately?

She wasn't finished. "So yes, I let you in because, beyond the personal details I don't know, I took one look at you and knew who you are. In a disaster, and when everyone else is scared or useless, you're the man I'd depend on to save my family."

He gave up. On trying to predict, or even to brace himself for what the next second would bring in this *Twilight Zone* of a household. He also gave up any preconceptions he'd unconsciously formed about Marta since she'd come rushing after Mauricio. Once he did, he let himself see beyond her apparent simplicity to the world of wisdom, born of untold ordeals, in her gaze. This woman had seen…and survived…too much.

A kindred feeling toward her swept him almost as powerfully as the one he'd felt toward Mauricio, if different in texture.

It seemed his weakness for Isabella extended to those who shared her blood. He might have a genetic predisposition to let anyone with her DNA influence his thoughts and steer his actions.

Marta tugged him again, and this time he let her lead him inside.

As they entered a family room at the center of a home right out of a syrupy family sitcom, she said, "Mauri never opens the door, either. I don't know why he did this time."

He pursed his lips as he sat on a huge floral couch that jarred him with its gaiety, considering the austerity he was used to. "He probably sensed that I'm the one to defend his home against invading alien armies…before he even saw me."

She spluttered, causing his own lips to twitch. He'd already known she wouldn't be offended when he poked fun at her, would relish his caustic humor.

Beaming, the eyes he was learning to read held something he didn't wish to translate. "You can joke about it, but you can actually be right. Mauri is an extremely...sensitive boy. There have been a lot of instances when he realized things he shouldn't or felt things before they happened."

Before he decided what to think, let alone formulate an answer, she clasped hands beneath her chin. "Now let me offer you something to drink. And you'll stay for dinner, yes?"

"Maybe Isabella won't want to have me."

"I want to have you for dinner. Mauri wants that, too. Bella can't say no to either of us. So you're safe."

Admitting that it was easier to decimate a squad of armed-to-the-teeth black ops operatives unarmed than resist this tiny woman, he surrendered. "Tea, please. If you have any."

"Bella has us stocked on every kind of tea on earth. It's the only thing she drinks."

It had been him who'd started her drinking tea, addicted her to it as per her admission. So she hadn't stopped. Just as she hadn't been able to stop her addiction to him.

He inhaled deeply, suppressing the acutely sensory memories that flooded his mind. "Earl Grey. Hot."

Clapping her hands, Marta rushed away. "Coming right up."

As she receded, Richard finally made a conscious comparison between her and her daughter.

She was much shorter and smaller, and her complexion, eyes and hair were darker. There were similarities in their features, but it was clear Isabella had taken after another relative, probably her father or someone from her father's side.

Marta was also different in other ways. Though she'd evidently lived a troubled life, she seemed more carefree, more optimistic than Isabella, even younger in spirit. If he'd ever imagined having an older sister, he would have probably wished for someone exactly like her.

He frowned at the strange idea, shaking it off. And all other distractions fell off with it, releasing his mind, letting it crash in the wreckage-filled abyss of reality.

Isabella had given birth to his son.

She'd been pregnant as she'd run for her life.

When had she found out? Before or after she'd fled?

If before, she would have had to run anyway to hide another betrayal from Burton. Or would she have aborted Mauricio, if he hadn't suspected her, to avoid his wrath?

That was a moot question. She'd had Mauricio, so she'd either discovered her pregnancy just as she'd run or afterward.

But why had she kept him? Had she wanted his child? Or had it all been about Mauricio himself? Had she wanted him?

That she'd had him proved it. Whatever she'd felt when she'd discovered her pregnancy, whatever dangers had been present, her desire to have him had trumped it all.

But she'd been on the run and pregnant, and hadn't considered asking him for help. Even before she'd realized he'd been the cause of her predicament.

So why? If she hadn't hated him then, why hadn't she run from Burton to him? He'd waited for her to, had left all channels open hoping she would. For some reason he couldn't fathom, she hadn't.

But if she had, and had told him about Mauricio, what would he have done? He had no idea.

He still had no idea. What to think, let alone what to do.

And here he was, after an explosive reunion with her that had plunged him right back into the one addiction of his life, sitting in her land of overwhelming domesticity, waiting for her mother to bring him tea and her son his portfolio. Not only had every single plan he'd had coming here been vaporized, every other one in his life had been, too.

What the blistering bloody hell would he do now?

What *could* he do?

Nothing. That was what. Nothing but sit back and observe, and make decisions as he went along. For the first time in a quarter of a century he wasn't steering everything and everyone wherever he wished. All his calculations had gone to hell the moment he'd laid eyes on her again. He expected them to remain there for the foreseeable future.

Making peace with that conclusion, he looked around the place. Murdock had said it had been turnkey, so he couldn't use it to judge anything about her or who she'd become.

Or maybe he could. She had chosen the finished product after all. It indicated this was what she wanted for herself, for her family now. The total opposite of what she'd had when she'd been with Burton, a fifty-bedroom mansion with two ballrooms and an attached garage for thirty cars. The demotion to a six-bedroom house with street parking was quite drastic. At most, he estimated this place to rent for six thousand a month, and to sell for a couple of million. While this neighborhood, though elegant, could as well be a row of hovels next to the outrageous hundred-acre estate of her former residence.

So was this what she wanted? An undistinguished upper-middle-class life? A safe, comfortable neighborhood for her family with good public schools for her child? Had she really changed her life so completely around? It appeared so.

And it appeared it had all been for Mauricio.

Mauricio. A son he hadn't known he had for seven years.

He couldn't get an actual grip on that. The shock of discovering Mauricio's existence would only deepen with time.

Almost as shocking had been Mauricio's and his grandmother's behavior with him. He couldn't rationalize, let alone cope with their instant acceptance. No one had ever reacted to him that way. He scared people on sight. At least awed them. He made the most hardened thugs wary, even before they knew who he really was and what he was capable of. So how had they taken to him so immediately?

Then it all happened at once. The sound of china rattling on a tray heralded Marta's approach. Stampeding feet down the stairs indicated Mauricio's. And the front door was opening.

Isabella.

The others, so focused on him as they rejoined him, missed her arrival until she entered the room. He held her eyes—her glorious, murderous eyes—as Mauricio foisted his precious load in his hands before hurtling himself at her. Her mother greeted her with as much joy. Isabella had eyes only for him.

If looks could kill, he would be a riddled corpse by now.

Mauricio fell over himself to fill her in on their whole meeting, word for word. Marta scolded her lovingly for never bringing Richard up. And though Isabella had brought her deadly displeasure with him under control and gave them a face he'd never seen—one of vivacious delight at being home—they seemed to realize that wasn't what she felt about his presence.

Not about to risk her spoiling their dinner plans, as Richard had intimated she might, Marta preempted her by announcing they'd have dinner at once and have tea later.

He had to give it to Isabella. All through what turned out to be an exceptional dinner, crafted to perfection by Marta, she somehow held back from doing what he could feel her seething to do: hurl a fork into his eye.

Along with discovering what superb home-cooked Colombian food tasted like, he found out the answer to a question he'd fumed over just last night. How a dinner could last four hours.

This one lasted even longer. And not because Isabella's younger sister, Amelia, and her two children arrived mid-dinner and extended the proceedings. That was the usual leisurely rhythm in this household. Something he was amazed to find he couldn't only tolerate, but enjoy. The experience was totally alien, but he still navigated it as if he had dinner with a household of women and children every night.

And like Mauricio and Marta, the newcomers immediately treated him as if they'd known him forever. Minutes after their arrival, he learned that Amelia's husband was finishing a contract in Argentina and would join them in the States next year. Until then, they were staying with big sister Isabella. As they had almost since the children were born.

Having grown up in a subdued household with a military father and a conservative mother, he had no idea how loud and lively a family could be. But it did seem everyone was more gregarious than usual on his account. Probably because an adult male presence was a rarity in their lives. The only other male in the family was Isabella's younger brother who lived abroad. But no matter how many men they'd been exposed to, they'd never seen anything like him. Everyone was so intrigued and awed by him and thrilled to have him.

Everyone but Isabella, of course. But she ignored him with such ingenuity, no one but him realized she hadn't given him one word or look all through dinner, even avoiding answering his direct questions without appearing to snub him.

He ate as much as all of them put together, to Marta's delight, who said she'd finally found someone with an appetite to do her efforts justice. When he said it was only expected, since he could probably house them all in his body, she laughed and was only happy her culinary artwork wouldn't have to be reduced, again, to the status of shunned leftovers.

After dinner they retired to the family room and he was served his promised Earl Grey. Mauricio solemnly told him he'd have to postpone showing him his drawings. He didn't trust the younger children to respect his works of art, and they wouldn't have the peace needed to discuss them anyway.

The evening progressed for another hour with everyone asking him a thousand questions, hanging on every word of his answers, laughing readily at his every witticism.

He sat there feeling like a sprawling lion after a satisfying meal, with a pride of lionesses lounging around him and cubs crawling all over him.

Then Mauricio and the younger children, Diego and Benita, started yawning. Marta and Amelia took them to bed, leaving Richard alone with Isabella for the first time.

Without turning her head toward him, just her baleful gaze, she seethed, "You'll get up now, and you'll get the hell out of here. And you will *never* come back."

Sighing in satisfaction that she'd finally talked to him, even to slash him before evicting him, he only sat forward to pour himself another cup of tea.

He settled back even more comfortably, slanting her a challenging glance. "Are you going to make me?"

"I'll do whatever it takes." Her usually velvety voice was a serrated blade. "I got my family out of a country full of thugs like you, and I am never letting one near them again."

Now, *that* piqued his interest. But direct questioning now wouldn't get her to elaborate. He had to get what he wanted indirectly, by giving her more chances to flog him.

"Thugs like me? What kind do you think I am?"

"I can *extrapolate* well enough."

"Shoot."

"If only I could. Right between your snake eyes."

This took him by such surprise he threw his head back and laughed. "If only you knew."

As if his merriment was the last straw, she turned to him, her body rigid with rage. "What's that supposed to mean?"

"Just that I was once code-named Cobra. So your assessment of my reptilian attributes is quite accurate."

"Of course I'm accurate. As for what kind of snake you are, I think you must have been Burton's rival gangster or you'd been sent by another cartel to destroy the competition.

Though your legitimate image was and remains flawless, I know what you really are. A criminal." At his ridiculing pout, she narrowed her eyes. "Don't bother spouting I'm a criminal, too. Take that to the law or shut up. But I'm telling you here and now, I'll go to any lengths to make certain you never come near my family again."

He sipped his tea, luxuriating in how fury intensified her allure. "You knew all that when you not only let me come near you, but let me be all over you and inside you."

"When it was between us, that was one thing. Now you've involved my family, all rules have changed. You don't want to find out what I'm capable of doing to protect them."

"But I do want to find out. Recount some of the unspeakable things you did in their defense. Who knows, maybe I can be deterred after all."

"Anything I previously did is irrelevant. What I'd do would be tailored to you. I'll keep that a surprise."

"Like you did with Mauricio?"

"Why would my adopted son be a surprise to you?"

That was the story she was going with?

From her immediate retort, she'd prepared that story in case he investigated her. He was sure she'd get her story straight with her mother and sister. She thought he wouldn't be able to find the truth in the void she'd created in her past. She had every reason to believe she'd get away with it since Mauricio looked nothing like him. But he wouldn't contest her claim, not now.

Maybe not ever.

She rose, flaying him with her antagonism. "Why did you come here in the first place?"

He drained his cup, put it on the tray and then rose to his feet. She took a step back, and he knew. She didn't fear him coming closer, but her own reaction to his nearness.

All he wanted was to take her against the nearest wall.

Since that was out of the question in her family-infested

home, he shrugged. "I came to find you, and they snared me. Your mother and son are inescapable. As you should know."

"Yeah, right, the unstoppable Richard Graves finally met his immovable objects."

"Very much so. Your mother and son are intractable. Your sister and her little urchins, too. What should I have done in your opinion to deter their determined attentions? Bared my fangs and snapped at them?"

"Gee, I'm sure they'll be thrilled with your opinion of them. But, yeah, one look at your real face and a swipe of your forked tongue and they would have run screaming. But you sat there purring all night like a lion ingratiating himself to a naïve, male-starved pride."

This time he guffawed. Their unlikely situation had made her think of that parable, too. "What can I say? Your mother's cooking can soothe even me, and your little tribe is quite…entertaining. They're such an exemplary audience. And they're yours, so it wasn't in my best interests to scar them for life with the sight of my hood spread out."

"News flash, playing nice with my family wouldn't ingratiate you to *me*, since that's the one thing I won't forgive you for." Before he could answer, her lips thinned. "Enough of this. Give me your word you won't come again."

His eyebrows rose. "You think my word is worth anything?"

"Yes."

Heat surged in his chest. She seemed to believe that, when she shouldn't believe he had any code of honor.

Not willing to corroborate her belief, he said, "Then, maybe you don't know anything about me after all."

Before she could blast him again, he brushed against her as her mother and sister walked in. He promised he'd be back in answer to their new invitation, then took his leave. The women saw him to the door and stood there until he drove away.

Isabella remained in the background. He was sure she was killing him a dozen horrific ways in her mind.

The stimulation of her murderous intentions only lasted a few blocks before reality all came crashing over him again.

He should heed her warning, should walk away. He'd seen her, he'd had her, and after he made sure she stayed away from Rose, he should disappear from her life again.

It shouldn't matter he felt he'd suffocate if he didn't have more of her. It shouldn't matter she'd had his son. A boy who provoked a thousand unknown stirrings inside him. For what would he do with those aberrant feelings?

She hadn't told him she'd had his son, seemed bound on never letting him know. Even without knowing what he *really* was, she knew she mustn't let him near a boy that age.

And she was absolutely right.

For the past seven years he hadn't known Mauricio existed, and Mauricio hadn't known he did.

He would keep it that way.

Six

After Richard left, her mother and sister pounced on her with questions. Isabella expended every drop of ingenuity she possessed into dodging them and validating none of their suspicions.

Those ranged from his being a suitor she wouldn't let close for reasons they couldn't imagine—since as did every woman on earth, they thought him a god and/or a godsend—to the truth. Her mother was the one whose eyes contained the suspicion...the *hope*, that he was Mauri's biological father.

She held it together until she was in her room, prepared for bed, then collapsed on it in a mass of tremors.

So much had happened so fast in that exhilarating, nauseating and terrifying roller coaster since he'd exploded into her life last night. Now his incursion had reached inside her home and within inches of the secret she'd thought safe forever. And it scared her out of her wits.

And that was before she considered that confounding evening he'd spent with them. Every second he'd spent charming her family like the snake he'd admitted he'd been labeled as, she'd felt a breath away from screaming with aggravation and swooning with dread. At the torture's end, she might have stood her ground, and Richard might have walked away, but she didn't think it would end that simply. He hadn't given his word he'd leave her family alone in his pursuit of her. And nothing involving Richard was without long-term repercussions. She was now terrified what his next blow would be and how he'd deal it.

At least she seemed to have steered him away from any suspicion he might have had about Mauri. His age alone must have been a red flag, and she'd gone light-headed holding her breath, expecting the worst. After all the suspense, he'd only made a passing comment and had taken her claim that Mauri was adopted without batting a lid.

But…maybe this very reaction indicated she was overreacting. Maybe even telling him the truth about Mauri would be the best way to end his infiltration of her life.

A man like him, who lived separate from humanity, without connections, who only cared about having the world at his feet, would probably be appalled at the news he'd fathered a son. His lack of curiosity, or the one that had been satisfied by a mere word, indicated that her assessment was probably correct.

Furthermore, this inexplicable visit itself might turn out to be a blessing in disguise. Maybe seeing her in her domestic milieu as a mother, especially to his biological son, would be a too-banal dose of reality, spoiling the fantasy of the wild affair he'd been planning to have with the mysterious femme fatale he seemed to think her. Maybe it would all douse his passion and make him walk away now, not later.

That sounded plausible. There was no way he would involve himself with her now that he'd seen her "tribe." Spending time with her family had probably been a quaint novelty to him, a field experiment in how the other half lived to add to his arsenal of analyzing human beings, to better devise strategies to control and milk them for all they were worth. But there was no way he'd want to repeat it.

He'd only said he would to punish her because she'd dared challenge him. But once he was satisfied he'd made her sweat it out long enough, he'd let her know he never intended an encore.

Once she came to this conclusion, exhaustion, emotional

and physical, descended on her like a giant mallet. She had no idea when sleep claimed her.

She woke up feeling as if she'd been in a maelstrom.

And she had been. Her dreams had been a vortex filled with Richard and their tempestuous time together, past and present. He'd always wreaked havoc inside her, awake or asleep. There'd never been any escaping him. Not in her psyche. She'd just have to settle for escaping him in reality.

By the time she headed to her office, her new conviction that he'd fade from her life again made her wonder if she should come clean to Rose and Jeffrey about her past.

She'd tried to after she'd left Richard yesterday, to deprive him of that coercion card. But their schedules hadn't allowed her to even broach the subject. So she'd scheduled a meeting with Rose first thing in the morning, the one sure way to get a hold of her.

But if Richard disappeared again, should she expose the ugly truth of her history to Rose and Jeffrey? Just the knowledge would scar their psyches. And what if they worried her past would catch up with her and they'd be standing too close when it did? *She* was certain there was absolutely no danger of that, or she wouldn't have taken their partnership offer. But what if they couldn't feel safe with her around?

She stood by her conviction they'd never judge her, would be more supportive than they already were. But if they worried about their family's safety at all, she'd have to leave.

And she didn't want to leave. Them, the practice, her new place. It was the first time she felt she had real friends, a workplace where she belonged and a home.

By the time she opened her office door she'd made her decision.

She'd wait to see what Richard did. If he disappeared again, that would be that. If he didn't…

No. She wouldn't consider that possibility until it came to pass.

Suddenly she found herself plucked from the ground and suspended against the door she'd just closed with two-hundred-plus pounds of premium maleness plastered against her.

"You're late."

A squeeze of her buttocks accompanied his reprimand before he crashed his lips over hers, invading her with the taste of him, the distillation of dominance and danger.

But he was invading more than her essence. He was breaching her last privacy, leaving her no place to hide. Just when she'd convinced herself he'd leave her alone, set her free.

She'd do anything to make him let her go. Even beg.

But his large hands were spreading her thighs around his hips, raising her to thrust his erection up at her core as he dragged her down on it. His tongue filled her again and again, drank her moans as they formed. Reality softened, awareness expanded to encompass his every breath and heartbeat. Nothing remained but Richard and her and their fusion.

"Richard..."

"Yes, let me hear your distress for me, make up for the agonizing night I spent, needing you under me, all around me."

Something shrill cut through the fog of sensations as he undid her blouse and bra, bent to engulf one nipple in his mouth. The first hot suckle almost made her faint with pleasure. Then the clamor rose again until she realized what it was—her mind screaming, reminding her of the threat he posed to her existence and everyone in it.

It finally imbued her with enough sanity and strength to push out of the craved prison of his arms and passion, to stumble away and put her clothes back in order.

"What are you doing here?"

At his question she turned to him with an incredulous huff. "I won't even dignify that by echoing it."

Lids heavy, his gaze swept her in ruthless hunger, strumming her simmering insanity. "I told you to end your partnership with the Andersons. And what did you do? You reported to work yesterday and again first thing this morning. When I made it clear this is the one thing I won't budge on."

She tossed him a contemptuous glance. "You don't have to budge. Only to bugger off, as you say in your homeland."

His lips twisted in that palpitation-inducing smile that seemed to come easier to him since yesterday. "Don't think that because I want you now more than ever I will bargain with you over this. It's not a matter of either you do it or you don't."

"You're right. It's not a matter of 'either or' but 'neither nor.'" At his arching eyebrow, she huffed. "You do know your grammar, don't you? The language *was* coined where you hail from. I will neither end anything with the Andersons nor start anything with you."

A theatric exhalation. "Pity. After everything that happened between us, I would have rather not forced you into complying. Oh, well."

He produced his phone from his pocket, pressed one virtual button. The line opened in two seconds and she heard a deep voice on the other end. She thought it said, "Sir."

Without taking his eyes off her, Richard got to the point of his call at once. "Murdock, I need a court order to shut down the Anderson Surgery Center in forty-eight hours."

With that he ended the call and continued looking at her.

So that was his extreme measure. If she wouldn't leave, he'd take everything from under her. And she had no doubt he could and would do it. And that would only be for starters. In case this somehow didn't work, he would only escalate his methods of destruction.

And none of it made any sense.

She cried out her confusion. "*Why* do you want me to stop working here? What is it to you? Is this even about me or..." A suspicion exploded in her mind. "Is this about

Rose? Did you discover her relationship to Burton and come here to clean up every trace of him, including anybody who knew him? If so, did you only want me out of the way so I wouldn't warn them about you? And now you've decided to strike directly since I didn't cooperate and spoiled your preferred stealth methods?"

As the conviction sank in her mind, from one breath to the next her desperation turned to aggression in defense of her friends. "Burton was a monster who deserved far worse than whatever you've done to him. But she was his victim. Besides that, Rose and Jeffrey are the absolute best people I've ever known, and I'd die before I let you near them. And that's *not* a figure of speech."

As if he hadn't heard her tirade, he cocked his head at her. "How did you come to know that couple?"

"Wh-what?"

"There was no evidence of when you met, or of your developing relationship, not even emails or phone calls, and I want to know how you did this."

"I—I met Rose in a conference in Texas four years ago."

"And? I want to know what led to their asking you to be their partner and not any of their long-term colleagues."

His icy focus shook her. Where was this interrogation heading? "I felt a…kinship to her at once. I guess she felt the same, since she told me her life story as we waited for a late lecturer. I was shocked to realize that Burton used to be her stepfather."

His eyes and jaw hardened. He gestured for her to continue.

"I didn't tell her about me, but that kindred feeling only grew when I knew both of our lives were blighted by that monster. Incredibly, she felt the same way. Afterward and for years, we talked for hours daily, using online video chat. We practically designed and decorated this place that way. She and Jeffrey kept pushing me to come live in the States and be their partner. The moment I could, I took my family and came back, thinking I was giving us all a new and safe life. Then *you* appeared to mess everything up."

His eyes grew heavier with so much she couldn't fathom. "I don't want to mess things up. Not anymore."

"Yeah, right. That's why you're going to shut down the practice Rose and Jeffrey worked for years to build and invested all their money in."

"It's all up to you. Walk out of here, and I do, too."

"You mean you'd leave them alone, for real? You wouldn't have done that eventually anyway?"

"I already said going after them was to force you to leave. I have no interest in sabotaging their business."

"So this isn't about Rose? You're not after her?"

"It is about her." Before his reply sent her alarm soaring again, he reached for her, dragged her against his rock-hard body. "But the one I'm after is you, as you well know. So I suppose we can negotiate after all. Taking everything into consideration, I'll make you a deal."

She squirmed against him. "What deal?"

"I want you out of here. And I want you, full stop. You want me, too, but need to be assured of your family's safety. So here's my deal. You will make use of everything I can give you, will be with me every possible minute that our schedules permit. And I promise to stay away from your family."

His hypnotic voice seeped through her bones with delicious compulsion, until she wondered why she'd ever put up a fight when being with him had always been all she'd ever wanted. And if he promised her family would be safe...

Then he added, "But only if you stay away from mine."

She pushed away to stare up at him, her mind shying away from an enormous realization.

Then he spelled it out. "Burton was my stepfather, too."

Richard had never intended to reveal that fact to Isabella. But he never did anything he intended where she was concerned. Nothing that was even logical or sane. He touched her, looked into her eyes, and his ability to reason was incinerated.

Not that he cared. As he'd told her, so many things had changed in the past forty-eight hours. His previous intentions weren't applicable anymore. He wanted her, had already decided to leave her family situation untouched. Laying down the card of his relationship to Rose now felt appropriate.

He'd always wondered if she'd ever worked out that his revenge on Burton had had a personal element, until last night when she'd made it clear she'd always thought it purely professional. He'd expected the truth to come as a surprise, but the avalanche of shock and horror that swept her at his revelation was another thing he'd failed to project.

Before he could think of his next move, the door opened after only a cursory knock.

And he found himself face-to-face with Rose.

His heart gave his ribs a massive thump as observations came like bullets from a machine gun. Rose's silky ponytail thudding over her shoulder with her sudden halt, the white coat swinging over a chic green silk blouse and navy blue skirt, her open face with its elegant features tensing and the eyes full of affection as she entered Isabella's office emptying to fill with surprise.

He'd checked her schedule, made sure she'd be occupied with patients during his visit. This confrontation hadn't been a possibility.

But it was a reality now.

And finding the sister he'd watched from afar for more than twenty-five years less than ten feet away was a harsher blow than he'd ever thought it could be.

Tearing his gaze away, he turned to Isabella, who was gaping at him as if she hadn't even noticed Rose's entry.

"I'll leave you to your visitor, Dr. Sandoval. We'll continue our business later."

He turned around and Rose blinked, moved as if coming out of a trance. "Don't go on my account."

He gave her his best impersonal glance. "I was just about to leave anyway."

Before either woman reacted, he'd almost cleared the door when Rose caught him by his sleeve.

Dismay soaring, he raised an eyebrow with all the cold impatience he could muster. He needed this confrontation to be over.

"Rex?"

Everything inside braked so hard he realized for the first time how people dropped unconscious from shock.

The sister who'd last seen him when she was six years old had recognized him on sight.

But it was still just a suspicion. Only he could solidify it. Or Isabella, now that he'd revealed his connection to Rose. But knowing her, she wouldn't be the one to do so. So it was up to him.

Feeling his insides clench in a rusty-toothed vise, he made his choice. "You must have mistaken me for someone else. The name is Richard. Richard Graves."

He flicked Isabella a warning glance, just in case. Not that he'd needed to. Isabella seemed to have lost the ability to speak or even blink. But when she regained the ability to talk, if she did tell Rose...

He couldn't worry about that now. He had to get the sodding hell out of there.

Not giving Rose a chance to say anything else, he turned and strode away, fighting the urge to break out into a run.

Once in his car, he drove away as if from an earth fissure that threatened to engulf everything in its path.

Which was a very accurate description.

Everything since he'd seen Isabella again *had* been like an earthquake that had cracked the ground his whole life was built on. He'd thought he could stem the spread of the chasms and return to a semblance of stability again.

But there was no fooling himself anymore. He'd set an unstoppable sequence of events in motion. And if he didn't stop the chain reaction, it would unravel his whole existence.

And everyone else's, too.

Two hours later in his penthouse, after a couple of drinks and a hundred laps in the pool, he had a plan in place.

He'd just gotten out of the shower when the intercom that never rang did.

The concierge apologized profusely, claiming that it was probably a false alarm, since he'd never allowed anyone up in the past six years, but a lady insisted he would want her up.

Isabella. She'd preempted him.

A wave of excitement and anticipation swept him as he informed the concierge that Isabella was always to be let up without question. He ran to dress, but she arrived at his door so fast he had to rush there barefoot in just his pants.

The moment he saw her on his doorstep, he wanted to haul her to bed, lose himself inside her and forget about all they had to resolve and all he had to do.

"Isabella…"

She pushed past him, strode inside. It took him a couple of minutes of following her through his penthouse to realize—to believe—what she was doing.

She was heading to his bedroom. And she was stripping.

Almost every surprise he'd ever had had involved her. This one almost had him launching himself at her as she passed one of the couches, tackling her facedown and thrusting inside her before they even landed on it.

He held back only because he wanted to let her take this where she wanted, to savor the torment of watching her disrobe for him, exposing her glory to his aching, covetous gaze. The contrast between the pitiless seduction of her action and her straitlaced stride made it all the more mind-meltingly arousing.

Once in his lower-floor bedroom, he could barely see her until he remembered he could turn on the lights with a whisper.

The expansive space filled with the subdued lighting he preferred, showcasing her beauty in golden highlights and arcane shadows. At the foot of his bed, she turned, wearing only white bikini panties and same-color, three-inch-heeled sandals. Her eyes were burning sapphires.

He approached, waiting for her to say or do something. She only stood there looking up at him.

Suddenly the urge to inspect her body, with the insight of new realizations, knowing she'd given birth to his child, overtook him. His eyes swept her voluptuousness, luxuriating in her as a whole before basking in each asset separately.

Her hips were lush with femininity, her waist a sharp concavity, her legs long and smooth, her shoulders square and strong. Every curve and line and swell of her was the epitome of womanliness, the exact pattern that activated his libido. Each inch of her had ripened to its utmost potential. He now realized it wasn't only time but motherhood that had effected the change.

Turning his savoring from visual to tactile, he caressed her buttocks, her back, leaving her firm belly for last. His skull tightened over his brain as he imagined her ripening every day with the child they'd made together during one of their pleasure-drenched deliriums. The idea of his seed taking root inside her, growing into a new life, that vibrant, brilliant boy who'd rocked the foundations of his world last night, turned his arousal into agony. He needed to claim her, to mark her with his essence again...*now.*

Wrestling with the savagery of his need, he skimmed his hands up to her breasts. Blood roared in his ears, his loins, as their warmth and resilience overflowed in his hands. He stared at the ripened perfection of her, the need to know if she'd breastfed Mauricio scalding him, the images searing him body and mind.

Unbidden, another image flared in his mind, heightening the imaginary inferno. Her, holding another baby, one he'd get to see her breastfeed.

Recoiling from the agonizing visions, he squeezed her supple flesh, his fingers unsteady with emotion and mounting hunger as he circled the buds he'd tasted during so many rides to ecstasy, thicker, darker now, and much more mouthwatering. And now he knew why.

Before he bent to silence the clamoring and engulf her nipples, she slithered from his hold and lowered to her knees.

Mashing her face into his loins, she kissed his erection, her hands trembling over the zipper, dragging his pants down.

"I didn't get to touch and taste you again…"

Her gasp of greed as he thudded heavily in her waiting grasp juddered through him. Relief and distress speared through him in equal measure as she worshipped him, the only touch and need he'd ever craved, measuring his girth, rubbing her face over his length, inhaling and smooching and nibbling. Then with a stifled cry of urgency, she opened her mouth over his crown, swirled her hot tongue over its smoothness, moaning continuously as she lapped up the copious flow of his arousal as if its taste was the sustenance she'd been starving for.

The sight alone, of her kneeling in front of him, of her gleaming head at his loins, of her lips, deep rose and swollen and wrapped around his erection, almost made him come.

Stepping out of what felt like burning cloth, he tried to savor it all, caressed the hair that rained over her face, held it away in one hand so he could revel in her every move and expression, bending to run his other hand over the sweep of her back, the flare of her hips. But she started rubbing herself sinuously against his legs like a feline in heat and he lost the fight.

He dragged her up, growling. Before he threw her back

on the bed and mounted her, she climbed him, wrapped her legs around his hips and ground her moist heat over his erection. He tore her panties off, digging his fingers into her buttocks, making her cry out, crash her lips into his.

Her tongue delved inside his mouth, tangling in abandon with his as if she was bent on extracting everything inside him. He let her storm him, show him the ferocity of her craving, rumbles of pained pleasure escaping from his depths.

Her voice, roughened by abandon, filled him. "Take me, Richard. Or should I call you Rex?"

He could swear he heard a crack as loud as a sonic boom. It was his control snapping.

He thrust up into her, invading her molten tightness, sheathing himself inside her to the hilt in one fierce stroke. Her scream felt as if it tore out of his own lungs. The very sound of unbearable pleasure, as his bellow had been.

On the second thrust he roared again and staggered with her to the bed, flinging their entwined bodies on it, loving her squeal as the impact emptied her lungs, then again as his weight crushed her next breath out of her.

He rose between the legs clamped over his back, holding her feverish eyes, tethering her head with a hand twisted in her hair, the other nailing her down by the shoulder.

Her swollen lips trembled over her anguished demand. "Do it, do it all to me."

He obeyed, pounding her, each ram wrenching from their bodies all the searing sensations they could experience or withstand.

Her shrieks of ecstasy rose until she mashed herself into him and he felt her shatter around him. Her inner flesh gushed hot pleasure over him, her muscles wrenching at his length in a fit of release. He rode the breakers of her orgasm in a fury of rhythm, feeding her frenzy.

"Come with me…"

He did, burying himself to her womb and surrendering to the most violent orgasm he'd ever known even with her, filling her with his essence in jet after excruciating jet.

Following the cataclysm, he couldn't separate from her. Couldn't imagine he ever would. He had to have her like this always, fused to his flesh through the descent, feeling her aftershocks and fulfillment.

He didn't think anything of her receding warmth until she shivered. Frowning, he rose off her to reach for the covers, groaning at the pain of separating from her body.

Securing her under them with him wrapped around her for extra warmth, he smiled in possession and satisfaction down at her. "I take it you've decided to take my deal?"

"No. This was actually the closure we both needed before I told you that I won't."

His hands, which had been caressing her back and buttocks, stilled. Her eyes were unwaveringly serious. She wasn't teasing or resisting. She meant this.

Then she told him why. "I can't have you in my life and hope it would remain normal. I've struggled too long and too hard, have too many people who depend on me to introduce your disruptive, destructive element in my life. I'm the pillar of my family and if you damage me, and I'm sure you will, everything will come crashing down. I won't have that."

Rising to look at her, he felt he'd turned to stone inside and out as she watched her rising, too.

"For closure to be complete, so we'd never have any loose ends tangling us in each other's lives, I'm also here to have everything out once and for all. It's the only way we could both finally let each other go. For good this time."

Seven

Richard let Isabella leave his side, a jagged rock in his throat. This felt real. And final.

Anything he did now to stop her would have to be true coercion. And no matter that he was losing his mind needing her, and she'd proved again she needed him as much, over-powering considerations had made her decide to quell that need. He *could* force her. But he couldn't. He had to have her not only willing, but unable to live without having him.

He watched her careful progress to the bathroom in only her sandals, what had remained on all through. She soon exited and, without looking at him, bent to pick up her panties, dropping them again when she realized they were ruined before walking out. Pulling on his pants, he followed her as she retraced and reversed her stripping journey.

Once beside the pool, she sat on the couch where they'd almost made love the first night and looked at him.

And the *way* she did…as if he was everything she wanted but could never have.

Before he charged her and overrode her every misgiving, her subdued voice stopped him in his tracks.

"I'll start." She stopped to swallow, her averseness to coming clean clearly almost overwhelming. "I'll tell you everything. My side of the story. But only if you promise you'll reciprocate and tell me the whole truth, too."

"What if I promise, and you tell me everything I want to know, but I don't deliver on my end of the bargain?"

Her shoulders jerked dejectedly. "I'd do nothing. I can do nothing anyway. The first truth I have to admit is that I am at your mercy. The imbalance of power between us is incalculable. I have so many vulnerabilities while you have none. You can force me to do anything you want."

He made her feel this way? Defeated? Desperate? He'd thought she needed his chase before she gave in to what she'd wanted all along. But if she truly hated it, this was as insupportable, as abhorrent, to him as when she'd thought he could harm her.

Feeling his guts twisting over dull blades, he came down to sit beside her. "You previously said you considered my word worth having. If you really think so, you have it. A caveat, though. You'll probably end up wishing you hadn't asked for the whole truth. It will horrify you."

"After what I've been through in my life, nothing ever would again." Her gaze wavered. "Can I have a drink first?"

Her unfamiliar faltering intensified his distress. He'd never seen her...defenseless before. Besides the shame that choked him for being what made her feel this way, a piercingly poignant feeling, akin to the tenderness only Rose had previously provoked, swamped him. For the first time he wasn't looking at Isabella as the woman who made him incoherent with desire, a woman he wanted to possess, in every meaning of the word, but a woman he wanted to... protect. Even from himself.

Especially from himself.

Stunned by the new perception, he headed to the bar and mixed her one of the cocktails she liked.

For a year after he'd left her, whenever he'd made himself a drink, he'd made her one, too, as if waiting for her to materialize and take it.

The day he'd thrown Burton in the deepest dungeon on the planet, he'd looked at the cocktail glass he'd prepared with such care and faced the stark truth that she never would. And he'd smashed it against the wall. Then he'd furiously and irrevocably terminated every method of communication she hadn't used. He'd been convinced she'd forgotten him. And he'd hated her then, with a viciousness he hadn't even felt for Burton. Because he hadn't been able to forget her.

And all that time she'd been running, pregnant with his child, giving birth to him, facing endless difficulties and dangers he could only guess at.

He didn't have to guess anymore. She'd finally tell him.

He poured himself a shot of whiskey, breaking his rule of not exceeding two drinks per day. He had a feeling he'd need as much numbness as he could get for the coming revelations.

It seemed she felt the same way as she gulped down the cocktail as soon as he handed it to her. Even with little alcohol, for a nondrinker like her, having it in one go would affect her as much as half a bottle of hard liquor would affect him.

As soon as he sat, struggling not to drag her onto his lap, she said, "To explain how I became Burton's wife, I have to start my story years earlier."

His every muscle bunching in dreadful anticipation, he tossed back his drink.

"You probably know my early history—that I was born in Colombia to a doctor father and a nurse mother and was the oldest of five siblings. My trail stops when I was thirteen, when my family was forced out of our home along with tens of thousands of others.

"Though we ended up living in one of the shantytowns around Bogota, my parents gave me medical training, while I home-schooled my siblings. Everybody sought our medical services, especially guerillas who always needed us to patch up their injured. Then one day, when I was nineteen, we went to tend to the son of our region's most influential drug lord, and Burton, who was there concluding a deal, saw me. He later told me I hit him here—" she thumped her fist over her heart "—like nothing ever had."

His own heart gave a clap of thunder he was surprised she didn't hear.

He wasn't ready to listen to this. Not just yet.

Rising, he strode to the bar to grab a tray of booze this time. He had a feeling he needed to get plastered. He only hoped he could achieve that.

He poured them both drinks. She took hers, sipped it, grimaced when she realized it was a stiff one, but took another swallow before she went on.

"He came to our domicile later to 'negotiate' with my parents for me. My father refused the 'bargain' point-blank and was so enraged he shoved Burton. Next moment, he was dead."

Richard stared at her, everything screeching to a halt inside him. Burton. He'd killed her father. Too.

She adjusted his deduction. "Burton's bodyguard shot him for daring to shove his master. Before I could process what had happened, Burton put a bullet through the killer's head then turned to me, apologizing profusely. My mother was frantically trying to revive my father, while I faced the monster who'd come to buy me.

"The sick infatuation in his eyes told me resistance would come at an even bigger price to the rest of my family. Though my soul wretched at being at this monster's mercy, I'd already dealt with the worst life had to offer and knew I could do anything to survive, and to ensure the survival of my family. And if I manipulated his infatuation, someone of his power could be used to save my family, and many, many others.

"So I swallowed my shock and anguish, said I believed he hadn't meant any of us harm, but to give me time to deal with my shock and loss and to get to know him. He was delighted my reaction wasn't the rejection he'd expected after the 'catastrophic mistake' of my father's murder and he promised me all the time in the world. And everything else I could want. I told him I only wanted my family to be taken to the United States, to live legally in safety and comfort. He told me that would only be the first of thousands of things he'd lavish on me.

"The next day I stood at my father's grave with the man who'd been responsible for his murder. Before Burton took us away, I promised my friends I'd be back to help as soon as I could."

His hand shaking with a murderous rage he'd never before suffered, he reached for the bottle. He took a full swig and savored planning the new horrors he'd inflict on Burton.

Isabella continued, "Within a year he got us permanent residences through an investment program. My sisters and brother were in school and my mother volunteered in orphanages and shelters. Burton pulled strings to equate my experience to college courses necessary for medical school. Then on my twentieth birthday, he proposed. Though he was like putty in my hands, from his murderous behavior with others, I didn't doubt he could kill us all if I wavered now that he'd fulfilled his end of the bargain. I was forced to accept. With an ecstatic smile."

This. The missing pieces. What explained everything. Rewrote history. Made everything he'd thought or felt or done not only redundant or wrong, but a crime. Against her.

And she wasn't finished telling him how heinous that crime had been. "After the lavish wedding, I played the part of the doting wife, capitalized on his abnormal attachment to me. Thankfully, I didn't have to suffer through many sexual encounters, as he rarely wanted full intimacy. I perfected the act of loving his constant pawing, though."

The rage that exploded inside him threatened to crack his head open as he imagined her succumbing to Burton's touch while her every fiber retched at the violation…

He hurled the half-finished bottle across the pool. His fling across dozens of feet was so forceful, the window smashed on impact, exploding outward. If not for the terrace, it would have rained shards on the street below.

Isabella's heavenly eyes turned black at his violence.

He gestured that he'd expended it, would rein it in now, and for her to continue.

So she did. "I was also thankful he'd had a vasectomy in his early thirties. When he said we could still have a child if I wished, I assured him my younger siblings always felt like my children, and I wanted to focus on my education, my humanitarian work, but mostly him. He was delighted, as he was with everything from me. I continued to perform the role of perfect wife to such a powerful man, appearing to make flamboyant use, as he wished me to, of his wealth, and managed to put aside millions. I wanted enough personal power, education-, money- and knowledge-wise, to plot my family's escape from this nightmare. Then you appeared in my life."

Before he found words to express the torrents of regret accumulating inside him, she looked away, eyes glittering.

"When you asked me to leave with you, promised to protect me, I believed you had no idea what you were getting yourself into, not knowing the extent of my vulnerability, or of Burton's power and obsession with me. I thought even if you'd managed to spirit my whole family away, he'd find us, and you wouldn't be able to protect yourself, let alone us, from his vengeance. Oblivious to your real powers, I thought you were no match for him, was certain I'd only doom all of us if I left with you.

"Then you were gone as I always knew you would be one day and I discovered what true misery was at last. It wasn't being trapped in this horror with my family eternal hostages, their lives depending on my ability to perfect my act forever. It was to know what passion was, then to lose it and return to my cage to pine for you forever."

"Isabella…"

Her hand rose, stopping his butchered groan. It seemed

she needed to spit this out, as she would venom. "When you put your plan in action, I knew once he became convinced I betrayed him, he would be as insanely vicious as he'd been irrationally indulgent, so I took my family and ran. Then around a year later, my 'lady in waiting' who was married to his new right-hand told me Burton's bank accounts had been emptied by unknown parties and he no longer had means to buy allegiance or even protection, and that just before she'd called me, he'd disappeared. She suspected he'd been killed.

"Not willing to gamble on that, I decided to go back to Colombia when friends enlisted my urgent assistance in relocating them. I employed all necessary secrecy methods, and used the money I'd taken from Burton to build shelters and medical centers for those I couldn't help personally.

"After three years of no developments, I dared to go back to the States for a conference, where I met Rose. Then four years later, when she kept persisting with her partnership offer, I made my most extensive investigations yet. It was then I discovered you'd thrown Burton into that off-the-grid dungeon for the world's most dangerous criminals and finally felt secure enough to come back. A week later...you appeared again. And here we are."

Richard stared at Isabella, every word of her revelations a shard shredding his guts.

He'd lived among corruption and perversion so long, he considered only the worst explanation for anyone's actions. He'd condemned her at face value, hadn't reconsidered when all his being had kept telling him otherwise.

But what she'd been through wasn't unique. He'd seen worse crimes perpetrated against innumerable individuals in the world he inhabited. It was what she'd achieved in spite of all the danger and degradation, the way she'd conquered all adversity, built unquestionable success and helped countless others that elevated her from the status of coping victim to that of hero.

And he was the villain. One of the major causes of her ordeals. Even worse, among her unimaginable sufferings, he'd been the one to cause her the most anguish.

And she had yet to mention what must have caused her the most turmoil.

"What about Mauricio?"

She turned, her eyes eclipsed by terrible memories. But there was no attempt to hide anything in them anymore.

"He's your son."

He'd already been certain. Still, hearing her say it was a bullet of shame and regret through the heart.

"I discovered my pregnancy just before Burton suspected I might have exposed his secrets. I would have had to run anyway even if he never did, since he would have considered I betrayed him in a way that mattered even more to him. I gave birth to Mauri four months afterward, almost three months before I was due. For weeks I thought I'd end up losing him or he'd suffer some major defects. It took the better part of a year before I was finally assured there were no ill effects of his being born so premature."

Their gazes locked over the knowledge of yet another crime on his record. Her emotional and physical distress as she'd escaped a madman's pursuit while carrying the burden of her whole family, not to mention her grief over losing him, must have caused her premature delivery. And what she'd suffered during and after... His mind almost shut down imagining the enormity of her torment.

"But as I said before, I hadn't put two and two together at the time. So I named him Ricardo, after you."

The consecutive blows had already numbed him. This new one gashed him the deepest. But he'd lost the ability to react to the agony, just welcomed suffering it.

"By the time I worked out what you'd done, and I couldn't bear being reminded of you every time I called him, he was two. It took him a year to get used to being called by his second name, my father's, and another to forget his first one."

So she'd cherished remembering him for two years every time she'd called their son, until she'd discovered his exploitation and the treasured memories had turned to bitterness and betrayal.

His eyes lowered, seeing nothing but a scape of roiling darkness where the most extreme forms of self-punishment swirled in his imagination like hideous phantasms.

"Now it's your turn."

Raising his gaze to hers, he no longer even considered not giving her the truth. Not only what she'd asked for, but *his* whole truth. Every single shred of it.

What no one else knew about him.

Isabella felt as if she'd just turned herself inside out.

But besides nearly collapsing after she'd poured everything inside her out to Richard, she felt…relieved. More. Freed. She'd never shared this with anyone. Even her mother and siblings. She'd protected them from the burden of the full truth. Though her mother suspected a lot, she'd never caused her the injury of validating her suspicions or inflicting the details on her.

Now only Richard knew everything about her.

His only overt reactions had been to bring half the bar over, guzzle down half a bottle, then smash a window fifty feet away. Apart from that, it was as if he'd turned to stone. He'd had no response to finding out Mauri was his.

He raised his gaze to her, his eyes incandescent silver, his face an impassive mask. And she knew he'd keep his word, would tell her his side of the truth. He'd warned it would horrify her. She'd claimed nothing ever could again.

But she'd lied. Her defenses were nonexistent where he was concerned. Anything with or from Richard devastated her. He was the only one who could destroy her.

Then he started.

"My father was in the Special Forces in the British army before he was dishonorably discharged. Bitter and suffering from severe financial problems after many failed investments, he joined a crime syndicate when I was six. He'd trained me in all lethal disciplines since I can remember, and I was so good that he involved me in his work. Not that I realized what we were doing for a couple of years. Then one day five years later, when Rose turned one, his partners came to tell us he'd been killed. Shortly thereafter, one of those partners started coming to our home. Then one day soon after that, my mother told me she and he just got married and the man—Burton—would now live with us."

Isabella sat forward, poured herself a drink, having no idea what it was. He'd already knocked her over with the disclosure that Rose was family and Burton had been his stepfather, too. She had a feeling she'd need anything to bolster her for the rest of his revelations.

"I knew Burton had killed my father because he wanted my mother. He'd been fixated on her as he had been with you. But because my mother was nowhere in your caliber, he soon began to mistreat her. And I could do nothing about it.

"Like you, I had a home filled with vulnerable targets, and though already a formidable fighter, I wasn't fully grown. Even if I could have killed him, that would have destroyed my family. I would have been put in a juvenile prison and my mother wouldn't have been able to carry on without me. So I did as you did. I played the part of the obedient boy who looked up to him, kept him placated every way I could. I tried to curb my younger brother, too, but Robert couldn't understand why I was being so nice to him. Rose soon took Robert's side, and it became Burton's favorite pastime to abuse them verbally, mentally and then, finally, physically. I hid my murderous hatred, channeled the perfect disciple, knowing it was the only thing that kept him in check, that he could easily kill them as he had our father."

She gulped down the horrible liquid in her glass, her eyes

filling. His gaze showed no indication of his thoughts as he continued recounting his atrocious past like a nuance-less automaton.

"When I was around sixteen, Burton started displaying signs of big money. I sucked up to him even more to find out its source, until he said he was now working for a major cartel just called The Organization, who turned abducted or sold children into mercenaries. He said he could make a bundle if he gave them Robert and Rose, that it would serve the two brats right.

"Knowing he'd do just that, I said surely their price would be a one-time thing, but if I became one of their 'handlers,' they'd pay me big money continuously, and he could have it all. Burton didn't like that it seemed I was protecting my siblings when I always said I could barely tolerate them. He also thought it fishy that I'd offer to give him the money I worked for. I allayed his suspicions, saying I considered it a benefit on all sides. I'd get out of the dump we called home, get rid of my clinging family, and get the best on-the-job experience. The money was in return for giving me this opportunity, as I wouldn't be doing anything with it for years, with all my needs paid for by my new employers."

Isabella had heard of The Organization many times during her marriage to Burton. The magnitude of evil they perpetrated was mind-numbing. To learn that Richard had volunteered to basically be sold to them to save his siblings, to save Rose, was…too much to contemplate, to bear.

"Buying my rationalization, and knowing how much The Organization would pay for my skill level, Burton jumped on my offer. I knew I'd leave my family behind, but the alternative was incomparably worse. The last time I saw them was the day I left to join The Organization. Robert was ten and Rose was six.

"I intended to amass enough power to one day assassinate Burton untraceably and disappear with my family. But he kept guarding against any counterstrikes. I know I never let my loathing show, but Burton, being the self-preserving parasite that he was, moved my family to places unknown, kept obliquely threatening me with their safety, providing me with evidence they were all well. As long as the monthly flow of cash continued."

She had the overwhelming urge to throw herself at him and hug the helplessness he must have felt out of him. But Richard wasn't one for human compassion, giving or receiving it. And if he ever were, she wouldn't be the one he'd seek that from.

Oblivious to her condition, he went on, clearly bent on giving her the whole story in one go, as she had been.

"What made that first year in The Organization survivable was a boy two years younger than myself. They called him Phantom, considered him their star future operative. Then Burton noticed the friendship we thought we'd hidden. He monitored us and overheard Phantom saying he was working on an escape plan. Burton told me if I reported him it would mean a higher place in The Organization at once and more pay. *He* couldn't do it, because he'd have to say how he'd found out, and I'd be punished for not reporting my *friend's* plans, would be demoted, or worse, when Burton wanted my paycheck to move to the six digits already. He had a lot of investments going. He made it clear it was Phantom...or my family."

Isabella struggled to hold back the tears. She'd always thought Richard made of steel, that he'd never felt love or fear for others, let alone could be held hostage by those feelings. And for him to have been just that, by the same man who'd caged her in the same way, was too much to contemplate.

"I knew Phantom, being prized, would be punished, tortured, but not killed. My family were nowhere as valuable. And there were three of them. Burton could hurt or even kill one to have me toe the line the rest of my life. So I reported Phantom. I let him think I did it to advance my stand-ing within The Organization so he'd hate me and show it, to further reinforce my coldblooded image, which every-thing depended on.

"Then I went all out to prove myself to be the absolute best they ever had. I applied my ruthlessness in ways you couldn't begin to imagine, my body count rivaling all the other operatives put together, until my monthly income was in the eight figures, with most of it going to Burton. I'd hoped to inundate him with far more money than he'd ever dreamed of so he'd let my family go, or at least treat them better until I got them out.

"But my escape and retaliation plans were further com-plicated when I was put in charge of another child—a boy they called Numbers, who reminded me so much of Rob-ert. I couldn't leave him or Phantom behind. But I finally gained enough autonomy so I could search for my family. I found them in Scotland…only too late. I pieced together that my mother tried to escape with my siblings. Burton pursued her and she lost control of her car and drove off the side of a mountain."

Isabella lost the fight, let the tears flow.

Richard didn't seem to notice as he continued reciting Burton's unimaginable crimes against him and the ghastly sequence of events of his loss.

"From what I learned, Burton hadn't bothered to help or to report the accident. He'd just walked away, since they'd already served their purpose. My mother and brother had died on impact. Only Rose had survived. I found her in an orphanage and arranged for her adoption by a kind and financially secure couple who'd been about to immigrate to the United States. I've been keeping an eye on her ever since."

And that, Isabella realized, was how he'd found her again. Even though the paranoid way she'd conducted her rela-tionship with Rose had kept her under his radar that long.

His dark voice interrupted her musings. "I never considered telling Rose I was alive. Then today… I can't believe she remembered me." He looked downward, his scowl deepening as if he was reliving those fraught moments. Without raising his face, he raised his eyes, impaling her with his glance. "What did you tell her after I left?"

She swallowed. "Nothing. I pretended I got an urgent call from my mother and ran out."

He only gave a curt nod. "It's best for her to remain ignorant of my existence."

She couldn't contest his verdict. Rose's life was the epitome of stability. The last thing she needed was his disruptive influence destroying her peace.

Although…he'd handled her crawling-with-kids-and-chicks household with stunning dexterity…

No. That had been a one-off. He'd sought her out the very next day to tell her he'd stay away from her family. Richard wouldn't want anyone permanently in his life. Not even his long-lost sister. Certainly not one who came with an extended family life right out of the textbook of normal and adjusted.

Considering he was done with that subject, he resumed his tale. "It was years before I could put my escape plan into action, after I made sure Numbers and Phantom and their team had escaped. I followed them, but as expected, they decided to kill me."

She gasped, blood draining. Phantom had been under the misconception he'd been his heartless enemy, a threat to their freedom and lives. As she'd been until an hour ago.

"Did you finally tell him the truth?"

He shrugged. "I saw no point."

"No point?" she exclaimed.

"Yes. I'd done everything they knew me to be guilty of, everything they hated me for. It didn't matter why I did it."

"Of course it matters. Knowing why always matters!"

He shook that majestic head of his in pure dismissal. "I don't believe so. I own my crimes, I don't excuse them."

He wouldn't ever think of asking forgiveness for them, either. "So if you didn't cite your extenuating circumstances to change their minds, how did you do it?"

"I told them it was in their best interest to back down, since it was them who wouldn't survive a confrontation."

A huff of incredulity escaped her. "I bet you weren't even exaggerating."

His look was what she expected a god would give a mortal who asked if he could smite him down. "I never exaggerate. They're formidable warriors, but their genius is in intelligence, applied sciences, medicine and subterfuge. My virtuosity is in termination."

"You're no slouch in intelligence and subterfuge yourself," she mumbled, remembering how he'd totally taken her in. Suddenly a terrible thought crossed her mind. "But since you survived without a scratch, does that mean…?"

An eyebrow arched. "You think I'd spend years planning to help them escape, only to kill them when they got their knickers in a twist?"

She exhaled in relief. "So how did it end with both sides alive, if you didn't put them straight and antagonized them in the most provocative method you could?"

"I was just stating facts. If they hadn't been using their macho hindbrains, they would have realized if I was the enemy, they would have all been already dead. Luckily, before I had to drive my point home, Numbers put himself between us and they backed down only for him. I let them continue thinking what they liked. I wasn't interested in becoming their friend, just in leading them in establishing our joint business."

"All your partners in Black Castle Enterprises are escapees from The Organization."

It wasn't a question but a realization. And it explained

everything. Those men were all larger-than-life; they must have been forged in the same hell Richard had been.

He nodded. "Once I made sure they were safe and our plan to dismantle The Organization was in motion, I could finally take my revenge on Burton. You know the rest."

No. She'd only thought she did.

It turned out she'd known nothing.

Now she did. And the more everything he'd just told her sank in, the more baffled and devastated she was. It *did* horrify her. But not in the way he'd thought.

He'd thought knowing he'd been the top executioner in such an evil establishment would validate her suspicions about him and...well, horrify her. What agonized her was realizing how much more nightmarish his life had been than hers. And that he'd had the best justification for all he'd done.

In fact, believing her to be Burton's willing wife, it was a wonder he hadn't punished her as viciously as he had him. It said a lot about the extent of his desire that it had curbed his killer instincts and stayed his hand.

Not that such desire mattered now. Those earth-shaking disclosures didn't change a thing.

While he might still want her, everything that had happened to him in the past had made him what he was now. If there was one man on earth who was unavailable for anything...human, it was him. That he hadn't said a thing about Mauri was proof positive of that.

So what she'd come here to tell him stood. She couldn't afford to have him in her life.

No matter that she craved him like a drug.

Her priority remained Mauri.

Inhaling a breath that burned like tear gas, she rose to her feet. He remained sitting, not even looking at her.

She waited until he looked up. "It's great we got things out in the open. But now you know my real history, you know I am not a danger to Rose, either myself or by association. Now we can go our separate ways, never to cross paths again."

Before he could say anything, she turned and rushed away.

It turned out she didn't have to worry. He just brooded after her in silence.

Once at the door, she remembered he had to open it for her. Before she could walk back to ask him to, the door opened. She hurried out, relieved, demolished.

This was it. It was over for good this time.

She'd never see Richard again.

Eight

When Rose entered her office the next morning, Isabella wasn't a mute, paralyzed mass like yesterday. She was a hopeless, miserable one.

She still struggled to smile as she received her treasured friend and colleague. Rose returned her kiss on the cheek before she pulled back, her blue-gray eyes filled with suppressed questions. She must be bursting to have her suspicion about Richard validated.

"Everything okay at home?"

In spite of the concern lacing the question, and the text message she'd sent her last night, Isabella believed Rose hadn't bought her excuse for running out yesterday one bit.

But Rose always made it clear that she was there for anything Isabella needed, and left it up to her to reveal any problems or worries. Isabella had never told her anything. Until now.

After she'd held it all in all these years, now that her family and those she'd struggled to help were safe, she could allow herself to consider her own needs. And now that the one she'd shared her innermost turmoil with had exited her life forever, she needed another confidante. Someone who wouldn't only listen in silence, offering not a word of sympathy or support, as Richard had. The only one who fit the bill was Rose.

She sat her down. "I need to tell you something—important. A lot of things, actually. About my past."

The worry hovering in Rose's eyes mushroomed into anxiety. "I always knew you were hiding something big, kept wishing you'd tell me."

Isabella reached for Rose's hands. "Before I do, I want you to promise to act according only to your and your family's best interests."

Rose grimaced. "Shut up and tell me everything, Izzy!"

And she did. Everything minus Richard.

All through her account, Rose's expressive face displayed her shock, horror, anguish and outrage on her behalf in minute detail. Her tears came at one point and wouldn't stop until Isabella fell silent and she hurled herself at her and crushed her in a nonending, breath-depleting hug.

"God, Izzy, you should have told me!" Rose sobbed between hard squeezes. "Why didn't you tell me?"

Isabella's tears flowed, too, as she surrendered to Rose's searing empathy. *This*…this was what she'd needed all these years, what she'd deprived herself of.

She thankfully let Rose inundate her with frantic reprimands before she finally pulled away, her tremulous smile teasing. "That's why I didn't tell you. I was afraid you'd drown me and flood the practice. Like you're doing now. When we've just finished decorating."

Rose burst out laughing. "God, Izzy, how dare you make me laugh after what you just told me?"

"Because it's all in the past. I just needed you to know everything about me, needed to share what I can't share with even my mother. But it is really all behind me."

Rose's resurging tears suddenly froze, her face filling with reproof again. "What did you mean by that prefacing warning? If you thought it a possibility this would change anything between us, you're stark raving mad!"

Isabella's heart expanded at the proof of her friend's magnanimity and benevolence. Then it compressed again. "Don't make any decisions now. Take time to think about it."

"The only thing I'll do with time is fume for months that you didn't come to me with this years ago!"

Isabella's lips spread at her friend's steel conviction. "At least wait until you see what Jeffrey thinks."

Rose's eyes widened. "You want me to tell Jeffrey?"

"I just assumed you would tell him."

Rose looked terminally affronted. "Of *course* I won't tell him!"

Isabella reached a hand out to hers. "I want you to tell him."

Rose snatched her hand, fisted it at her chest. *"No."*

It was Isabella's turn to burst out laughing at the growling finality in Rose's usually gentle, cheerful voice and the furiously obstinate expression that gripped her gorgeous if good-natured face. She looked like a tigress defending her cub. Isabella's laughter made her crankier.

Isabella tried to suppress her smiles. "I consider Jeffrey part of you. Not to mention a part of us, our team."

"I said no. You told *me* because you needed to purge the burden from your system by sharing it with someone who's strong enough to carry it with you, someone you fully trust."

"That's absolutely right, but Jeffrey—"

Rose cut her off. "You also needed to have someone fully appreciate what made you the wonderful human being you are."

"Uh…not that I'm not delighted you think I'm wonderful, but that's not how I…"

Again Rose bulldozed over her protests. "I tell Jeffrey all my secrets not because he's my husband and soul mate, but because they might impact him, so he's entitled to a heads-up. But if you really wanted him to know, and thought he should, as himself, not as a part of me or our team, you would have sat us both down and told us both all that. But you chose to tell only me."

Isabella shook her head at the incredible combination her friend was. The most romantic person on earth who melted with love for her husband, and the most no-nonsense prag-matist around. And as she'd always known, the best, stron-gest, most dependable friend anyone could aspire to have. She always felt the fates had chosen to compensate her for all the hardships of her life with Rose. And now she'd unbur-dened herself to her, not to mention knowing her relation-ship to Richard and therefore to Mauri, she felt the uncanny bond they'd shared from the start had become even deeper.

"And you did because I'm your closest friend. We're even closer than I thought. We both had our souls almost shat-tered by the same monster. And we both survived him." Rose's eyes shone with admiration. "Though I can't begin to compare our ordeals at his hand. I didn't fight for my life and that of my family for years like you did. I survived by accident."

Isabella now knew that wasn't true. Beyond escaping death in her family's car crash, Rose's survival had been no accident. She'd been saved. By Richard. He was the one who'd created her second chance in life. He was the real difference between their lives. She hadn't had a savior and champion like him.

She couldn't tell Rose that. The older brother who'd been looking out for her since she was ten didn't want her to know.

But although she'd always thought he'd played the oppo-site role in her life, that of conqueror and almost destroyer, it was still him who'd rid her of Burton forever. That made him the one who'd given her this new lease on life.

"What about Mauri? Is he...?" Rose choked. She couldn't even say Burton's name.

"*No.* I would have never let myself get pregnant by him."

But she *had* let herself get pregnant by Richard. When she'd discovered her pregnancy, even after he'd left, even knowing the danger she'd put herself in, she'd been giddy with delight that she'd have a part of him with her always.

So far, she'd risked it again. Four times, if she wanted to be accurate.

Rose's voice dragged her out of her turbulent musings. "Whew. It's a relief to know that monster didn't manage to perpetuate his genes."

Grabbing the opportunity to steer the conversation in a less-emotional direction, she pulled a face at Rose. "You should know me better than to think I'd inflict those on my child."

Rose pounced, hugging the breath out of her before pulling back. "But you're so amazing your genes would vaporize any dirt or perversion in any others. Mauri would have turned out to be the awesome kid he is just because you're his mom."

Feeling suddenly lighthearted, when she'd thought she'd never feel that way again after losing Richard for the second and last time, Isabella dragged Rose closer and smacked kisses on both her cheeks.

"Have I told you lately just how much I love you?"

Rose gave her a mock scolding glare. "When have you ever told me that?" When Isabella started to protest, Rose pulled her into another hug. "You never needed to tell me. I always knew. And I love you, too. Now more than ever."

Isabella hadn't expected to go home happy. But thanks to Rose, and to work, not to mention to Prince Charming Jeffrey, the day she'd predicted would be an endless pit of gloom had turned out to be the best she'd had in a couple of decades.

She didn't expect her buoyant condition to continue, knew misery would descend on her more aggressively than it had the first time she'd lost Richard. Back then, there'd been distractions vying for her mental and emotional energy, fractioning her turmoil over him. Now, without anxieties consuming her focus, she'd experience the full measure of it.

There was another reason she was certain her despondency would only deepen. Before she'd met him again, she'd had this vague hope she'd find love again. She now knew this was an impossible prospect.

Richard would remain the one who could make her turn off the world and lose herself in his ecstasy. She didn't want—couldn't stomach—anything less than that. So now she knew. She'd spend the rest of her life as a mom, a daughter, a sister, a friend and a doctor. But the woman part of her was over. Only Richard had the secret code to this vital component of her being. And he was gone. Forever this time.

Turning onto her street, she shook herself. She was sliding again, and she owed it to Mauri and her family not to expose them to her dejection. She'd promised them a shining new beginning and she'd be damned if she didn't deliver.

And then she had to count her blessings. She'd unburdened herself to Rose, their bond had become more profound, her family was safe, they loved their new home and she loved her new workplace. If she obsessed over Richard more than ever, if her body demanded its mate and master now that she could no longer swat her hunger away with hatred...tough.

She'd just mentally slapped some sense into herself when she saw it.

Richard's car. Parked—again—in her spot.

Her heart followed the usual drill when it came to Richard. It crashed to a halt before bursting out in mad gallop, stumbling like a horse on ice.

She didn't know how or where she ended up parking, or how she made it inside the house. The empty house. Where was everyone...?

Shouts burst from the kitchen. Her heart almost exploded from her chest as she burst into a run, then she heard... clapping. *Clapping?*

Screeching to a halt at the threshold, she saw...saw...

Richard was in her kitchen. He had every member of

her household at the huge semicircular counter island and he was…

Performing for them. Knife tricks.

He was swirling knives with such speed and skill, his hands were a blur; the feats he performed with four—no, five…*six* knives nothing short of impossible. He made it look effortless. His captive audience was openmouthed and glassy eyed.

She sympathized. She would have done the same if she wasn't shocked out of her wits.

With everyone hypnotized by his show, they didn't notice her. Only he slunk her a sideways glance, that half smile that reduced her brain functions to gibberish on his lips. She stopped behind Mauri, and Richard escalated the level of difficulty, catapulting knives above his head, behind his back, turning this way and that to show them the intricate, mesmerizing sequence.

At the crescendo of his routine, he tossed what looked like a fish filet in the air, threw the knives in blinding succession after it, slicing it to equal pieces in midair. After catching the plummeting knives in one hand and the fish pieces in the other, he spread his arms and took a bow.

A storm of applause and yells erupted. She almost clapped and cheered, too. Almost. It was a good thing she was still breathing and on her feet.

Everyone's excitement intensified when they noticed her. Richard slinked a tea towel over his shoulder as he approached her, his gaze unreadable, his mouth curved in that devastating smile. Her head filled with images of her winding herself around him, dragging that arrogant head down and taking those cruelly gorgeous lips.

"Did you catch Richard's unbe*lievable* show?" Amelia exclaimed.

"I caught a slice of it." Everyone laughed at her reference to his closing act. Including him. She wanted to be mad at him for crashing her home again, but couldn't. But that didn't mean she couldn't still reprimand him. "How will I convince the kids not to play with knives now?"

He waved away her concern. "I already took care of it."

"Oh, how did you do that?"

"I told them only I was allowed to do such things, as I spent more years than they've been on this earth practicing."

"And this convinced them?"

"They are extremely obedient cubs."

She blinked. "Uh, are we talking about the same trio?"

"*Or* I'm too intimidating even when I'm trying not to be."

Said trio was flitting around preparing the kitchen table, their awed eyes almost never leaving Richard. "They don't look intimidated, they look enthralled."

"Same result." His smile grew placating. "Don't worry. I got their promise they'd never try anything with sharp objects. I promised Mauricio I'd teach him to juggle. With environmentally safe plastic."

Before she could hiss his skin off for making Mauri such a promise, he turned to his audience.

"Now, to the second part of my show. Food."

Her mouth hung open as her mother and sister rushed to empty three huge brown bags on the other counter.

"Richard brought everything to make sure his recipe is just right," her mother explained, her smile so wide it hurt Isabella. "We're having a cooking contest. You'll grade his efforts tonight against mine in our first dinner face-off."

As Richard started preparing his ingredients, Isabella closed her mouth to keep her jaw from dragging on the floor.

Was that really him? Was this even her home? Or had she stepped into some parallel universe?

He wasn't kidding about this being the second part of the show. He turned preparing seafood into feats of speed and precision. She was sure he assembled weapons and dismantled bombs with the same virtuosity.

All the time he quizzed the kids about the seafood, spices, herbs and vegetables he used. Their excitement at the informative and entertaining Q and A session was almost palpable. She'd never seen them so taken with an adult. Mauri asked him more personal questions than she'd thought possible, down to how he chewed his food. Richard was a good sport, rewarding Mauri's boundless curiosity with amusing, frank, yet age-appropriate answers.

Seeing them interact the first time had been disturbing. Now it plain hurt.

After Richard started cooking, he said, "Somebody recently taught me that recipe. I was the sous chef during its preparation. Now I get to be the chef and, fingers crossed, I won't turn what was a magical seafood feast into a curse."

Amelia, who'd taken her eyes off Richard only to swing them to Isabella for a silent verdict on how things stood between them, piped in at once, "You have nothing to worry about. The aromas alone are a powerful spell."

"Who taught you this recipe?" That was Mauri, of course.

"A lovely lady called Eliana."

If he'd thrown that knife he wielded into her heart it wouldn't have hurt more. Hearing him mention another woman with such indulgence made something she'd never felt on his account sink its talons into her gut.

Jealousy. Acrid, foul. And totally moronic. She was the one who'd turned down his offer to continue their intimacies.

But…he'd never cooked with her!

Well, he was cooking for her whole family now.

As if he could feel her burning envy of that woman who'd taken him into her kitchen and made him follow her orders, his steel-hued gaze targeted her. "She's almost like a sister to me since she married a man I consider a brother."

The tension drained from her muscles, forcing her to sit.

Mauri's next question came at once. "What's his name?"

"Rafael. Ah-ah…" Richard raised his hand, anticipating and answering Mauri's next batch of questions. "Rafael Moreno Salazar. He's from Brazil and he's my partner.

He's ten years younger than me. And *he* is a magician with numbers."

Numbers. The boy Richard wouldn't leave behind in The Organization, the one he'd postponed his own escape for.

Forever needing more info about Richard, Mauri lobbed him another question. "Do you have other friends?"

"I have six partners, including Rafael. One I considered my best friend. He doesn't like me back now."

And that had to be Phantom.

Before Mauri pounced to extract that story, Richard gave him what she could only call a man-to-man look that said, "Later." And wonder of wonders, it worked. Well, almost.

Mauri swerved into another tack. "What's his name? Where's he from?"

"Numair Al Aswad. That means *black panther* in Arabic. He's a sheikh from a desert kingdom called Saraya."

Everyone's eyes got even wider. It was still Mauri who asked what she thought was on everyone's mind. "Is each of your friends from a different country?"

Richard chuckled as he began to distribute food on plates. "Indeed. Black Castle Enterprises is a mini United Nations. We also have a Japanese chap, a Russian, an Italian and a Swede. My right-hand man, Owen Murdock, is an Irishman. I trained him like I trained Rafael."

"Like you'll train me?"

It felt as if everyone, except Benita and Diego, who chose this moment to bicker, held their breath for Richard's answer.

He considered Mauri for a moment. "We'll see if you've got what it takes first."

"I got it!"

The kids giggled at Mauri's impassioned claim but stopped at once. It wasn't Mauri's scolding look that made them look so sheepish and contrite. They never reacted like that to his "older brother" exasperation. It was Richard. He didn't level any disapproval or reprimand at them, just a look.

She fully sympathized. Just a look from him took control of her every voluntary and involuntary response.

Her mother and sister intervened to end Mauri's bombardment of Richard, and they all sat to eat.

It did turn out to be a magical meal, on all counts. The food was fantastic, making everyone want to meet the Eliana who'd invented the recipe, with her mother the first to declare Richard the winner of their contest. The constant mood was one of prevailing gaiety and excitement, again thanks to Richard. He was a maestro in handling people of all ages, compelling, constantly surprising, making each person feel they had his full attention, and causing them to fall over themselves to win his approval.

Although she knew this was just his expert manipulation skills, she couldn't help but enjoy it. Delight in it. But both his behavior and her reaction to it made her more nervous.

What *did* he want?

Then she was finally getting the chance to find out.

After dinner, her mother and sister insisted she and Richard retire to the living room while they cleaned up. Mauri agreed to stay behind only after Richard promised a drawing session afterward.

The moment they were out of earshot, she pounced. "Any explanation for…all of this?"

A smile that should be banned by a maximum-penalty law dawned on his face. It was different from what he'd flooded her family and house with all evening. A mixture of wickedness and provocation. One of those would have been more than enough for her to handle. Together, as with everything about him, they were overkill.

He only answered after he sat. "Your family invited me, remember?"

"And since when do you answer anyone's invitations?"

"You have no idea what I've had to do in the past months with Rafael's marriage. Then Raiden, another of the Black Castle blokes, the Japanese-by-birth guy I mentioned, followed suit. Both their weddings had me putting up with human beings all the time. Then came Numair's. That one rewrote the fundamental rules of existence for me. He was the one I thought would be the last man on earth to succumb to the frailties of our species or fall into the trap of matrimony. Nothing was sacred after that, and I've been open to anything ever since. Even cooking dinner from a minitribe of women and children."

So all his friends had married. Was that what was making him dip his foot in the land of domesticity? To see if it was for him? And he thought her household was the most convenient testing ground, since he already had a son and a lover there? Did he think she'd let him experiment on them?

Gritting her teeth, she sat beside him. "You said you'd leave my family alone."

"That was only in return for leaving mine alone."

"But you now know your concern for Rose is misplaced."

"I do. I no longer want you to stay away from Rose."

"Well, *I* want you to stay away from my family."

"I no longer want to do that, either."

"Why? You only involved my family as a pressure card."

"I did?" He cocked his head at the grinding of her teeth. "By 'family' you mean Mauricio. You want me to leave *him* alone."

"Who else?"

At her exasperated answer, he shrugged. "I don't want to do that, either."

"Why?" she snapped. "What's new? You didn't bat a lid when I told you he was your son."

"I didn't because I've already been immunized against the shock, having contracted it full-force the day before. I knew he was my son the moment I saw him."

"No *way* you knew that. He looks nothing like you."

He produced a picture from his inner pocket, handed it to her. If she wasn't certain Mauri never had clothes like that, and this photo was in a place they'd never been and looked from another era, she would have sworn it was him.

"That's my younger brother, Robert. He looked exactly like our mother. I took after my father. Rose was a mix of the two."

Stunned, she raised her eyes, a memory rushing in. "Rose once told me Mauri so reminded her of one of her dead brothers. I didn't make anything of it, as it never occurred to me to tie you to her."

His face darkened. "So she believed I was dead."

She swallowed. "She did only because it was the only thing to explain why you didn't search for her."

His jaw muscles bunched. She winced at the pain she felt for both Rose and him. This wasn't right. That he'd deprived Rose of knowing he was alive. Rose suffered the loss of her biological family even now. And he might have suffered even more watching her from afar.

"But she didn't hesitate to identify you, which means she's been clinging to the hope that you're alive. You probably look very much like she remembers you."

"I was sixteen. I looked nothing like this." He lowered his gaze, as if remembering those moments they'd all been frozen with shock, each for their own reasons. "Did she ask you about me again?"

"I didn't give her a chance. I told her everything about me, so she was too busy with my revelations to think of you. But I'm sure she will. What do you want me to say when she does?"

"What do you want to tell her?"

That was the last thing she'd expected he'd ask. "I...I honestly don't know. I think she deserves to know the brother she loved and clearly still misses terribly is alive. But you probably have nothing in common with that brother, so maybe it's not in her best interests to know you. It's your call."

"Don't tell her."

Hating that this was his verdict, but conceding it was probably the right one, she nodded.

Then her original point pushed to the forefront again. "So you knew about Mauri all the time you were here before, and as I told you everything about myself. Yet you gave no indication that you were in the least interested."

"I wasn't." Before her heart could contrarily implode with dismay, he added, "I was flabbergasted."

That astounded *her*. "I didn't know anything could even surprise you."

"Finding a seven-year-old replica of my dead brother on my ex-lover's threshold? That's the stuff strokes are made of."

The "ex-lover" part felt like a blow to her heart.

Sure, she'd walked away this time, saying it was over. But was that what he already considered her? What he'd decided she was? When they'd made love…had earth-shattering sex…just yesterday? If he wasn't here to pursue her, then why was he here?

"I walked out of here intending not to come back."

"And that was the right decision. Why are you back?"

"Because the facts have been rewritten. Now instead of wanting to end your friendship with Rose, I want to be your and your family's…ally."

Ally? *Ally?* That was downright…offensive after what had happened the past couple of days. Not to mention in the past.

"I don't need allies."

"You never know when and how you might. Having someone of my influence on your side can be more potent than magic."

She tamped down the need to blast his insensitive hide off his perfect body. "I have no doubt. But I don't need magic. I work for what I have. And I have more than enough to give my son the best life and to secure his future."

"Even if you don't want or need my alliance, you don't

have the right to make that decision for Mauricio. The fact remains, he's my flesh and blood. And my only heir."

After a moment of gaping at him, her nerves jangling at his declaration, she choked out, "Are you here because you decided to tell him that?"

Mauri chose this crucial moment to stampede into the living room. "I got all my drawing stuff!"

Before she could say anything more, Richard turned his attention to Mauri.

Brain melting with exasperation and trepidation, she could only watch as father and son ignored her and got engrossed in each other. She had to wait to get her answer.

A no would mean resuming her life as it was. A yes would turn it upside down. And it was all up to Richard.

As it had always been.

Richard had swung around at Mauricio's explosive entry, infinitely grateful for the distraction.

As heart-wrenching as the sight of him, the very idea of him, still was, right now he'd take anything over answering Isabella's question. Since he didn't have an answer for it.

He had no idea what he was doing here, or what he would or should do next.

In the distraction arena, Mauricio was the best there was. The boy—his *son*—wrenched a guffaw from his depths as he hurled himself at him, dropping his armful of drawing materials in his lap.

Crashing to a kneeling position at his feet, Mauricio anchored both hands on his knees and looked up at him with barely contained eagerness. "Tell me your opinion of my work. And teach me to draw something."

"You can draw?"

That was Isabella. She would have asked if he could turn invisible with the same incredulity.

Richard slid her a glance. "I have many hidden talents."

"I'm sure." She impaled him on one of those glances that

made it an achievement he hadn't dragged her out of that kitchen and buried himself inside her.

Mauricio dragged his focus back, and his angelic face, overflowing with inquisitiveness and determination, sent a different avalanche of emotions raging through him.

His throat closed, his voice thickened. "Why don't you show me your best work?"

Mauricio rummaged through the mess on his lap, then pulled out one sketchbook and thrust it at him. "This."

With hands he could barely keep from trembling, Richard leafed through the pages, his heart squeezing as he perused each effort, remarkable for a boy of his age, testimony to great talent...and turmoil.

Had the latter manifested itself in response to their lifestyle, as Isabella kept relocating them to keep them safe? He was sure she'd shielded her son and family from the reality of their situation. But he believed Mauricio was sensitive enough he'd felt his mother's disturbance, and felt the dangers she'd paid so much of her life to protect him and their family from.

There was also a searing sense of confusion in the drawings, an overwhelming inquisitiveness and the need to know, what *he'd* experienced firsthand. Was that a manifestation of his growing up fatherless? Was he constantly wondering about the father he'd never known, or even known about? Did a boy of such energy and intelligence miss a stabilizing male influence, no matter how loving and efficient the females in his life were?

He pretended to examine each drawing at length, trying to bring his own chaos under control.

At last he murmured, "Your imagination is quite original and your work is extremely good for your age."

Mauricio whooped. "You really think I'm good?"

Though the boy's unrestrained delight made him wish to give him more praise, he had to give him the qualification of reality. "Being good doesn't mean much without hard work."

"I work hard." Mauricio tugged at Isabella. "Don't I?"

Her eyes moved between them, as if she was seeing both for the first time. "You do, when you love something."

Richard retuned his gaze to Mauricio before he plunged into her eyes. "When you *don't* love something, you must work even harder. When you're lucky to love something, it only makes the work *feel* easier because you enjoy it more. But you must always do anything, whether you enjoy it or not, to the very best of your ability, strive to become better all the time. That's what I call 'got what it takes.'"

Mauricio hung on his every word as if he was memorizing them before he nodded his head vigorously.

Isabella's gaze singed every exposed inch of his skin.

The burning behind Richard's sternum intensified as he turned a blank page. "What do you want me to teach you?"

Mauricio foisted the colors at him. "Anything you think I should learn."

Richard gave him a considering look. "I think you need a lesson in perspective." As soon as the words left his lips, Richard almost scoffed. No one needed that more than him right now.

"What's that?" Mauricio asked, eyes huge.

"I'd rather show you than explain in words. We'll only need a pencil, a sharpener and an eraser."

Richard blinked at the speed with which Mauricio shoved the items in his hand then bounced beside him on the couch, bubbling over with readiness for his first drawing lesson.

Gripping the pencil hard so the tremor that traversed him didn't transfer onto the paper, Richard started to sketch. Mauricio and Isabella hung on his every stroke.

Before long Mauricio blew out a breath in awe. "Wow, you just drew some lines and made it look like a boy!"

Richard added more details. "It's you."

"It does look like me!" Mauricio exclaimed.

Richard sketched some more. "And that girl is Benita."

"But she's not that much tinier than me."

"She's not tiny, she's just far away. Watch." He drew a few slanting, converging lines, layered simple details until he had a corridor with boy in front, girl in back. "See? We have a flat, two-dimensional paper, but with perspective drawing, we add a third dimension, what looks like distance and depth."

Mauricio's eyes shone with the elation of discovery, and something else. Something he'd once seen in Rafael's eyes. Budding hero worship. He felt his lungs shut down.

"I get it!" Mauricio snatched another sketchbook, showed him that he did before raising validation-seeking eyes to him. "Like this, right?"

Richard felt the smile that only Mauricio, and his mother, provoked spread his lips. "Exactly like that. You're a brilliant lad. Not many people get it, and most who do, not that quickly."

Mauricio fidgeted like a puppy wagging his tail in exultation at his praise. "*I* didn't know anyone could draw so quickly and so great! Can you do everything that good?"

"As I told you, whatever I do, I do to the best of my ability. I'm the best in some things, but certainly not in drawing. Plenty can do far better." Mauricio's expression indicated he dismissed his claim, making his lips widen in a grin once again. "There *are* people who make it seem as if they're pouring magic onto the pages. But what they and I can do comes from a kernel of talent, and a ton of practice. The talent you have. Now you have to practice. It will only become better the more you do it."

Isabella's gaze locked with his and the meaning of his motivational words took a steep turn into eroticism. It had been incredible between them from the first, but only kept getting more mind-blowing with "practice." That last time had been their most explosive encounter yet. He couldn't wait to drag her into the inferno of ecstasy again.

Suppressing the need, he continued to give Mauricio ex-

OLIVIA GATES

amples while the boy emulated him. Isabella watched them, the miasma of emotions emanating from her intensifying.

Mauricio finally exhaled in frustration, unhappy with his efforts. "You make it look so easy. But it isn't."

"You'll get there eventually. What you did is far better than I expected for a first time."

Mauricio eyed his drawing suspiciously. "Really?"

"Really. Draw a lot, draw everything, and you'll be superlative, if you want to be."

"Oh, I want!"

"Then, you will be. Trust me."

"I trust you."

A jolt shook Richard's heart. Hearing Mauricio say that again, with such conviction, made him want to go all out to deserve that faith and adulation.

Should he be feeling this way? Was it wise? Could he stop it or had he put in motion an unstoppable chain reaction?

"I want you to teach me everything you know."

Richard laughed. The boy kept squeezing reactions of him that he didn't know he was capable of. "I doubt you'd want to learn most of the things I do."

"I do!"

He slanted a glance at Isabella. "I don't think your mother would appreciate it, cithcr."

"Because it's dangerous stuff?"

"To say the least." Before Isabella burst with frustration he looked at his watch. "And that's a discussion for another day, young man. We agreed we'd do this until your bedtime. Now you need to go to sleep and I need to get going."

Without trying to bargain for more time, Mauricio stood and gathered his things, looking like a stoic knight's apprentice. He had an acute sense of dignity and honor. Once he gave his word, he kept it. It made Richard...proud?

Before he could examine his feelings, Marta came to take Mauricio to bed. Handing his grandmother his things, he came back to say good-night. After he hugged his mother, he threw himself at Richard, clung around his neck.

"Will you come again?"

Feeling the boy's life-filled body against him, the tremor of entreaty in his voice, was like a fist closing over his heart.

Richard looked over the boy's head at Isabella. Her eyes were twin storms. She was terrified. Of where this might lead. Truth be told, he had no idea where it would. And was just as afraid.

But he had only one answer. "Yes, I will."

Planting a noisy kiss on Richard's cheek, Mauricio slipped free, flashing him a huge grin before skipping off.

The moment she could, Isabella hit him with the burning question she'd postponed for the past hour. "*Do* you intend to tell Mauri the truth?"

There was only one answer to that, too.

"No. Not yet."

Nine

Not yet.

Every time those two words reverberated in Isabella's mind, which was all the time, it made her even more agitated.

Not yet implied he would tell Mauri the truth eventually.

But he'd also implied that even if he did, it wouldn't mean anything would change. Mauri would only know he had a father, and would get the benefit of all his wealth and power.

As if *that* wouldn't change everything.

Before he'd left that night, he'd confessed he hadn't thought this through, didn't know what to expect himself. But the fact remained that Mauri had a right to everything he had as his only heir. While he…he only wanted to know his son. Only time would tell how that would translate into daily life or in the long term. They'd just have to wait and see how things worked out.

She had no other choice but to do just that. Now that he'd expressed the wish to know his son so unequivocally, she'd been unable to deny him his desire.

Ever since that day three weeks ago, she'd succumbed and gone along for the roller-coaster ride of having Richard in her family's everyday life. And he'd been with them every possible minute. After their workdays, from early evenings to past the children's bedtime, he'd been there. And he'd shocked her more with each passing minute.

His unstoppable charm continued on full-blast. But she could no longer believe it to be anything but genuine. Though he dazzled them all, she was now certain it wasn't premeditated. He clearly liked being with her family. He really was interested in all of their concerns and indulgent of all their quirks.

But with Mauri, he was something she'd never seen a man being toward a child, not even her own loving father.

That almost tangible affinity they shared had disturbed her, worried her from that first day. It shook her to her core to see it growing every day, in Richard's eyes, in his vibe. Such absolute focus, such a heart-snatching level of emotion.

What shook her as much was seeing *him* through new eyes. There was far more to him than the lethal seducer who'd taken her heart and body by storm, or the merciless void who'd taken Burton apart, or the ruthless manipulator who'd threatened to tear her life apart when he'd first returned. There were depths and passions in him she doubted even he knew he possessed. And no one seemed more surprised to discover these hidden qualities than Richard himself.

Just today, he'd done something she was certain he'd never contemplated within the range of possibilities.

He'd taken them shopping.

She'd agreed only after he'd promised no splurging. After the fact, she'd kicked herself for not defining *splurging*. To him, it could be keeping it under a million dollars.

As it had turned out, she shouldn't have worried.

Thinking they were shopping—rightfully so—with the genie of the lamp, the kids had asked for things they wouldn't dare ask of their family. She'd bated her breath, hating to have to shoot him down in front of them if he succumbed to their demands. But he'd only given them the most subtle but stern lesson in needless excess and its detriments. After that, they'd let him choose, and he'd picked reasonably priced stuff they'd been delighted with, but would also truly enjoy *and* benefit from.

Mauri was the one who didn't ask for anything, excessive or otherwise. He was overwhelmed each time Richard picked something out for him that he revealed he'd intensely wished for. What he'd never asked her for. Mauri never asked for anything, as if he was aware of her burdens and never wanted to add to them, even when she entreated and cajoled him to ask for anything. It forced her to try to predict his desires. Clearly very inaccurately. It upset and stirred her in equal measure that Richard, after such short if intense acquaintance, was the one to read him so accurately.

After the shopping for the kids was concluded, she told Richard he was forbidden from buying the adults anything. He again said she didn't have a right to dictate terms on the others' behalf. She grudgingly conceded that his relationship with her family should remain independent of theirs.

Especially since *that* was now nonexistent.

Ever since he'd come offering his so-called alliance, there'd been no hint of the voracious predator he'd been. Each day, each *hour* that passed without him bringing up his desire for a continuation of their affair left her partially relieved...but wholly distraught. For she wanted him now, this new him she could admire and respect, far more than she'd ever wanted him before. But it seemed her earlier assumption had been correct. The reality of her being the mother of his son, the domesticity of her life situation, seemed to have doused his passion irreversibly.

Just as she was considering putting herself out of her misery and asking him what his intentions were, she found Rose and her family right in their path.

Rose hadn't asked her about Richard again. To her relief. And astonishment. Isabella surmised she hadn't because she feared Isabella knew nothing about his real identity, and didn't want to cause him trouble since he was hiding it.

Following the same rationalization, Rose probably wouldn't bring up her suspicion again in everyone's presence.

As Jeffrey and their kids, Janie and Robbie—named after Rose's mother and brother, Janet and Robert, as Isabella only now realized—rushed to greet them, Rose stood behind, staring at Richard. Richard, after shaking hands with Jeffrey at Isabella's brief introduction, stared back.

After her mother and sister took the kids and went to the food court, only the four of them remained. Jeffrey's animated conversation petered out when he realized it was a monologue and finally noticed the turmoil in his wife's eyes as she stared at the stranger.

Before he could react, Rose threw herself at Richard, clung to him with all her strength.

Isabella's lungs almost burst. Richard looked as if he'd turned to stone the moment Rose touched him.

Then Rose's incoherent whimpers started to make sense. "Don't tell me you're not Rex…don't you dare."

Richard squeezed his eyes shut, bared his teeth as if straining under an unbearable weight.

Rose suddenly pulled back, features shaking out of control, eyes reddened and pouring tears as she grabbed his arms in trembling hands. "You're my brother. *Say* it."

Richard breathed in sharply, emptied his massive chest on a ragged exhalation and nodded. "I'm your brother."

A sob tore out of Rose's depths and she flung herself at Richard again. Among the cacophony filling her ears, Isabella heard Jeffrey exclaiming a string of hells and damns.

As Rose wept uncontrollably, mashing her face into her brother's chest, this time Richard contained her in his great embrace, stroked her gleaming head soothingly, his hands trembling. Isabella remembered to breathe only when she felt the world dimming.

Richard had decided to stop hiding, to let his sister have him back.

A week ago she'd asked him why he'd never done that.

He'd said so he wouldn't taint Rose's life with his darkness. When she'd said that same fear should apply to her and her family, he'd assured her he'd installed every precaution, would never impact them negatively in any way. When she'd countered he should do the same with Rose and come clean to her and his response had been a silent glance, she'd figured it was only a matter of time before he did.

Suddenly it hit her. This was all his doing. He was the one who'd chosen the mall and decided when to stop shopping and walk around. He must have known Rose and her family were coming, had wanted to set this up to see where it would lead. But it seemed Rose had still surprised him with her unrestrained reaction.

Richard now stepped back from the sister who clutched him as if afraid he'd disappear again if she let him go. What Isabella saw in his eyes almost knocked her off her feet.

Such...*tenderness.*

She'd seen nothing like that in his eyes before. Not even toward Mauri. With him there was indulgence, interest, and when no one noticed, stark, fierce emotions that left her breathless. He'd certainly never looked at her—before his current careful neutrality—with anything approaching this...sheer beauty. She hadn't thought him capable of it.

But she'd never inspired such depth and quality of emotion in him.

His voice was a gruff rasp as his gaze moved from Rose to Jeffrey and back. "We have much to talk about. How about we do it over lunch? Isabella wanted to have sushi today."

Nodding feverishly, looking up at him as if at everything she'd ever wished for had come true, Rose clung to his arm, let him steer her away. Isabella and Jeffrey followed the newly reunited siblings in a trance.

Richard spent the first hour telling the Andersons everything. The next two were consumed with Rose's nonstop questions and his attempts to answer each before she hit him with the next.

He left out strategic areas. Such as how many monsters he'd eliminated. And how he'd gotten the info to bring Burton down, making it sound as if Isabella had cooperated knowingly, as if there'd been nothing beyond this goal between them. Rose must have been too dazed to remember her earlier observation that Mauri looked like their dead brother to come up with the right conclusion. But Isabella felt it was only a matter of time before she did. Or before Richard told her.

Jeffrey finally shook his head. "So you removed every obstacle from our path in our known history! I thought we were plain lucky, but Rose always said she had her own guardian angel, and me by association. Turns out she was right."

Richard huffed. "More like a guardian devil."

Rose's eyes filled again as she squeezed his hands. "You've always been an angel to me, from the first moment I can remember, till that day you went away. But I always felt you watching over me, and that's why I never believed in my heart that you were dead. It's only because you never came forward that I had to tell myself that you were. But I lived feeling I'd one day see you again. That's why I knew you the moment I saw you. Because I've been waiting for you."

"I'm glad you did." Richard's smile was tight with emotion. "And I'm sorry I made you wait that long."

She lunged across the table, knocking things over to plant a tear-smeared kiss on his cheek before subsiding. "Never be sorry. I'll be forever grateful you're alive, that you found me back then and that you're here now. I can't ever ask for more than that."

"Can *I* ask you to forgive me for ever doubting you?" Jeffrey hugged his wife to his side lovingly before returning his gaze to Richard. "Rose always talked about her biological family, but mostly about you. Though she had more years with your mother and brother, she remembered you most of all. She always said you were the best at everything, couldn't believe you *could* die. She painted this Superman image of you, and what do you know? She was right. I have a bona fide double-oh-seven for a brother-in-law."

"I bet Rex would put him to shame…uh…" Rose stopped and smiled goofily at Richard, squeezing his hand again as if to make sure he was really sitting across from her. "I don't know if I can get used to calling you Richard."

His free hand cupped her cheek, and the look in his eyes almost uprooted Isabella's heart all over again.

What she'd give to have him look at her that way.

"You have to in front of others." His gaze suddenly turned deadly serious. "It's beyond vital I'm never associated with Cobra, The Organization's operative. Though I wiped every shred of evidence they had on me, changed radically from the bald-shaven, crooked-nosed, scarred boy and man they knew, and no one suspected me in the past ten years, I can't risk any mistakes that might lead to my exposure. The consequences to everyone I know would be unspeakable."

At his ominous declarations, what shook her most was finding out he'd been mutilated by his years as his father's, Burton's and The Organization's weapon. She'd only known him after he'd fixed the damages—at least the physical ones—but now she realized more than ever how deep they'd run.

At the couple's gaping horror, he exhaled. "This is why I didn't want to burden you with my existence. Maybe it's advisable that I continue watching over you from afar without entering your lives at all."

"No!" Rose's cry was so alarmed, so agonized, it was another blow to Isabella. "I *must* have you in my life. We'll do everything you need us to do." She tugged at her husband, eyes streaming again, imploring. "Won't we, Jeff?"

Jeffrey nodded at once, eager to allay his wife's agitation. "It goes without saying, man. Your secret is our secret." Then he grimaced. "But what are we going to tell the kids?"

"Oh, God…I hadn't thought of that," Rose sobbed, the realization bringing on another wave of weeping. "We can't tell them you're their uncle!"

Richard engulfed her hands in his, as if to absorb her anguish. "It's not important what they think I am as long as I become part of their lives." Richard looked at her, no doubt correlating how the same applied to Mauri. Turning his gaze back to the distraught Rose, his lips crooked in a smile. "Tell them I was your dearest friend when you first got adopted. They'll end up calling me uncle anyway."

Just as tremulous relief dried Rose's tears, Isabella's mother and Amelia came back with the kids for the second time. Richard suggested they all adjourn to his place for the rest of the evening. Everyone agreed with utmost enthusiasm, Rose and Jeffrey's kids squealing in delight when Mauri told them he had a pool in his apartment.

As they all headed for their cars, Isabella hung back, looking at Richard. This lone predator who was now suddenly covered in family. And appearing to delight in them as they did in him.

Only she felt like the odd woman out. As she was.

If he no longer wanted her, and it was clear he didn't, she'd always be left out in the cold.

Over the next few weeks it seemed as if an extended family had mushroomed around Isabella's immediate one. Rose's adoptive family, Richard's friend Rafael and his wife, Eliana—the recipe fairy, as she'd come to be known in their household—and Isabella's own siblings. With the latter now living abroad, two in France and one in Holland, they'd all come to visit on her return to the United States and were delighted with her new status quo.

She was the one who suffered more the better things got.

Not that she felt alienated by everyone's focus on Richard. *That* pleased her, for him, and for everyone else. It was Richard's distance from her that was killing her inch by inch every day.

Today, as with every Saturday, Richard was coming to take them to spend the day with everyone who could make it. He'd been taking them on outings that only a man of his imagination and influence could come up with and afford. She'd cautioned him he'd been overdoing it, building unrealistic expectations that he'd always be that available, that accommodating.

His answer had shaken her, since it was the very reason she wanted to make every second with Mauri count. He said that Mauri would be seven only once, that soon he wouldn't think it cool to hang around with him or be as impressed or as easily pleased by him. But he had another reason she didn't. He had seven years of absence to make up for.

He'd ended the discussion by reassuring her that Mauri understood he might not be able to keep up this level of presence, that he'd managed to clear his calendar to spend this time with them, but that that might not always be the rule.

Then she'd tried to call him out on his extravagance. Though his trips were fun and enriching for all of them, they cost a ton. He'd waved her concern away. He already owned the transportation and commanded most of the personnel and services involved. He'd insisted she sit back and enjoy someone doing things for her for a change.

She would have enjoyed the hell out of it, had it been meant for her. Or even partially for her. But she was incidental to him as Mauri's mother. And she could no longer take it. If he wanted to be with his son, he should be, without dragging her along.

Decision made to tell him this today, she rushed to hide the signs of her tears when she heard the bell ring. He was already here.

Mauri stampeded down the stairs to open the door to the man she now lived to anticipate.

Tears welling again, she listened to the usual commotion of father and son meeting. This time it was even more enthusiastic, as if it was after a long absence when they'd seen each other forty-eight hours ago. Yesterday was the first time in weeks Richard hadn't spent the evening with them.

When she brought herself under control, she walked down to excuse herself from their planned outing. Both of them would probably welcome that, must be unable to wait to be alone together.

Before she took the turn into the living room, she froze.

Mauri's voice carried to her, serious, almost agitated.

"Do you know that my real name is Ricardo? Today I discovered it's Spanish for Richard. Mom used to call me Rico until I was two, then started calling me Mauri. But I always hated Mauri. I always wanted to be Rico."

Slumping against the wall, tears stung her eyes again. She hadn't even realized that Mauri—Rico—remembered. What had she done to her own son to ameliorate her own suffering?

There was absolute silence. Richard, for the first time, had no ready answer.

So Mauri…Rico just hit him with his next question.

"You're my father, right?"

That question had come much later than she'd anticipated. Her knees still almost gave at finally hearing it.

Every nerve quivered as she waited for Richard's answer.

By now she knew anything she'd ever feared on Mauri's…*Rico's* behalf would never come to pass. Richard, for all his darkness and complexities, was proving to be a better father to Rico than she could have ever wished for. He was beyond amazing with him. She believed he either loved their son or felt all he was capable of feeling for him. Rico would be safe and cherished with him. And Richard had revealed himself to be a tremendous role model, too.

Powerful, resolute, committed, brilliant, everything a boy could look up to and wish to emulate. Not to mention that she didn't think Rico could go back to a life without him.

What she feared now was all on her own behalf.

If Richard revealed the truth and demanded to be in his son's life indefinitely, she could only continue to do what she'd been doing. Make his presence in their lives as welcome as could be. She wanted Rico to have his father.

But his desire for her had come to an abrupt end the moment she'd gone from black widow in his eyes to hardworking doctor and the steadfast mother of his child.

She could have lived with that, if only she didn't yearn for him. More than ever. For against all her efforts and better judgment, what she felt for him made her previous emotions fade into nothing. If she'd loved him before, she worshipped him now, while he'd never felt anything beyond desire for her. A desire that had ceased to exist.

But she might have been able to put up with seeing him regularly, as she'd been doing so far, even knowing he'd rather she wasn't part of the equation. What made it untenable was the thought that he might, probably would, one day find the one woman for him, fall head over heels in love with her as his friends had with their wives and marry her.

How could she survive watching him with another woman up close for the rest of her life, the life she knew she'd spend alone if she couldn't have him?

A one-note ring made her jump. She felt around in her pocket frantically before she realized it was Richard's phone.

He answered at once. "Numair?" After moments of silence, he exhaled. "Mauricio...Ricardo, I'm sorry, but I have to run. Numair, the partner I told you about, said it's an emergency. I don't know if I'll be back in time to have our outing, but we'll continue our discussion later, I promise."

Isabella stumbled away, ran into the study. Listening to him practically run out of the house, she sagged down.

She'd thought Richard would finally tell Rico the truth

and she'd start dealing with the new reality, for worse, or worst, and be done with it.

Now she had to wait. For his return.

To start a new chapter with his son.

And to close hers forever.

Ten

Richard didn't know whether to feel thankful or enraged at Numair's summons. He'd interrupted one of his life's most crucial moments.

But there was one rule they lived by in Black Castle. If one partner called, everyone dropped everything *at once* to answer.

But what would he have done if Numair's call hadn't taken precedence over even Mauricio's...Ricardo's...*Rico's* question?

He'd wanted to snatch him in his arms and tell him, "*Yes. I'm your father. And I'm never leaving your side ever again.*"

Now he'd never know if he would have.

Those past weeks with him, with Isabella, had turned him inside out. He felt raw, giddy, ecstatic, off balance. And terrified. As much as he'd once been for his family's safety.

He'd been scared of making one wrong move and shattering that unexpected perfection that had sprung between them all. He'd battered his way through every personal situation in his life, because he'd been dealing with men who thrived on adversity, equals who only got stronger with conflict. But mainly because he'd known when all was said and done, he'd mattered to no one. So nothing had really mattered.

But although he'd been in constant agony needing Isabella, he'd been unable to reach out and take her. Even if she still wanted him, he'd feared reintroducing such tempestuous passion would destroy their delicate new status quo, messing up this harmony he hadn't dreamed they could ever have.

That had only been his initial fear. He'd progressed to worse possibilities soon after. That if he pursued her, she'd let him have her again, but that intimacies would never let her see him beyond sex. Knowing the real her now, that would have never been enough. He feared she would have pushed him away sooner or later, but remained always near for Rico's sake. He had no doubt someone as magnificent as her would have eventually found someone worthy to worship her.

He didn't want to imagine what he was capable of doing if he saw her in another man's arms.

Everything inside him roiled until he reached Numair's penthouse.

The door opened before he rang the bell and, without a glance, Numair turned and left Richard to follow him inside.

A melodious voice heralded the approach of what he'd once thought an impossibility. Numair's bride.

Before she noticed his presence, Jenan clung to her husband's neck and they shared a kiss like the one he'd seen them exchange at their wedding. A confession of ever-present hunger, a pledge of ever-growing adoration.

The sight of his former friend so deliriously in love with his princess bride had been a source of contentment before. Now it tore the chasm of desolation inside him wider.

He longed to have anything even approaching this bond with Isabella. But there was no chance for that. He'd done her so many wrongs, he couldn't dare hope she'd ever forgive him, let alone love him as he loved her.

Yes, he'd long admitted the overpowering emotions he felt for her were love. Far more. Worship and dependence that staggered him with their power. He believed he'd always felt all that for her, with the events of the past weeks turning their intensity up to a maximum. He'd only spent years telling himself she was nothing to him so he could live on without her. But while he'd destroyed Burton, he'd also damaged something infinitely more vital. Isabella's budding love. Which had only been possible when she'd been oblivious of his true nature. He'd made reclaiming it far more impossible since he'd barged into her life…

"Richard, what a great surprise!"

He blinked out of his oppressive musings as Jenan strode toward him, still spry in her third trimester of pregnancy. Her hand embraced her husband's, as if they couldn't bear not connecting. She glowed with Numair's love, her body ripe with its evidence. It was literally painful to look at her.

He'd missed it all with Isabella. He hadn't been there to cherish and protect her while she'd carried their child. Instead, his actions had put her in distress and danger. If not for her strength and resourcefulness, the outcome could have been catastrophic. As it was, he'd caused her years of strife and misery, had caused Rico's premature birth. He could have caused his death, and Isabella's.

"If my presence is a surprise—" he growled his pain "—then your beloved husband neglected to tell you that he made me drop a crucial matter to answer his clearly fraudulent red alert."

Jenan pulled a leave-me-out-of-it face. "*And* that's my cue to leave you colossal predators to your favorite pastime of snapping and swiping at each other." Planting a hot kiss on her husband's neck, she murmured, "No claws or fangs, hear?"

Numair's love-filled gaze turned lethal the instant he directed it at Richard. "No promises, *ya habibati.*"

Chuckling, supremely confident in her husband's ultimate benevolence, Jenan passed Richard, dragging him down for an affectionate peck before striding out of the penthouse.

The moment she closed the door, Numair growled, "What the *hell* is the matter with you?"

"With *me*?" Richard's incredulity immediately turned to anger. "Numair, you've never caught me at a worse time—"

"Tell me about it," Numair interrupted.

"*And* it's not in your best interest to provoke me after—"

Numair talked over him again. "After I almost took a bullet for you."

Everything went still inside Richard. "What?"

"I trust you remember Milton Brockovich?"

Richard frowned, unable to even guess at the relevance of Numair's question. He had no idea how he knew of Brockovich.

Four years ago Brockovich's older brother had raped and almost killed a client's daughter. Richard had saved the girl, would have preferred to take the scum in, but he'd pulled a gun on him. So Richard had put a bullet between his eyes. He'd seen the younger unstable Brockovich in the precinct, and he'd ranted that he'd get even with him.

Richard had considered liquidating him as a preemptive measure, before dismissing him. He'd decided the airtight security measures he constantly varied would take care of Brockovich if he ever developed into an actual threat.

"And do you remember forcing me to pledge to fulfill any one demand in return for information leading to Jenan's whereabouts when she disappeared?"

"You mean when she discovered you were using her?"

Numair sneered. "I hated being indebted to you. So when Rafael told me of your domestic adventures with those suburban doctors, I knew something was wrong. I watched you, looking for an opening to do something big enough, preemptively, to fulfill my obligation to you. And I discovered you've converged massive security on those people, for no apparent reason...and neglected your own."

Richard frowned. Numair was right. His personal team did nothing without constantly updated orders. The ones

he'd forgotten to give them...for weeks now. Not that this
should matter. His personal security was a matter of paranoia on his side, not an actual necessity.

Numair went on. "I know you're probably one of the most
unassailable men on earth, but I had a bad feeling about this.
Knowing you're at your headquarters early on Saturdays,
I decided to confront you. I caught up with you as you left
the building—just in time to see Brockovich pull a gun on
you. The Cobra I know would have sensed him a mile away.
Wouldn't have let him breach that mile in the first place.
You didn't even notice him as he passed you. He turned to
shoot you and I was on top of him, diverting the bullet and
knocking him out. You were gone by then without noticing
a thing. I put him someplace where he won't cause anyone
trouble again, but I got this—" he held up a bandaged forearm "—from a ricocheting piece of pavement. And I had
to lie to Jenan about it."

Richard could only stare at him.

"You didn't hear the silenced gunshot or notice the commotion behind you in an almost empty street."

Richard shook his head, dazed. "You saved my life."

Numair gave a curt nod. "And since you saved mine
when you reconnected me with Jenan, this repays my debt."

Unable to stand anymore, Richard sagged on the nearest
horizontal surface, dropping his head in his hands.

Numair came down beside him. "What the *hell* is going
on with you, Cobra?"

He slanted him a glance without raising the head that felt
as if it weighed half a ton. "Don't tell me you care."

"To borrow what you said—when you helped me resolve
Zafrana's debts, saving Jenan's kingdom and its king, her
father—if I didn't, I wouldn't have intervened on your behalf."

"You didn't do it for me. You were just discharging your
debt. You're terminally honorable that way."

"That notwithstanding, and though I might have seriously considered killing you before, I wouldn't want your life to end at the hands of such a worthless scumbag."

"You think I deserve a more significant end, eh?"

"Definitely a spectacular one." Numair's expression suddenly grew thunderous. "Will you tell me what the hell is wrong with you? Are you...sick?"

Richard's breath left him in a mirthless huff. "You can say that." Before Numair could probe, Richard sat forward, deciding to end this meeting. "Thanks for bringing this to my attention. And for saving my life. I'm in your debt now. You know the drill. You can ask for anything and it's yours."

"Again, to echo what you said to me before, I'll collect right now. Answer my questions."

"Why? Really, Phantom, what do you care?"

"Let's say now I've found this hugely undeserved bliss with Jenan, and you do have a hand in it, I can no longer hang on to my hatred of you. I don't want to. I want to wipe the slate clean, don't want to let old animosities taint the new life where our child will be born. Especially since you turned out to be human after all, apparently wanting a woman so much you've been putting up with her family and friends for weeks on end. Not to mention slipping up like mortals do. So just tell me the truth, dammit."

Richard had long thought it pointless to tell Numair why he'd betrayed him, causing him to be punished within an inch of his life for two months straight. But he wanted to stop hiding from him, as he'd stopped hiding from Rose, and from himself. He needed to resolve the issues between them, once and for all.

So he told him the truth. About everything.

To say Numair was stunned would be an understatement.

Suddenly heaving up, Numair dragged him with him by his lapels, his teeth bared, his shout like thunder. "All these years...you *crazy* bastard...you let me think you betrayed me, made us live as enemies...*all these years*."

This wasn't among the possible reactions he'd expected. Numair was enraged…but not as he'd thought he would be.

Richard swallowed the thorns that had sprouted in his throat. "I did betray you. I almost had you maimed. I did get you scarred. And it didn't matter why I did."

Shock expanding in his eyes, Numair shook him, hard. "Are you mad? Nothing else mattered. You had no other choice. Your family had to come first. You did the only thing to be done, sacrificing the one who could take the punishment for those who couldn't. I'm only damned sorry it didn't save your family. I would have taken far more damage if it had ultimately spared their lives."

Richard tore himself from Numair's furious grip, sagged again to escape the contact, the crashing guilt, the crushing futility. Numair's hands descended heavily on his shoulders.

"Look at me." He did, letting Numair see the upheaval filling his eyes. Numair winced. "I went mad all these years, hated you as fiercely as I once loved you for never giving me an explanation, not for the betrayal itself. You were the first person who ever gave me a reason to cling to my humanity, the one I looked up to, the one who gave me hope there'd one day be more for me than being The Organization's slave. Because there was more with you, a friendship that I thought would last as long as we both lived. I hated you, not because I got scarred, but because I thought you took all that, my belief in you, in our bond, the strength and stability it brought me, away from me."

Moved beyond words, Richard stared up at Numair, the stinging behind his eyes blurring his vision.

Numair sat, fervor replacing the fury on his face. "But I have my friend back now. And you have me, too. It's twenty-six freaking years too late, but better late than never. You damn self-sacrificing jackass."

Richard coughed. "That was no self-sacrifice. I just believed there was no forgiving my crimes. I only hoped you'd consider, after all I did over the past ten years, that I atoned for them, at least in part. But you're as unforgiving as your homeland's camels."

Numair arched a teasing eyebrow. "What, pray tell, did you do to atone? It was *I* who deigned to put my hand in that of my betrayer to build Black Castle Enterprises for us all."

"You deigned nothing. You couldn't do it without me."

Numair's face opened on a smile Richard hadn't seen since he'd been fourteen. "No, I couldn't. And I now believe what Rafael kept telling us all these years. That my escape plan wouldn't have worked, certainly not as perfectly as it had, without your help." Suddenly a realization dawned in Numair's eyes. "You waited until we were all out before you left, too, didn't you?"

Letting him read his answer in his eyes, Richard attempted a smile. "We didn't do too shabbily for sworn enemies, did we?"

Numair clapped him zealously on the back, imitating his accent. "We did splendidly, old chap."

The knife embedded in his chest only twisted at Numair's lightheartedness. "At least, you did. You're there for the woman you love every moment she needs you, to love and protect her. You'll share with her every up and down of childbirth and child rearing. You'll never leave her to face a merciless world alone, like I did with Isabella."

Numair frowned again. "You had reasons for your actions, and she understands them like I do now. The fact that she let you in your son's life attests to that."

"She may understand, even forgive, but she'll never forget, not what I did in the past, or what I did when I first invaded her life again. She'll never love me again."

Numair grabbed his shoulder, turning him fully to him. "When has *never* been a word in your vocabulary? You keep after something until it happens. So you lost seven years of your son's life…"

Unable to bear Numair's placation, he tore his hand off, stepping away from him. "I didn't lose them, I *threw* them away. When I didn't give her the benefit of the doubt, didn't trust my heart about her, when I left her in the hands of the monster who'd destroyed my family. I almost cost her, and Rico, their lives…"

"Stop it, Richard," Numair roared, bringing his tirade to an abrupt end. He'd never called him Richard before. "You won't serve them by wallowing in guilt. From now on, you'll live to make it up to her, and to your son. From what Rafael tells me, the boy worships you. And she's trusting you to be around him. This says a lot about her opinion of you as you are now, and of your efforts to *atone*. Keep at it, prove to her how much you love her and your son. When she realizes the best thing for her is to open her heart to you again, she will. Hang in there. When she bestows her love and trust on you again, nothing will ever touch that blessing. I know."

Richard only nodded so Numair would let this go. He couldn't bear one more word on the subject.

Satisfied that he'd talked him down, Numair let Richard divert their conversation to their own shattered relationship. Numair did more than wipe the slate clean. He pushed a re-start button where they'd left off as teenagers.

Numair finally let him go two hours later, and only one thing he'd said looped in his mind until it almost pulped it.

When she realizes the best thing for her is to open her heart to you again, she will.

What Numair thought would bolster his hope for a future with Isabella had only pulverized it, since she undoubtedly realized the best thing for her would be to never open her heart to him again, to stay as far away from him as possible.

When he finally worked up enough nerve to go back to Isabella's home, it was she who let him in. She'd sent Mauri out with Rose's family and stayed behind to talk to him.

With foreboding descending on him like a suffocating shroud, he followed her into the living room.

Once they sat, the voice he now lived to hear washed over him, a tremor traversing it.

"I overheard you and Mauri…and *Rico*…earlier today."

So she'd heard their son's desire to be called Rico again. And his demand for Richard to admit that he was his father.

Would she forbid him to do so, revoke his privilege to come to her home and spend time with Rico? Would she cast him out?

Isabella's hushed words doused his panic. "If you need my blessing to tell Rico the truth, you have it, Richard. I will accommodate your every desire to be with him."

The delight that detonated within him almost blanked out the world.

She wasn't casting him out but letting him further in. As Numair had said, she'd grown to trust him with Rico, was giving him the ultimate privilege of claiming his son.

But…was she telling him that was the extent of their relationship? He'd only be Rico's father, but…nothing to her?

In the past he'd been worse than nothing, her bane, steeping everything between them in deceit and manipulation, then in lust and degradation. If he'd intentionally set out to destroy her feelings for him, he couldn't have done a more complete job. If she wanted something real and lasting with a man, she'd look for it anywhere else but with him. She *deserved* the real thing. The best there was. And he wasn't it. He had sinned against her beyond forgiveness, was tainted beyond retrieval.

But since he was, what right did he have to Rico? Wouldn't he be better off without a father like him? It was even worse now that his turmoil over them could have gotten him killed today. What would that have done to Rico if he'd already known Richard was his father?

Why had he invaded their lives? What had he been searching for? Redemption? When he'd long known he was beyond that? Love? When he knew he didn't deserve it?

If he loved them, and he loved them far beyond anything

he'd thought possible, he had to make them happy. To keep them safe. There was only one way he could do that.

He rose, in an agony worse than when multiple bullets had torn through his flesh, looked down into Isabella's searching gaze and dealt himself a fatal injury. That of saying goodbye. Forever this time.

"Actually, I think you were right not to want me near your family. I'm glad that interruption stopped me from making an irretrievable statement, gave me time to realize it's not in Rico's best interests to have me in his life. Nor is it in Rose's and her family's. I'm sorry I forced myself into your lives and disrupted your peace, but I promise to leave all of you alone from now on. Once you tell Mauricio I'm not his father, he'll reconsider being called Rico, and there won't be any irreversible damage when I disappear from his life."

Shocked to her core, Isabella watched Richard walk away, feeling as if he was drawing her life force out with him.

Then the front door clicked shut behind him and everything holding her up snapped. She collapsed on the couch in an enervated mass.

She'd thought he'd be delighted with her blessing, had been about to follow it with a carte blanche of herself, if he'd consider her as a lover again.

She'd been ready with assurances that whether or not it worked out between them, it wouldn't impact the lifelong relationship she'd been sure he'd wanted with his son. The worst she'd thought would happen was his rejection of her, had been prepared to put up with anything, even watching him find love with another woman, so Rico would have his father, and she'd have him in her life at all.

She hadn't even factored in the possibility that within hours he'd decide he didn't want Rico, either.

There was only one explanation for this. He'd given the domestic immersion a go, and when the moment of truth had come, he'd decided he couldn't have her and Rico in his life on an ongoing basis. He didn't need them the way they both did him.

So he'd decided to walk away, thinking it the ideal time to curtail damages. Little did he know he'd been too late. Mauri was already so deeply attached she dreaded the injury the abrupt separation would cause him.

As for her, he'd damaged her eight years ago. But now… Now he'd finished her.

On Mauri's return, she rushed to her room to postpone the confrontation until her own upheaval had settled. But he came knocking on her door, something he never did, bounding inside, asking when Richard would be coming the next day.

Sticking hot needles into her flesh would have been easier than telling him Richard wouldn't come at all.

Rico's reaction gutted her.

He wasn't upset. He was hysterical.

"He wouldn't leave me!" he screamed. "He promised me he'd come back to tell me everything. It's you who never wanted to tell him about me. You don't like him and keep silent when he's here, no matter how nice he is to you. You kept looking at him with sad eyes until you made him go away. But I won't let him go. He's my father and I know it and I'll go get him back!"

"Mauri…darling, please…"

"My name is Rico!" he screamed, and tore out of her grasp.

It was mere seconds before she realized he hadn't bolted to his room, but downstairs and out of the house. She hurtled after him, spilled outside in time to see him dart across the street. She hit the pavement the moment a car hit him.

Eleven

It was true that catastrophes happened in slow motion.

To Isabella's racing senses, the ghastly sequence as her son flew into the trajectory of that car, the shearing dissonance of its shrieking brakes, the nauseating brunt of its unyielding metal on Rico's resilient flesh and fragile bones was a study in macabre sluggishness. It had been like that when her father had been shot dead a foot away from her.

Then her son's body was hurled a dozen feet in the air, with all the random violence one would toss a scrunched piece of paper in frustration. He impacted the asphalt head-first with a hair-raisingly dull crunch, landing on his back like one of his discarded action figures. At that point, everything hit an insane fast-forward, distorting under the explosion of horror.

She hadn't moved, not consciously, but she found herself descending on him, crashing on her knees beside him, her mind splintering.

The mother in her was babbling, blubbering, falling apart in panic. The woman whose life had been steeped in tragedy and loss looked on in fatalistic dread. The doctor stood back, centered, assessing, planning ten steps ahead.

The doctor won over, suppressing the hysterical mother under layers of training and experience and tests under fire.

From the internal cacophony and external tumult rose her mother's voice, as horrible as it had been when her husband lay dying in her arms, shouting that they were a doctor and a nurse, and for everyone to stand back. Everything stilled as she accessed the eye of the storm inside her, examined her unconscious son as detachedly as she would any critical case.

Her hands worked in tandem with her mother's as they zoomed through emergency measures, tilting his head, clearing his airway, checking his breathing and circulation. Then she directed her mother to stabilize his neck and spine, stem his bleeding while she assessed his neurological status. The ambulance arrived and she used all its resources and personnel as extensions to her hands and eyes in immobilizing, transferring and resuscitating Rico.

Then there was nothing more to do until they reached the practice. Nothing but call for reinforcements.

She knew she should call her partners. But the first call went to the only one she needed with her now.

Richard.

Even if he'd walked away, half of Rico remained his. Even if he'd chosen not to be Rico's father, he'd once told her he wanted to be her ally. Only an ally of his clout would do now.

While she was a pediatric surgeon with extensive experience in trauma, this was beyond her ability alone. Rico needed a multidisciplinary approach, with a surgeon at the helm who counted neurosurgery as a top specialty. Only one surgeon with the necessary array of capabilities came to mind. Someone only Richard could bring her.

The line opened at once and a butchered moan escaped her lips.

"Richard, I need you." This sounded wrong, was irrelevant. She tried again. "*Rico* needs you."

The moment Richard felt his phone vibrate he just knew it was Isabella. Even if the look in her eyes as he'd walked away had told him he'd never hear from her again. If he was right, and it was her calling him now, then something terrible must have happened.

Then he'd heard her voice, sounding like the end of everything. *Richard, I need you. Rico needs you.*

He listened to the rest and the world did come to an end around him.

Rico. His son. Their son. In mortal danger.

Without preliminaries, she ended the call. The worst possible scenario lodged into his brain like an ax.

No. No. *He's fine. He* will *be fine.* She'll save him. *He'll* save him. Antonio. He *must* get Antonio.

Barely coherent as he tore through traffic on his way to her, to his son...to his *family*, he called Antonio. He was Black Castle's resident omnicapable medical genius, who'd saved each member of the brotherhood, except him, as he'd never been part of it, from certain death at least once. After Isabella herself, he'd trust no one else with his son's life.

As per their pact, Antonio answered at once. In his mounting panic, everything gushed out of him. Antonio calmly estimated he'd be in New York with his fully equipped mobile hospital in an hour. But if the condition was critical, they must start without him.

Richard called Isabella back, including her in a conference call so she could give Antonio her diagnosis directly, as the expert, and the one who'd been at the accident scene.

But that had been no accident. He'd done this. Every time he came near her—them, he almost destroyed them.

In a fugue of murderous self-loathing he heard Isabella give Antonio a concise, comprehensive report of Rico's injuries and her measures to save him, her voice a tenuous thread of control.

Isabella... This miracle fate had given him when he'd never deserved her, who'd given him another miracle, only for him to throw her—throw them away, time and again.

His mind fragmenting under the enormous weight of guilt and dread, he'd almost succumbed to despair when

Antonio's authoritative tone dragged him back to focus with the first ray of hope. His verdict.

"From his signs, your diagnosis of a subdural hematoma with a coup-counter-coup cerebral contusion is correct. From his vitals, your measures have stabilized him and stopped the brain swelling, which will resolve over time. But he will need surgery to drain the hematoma and cauterize the bleeders. It's not as urgent as I feared, so I can be the one to perform it. Bring him to the tarmac. I'll have the OR ready."

The terrible tension in Isabella's voice rose. "We're already at the practice, and I wouldn't move him again. Our OR is fully equipped. I'll prep him and wait for you there."

Antonio didn't argue. "Fine. I'll bring my special equipment. Continue to stabilize him until I arrive. Richard—send a helicopter to the jet."

Emerging from the well of helplessness, latching on to something useful to do, Richard pledged, "I'll get you to the OR ten minutes after you land."

Once at the practice, Rose intercepted him, restraining him from stampeding in search of Rico and Isabella.

They were in the OR, and the most she could do was take him to the lounge where surgical trainees observed surgeries, *if* he promised not to distract Isabella or to agitate her, when she was miraculously holding it together.

Ready to peel his skin off to bolster Isabella, he gave Rose his word. Once they arrived, nothing could prepare him for what he saw through the soundproof glass. It would scar his psyche forever.

Rico, looking tinier than the strappy, big-for-his-age boy he adored, lying inert and ashen on the operating table. Isabella in full surgical garb, orchestrating the team swarming around him: Jeffrey, Marta, other nurses, an anesthesiologist.

Then Isabella raised her head. The one part of her visible,

her eyes, collided with his. What he saw there before she turned back to their son almost brought him to his knees.

"He'll be fine." Rose caressed his rock-tense back, tugging him to sit on the viewing seats.

His eyes burned. "Will he?"

Assurance trembled on Rose's lips. "She already saved him from the worst at the accident scene. The surgery is necessary, but I believe the life-threatening danger is over."

A rough groan tore from him, and he dropped his head into his hands, unable to bear the agony of hope and dread.

"She's amazing, isn't she?"

Rose's deep affection made him raise his head and look down at Isabella once more. He wondered again how fate had found it fit to bless him with finding her. His only explanation was so he'd lose her, the worst punishment it could have dealt him. But that was what he deserved. Why had fate chosen to punish *her* by putting him in her path time and again?

"Look at her—functioning at top efficiency even though it's her son on that table. I don't think I would have held together in her place. But Isabella's survived and conquered so much, she channeled that strength to take on the unimaginable responsibility of Rico's life."

Realizing she'd just said Rico's name, he looked at her.

A smile of reproach quivered in her tear-filled eyes. "I almost fainted when Isabella finally told me the truth. It's why I am up here, not down there." A beat. "Not that I didn't know it from the first moment I saw you together. I kept hoping you'd tell me all this time. Why didn't you?"

"I...I...left it up to her to tell you." It hurt to talk, to breathe, to exist. And he deserved far worse, a life of constant agony. "I was on probation, and she didn't know if I'd work out. I didn't. I was a catastrophic failure. I was leaving them, leaving all of you. I'm the reason this happened. I almost ended up killing my son."

"You were leaving? God, Rex, why—?"

Rafael, Eliana, Numair and Jenan walked in, cutting off Rose's anguished exclamation.

Eliana rushed to hug him. "Antonio called us."

Rafael hugged him, too, and he saw in his eyes that Numair had told him everything. But there was no surprise there, just reaffirmed faith. Rafael had always believed in him, no matter the evidence against him.

"I called him as I walked in, and he said he'll be landing in a few minutes," Rafael said. "My helicopter is waiting beside his landing lane. He said he'll drop off with his gear outside the practice like he does on missions. I coordinated with the police so they don't pursue him or my pilot."

Numair added, "The others are on their way. Is there anything else we can do?"

Richard shook his head, choking on too many brutal emotions to count. His son lying there, his fate undecided. The love of his life doing what no mother should, fighting for her son's life. The unwavering support of Isabella's and Rose's families. All his friends rallying around him.

Yes, friends. Brothers-in-arms. Just…brothers.

And he again wondered…how he deserved to have all these people on his side when he'd done nothing but waste opportunities and make horrific decisions.

Suddenly, Antonio rushed into the OR already gowned. And as if they'd always worked together, he and Isabella took their places at the table. After Isabella filled him in as he set up his equipment and examined scans, Antonio looked up, gave Richard a nod, a promise. His son would be fine.

Isabella looked up, too, sought only his eyes, and he wanted to roar for her to leave it all to Antonio. She'd suffered enough. But he knew she'd see it through, could only be thankful his son had such a mother.

"All right, everyone…" Antonio's voice filled the lounge. "Out." Before Richard could protest, he pinned him in his uncompromising gaze. "Especially you, Richard."

Everyone rushed out immediately, but Richard stood rooted, even as Rose and Rafael tried to pull him away. He couldn't leave Rico. He *wouldn't* leave *her*.

He'd never leave either of them again.

His gaze locked with Isabella's, imploring her.

Let me stay. Let me be there for both of you.

Her nod of consent was a blessing he didn't deserve, but he swore he'd live his life striving to.

She murmured and Antonio exhaled. "Dr. Sandoval decrees that you stay. But make one move or sound and you're out." At Richard's eager nod, Antonio looked at Rose. "Sorry I kicked you out with the rest, Dr. Anderson, but I did only so you'd keep your big brother on a leash. Now you'll do it in here."

Rose's relief was palpable as she dragged him to sit down. He sank beside her, clinging to Isabella's eyes in one last embrace, trying to transfer to her his every spark of strength, pledging her every second he had left on this earth, whether she wanted it or not. She squeezed her eyes, as if confirming she'd received it all.

Then the procedure started.

Richard had been in desperate situations too many times to remember. But none had come close to dismantling him like the two heart-crushing hours before Antonio announced he was done, and they wheeled Rico to Intensive Care.

Richard found himself there, pushing past Antonio as he came out first. "I must see him."

Antonio clamped his arm. "I let you watch the surgery against my better judgment already, because Dr. Sandoval needed your presence. But if I let you back there, she'll go back, too, and I barely managed to tear her from your son's side. I don't want her around him while he's still unconscious one more second. She's been through enough."

As Richard struggled with his rabid need to touch his son,

to feel him breathe and to spare Isabella further anguish, Antonio's gaze softened as she and the others came out.

"The surgery went better than even I projected. Seems Rico has his father's armored head." Rose and his Black Castle friends who'd caught up gave drained smiles as Antonio's gaze turned to Isabella. "But seriously, Dr. Sandoval's impeccable damage control presented me with a fully stable patient." His gaze turned to Richard, hardening. "Without her, the prognosis wouldn't have been the perfect one it is now. Rico is a lucky boy to have his mom's healing powers and nerves of steel."

Another breaker of guilt crashed over Richard. He wanted to snatch Isabella in his arms, beseech her forgiveness. Only knowing she wouldn't appreciate it held him back.

Antonio extended a hand to Isabella. "It was a privilege working with someone of your skill and grace under fire, Dr. Sandoval, though I wish it wasn't under these circumstances."

Seeming to operate on autopilot, Isabella took his hand. "Isabella, please. It's me who's eternally in your debt. You were the only one I could trust my son's life with."

Antonio waved him off. "Any neurosurgeon worth his salt would have done as good a job. His condition, thankfully, didn't require my level of expertise. But it was a privilege to operate on him. He's sort of my nephew, too, you know. Whether Richard likes it or not, he's been drafted into our brotherhood."

Richard stared at him, overwhelmed all over again as everyone murmured their corroboration.

Antonio turned to Richard. "Any debt here is all yours, buddy."

Richard's nod was vigorous. "Unequivocally. I'm indebted to *everyone* here, and to the whole world, an unrepayable debt in the value of Rico's invaluable life."

Antonio chuckled, no doubt enjoying seeing Richard,

who always antagonized everyone, so ready to be everyone's eternal slave.

Richard only dragged him into a hug. He even kissed him.

Pulling back, blinking in surprise, Antonio laughed. "Whoa. Who are you, and where's the lethal and exasperating Richard Graves I know and love, and occasionally loathe?"

Richard exhaled. "He doesn't exist anymore."

Antonio laughed. "Nah, he's still in there. But I bet he'll never again emerge around our current company." He wiggled an eyebrow at him. "I would have loved to squeeze you for an installment on your debt, but there'd be no fun in that when you're beyond collapse." He pulled Richard's hand, wrapped it around Isabella's. "Go get some rest."

"But…"

"But…"

Hand raised, Antonio ended their protests. "I'll hold the fort here, not that I need to. Rico is stable, but I'll keep him sedated until his brain edema totally resolves. I'd rather you don't look ninety percent dead, as you both do now, when he wakes up." He shoved them away. "Go home…now."

Twelve

All the way to Isabella's house she sat beside him, unmoving, unresponsive. Not that he'd tried to make her respond. She'd been shattered, had put herself back together so many times, he could barely breathe around her in fear that she'd finally come apart for good.

Once inside, she stopped at the living room, her eyes glazed, as if she was envisioning their evenings spent there. Without warning, a sob tore out of her, sounding as if it actually ripped things inside her to break free.

She'd held it all in until this moment. Before another thought or reaction could fire inside him, she was a weeping heap on the ground.

Crashing to his knees in front of her, he wrapped himself around her, reciting her name over and over, hugging and hugging her, as if he'd integrate her whole being into his own, or at least absorb all traces of her ordeal.

She suddenly exploded out of his arms. His heart almost ruptured. She hated his touch, couldn't bear his consolation.

But instead of pulling away, she tackled him. Stunned for seconds before relief burst inside him, he let her ram him to the ground, needing her to take her revenge, expend her rage, cause him permanent damage as he'd done to her. Hoping he'd finally atone for a measure of his crimes against her, he opened himself completely to her punishment.

She only crashed her lips over his.

Going limp with shock beneath her, he surrendered to her

as she wrenched at him with frantic, tear-soaked kisses that razed whatever remained intact inside him. Then she was tearing at his clothes, clawing at his flesh in her desperation, bathing him in her tears, her pleas choking.

"Give me…everything…I need it all…now, Richard… *now.*"

That was what she needed? To lose herself in him, to ameliorate her ordeal and douse her pain?

This was an offering he didn't deserve. But it was the least of her dues. To have everything that he had. He'd give it all to her, now and forever, to do with what she would.

The barbed leash he'd been keeping on his need snapped. He completed her efforts to tear his clothes off, ripped her out of hers and surged to meld their naked bodies, squashing her against him as if he'd absorb her.

Nothing, starting with him, would ever harm her again. Or Rico. Not while he had breath left in his body.

She met his ferocity halfway, the same remembered horror reverberating in her every nuance, the same need to extinguish it driving her. She sank her teeth into his lips, whimpering for his reciprocation. Giving her what she needed, he twisted his fist in the silk of her hair, imprisoning her for his invasion. She fought him for more, urged him deeper until the stimulation of their mouth mating became distress. Tearing her lips away, she bit into his deltoid, broke his skin as she crushed herself to him. Growling his painful pleasure, the bleakness of despair shattered inside him as her unbridled passion pulsed in his arms, dueled with his, equal, undreamed of. He'd do anything…*anything*… to make it permanent.

He heaved up with her bundled in his arms. "Bed— Isabella…where's your bed?"

"No…here…I need you inside me…*now.*"

Her keen sent the beast inside howling to obey her. Running to the closest horizontal surface, he lowered her there, flung himself over her even as she dragged him down. Madness burgeoned between them as she rewarded his every nip and squeeze with a fiercer cry, a harder grind of her core into his erection, a more blatant offering of herself. Her readiness scorched his senses, but it was her scream for him to *fill* her that slashed away his sanity, made him tear inside her.

He swallowed her scream, let it rip inside him as her unbearably tight flesh yielded to his shaft, sucking him into their almost impossible fit, hurling him into the firestorm of sensation he craved. The carnality, the reality, the *meaning* of being inside her again… This was everything.

And he'd always cede everything to her, the one he'd been made for.

He withdrew, his shaft gliding in the molten heat of her folds. She clung to him, demanding his return, her piercing cry harmonizing with his tortured groan.

Sanity receding further, he thrust inside her once more. She collapsed beneath him, an amalgam of agony and ecstasy slashing across her face, rippling through her body, hot passion gusting from her lungs.

"Give me all you've got… Don't hold anything back…"

Her need rode him, making him ride her harder. The scents and sounds of her pleasure intensifying, her flesh became an inferno around him, more destructive than everything he'd ever faced combined. And the one thing that made him truly live.

With every squeeze of her flesh welcoming him inside her, needing what he gave her, another fraction of the barrenness of his existence, the horrors he'd seen and perpetrated, dissipated. The poignancy, the liberation, sharpened until he bellowed, pounding into her with his full power. Crying, begging, she augmented his force, crushed herself against him as if to merge their bodies.

Knowing she was desperate for release, he sank his girth inside her to the root. She bucked so hard, inside and out it was like a high-voltage lash. It made him plunge ever deeper inside her, sending her convulsions into hyperdrive, suffocating her screams. The gush of her pleasure around his thickness razed him, the force of her orgasm squeezing his shaft until her seizure triggered his own.

His body felt as if it detonated from where he was buried deepest in her outward. Everything inside him was unleashed, scorching ecstasy shooting through his length and gushing deep inside her as if to put out the flame before it consumed them both.

At the end of the tumult, she slumped beneath him, unconscious, her face streaked in tears. He could barely hang on to his own consciousness enough to gather her and go in search of her bedroom.

Once there, he laid her on her bed, every vital piece of him that had gone missing without her back in place. She'd tell him when she woke if they were back for good, or only temporarily. If she'd bestow another chance at life, or if she'd cut it short.

Isabella felt for her phone before she opened her eyes.

Finding it on her nightstand, where she didn't remember putting it, she grabbed it in trembling hands, sagged back in a mass of tremors, tears overflowing. There were a dozen messages from her mother and Antonio throughout the night, the latest minutes ago. Rico was perfectly fine.

Before she could breathe, another blow from her memory emptied her lungs again. *Richard.*

She'd almost attacked him, made him take her...then she remembered nothing. The explosive pleasure his possession had given her had knocked her out. Afterward he'd put her in bed and...left?

Before mortification registered, a silent movement did, making her sag deeper in bed. Richard...in only pants, walking in...with a tray. The aromas of fresh-brewed coffee and hot croissants made her almost faint again. She was that hungry.

She was hungrier for him. Not that she'd jump his bones again. The overwrought situation, her excuse and what had ignited him, was over. He'd decided to walk away, and she had to tell him he was free to go. She'd be damned if she clung to him through his guilt over Rico, or any obligation to her. Being unable to stop wanting him was her curse.

Suffocating with heartache, she struggled to find words to breach the awkwardness as Richard put the tray beside her then sat on the bed. His eyes downcast under a knotted brow, he silently poured her coffee, buttered a croissant, adding her favorite raspberry jam. His heat and scent and virility deluged her, hunger a twisting serpent in her gut.

Cries bubbled inside her: that he didn't need to stick around, or coddle her, that she was okay now—*they'd* be okay. Before any escaped, he put the croissant to her lips. But it was the look in his eyes that silenced her, made her bite into the delicious flaky warmth, her senses spinning.

It felt as if he was showing her inside him for the first time. It was dark and scarred and isolated in there. A mirror image of her own insides. She'd already worked all that out, but she'd thought he'd grown so hardened, was so formidable, that his demons were just more fuel for his power, that he didn't suffer from his injuries the way she did. But he was exposing facets of himself she would have never believed existed—wounded, remorseful…vulnerable.

Enervated by the exposure, she could only eat what he fed her and drown in his gaze, in a world of aching entreaty, and what she'd despaired of seeing directed to her… tenderness.

Then he began speaking. "I've been damaged in so many ways, been guilty of so much, I can't begin to describe it. But Rico…he's purity and innocence and love personified. And you…by God, Isabella, *you*. Against all odds and in spite of all you've suffered, you are all that and everything that's shining and heroic. And while I can't breathe without you…"

That statement was so…enormous it had her pent-up misery bursting out. "B-but you didn't come near me for weeks!"

His gaze flooded with incomprehension, then incredulity. "Didn't you feel me *warring* with myself not to?"

She shook her head, every despair she'd been resigned to evaporating, bewilderment crashing in its place. *"Why?"*

"Because I spoiled everything, in every way possible. In the past and in the present. But even after I discovered the extent of my crimes against you, you still gave me another chance—but only for Rico's sake. I was going out of my mind needing you, but though I knew you wanted me still, physical intimacy had so far only driven you further away, made you despise me, and yourself. And I didn't blame you. I didn't know if I had more in me than what you already rejected. So I enforced the no-touching rule on myself to see if I could offer you what I never did, if I had something inside me that was worthy of you, of Rico…of the extended family who'd reached out and accepted me as one of their own because of you."

Every word unraveled the maze of confusion she'd been lost in, shattered the vice of anguish gripping her insides.

He'd been holding back. He still wanted her.

He went on, dissolving the last of her uncertainties, giving her far more than she'd dared dream of. "But as I fully realized the extent of my emotions for you, I started to worry about the sheer depth of my attachment to Rico, the staggering *force* of my love for you. I started to fear myself. Then Rico asked if I was his father and Numair summoned me, and it all spiraled out of control in my mind."

The staggering force *of my love for you… My love for you.*

The words revolved in her mind, spinning an all-powerful magical spell, enveloping her whole being.

Richard loved her.

As mind-blowing and life affirming as this realization

was, the more pressing matter now was his distress. The need to defuse it was her paramount concern. Her trembling hand covered his fisted one. "What happened? I could have sworn you'd come back to tell him the truth."

He continued staring at her, adrift in his own turmoil. "I was so lost in you, in my yearnings for a future together as a family, I totally dropped my guard. I almost got myself killed. And I didn't even notice it. Numair saved my life unbeknownst to me."

Each nerve in her body fired, every muscle liquefied. A wave of nausea and horror stormed through her at the idea that he could have been...been... The images were... unbearable, unsurvivable...

"That was the last straw. It made me believe that whatever I do, just because of what I am, I'd only blight your lives, cause you even more untold damages. I had to keep you safe, from myself most of all. That was why I had to walk away."

Another surge of dread smashed into her.

He believed his love, his very life, would be a source of threats to them? And that was why he'd still walk away?

His eyes were haunted, desperate, as they left hers, searched space aimlessly. "I thought my control and strength of will limitless. But it all crumbled in the face of my need for you. What can I do now when it's beyond me to leave you?"

The heart that had been pulping itself against her ribs did a full somersault. She swore.

And she did what she'd told herself she couldn't do again. She launched herself at him, over the tray, knocking everything over, tackling him down to the bed, bombarding him with kisses and raining now-ready tears all over him.

"You can do only one thing for the rest of our lives. You can love, love, *love* me, and Rico, as much as we love you."

Richard, lying speechless beneath her unrestrained passion and relief, looked as if he was coming out of a fugue.

"You *love* me?" If she'd told him she could stick to walls he wouldn't have looked more stunned. "*You* love me? How? When I did everything to deserve your loathing?"

His guilt, his hatred of himself, his conviction he didn't deserve her love felt so total, she knew he'd need a lengthy argument to persuade him otherwise. She wasn't up to that now.

She wanted to get to the good part at once. At last.

So she asked one simple question. "Do you love us? Me?"

And if she had any doubt, what came into his eyes now put it all to rest forever. It *was* staggering, the purity and totality of emotions that deluged her.

"I far more than love you. *You*. I've *always* loved you… from the first moment I saw you. But I thought you never really wanted me, and that was why you didn't come with me, never sought me again. I fought admitting my love for years, so I could move on. But I was done fighting weeks ago. I only want to worship you forever, and be the father Rico deserves, and never let you go."

Crying out, she snatched a kiss from those lips that had been the cause for her every ecstasy and agony.

"You want to know how I could love you? *That's* how. I loved you from the first moment, too. I must have *felt* your love, and it kept me bound to you, even through the misconceptions and estrangement." She melted caresses over the planes of his rugged face, sizzling in delight at the open adoration in his eyes. "And if I loved the old you with all my heart, I adore the new you that Rico unearthed, the magnificent man and human being your terrible life had buried deep within you, with all my being."

He shook his head adamantly. "Rico only melted what remained of my deep freeze, but the one who brought the whole iceberg crashing down into tiny fragments has always been you. The moment I saw you again, it was over for me." He heaved up, had her beneath him in a blink. "I want you certain of one thing. I would have admitted it sooner rather than later that I wanted nothing but to be yours, to make it all up to you, even if we didn't have Rico." His face twisted. "But we do have him, and you saved him… You saved all of us."

He buried his face in her bosom and she felt another thing she'd never thought possible. His tears.

Crying out, as if they burned her, she dragged his head up, her hands and lips trembling over his face, needing to wipe them and the pain behind them away.

No longer hiding anything from her, his emotional state or anything else inside him, he worshipped her in return. "This perfection makes me even more terrified. I don't deserve a fraction of it. How could I possibly have all this?"

After another fervent kiss, she looked into his eyes, intoxicated with the freedom of showing him everything in her heart. "You better get used to it. You have all of me forever. And Rico. And you also have Rose and her family. And my family. *And* your best friend back. Not to mention that army of partners who drafted you into their brotherhood."

His eyes turned into shimmering pools of silver. This time she knew it was with joy and gratitude.

His next words confirmed her suspicion. "It's too much."

Wrapping his massive frame in a fierce embrace, she pressed his head to her fluttering heart. "No, it isn't. You see only the bad things you did, when you had overpowering reasons…or at least was under as powerful misconceptions. But you also did so many incredible things for so many people. You sacrificed yourself for your family, then for Rafael and Numair and their—your brotherhood, then you gave Rose a second chance and watched over her all her life."

He pushed himself off her, as if unable to bear her exoneration. "But what I did to you…"

She pulled him back, never intending to let him go again. "I don't care anymore what you did when you thought I was Burton's accomplice. Neither should you." He shook his head, face gripped in self-loathing. She grabbed his face, made him look at her. "What matters is that you gave me everything."

A spectacular snort answered her claim.

It made her burst out laughing. His scowl deepened, not accepting that she should make light of it. Her lethal Cobra had turned out to be a noble knight after all.

Grinning so widely it hurt, she stabbed stinging fingers into the mane he'd let grow longer, as she loved it, which she'd been dying to do since he'd imposed the no-touching ban.

"You have," she insisted. "You've given me passion and pleasure like I never dreamed possible. And you did something else no one could have—you freed me from Burton, opened up my life to new possibilities."

"That was totally unintentional!" he protested.

She overrode his protest. "You did try to save me, and if I hadn't been so busy protecting you, I would have come with you, or I would have at least sought you, and you would have protected me." As he looked about to reject her qualifications, she tugged on his hair, stopping him. "But the greatest gift you gave me is Rico. And since your return, you've given me our own small family, and an extended one. Now you're giving me your love, this incomparable gift you've never given another."

Listening to her enumerate his countless contributions to her life, his expression softened with that tenderness she was already addicted to.

"I'm giving you *everything* I have and am. You already have it, will always have it. You can weed through the mess and extract only what you like. You can toss out the rest." Just like that, he was the uncompromising Richard Graves again.

Laughing, her heart hurting with too much love and exultation, she stormed him with kisses again. "I'm hoarding every single thing about you. I love every gnarled shred of what makes you the man I worship."

He only got more serious. "I mean it, Isabella. Just tell me everything on your mind the moment you think it, and whatever it is, it's yours, it's done or it's gone."

As he melted back to the bed, taking her with him, she luxuriated in his sculpted magnificence, her pleasure magnified unto infinity now that she knew this majestic being was hers as she was his and she'd always have the right to revel in him.

"As long as this is a two-way street and you tell me anything you want different."

"You're beyond perfect just the way you are." He looked alarmed. "Never change!"

She chuckled, delirious with his new transparency. "I guess I'll have to one day. I'll grow older."

"I already told you, you will only grow better."

"It's *you* who is growing so much better with age. There should be a law to curb your improvement." She nipped his chin, caught his groan of pleasure in hungry lips. "I constantly want to devour you."

Hunger blazing in his eyes, he pressed himself between her spreading thighs. "Devour away. I'm self-regenerating." He suddenly groaned, grimaced. "I didn't promise you the most important thing."

She wrapped her legs around his hips, pulling him back to her. "Nothing is more important than having you."

"Yes, there is. Safety. Yours, Rico's and that of everyone you love. I promise you my near-fatal slipup will never be repeated. If I feel I can't be sure of that, I'll scrap this identity and start from scratch."

Terrified all over again, she clung to him. "Oh, God, Richard, how did it happen?"

He told her and she sank back in relief. "You don't have other people who want to kill you, do you?"

"Actually, it's in everyone's best interest to keep me safe…so I can keep them safe."

"If so, what's with your security fetish?" At his rising eyebrows, she grinned. "Yes, I've noticed our security detail everywhere. I know if I'm being watched. Comes from my years in Colombia and then on the run."

He groaned, the knowledge of her ordeals something she knew would hurt him forever. "It's been a well-established paranoia since I escaped The Organization. Knowing what it would mean if they ever found out I defected, and who I am now, I'd rather always be safe than sorry."

"But you *are* generally safer than anyone on earth, barring that aberrant situation, which could have happened to anyone."

"It should have never happened to me."

"And it won't happen again, if I know anything about you. So we're not in any danger by association. What are you worried about, then?"

His lips twisted, as if she'd asked him why he breathed. "I'll *always* worry, because you and Rico are not inside my body, where I can monitor where you are at all times, and where I can keep you safe every second of every day for the rest of my life."

After another ferocious hug, she pulled back, grinned up at him. "Welcome to love. And to parenthood."

He squeezed his eyes, gritted his teeth. "It's always that bad, isn't it?"

"Far worse."

His eyes opened, blasting her to her marrow with his adoration. "I love it. I love *you*. Darling…"

Her phone rang. They froze for a heartbeat before they both lunged for it.

It was Rico. Shaking, Isabella put him on speaker. He sounded sleepy, but exactly like their perfect little boy.

"Uncle Antonio told me who he is and what happened and that he didn't expect me to wake up so soon, and that my head is as hard as my father's. You're my father, Richard, right?"

Richard covered his face with his hands for a second, dragged them down over it, his eyes filling again. "I am your father, Rico. And *Father* is what I want you to call me from now on. I'm sorry I left, but your mother and I are coming right now, and I'll tell you everything as soon as you can handle long talks. But I want you to know one thing. I'm never leaving you again. *Ever.*"

Rico's squeal of delight was cut short before he slurred for them to hurry up. Antonio came on and told them to come only if they were rested, as Rico was already asleep again.

With the call over, Richard looked at her, his eyes reddened, his expression disbelieving again. "This *is* too much, my love. Too many blessings."

Overwhelmed by everything, too, Isabella clung to him. "Can you handle one more? You might have to make space inside yourself for one more person who'll love you forever." He pulled back, eyes wide in shock. She bit her lip, pulled at a patch of his chest hair. "I suspect we made another baby."

"You suspect?" he rasped, looking shell-shocked.

"Want to find out for sure?"

He exploded from her side, cursing that he'd shredded his clothes, called Murdock, told him to get him intact ones and the helicopter.

She giggled at seeing him all over the place, flustered, no doubt, for the first time in his life. "What are you *doing*?"

"I'm going to buy a pregnancy kit."

"By helicopter?"

"That's to go to Rico."

"But we're not in such a hurry anymore." He looked as if this possibility hadn't even occurred to him. "And there's a kit in the top drawer of my bathroom cabinet."

Before she finished talking, he hurtled to where she'd indicated, coming back with it in seconds.

Trembling, she rose, took it from him, her smile shaky. "I had to go to the bathroom anyway."

"Why?" Then he groaned. "Bloody hell, yes, of course, by all means. I think my mind has been irreversibly scrambled."

She planted a kiss on his chest as she passed him. "No way. But I love you even more because it's scrambled now."

Heart drumming madly, she ducked into the bathroom. In minutes, she exited, the strip held tight in her hand.

"Tell me." His voice was a ragged rumble.

She walked into his arms before she held up her fist. "I wanted to find out with you."

"Do it."

She opened her fist. The two pink lines were as clear as they had been when she'd found out she was pregnant with Rico.

On a triumphant growl, Richard crushed her to him.

Many hot tears and kisses later, Richard raised his head, scorched her to her soul with the power of his love. "I'll always live with the regret that I wasn't there for you when you were carrying Rico, that I lost the first seven years of his life." His finger on her lips silenced her protest. "But now fate has given me more than the everything it has already given me—another miracle, and a chance to fix all my mistakes. Now I get to share our new baby with you, and with Rico, from the first moment. I will be there for you, for all of you, every single second, for the rest of my life. This time, I'll do everything right."

Aching with thankfulness, she clung to him, the man she was fated for, the father of her son and of her unborn baby. "Just love me, just love us. You're all I need. All our children will ever need. If we have you, everything will always be right with the world."

Looking down at her, that god among men who loved her, he lavished hunger and tenderness and devotion on her, his every look and word a pledge. "I will live to love you. And you have me, all of me. I'm all yours, forever."

* * * * *

"Stop thinking that you don't measure up somehow, because you're wrong."

Serafia gasped at his bold words. She couldn't hold back any longer. She lunged forward, pressing her lips against his before she lost her nerve. It had been a long time since she had trusted herself in all the various areas of her life, and romance had fallen to the bottom of the stack. What good was she to a man in the state she was in? Especially a prince? Still, she couldn't help herself.

And neither could Gabriel.

He met her kiss with equal enthusiasm. He held her face in his hands, drawing her closer and drinking her in. He groaned against her lips and then let his tongue slip along hers. His touch made her insides turn molten with need and wore away the last of her self-control.

At last, Gabriel pulled away, their rapid breaths hovering between them in the night air. "Is it too early to make our exit?" he asked.

Serafia shook her head and looked into his eyes. "I think the prince can leave whenever he wants to."

***

Seduced by the Spare Heir
is part of the series Dynasties: The Montoros—
One royal family must choose between
love and destiny!

SEDUCED BY THE SPARE HEIR

BY
ANDREA LAURENCE

MILLS &
BOON

Published in Great Britain 2015
by Mills & Boon, an imprint of Harlequin (UK) Limited,
Eton House, 18-24 Paradise Road, Richmond, Surrey, TW9 1SR

© 2015 Harlequin Books S.A.

Special thanks and acknowledgement are given to Andrea Laurence for her contribution to the Dynasties: The Montoros series.

ISBN: 978-0-263-25268-2

51-0715

Andrea Laurence is an award-winning author of contemporary romance for Mills & Boon® Desire™ and paranormal romance for Mills & Boon® Nocturne. She has been a lover of reading and writing stories since she learned to read at a young age. She always dreamed of seeing her work in print and is thrilled to share her special blend of sensuality and dry, sarcastic humor with the world.

A dedicated West Coast girl transplanted into the Deep South, Andrea is working on her own happily-ever-after with her boyfriend and their collection of animals, including a Siberian husky that sheds like nobody's business. If you enjoy Gabriel and Serafia's story, tell her by visiting her website, www.andrealaurence.com; like her fan page on Facebook at facebook.com/authorandrealaurence; or follow her on Twitter, twitter.com/andrea_laurence.

To my fellow authors in the Montoros series—
Janice, Katherine, Kat, Jules and Charlene.
It was a joy working with all of you. Thanks for
tolerating my eighty million questions on the loop.

And to our editor, Charles—You're awesome, as always.
I look forward to working with you again.

One

This party was lame. And it was *his* party. How could his own party be lame?

Normally parties were Gabriel Montoro's thing. Much to the chagrin of his family, he'd earned quite the reputation as "Good Time Gabriel." Music, alcohol, dim lighting, superficial conversation... He was the king of the party domain. But now that Gabriel had been tapped as the new king of Alma, everything had changed.

Gabriel gripped his flute of champagne and looked around the ballroom at his family's Coral Gables estate. Their tropical retreat seemed incredibly stuffy tonight. There wasn't a single flip-flop in the room, much less one of the feral parrots that lived on their property and flew in the occasional open door. His family had always had money, but they hadn't been pretentious.

But things had changed for the Montoro family since the tiny European island nation of Alma decided to restore their monarchy. Suddenly he was Prince Gabriel, third in line to the throne. And before he could adjust to the idea of that, his father and his older brother were taken out of the running. His parents had divorced without an annulment, making his father ineligible. Then, his ever-responsible brother abdicated and ran off with a bartender. Suddenly he was on the verge of being King Gabriel, and everyone expected him to change with the title.

This suffocating soiree was just the beginning and he knew it. Next, he'd have to trade in his South Beach penthouse for a foreign palace and his one-night stands for a queen with a pedigree. Everything from his clothes to his speech would be up for public critique by "his people." People he'd never seen, living on an island he'd only visited once. But his coronation was only a month or two away. He left for Alma in a week.

That was why they were having this party, if you could even call it that. The music was classical, the drinks were elegant and the women were wearing far too much clothing. He got a sinking feeling in his stomach when he realized this was how it was going to be from now on. Boring parties with boring people he didn't even know kissing his ass.

There were two hundred people in the room, but there were more strangers than anything else. He found that terribly ironic. People had come out of the woodwork since his brother, Rafe, abdicated and Gabriel was thrust into the spotlight. Suddenly he wasn't just the vice president of South American Operations, cast into the Southern Hemisphere where he couldn't embarrass the family; he was the hot ticket in town.

Him! Gabriel—the middle child whom no one paid any attention to, the one dismissed by his family's society friends as the bad boy, the spare heir and nothing more. Now that he was about to be king, he had strangers at every turn fighting to be his new best friends.

He hated to break it to them, but Gabriel didn't have friends. Not real ones. That required a level of trust in other people that he just didn't have. He'd learned far too young that you can't trust anyone. Even family could let you down when you need them the most.

Speak of the devil.

From across the room, his cousin Juan Carlos spied him and started in his direction. He was frowning. Nothing new there. Ever serious, Juan Carlos never seemed to have any fun. He was always having business discussions, working, being responsible. He was the kind of man who should be the king of Alma—not Gabriel. After hundreds of years, why hadn't people figured out that bloodlines were not the best indicator of leadership potential?

"You're not talking to anyone," Juan Carlos noted with a disapproving scowl as he loomed over his cousin. At several inches over six feet, he had a bad habit of hovering over people. Gabriel was never quite sure if his cousin deliberately tried to intimidate with his size or if he was unaware how much it bothered people when he did that.

Gabriel wasn't about to let his cousin's posture or his frown get to him. He tended not to worry too much about what his cousin thought, or what anyone thought, really. When it came down to it, Juan Carlos was serious enough for them both. "No one is talking to me," he corrected.

"That's because you're hiding in the corner sulking."

Gabriel scoffed at his blunt observation. "I am not sulking."

His cousin sighed and crossed his arms over his chest. "Then what would you call it?"

"Surveying my domain. That sounds kingly, right?"

Juan Carlos groaned and rolled his eyes. "Quit it. Don't even pretend you care about any of this, because I know you don't. You and I both know you'd much rather be in South Beach tonight chasing tail. Pretending otherwise is insulting to your family and insulting to your country."

Gabriel would be lying if he said the neon lights weren't beckoning him. There was nothing like the surge of alcohol through his veins and the thumping bass of music as he pressed against a woman on the dance floor. It was the only thing that could help him forget what a mess he was in, but after the drama with Rafe, he'd been on a short leash. The family couldn't take another scandal.

That didn't mean he felt like apologizing for who he was. He wasn't raised to be king. The Alman dictatorship had held strong for nearly seventy years. Who would've thought that when democracy was restored, they'd want their old royal family back? They hadn't anticipated this summons and he certainly hadn't anticipated his brother, the rightful king, would run off with a Key West bartender and send Gabriel's life into a tailspin. "I'm sorry if that offends your sensibilities, J.C., but I didn't ask to be king."

"I know you didn't ask to be king. It is plainly obvious to every person in this room that you don't want the honor. But guess what? The crown has landed in your lap and you've got to step up and grow up." Juan Carlos sipped his wine and glared at Gabriel over the rim. "And what have I told you about calling me that?" he added.

That made Gabriel smile. Annoying his cousin was one of his favorite pastimes since childhood. The smile was short-lived, though.

It wasn't the first time he'd been told to grow up. What his family failed to realize was that Gabriel had grown up a long time ago. They all liked to pretend it didn't happen, but in a dark room with thick rope cutting into his wrists, he'd left his childhood and innocence behind with his captors. If his family had wanted him to act responsibly, they should've done more to rescue him. He'd survived because of his own quick thinking and his first choice as an adult was to live the life he wanted and not care what anyone else thought about it.

Grow up, indeed. Gabriel took a large swallow of his champagne and sighed. The days of living his life as he chose were numbered. He could feel it. Soon it wouldn't just be his father and cousin trying to tell him what to do.

"Always good talking with you, cuz. Don't you have someone to schmooze?"

Juan Carlos didn't respond. Instead he turned on his heel and walked over to the dessert table. Within seconds, he was chatting with someone influential, whose name Gabriel had forgotten, over silver platters of chocolate truffles and cream puffs.

Gabriel turned away, noticing the side door that led

out to the patio and garden pavilion. Hopefully he could make it out there before someone noticed.

Glancing around quickly, he spied his father with his back to him. His sister was chatting with a group of ladies in the corner. This was his chance. He moved toward the door and surged through it as fast as he could.

Gabriel was immediately rewarded with the oppressive wave of heat that July in Miami was known for. The humid blast hit him like a tsunami after the air-conditioned comfort of the ballroom, but he didn't care. He moved away from the door and out into the dark recesses of the patio.

There were some tables and chairs set up outside in case guests wanted to come out. They were draped with linens and topped with centerpieces of candles and roses. All the seats were empty. Gabriel was certain none of the ladies were interested in getting overheated in their fancy clothes with their meticulously styled hair and makeup.

Glancing over at the far end of the semicircular patio, he spied someone looking out into the gardens. The figure was tall, but slender, with the moonlight casting a silver silhouette that highlighted the bare shoulders and silk-hugging curves. She turned her head to watch a bird fly through the trees and he was rewarded with a glimpse of the cheekbones that had made her famous.

Serafia.

The realization sent a hot spike of need down his spine and the blood sped through his veins as his heart beat double-time. Serafia Espina was his childhood crush and the fantasy woman of every red-blooded man who had ever achieved puberty. Eight years ago,

Serafia had been one of the biggest supermodels in the industry. Like all the greats, she'd been known by only her first name, strutting down catwalks in Paris, New York and Milan wearing all the finest designers' clothes.

And she'd looked damn good in them, too.

Gabriel didn't know much about what had happened, but for health reasons, Serafia had suddenly given up modeling and started her own business of some kind. But judging by the way that red dress clung to her curves, the years hadn't dulled her appeal. She could walk the catwalk right now and not miss a beat.

He hadn't spoken to Serafia in years. When his family was overthrown by the Tantaberras, they had fled to the United States and the Espinas moved to Switzerland. In the 1980s, they'd moved to Spain and their families renewed their friendship. When Gabriel and Serafia were children, their families vacationed together on the Spanish Riviera. Back then, he'd been a shy, quiet little boy of ten or eleven and she was the beautiful, unobtainable older woman. She was sixteen and he was invisible.

This was a fortunate encounter. They weren't children anymore and as the future king of their home country, he was anything but invisible. As Mel Brooks famously said, "It's good to be the king."

Serafia felt the familiar, niggling sensation of someone's eyes on her. It was something she'd become keenly attuned to working in the modeling business. Like a sixth sense, she could feel a gaze like a touch raking over her skin. Judging. Critiquing.

She turned to look behind her and found the man

of the evening standing a few feet away. Gabriel had
certainly grown up a lot since she saw him last. He
was looking at her the way most men did—with un-
masked desire. She supposed she should be flattered
to catch the eye of the future king, but he was in his
twenties, just a baby. He didn't need to get involved
with an older, has-been model with enough baggage
to pack for a long vacation.

"Your Majesty," she replied with a polite bow of her
head.

Gabriel narrowed his gaze at her. "Are you being
sarcastic?" he asked.

Serafia's mouth dropped open with surprise, her response momentarily stolen. That wasn't what she was
expecting him to say. "Not at all. Did it come out that
way? If it did, I sincerely apologize."

Gabriel shook his head dismissively and walked toward her. He didn't look like any king she'd ever seen
before. He exuded a combination of beauty and danger, like a great white shark, gliding gracefully across
the stone patio in a tailored black suit and dress shirt.
His tie was bloodred and his gaze was fixed on her as
if she were prey.

She felt her chest tighten as he came closer and she
breathed in the scent of his cologne mingling with the
warm smell of the garden's exotic flowers. Her fight-
or-flight instincts were at the ready, even as she felt
herself get drawn closer to him.

He didn't pounce. Instead he leaned down, rested
his elbows on the concrete railing and looked out into
the dark recesses of the tropical foliage. "It's not you,
it's me," he said. "I still haven't quite adjusted to the
idea of all this royalty nonsense."

Royalty nonsense. Wow. Serafia's libido was doused with cold water at his thoughtless words. That wasn't exactly what the people of Alma wanted to hear from their new king. After the collapse of the dictatorship, restoring the monarchy seemed like the best way to stabilize the country. The wealthy Alma elite would get a little more than they bargained for with Gabriel Montoro wearing the crown. He didn't really seem to care about Alma or the monarchy. He hadn't grown up there, but neither had she. Her parents had raised her to value her heritage and her homeland, regardless.

Perhaps it was just his youth. Serafia knew how hard it was to have the spotlight on you at such a young age. She'd been discovered by a modeling agency when she was only sixteen. Whisked away from her family, she was making six figures a year when most teenagers were just getting their driver's licenses. By the time she was old enough to drink, she was a household name. The pressure was suffocating, pushing her to her personal limits and very nearly destroying her. She couldn't even imagine what it would be like to be the ruler of a country and have over a million people depending on her.

"I think you'll get used to it pretty quickly," she said, leaning her hip against the stone railing. She picked up her glass of wine and took a sip. "All that power will go to your head in no time."

Gabriel's bitter laugh was unexpected. "I doubt that. While I may be king, my family will ensure that I'm not an embarrassment to them."

"I thought a king can do what he likes."

"If that was true, my father or my brother would still be in line for the crown. In the end, even a king has a mama to answer to." Gabriel looked at her with a charming smile, running his fingers through his too-long light brown hair.

It was shaggy and unkempt, a style popular with men his age, but decidedly unkingly. The moonlight highlighted the streaks of blond that he'd probably earned on the beach. She couldn't tell here in the dark, but from the pictures she'd seen of him in the papers and online, he had the tanned skin to match. Even in his immaculate and well-tailored suit, he looked more like a famous soccer player than a king.

"And I know your mama," she noted. Señora Adela was a beautiful and fierce woman who lived and loved with passion. She'd also been one to give the lecture of a lifetime while she pulled you down the hallway by your ear. "I'd behave if I were you."

"I'll try. So, how have you been?" he asked, shifting the conversation away from his situation. "I haven't seen you since you became a famous supermodel and forgot about all of us little people."

Serafia smiled, looking for the right answer. She knew people didn't really want to know how she was doing; they were just being polite. "I've been well. I started my own consulting business since I left modeling and the work has kept me fairly busy."

"What kind of consulting?"

"Image and etiquette, mostly. I traveled so extensively as a model that I found I could help companies branch out into unfamiliar foreign markets by teaching them the customs and societal norms of the new country. Other times I help wealthy families groom their daughters into elegant ladies."

Although families mostly paid her to teach etiquette

and poise and give makeovers, she also spent a lot of time trying to teach those same girls that being pretty wasn't all they had to offer the world. It was an uphill battle and one that had earned her the label "hypocrite" more than a time or two. Sure, it was easy for a super-model to say that beauty wasn't everything.

"Do me a favor and don't mention your consulting business around my father or Juan Carlos," Gabriel said.

Serafia's dark eyebrows knit together in confusion. "Why is that? Do they have daughters in need of a makeover?" Bella certainly didn't need any help from her. The youngest Montoro was looking lovely tonight in a beaded blue gown with her golden hair in elegantly twisted curls.

Serafia had heard rumors that the Montoro heirs had been allowed to run wild in America, but from what she had seen, they were no different from the youths of any other royal family. They wanted to have fun, find love and shirk their responsibilities every now and then. Until those desires interfered with the crown, as Rafe's abdication had, there was no harm done.

Gabriel shook his head and took a large sip of his champagne. "No daughters. They've just got *me*. I wouldn't be surprised if they'd jump at the chance to have you make me over. I don't really blame them. I'm about to be the most unsuitable king ever to sit upon the throne of Alma. The bad boy…the backup plan… the worst possible choice…"

Her eyes widened with every unpleasant description. "Is that their opinion or just your own?"

He shrugged. "I think it's everyone's opinion, in-cluding mine."

"I think you're exaggerating a little bit. I'm not sure

about what your family thinks behind closed doors, but I haven't heard anything about you being unsuitable. Everyone is surprised about Rafe abdicating, of course, but I just came from Alma and the people are very excited to have you come home and serve as their monarch."

She hadn't originally planned on visiting Alma, but she'd gotten a call from a potential client there. She was already coming to Florida to consult with a company in Orlando, so she made a stop in Alma on the way. She was glad she had. It was inspiring to see an entire country buzzing with hope for the future. She wished she saw some of that same excitement in Gabriel.

He narrowed his gaze, seemingly searching her expression for the truth in her words, but he didn't appear to find it. "That won't last long. I wouldn't be surprised if they'd start begging for the dictatorship to come back within a year of my reign beginning."

And Serafia had thought she was the only one around here with miserably low self-esteem. "The people of Alma fought long and hard to be free of the Tantaberras. You would have to be a wicked, bloodthirsty tyrant for them to wish his return. Is that what you have planned? A reign of terror for your people?"

"No. I guess that changes things," he said with a bright smile that seemed fake. "I didn't realize they had such low expectations for their king. As long as I don't decapitate all my enemies and force my subjects to cower in fear, I'll be a success! Thanks for letting me know that. I feel a lot better about the whole thing now."

Gabriel was leaving for Alma in a week, and that attitude was going to be a problem. Before she could curb her tongue, Serafia leaned in to him and plucked the champagne glass from his hand. "The citizens of Alma have been through a lot over the last seventy years. While the wealthy upper class could afford to flee, most of the people were trapped there to suffer at the hands of Tantaberra and his sons. They're finally free, some of them having waited their whole lives to wake up in the morning without the oppressive hand of a despot controlling them. These people have chosen to restore your family to the throne to help them rebuild Alma. They can probably do without your sarcasm and self-pity."

Gabriel looked at her with surprise lighting his eyes. He might not be comfortable with the authority and responsibility of being king, but he seemed shocked that she would take that tone of voice with him. She didn't care. She had lived in Spain her whole life. She wasn't one of his subjects and she wasn't about to grovel at his feet when he was being like this.

She waited for him to speak, watching as the surprise faded to heat. At first she thought it was anger building up inside him, but when his gaze flicked over her skin, she could feel her cheeks start to burn with the flush of sexual awareness. She might have been too bold and said too much, but he seemed to like it for some reason.

At last, he took a deep breath and nodded. "You're absolutely right."

That was not what she'd expected to hear at all. She had braced herself for an argument or maybe even a come-on line to change the subject, but she certainly didn't think he would agree with her. Perhaps he wasn't doomed to failure if he could see reason in her words.

She returned his glass of champagne and looked out into the garden to avoid his intense stare and hide her blush. "I apologize for being so blunt, but it needed to be said."

"No, please. Thank you. I have spent the days since my brother's announcement worried about how it will impact me and my life. I've never given full consideration to the lives of all the people in Alma and how they feel. They have suffered, miserably, for so long. They deserve a king they can be proud of. I'm just afraid I'm not that man."

"You can be," Serafia said, and as she spoke the words, she believed them. She had no real reason to be so certain about the success of the Montoro Bad Boy. She hadn't spoken to him in years and he was just a boy then. Now there were only the rumors she'd heard floating across the Atlantic—stories of womanizing, fast cars and dangerous living. But she felt the truth deep in her heart.

"It might take time and practice, but you can get there. A lesser man wouldn't give a second thought to whether he was the right person for the job. You're genuinely concerned and I think that bodes well for your future in Alma."

Gabriel looked at her and for the first time, she noticed the signs of strain lining his eyes. They didn't entirely mesh with the image that had been painted of the rebellious heir to the throne. He seemed adept at covering his worry with humor and charming smiles, but in that moment it all fell away to reveal a man genuinely concerned that he was going to fail his country. "Do you really believe that?"

Serafia reached out and covered his hand with her

own. She felt a warm prickle dance across her palm as her skin touched his. The heat of it traveled up her arm, causing goose bumps to rise across her flesh despite the oppressive Miami summer heat. His gaze remained pinned on her own, an intensity there that made her wonder if he was feeling the same thing. She was startled by her reaction, losing the words of comfort she'd intended to say, but she couldn't pull away from him.

"Yes," she finally managed to say in a hoarse whisper.

He nodded, his jaw flexing as he seemed to consider her response. After a moment, he slipped his hand out from beneath hers. Instead of pulling away, he scooped up her hand in his, lifting it as though he was going to kiss her knuckles. Her breath caught in her throat, her tongue snaking out across her suddenly dry lips.

"Serafia, can I ask you something?"

She nodded, worried that she was about to agree to something she shouldn't, but powerless to stop herself in that moment. The candlelight flickering in his eyes was intoxicating. She could barely think, barely breathe when he touched her like that.

"Will you…" He hesitated. "…help me become the kind of king Alma deserves?"

Two

Gabriel watched as Serafia's expression collapsed for a moment in disappointment before she pulled herself back together. He couldn't understand why he saw those emotions in her dark eyes. He thought she would be excited that he wanted to step up and be a better person for the job. Wasn't that what she'd just lectured him about?

Then he looked down at her hand clutched in his own, here in the candlelight, on the dark, secluded patio, and realized he had a pretty solid seduction in progress without even trying. That might be the problem. He'd been too distracted by their conversation to realize it.

He had to admit he was pleased to know she responded to him. In the back of his mind, he'd considered Serafia unobtainable, a childhood fantasy. The moment she'd turned to look at him tonight, he felt his heart stutter in his chest as if he'd been shocked by a defibrillator. Her stunning red silk gown, rubies and diamonds dangling at her throat and ears, crimson lipstick against the flawless gold of her skin...it was as though she'd walked out of a magazine spread and onto his patio.

She was poised, elegant and untouchable. And bold. With a razor-sharp tongue, she'd cut him down to size, sending a surprising surge of desire through him instead of anger. She didn't care that he was the crown prince; she was going to tell it the way it was. With everything ahead of him, he was beginning to think he needed a woman like that in his life. Gabriel was already surrounded by too many yes-men or needling family members.

Serafia was a firecracker—beautiful, alluring and capable of burning him. A woman like that didn't exist in real life, and if she did, she wouldn't want anything to do with a man like Gabriel. Or so he'd always thought. The disappointment in her dark eyes led him to believe that perhaps he was wrong about that.

He wasn't entirely sure that a haircut and a new suit would make him a better king, but he was willing to give it a try. It certainly couldn't hurt. Working with a professional image consultant would get his father and Juan Carlos off his back. And if nothing else, it would keep this beautiful, sexy woman from disappearing from his life for at least two more weeks. It sounded like a win-win for Gabriel.

"A makeover?" she said after the initial shock seemed to fade from her face. She pulled her fingers from his grasp and rubbed her hands together for a moment as if to erase his touch. Serafia didn't seem to think his plan was the perfect solution he'd envisioned. "For you?"

"Why not? That's what you do, right?"

Her nose wrinkled and her brow furrowed. "I teach teenage girls how to walk in high heels and behave themselves in various social situations."

"How is what I'm proposing any different? Obviously I don't need the lesson on heels, but I'm about to face a lot of new social situations. With the way my family has been nagging at me, there seem to be a lot of land mines ahead of me. I could use help on how I should dress and what I should say. And I think you're the right person for the job."

Serafia's dark eyes widened and she sputtered for a moment as she struggled for words to argue with him. "I thought you didn't want a makeover," she said at last.

Gabriel crossed his arms over his chest. "I didn't want my family to force me into one. There's a difference. But you've convinced me that it's needed if I'm going to be the kind of king Alma needs."

"I don't know, Gabriel." She turned back to the gardens, avoiding his gaze. She seemed very hesitant to agree to it and he wasn't sure why. She'd pretty much dressed him down and chastised him for being a self-centered brat. Her words were bold and passionate. But then, when he asked for her help, she didn't want to be the one to change him. He didn't get it. Was he a lost cause?

"Come on, Serafia. It's perfect. I need a makeover, but I don't want everyone to know it. You're a friend of the family, so no one will think twice of you traveling with me or being seen with me. No one outside of the family even needs to know why you're here. We can come up with some cover story. I've got a week to prepare before I leave for Alma and another week of welcome activities once I arrive before things start to settle down. I'm not sure I can get through all that without help. Without *your* help."

"I can't just drop everything and run to your side, Gabriel."

"I'll pay you double."

She turned back to him, a crimson frown lining her face. Even that didn't make her classic features unattractive. "I don't need the money. I have plenty of that. I don't even have to work, but I was tired of sitting around with my own thoughts."

He wasn't sure what kind of thoughts would haunt a young, successful woman like Serafia, but he didn't feel that he should ask. "Donate it all to charity, then. I don't care. It's good for your business."

"How? I'd be doing this in secret. That won't earn me any exposure for my company."

"Not directly, but having you by my side in all the pictures will get your name in the papers. After you're seen with royalty, maybe your services will be more in demand because you have connections."

Serafia sighed. She was losing this battle and she knew it.

Gabriel looked at her, suppressing a smile as he prepared to turn her own argument against her and end the fight. "If for no other reason, do it for the people of Alma. You yourself just said how much these people have suffered. Do your part and help me be the best king I can possibly be."

She tensed up and started biting her lower lip. Picking up her wineglass, she took a sip and looked out at the moon hovering over the tree line. At last, her head dropped in defeat. The long, graceful line of her neck was exposed by the one-shoulder cut of her gown and the style of her hair. The dark, thick strands were twisted up into an elegant chignon, leaving her flawless, honey-colored skin exposed.

He wanted to press a kiss to the back of her neck and wrap his arms around her waist to comfort her. His lips tingled as he imagined doing just that, but he knew that would be pushing his luck. If she agreed to work with him over the next few weeks, there might be time for kisses and caresses later. It couldn't take every hour of the day to make him suitable. But if she left now, he'd never have the chance.

Taking a deep breath, she let it out and nodded. "Okay. We start tomorrow morning. I will be here at nine for breakfast and we'll begin with table manners."

"Nine?" He winced. Most Saturday mornings, he didn't crawl out of bed until closer to noon. Of course, he wouldn't be closing down the bars tonight. If he left the family compound, they'd likely release the hounds to track him down.

"Yes," she replied, her voice taking the same tone as the nuns had used when he was in Catholic school. Serafia didn't look a thing like Sister Mary Katherine, but she had the same focused expression on her face as she looked him over. The former supermodel had faded away and he was left in the presence of his new image consultant.

"Modern kings do not stay up until the wee hours of the morning and sleep until noon. They have a country to lead, meetings to attend and servants that need a reliable schedule to properly run the household. After breakfast, you're getting a haircut." She reached out for his hand, examining his fingernails in the dim lights. "And a manicure. I'll have someone come in to do it. If we went to a salon, people would start talking."

Getting up early, plus a haircut? Gabriel self-consciously ran his fingers through the long strands of his hair. He liked it long. When it was short, he looked too much like his toe-the-line brother, CEO extraordinaire Rafe. That wasn't him. He was VP of their South American division for a reason. Since the news of Alma's return to monarchy, he'd spent most of his time in Miami, but he preferred his time spent south of the equator. Life down there was more colorful, less regimented. He didn't even mind the constant threat of danger edging into his daily routine there. Once you'd been kidnapped, beaten and held for ransom, there wasn't much else to fear.

All that would end now. A new VP would take over South American Operations and Gabriel would take a jet to Alma. He'd be ruling over a country with a million citizens and dealing with all the demands that went with it.

What had he signed himself up for?

"I wish I had my tablet with me, but I'll just have to make all my notes when I get back to my hotel. Sunday, we're going through your wardrobe and determining what you can take with you to Alma. Monday morning, I'll arrange for a private shopper to come to the house and we'll fill in the gaps."

"Now, wait a minute," he complained, holding up his hands to halt her long list of tasks. He knew he could use some polishing, but it sounded as if Sera-fia was preparing to gut him and build him up from scratch. "What is wrong with my clothes? This is an expensive suit."

"I'm sure it is. And if you were the owner of an exclusive nightclub in South Beach, it would be perfect, but you are Prince Gabriel, soon to be King Gabriel."

He sighed. He certainly didn't feel like royalty. He felt like a little boy being scolded for doing everything wrong. But he'd brought this pain upon himself. Spending time with his fantasy woman hadn't exactly gone to plan. It had only been minutes since he made that decision and he was already starting to regret it.

"Are you dating anyone?"

Gabriel perked up. "Why? Are you interested?" he said with the brightest, most charming smile he could conjure.

Serafia wrinkled her nose at him and shook her head. "No. I was just wondering if I needed to work with you on dealing with any sticky romantic entanglements before you leave."

That was disappointing. "I'm not big on relationships," he explained. "There are plenty of women I've seen on and off, but there shouldn't be any heartbroken women trying to follow me to Alma."

"How about pregnant bartenders?" she asked pointedly.

Gabriel chuckled. His brother's relationship drama had everyone in the family on edge. If he didn't work out, the crown would be dumped on Bella and she was only twenty-three, barely out of college. "No pregnant bartenders that I am aware of," he answered. "Or dancers or cocktail waitresses or coeds. I'm extremely careful about that kind of thing."

"You always use protection? Every time?"

Gabriel stiffened. "Do we really have to talk about my sex life?"

Serafia sighed and shook her head. "You have no real idea what you've gotten yourself into, do you? From now on, your sex life is the business of a whole country. Who you're seeing and who might be your future queen will be one of the first issues you'll tackle as king. After that, fathering heirs and continuing the Montoro bloodline will be the chief concern of each of your subjects. Every woman you're seen with is a candidate for queen. Every time your wife turns down a glass of wine or puts on a few pounds, there will be pregnancy rumors. Privacy has gone out the window for you, Gabriel."

"There's not going to be someone in the room while I *father* these heirs, is there?"

At that, Serafia smiled. "No. They have to draw the line somewhere."

That offered little comfort to Gabriel in the moment. Each step he took toward being king, the more concerned he became. He wanted to be a good leader, but the level of scrutiny in every aspect of his life was suffocating. His hair, his clothes, his sex life… He could feel the pressure crushing against his chest like a pile of stones.

Serafia pointed to a pair of chairs nearby. "Why don't we sit down for a minute. You look like you're about to pass out and these shoes are starting to pinch."

Gabriel pulled out a chair for her and took the one beside her. "I guess I just never thought about all this before. A few weeks ago, I was just a VP in my family company, someone with far-off ties to a country and a history most of us have forgotten all about. Then, boom, I'm a prince. And before I can adjust to that, I find out that I'm going to be king of the place. My life has taken a strange turn."

She nodded sympathetically. "I hate to be the one to tell you this, but it's just going to get worse. Once you're in the spotlight, your life is no longer your own. But from someone who's lived through it, know that the sooner you adjust to the idea of it, the better off you'll be."

Serafia hated to see Gabriel like this. He seemed like such a vibrant, fun-loving man, and the weight of his future was slowly crushing him like a bug. She was pushing him. Maybe more than she had to, at least at first, but he needed to know how things were going to be now. He would adjust to the crown much more easily if he understood the consequences of it.

"Is that what it was like for you? Is that why you gave up modeling?"

Serafia couldn't help the pained expression she felt crossing her face. It happened every time her old career came up. She smiled and shook her head. "That was just a part of it."

"Do you miss modeling?" he asked.

"Not at all," she said a touch too quickly, although she meant it. It wasn't the glamorous business everyone thought it was. It was harsh, and despite how many millions she made doing it and how famous she became, there were still days where she was treated like little more than a walking coat hanger. And a fat one at that. "I'm not really interested in being in the spotlight anymore. It is both a wonderful and terrifying place to live."

Gabriel nodded thoughtfully. "The runways and magazine covers suffer for your absence. I understand why you stopped after what happened to you on the runway, though. I can imagine it's scary to come that close to death without any kind of warning. I mean, to go all that time without knowing you had...what was it, exactly?"

"A congenital heart defect," she replied, the lie slipping effortlessly off her tongue after all these years.

"Yeah, that's terrifying to think your own body is just waiting to rebel against you."

Serafia stiffened and tried to nod in agreement. That would be frightening, although she really wouldn't know. Her parents had done an excellent job spreading misinformation about her very public heart attack. Why else would a perfectly healthy twenty-four-year-old woman go into cardiac failure on the runway and drop to the floor with a thousand witnesses standing by in horror?

She could think of a lot of reasons, and for her, all of them were self-inflicted. Serafia had fallen victim to an industry-endorsed eating disorder, which had spiraled out of control leading up to that day. Anorexia was a serious illness, an issue that needed more visibility in the cutthroat modeling industry, but her family wanted to keep the truth out of the papers for her own protection. At the time, she had been in no condition to argue with them on that point.

Instead the word was that she'd retired from the modeling business to get treatment for her "heart condition" and no one ever questioned it. Instead of surgeries, her actual treatment had included nearly a year of intensive rehabilitation. She had to slowly put on thirty pounds so she didn't strain her heart. Then she learned to eat properly, how to exercise correctly and most important how to recognize the signs in herself that she was slipping into bad habits again.

"Are you better now?" he asked.

That was debatable. With an eating disorder, every day was a challenge. It wasn't like being an alcoholic or a drug user, where you could avoid the substance of choice. She had to eat. Every day. She needed to exercise. Just not too much. She had to maintain her weight and not swing wildly one way or another, or she'd put too much strain on her damaged heart. But she was managing. One day at a time, she reminded herself. "Yes," she said instead. "The doctors got me all fixed up. But you're right, I couldn't face the catwalk again after that. After nearly dying, I realized I wanted to do something else with my life. I'm much happier with what I'm doing now."

"Gabriel Alejandro Montoro!" a sharp voice shouted through the doorway to the patio. It was followed by several loud steps across the stone and a moment later, the figure of his younger sister, Bella, appeared.

"There you are. Everyone has been looking for you."

Gabriel shrugged, unaffected by his sister's exasperation. "I've been right here the whole time. And since when do you get to call me by my full name? Only Mama gets to do that."

"And if Mama were here, she'd haul you back into the house by your ear."

Serafia chuckled. Her memories of Adela were spot-on. "I'm sorry to monopolize Gabriel's time," she said, hoping to draw down some of his sister's ire. "We were discussing the plans for his royal transformation."

Bella eyed Serafia suspiciously, then turned to look at Gabriel. "Good luck with that. Either way, Father wants you inside, and now. He's wanting to do some kind of toast and then he wants to see you out on the dance floor. The press wants a shot of you dancing."

Gabriel stood with a reluctant sigh, reaching out his hand to help Serafia up. "And so it begins. Would you care to join me inside?"

"Absolutely." Serafia slipped her arm through his and they walked back into the house together.

There were even more people in the room now than there were when she'd decided it was too crowded and gone outside. Nothing she could do about it, though. She stayed by his side as they cut through the crowd in search of his father. They found him standing by the bar with Gabriel's cousin, Juan Carlos.

Serafia had never had much contact with the Salazar branch of the Montoro family, but she had heard good things about Juan Carlos. He had a good head on his shoulders. He was responsible and thoughtful. To hear some people talk, he was Gabriel's polar opposite and a better choice for king. She would never tell Gabriel that, though; he had enough worries. Perhaps Juan Carlos would accept a post as the king's counsel. He would make an excellent adviser for Gabriel or royal liaison to Alma's prime minister.

"There you are," Rafael said once he spied them. "Where have you..." He paused when his gaze flicked over Serafia. "Ah. Never mind. Now I know what has occupied your time," he said with a smile.

"It's good to see you again," she said, returning his grin and leaning in to hug her father's oldest friend.

"Too long!" Rafael exclaimed. "But now that some

of us will be back in Alma, that will not be the case. Your father tells me he's considering moving back if the monarchy is stable."

"He told me that, as well." Her dad had mentioned it, but the Espina family was a little gun-shy when it came to their home country. Their quick departure from Alma in the 1940s had been a messy one. There were rumors and accusations thrown at anyone who fled before Tantaberra rose to power, and her family was not immune. Serafia knew they would move slowly on that front and some might never return. Spain was all she had ever known and she had fallen in love with Barcelona. It would take a lot to lure her away from her hacienda with beachfront views of the Mediterranean.

Rafael clapped his son on the back. "Now that you're here, I want to make a small speech, do a toast, and then maybe you can take a spin around the dance floor and encourage others to join you. The party is getting dull."

Gabriel nodded and Juan Carlos went over to silence the band and bring Rafael the microphone. The music stopped as Rafael stepped onto the riser with the band and raised his hand to get the crowd's attention. He had such a commanding presence; the whole room went deathly silent in a moment. He would've made a good king, too. Alma's archaic succession laws needed to be changed.

"Ladies and gentlemen," Rafael began. "I want to thank all of you for coming here tonight. Our family has waited seventy years for a night like this, when we could finally see the monarchy restored to Alma. With it, we hope to see peace, prosperity and hope restored for the people of Alma, as well. I'm thrilled to be able to stand up here and join all of you in wishing my son and future king, Prince Gabriel, all the success in the world as he returns to our homeland."

Several of the people in the crowd cheered and applauded Rafael's statement. Gabriel stood stiff at Serafia's side, his jaw tight and his muscles tense. He didn't seem to be as excited as everyone else. After their discussion outside, she understood his hesitation. Still clinging to his arm, she squeezed it reassuringly and smiled at him.

"I ask everyone here to raise their glass to the future king of Alma, Gabriel the First! Long live the king!"

"Long live the king!" everyone shouted as they held up their glasses and took a sip. Serafia raised her glass as well, drinking the last of her wine.

"Now I would like to ask Gabriel to step out onto the dance floor and show us a few moves. Everyone, please, join us."

"Looks like I have to ask a lady to join me on the dance floor." Gabriel leaned in closer to her, a sly smile curling his full lips. "Have your doctors cleared you for vigorous physical activity?"

Serafia smiled at Gabriel and nodded. "Oh yes, I've got a clean bill of health. I could go all night on the dance floor if you can keep up with me."

Gabriel took her hand and led her out into the center of the room. As the band started playing an upbeat salsa tune, his hand went to her waist and tugged her body tight against his. "Is that a challenge?" he asked.

The contact of his hard body against hers sent a shock wave through her system that she had little time to recover from. He was no longer the mop-topped little boy she remembered running up and down the beach with his kite. Now his green eyes glittered with attraction and a flash of danger. And he *was* dangerous. She might not have finished high school, but she read enough history to know that getting involved with a king never ended well.

Before she could answer him they started moving in time with the music. It had been a long time since she'd danced, but the movement came easily with his strong lead. She almost seemed to float across the wooden floors, the rhythm of the music pulsing through their bodies. The crowds and the cameras around them faded away as they moved as one.

Soon other couples joined them on the dance floor and she didn't feel so exposed. The people around her made her feel better about the prying eyes, but being in Gabriel's arms was still a precarious place to be. The way he held her, the way he looked at her… The next two weeks were going to be a challenge to her patience and her self-control. Gabriel wanted more from her than just a makeover, and when he held her, she felt the same way. She never should've accepted the job, and she knew that now.

This was no teenage girl or Spanish businessman she was dealing with here. Gabriel Montoro was a sexy, rebellious handful and if she wasn't careful, she was going to get in way over her head.

Three

"You're late. Again."

That wasn't anything Gabriel didn't already know. After the last few days he'd had, he wasn't really in the mood to hear it. He'd signed himself up for this nightmare, but he was almost to the point where he'd pay Serafia more to leave him alone than to stay. He was used to the constant criticism of his family, but for whatever reason, Serafia's critical comments grated on him. He just didn't want a woman like her pointing out his faults. He wanted her nibbling on his ear. Unfortunately critiquing him was her job.

"Thanks for the information," he snapped. "When I'm king, I will have you named the official court time-keeper."

He expected her to respond with a smart comment, but instead she turned on her heel and walked across the room. She returned a moment later with a velvet-covered tray in her hands. Laid across it were four different styles of watches.

"One of these, actually, will be the official court timekeeper. I had them brought over from a local jeweler for you to choose the one you like."

His cell phone chimed and he looked down at the screen to avoid the display of watches in front of him. It was a text from a woman he'd gone out with a few weeks ago: a brunette named Carla. He opted to ignore it. He'd been getting a lot of those texts lately and he couldn't do anything about them now that he was on house arrest. What would he say, anyway? "Sorry, love, I've got to fly to a country you've never heard of and be king"?

Slipping the phone back into his pocket, he sighed when he realized the tray of watches was still there, waiting on him. *Watches.* Gabriel hated watches. He didn't wear one, ever. And why did he need to with the clock on his cell phone? "I don't need a watch."

Her resolve didn't waver. "You say that, and yet I've noticed punctuality seems to be a problem for you."

Was she an image consultant or a drill sergeant? "It's not a problem for me. I'm fine. It seems to be more of a problem for you."

Serafia's pink lips tightened as she seemed to fight a frown. "Please choose one."

"I told you, I'm not going to wear a watch." Gabriel couldn't stand the feel of something on his wrists. He'd worn watches all through high school and college, but after his abduction, he gave them all away. Even the nicest watches reminded him of the restraints he'd worn for too long. In an instant, he was back in that cold, dark basement and he never ever wanted to go back to that place.

"There's a Ferragamo, a Patek Philippe and two Rolexes. How can you turn your nose up at a Rolex?" Serafia reached down and plucked one off the tray. "Try this on. It's steel and yellow gold, so it will coordinate nicely with whatever you might be wearing. The faceplate is surrounded by pave diamonds and there are diamonds on the hours. I think it will really look elegant—"

Gabriel didn't move fast enough and before he knew what she had planned, he felt the cold steel of the metal at his wrist. His whole body tensed in an instant. On reflex, he hissed and jerked away from her. He was instantly transported back to Venezuela and the dark, claustrophobic room he was held in for almost a week. He could smell the mildew and filth, the air stale and thick with humidity.

"I said no!" he shouted without intending to. His eyes flew open, taking in the open, airy bedroom. He drew in a deep breath of air scented with hibiscus flowers and felt the tension fade from his shoulders. Looking at Serafia, he immediately regretted his reaction. There was fear as real as his own reflected in her dark eyes. "I'm sorry to yell," he said, but it was too late. The damage was done.

She shied away from him, turning her back and carrying the hundred thousand dollars' worth of watches back to the desk. She didn't speak again until she returned, more composed. It was amazing how she always seemed so put together. He could rattle her for a moment, but she always seemed to snap right back.

That was one skill he could use, but she hadn't taught him that yet.

She crossed her arms over her chest and looked at him. "What was all that about?"

Gabriel didn't like talking about his abduction. And his family had done a good job keeping the story out of the media. "I...I just don't like to wear a watch. I don't like the feel of anything around my wrists." He didn't want to elaborate. She already looked at him as if he was flawed. She had no idea how truly flawed he was. He was broken.

Serafia sighed, searching his face for answers he wasn't going to give her. "Okay, fine. No watch." She picked up her tablet and tapped through a few screens. "Your first public event in Alma will be a party hosted by Patrick Rowling. We need to get you fitted for your formal attire."

Patrick Rowling. Gabriel had heard his father and brother talking about the man, but he hadn't paid any attention. "Who is Patrick Rowling?"

"He's one of the richest men in Alma. He's British, actually, but when oil was discovered in Alma, his drilling company led the charge. He owns and operates almost all the oil platforms and refineries in the country. He's a very powerful and influential man. This party will be your first introduction to Alman society. Forging a solid relationship with the Rowlings will help secure a strong foothold for the monarchy."

Gabriel would be king, but somehow he got the feeling that he would be the one kissing Patrick's ring and not the other way around. He was already dreading this party and he didn't know anything about it.

"Now, this is a formal event, so custom dictates that you should wear ceremonial dress."

Serafia swung open the door of the armoire and pulled out a navy military uniform that looked like something out of an old oil painting in a museum. It looked stiff and itchy and he had absolutely no interest in wearing it.

"All right, now," he complained. "I've been a really good sport about most of this makeover stuff, but this is going too far." Gabriel frowned at Serafia as she held up the ridiculous-looking suit. "I let you cut my hair, give me a facial, a manicure, a pedicure and all other kinds of cures. You've given half my wardrobe to charity and spent thousands of dollars of my own money on suits no man under sixty would want to wear. I've tried to keep my mouth shut and go with it. But that... that outfit is ridiculous."

Serafia's eyes grew wider the longer he complained. "It's the ceremonial dress of the king!" she argued.

Of course it was. "It's got ropes and tassels and a damn baby-blue sash. I'm going to look like Prince Charming at the ball."

Serafia frowned. "That's the point, Gabriel. You are going to be *Su Majestad el Rey Don Gabriel I.* That's what kings wear."

"Maybe in the 1940s when my great-grandfather was the king. It's old-fashioned. Outdated."

"It's not for every day. It's for events like coronations, weddings and formal events like this party at the Rowling Estate. The rest of the time you'll wear normal clothes."

"Normal clothes you picked out," he noted. Not much better in his estimation.

Serafia sighed and returned the suit to the armoire. When she shut the door, she slumped against it in a posture of defeat. Closing her eyes, she pinched the bridge of her nose between her fingers. "We leave for Alma in two days and we have so much to cover. At this rate, we're never going to get it all done. You hired me, Gabriel. Why are you fighting me on every little thing?"

He didn't think he was fighting her on everything. The watch issue was nonnegotiable, but they'd gotten that unpleasantness out of the way. The clothing was just a hard pill for him to swallow. "I'm not intentionally trying to make your job more difficult. It just seems to be a gift I have."

Serafia rolled her eyes. "So it seems. Admittedly, you appear to enjoy getting me all spun up. I've seen you smile through my irritation."

Gabriel had to admit that was true. There was something about the flush of irritation that made Serafia even that much more beautiful, if it was possible. In his mind, he imagined the same would hold true when she was screaming out in passion, clawing at the sheets. The woman who had sashayed down the runway all those years ago had nothing on the vision in his mind as he thought of her at night.

And he had. Since the night on the patio, he'd lain alone in bed every night thinking about her. He hadn't intended to. Serafia was a fantasy from his younger years; the image of her in a bikini was the background of his first computer. It had been a long time since he'd had a crush on Serafia, and yet those desires had rushed back at the first sight of her.

It was probably his family-imposed curfew. The day his brother abdicated, he was practically dragged from his penthouse to the family compound. He'd gone weeks with no clubs, no bars, no socializing with friends at parties. His every move was watched and that meant he was on the verge of his longest dry spell since he broke the seal on his manhood.

It didn't really matter, though, at least where Serafia was concerned. He could've bedded a woman this morning and he would still want her the way he always had wanted her.

"Yes," he admitted at last. "I get pleasure from watching you spin."

"Why? Are you a sadist?"

Gabriel smiled wide and took a few steps closer to her. "Not at all. It might be cliché to say it, but, Serafia, you are even more beautiful when you're angry."

Serafia rejected the flicker of disbelief in the back of her mind and silenced the denial on her lips. As her therapist had trained her, she identified the negative thoughts and reframed them. She was a healthy, attractive woman. Gabriel found her eye-catching and it wasn't her place to question his opinion of her. "Thank you," she said. "But please don't spend the rest of our time together trying to annoy me. You might find I'm more attractive, but it's emotionally exhausting."

Gabriel took another step toward her, closing in on her personal space. With her back pressed against the oak armoire, she had no place to go or escape. A part of her didn't really want to escape, anyway. Not when he looked at her like that.

His dark green eyes pinned her in place, and her breath froze in her lungs. He wasn't just trying to flatter her with his words. He did want her. It was very obvious. But it wasn't going to happen for an abundance of reasons that started with his being the future king and ended with his being a notorious playboy. Even dismissing everything in between, it was a bad idea. Scrafia had no interest in kings or playboys.

"Well, I'll do my best, but I do so enjoy the flush of rose across your cheeks and the sparkle of emotion in your dark eyes. My gaze is drawn to the tension along the line of your graceful neck and the rise and fall of your breasts as you breathe harder." He took another step closer. Now he could touch her if he chose. "If you don't want me to make you angry anymore, I could think of another way to get the same reaction that would be more...*pleasurable* for us both."

Serafia couldn't help the soft gasp that escaped her lips at his bold words. For a moment, she wanted to reach out for him and pull him hard against her. Every nerve in her body was buzzing from his closeness to her. She could feel the heat of his body radiating through the thin silk of her blouse. Her skin flushed and tightened in response.

One palm reached out and made contact with the polished oak at her back. He leaned in and his cologne— one of the few things she hadn't changed—teased at her nose with sandalwood and leather. The combination was intoxicating and dangerous. She could feel herself slipping into an abyss she had no business in. She needed to stop this before it went too far. Serafia was first and foremost a professional.

"I'm not sleeping with you," she blurted out.

Gabriel's mouth dropped open in mock outrage. "Miss Espina, I'm shocked."

Serafia chuckled softly, the laughter her only release

for everything building up inside her. She arched one eyebrow at him. "Shocked that I would be so blunt or shocked that I'm turning you down?"

At that, he smiled and she felt her knees start to soften beneath her. Much more of that and she'd be a puddle in her Manolos.

"Shocked that you would think that was all I wanted from you."

Serafia crossed her arms over her chest. She barely had room for the movement with Gabriel so close. She needed the barrier. She didn't believe a word he said. "What exactly were you suggesting, then?"

His jewel-green gaze dropped down to the cleavage her movement had enhanced. She was clutching herself so tightly that she was on the verge of spilling out of her top. She relaxed, removing some, if not all of the distraction.

"I'm feeling a little caged up. I was going to suggest a jog around the compound followed by a dip in the swimming pool," he said.

"Sure you were," she replied with a disbelieving tone. "You look like a man who's hard up for a good run."

He smiled and she felt a part deep inside her clench with need. Desire had not been very high on Serafia's priority list for a very long time. She was frustrated at how easily Gabriel could push her body's needs to the top of the list.

"The king's health and well-being should be at the forefront of the minds of the Alman people. Long live the king, right?"

"Long live the king," she responded, albeit unenthusiastically.

"So, how about that run?"

The way he looked at her, the way he leaned into her, it felt as if he was asking for more than just a run. But she answered the question at hand and tried to ignore her body's response to his query. "First, you need your ceremonial dress tailored. It will take a couple days to get it back and we need it before we leave. Then you can run if you like."

"And what about you? Don't you need a little rush of endorphins? A little...release?"

"I exercised when I got up this morning," she replied. And she had. Every morning when she woke up, she did exactly forty-five minutes on her elliptical machine. No more, no less, doctor's orders. Her treadmill at home was gathering dust, since running was out of the question unless her life was in danger.

His gaze raked over her, making every inch of her body aware of his heavy appraisal before he made a sucking sound with his tongue and shook his head. "Pity."

He dropped his arm and took a step back, allowing her lungs to fill with fresh oxygen that wasn't tainted with his scent. It helped clear her head of the fog that had settled in when he was so close.

The persistent chirp of his cell phone drew his attention away and for that, Serafia was grateful. Apparently Gabriel's harem of women were lonely without him. Since they'd begun this process four days ago, he averaged a text or two an hour. Most of the time he didn't respond, but that didn't stop the messages from coming in. She didn't care about what he'd been involved in, but she couldn't help noticing all the different names on the screen.

Carla, Francesca, Kimi, Ronnie, Anita, Lisa, Tammy, Jessica, Emily, Sara…it was as if his phone was spinning through a massive Rolodex of names. His little digital black book would be ungainly if it were in print.

"I'm going to go see if the tailor has arrived," she said as he put the phone away again. "Do you think you can fight off all your lovers long enough to get this jacket fitted properly?"

Gabriel narrowed his eyes at her and slipped his phone into his pocket. "You sound jealous."

Maybe a little. But that was none of his concern. She would deal with it accordingly. "Not jealous," she corrected. "I'm concerned."

He frowned at her then. "You sound like my father. Why would you be concerned with my love life?"

"It's like I told you that first night, Gabriel. Your life is no longer your own. Not your relationships or your free time or even your body. You can't drive your sports cars around like a Formula One driver and put the king's health at risk. You can't party every night with a different woman and put the future of your country in the hands of a bastard you father with some girl you barely remember. You can't waste the realm's money on the hedonistic pleasures you've built your whole life on."

"From what I learned in school, that's what most kings do, actually."

"Maybe four hundred years ago, but not anymore. If King Henry the Eighth had to deal with the modern press, things would've ended very differently for him and all his poor wives."

"So you're saying it's all about appearances? I have

to be squeaky clean on the outside to keep the press and the people happy?"

"It's bigger than that. Your recklessness is indicative of an emotional disconnect. That's what worries me. You need to prepare yourself for the marriage that is just around the corner for you. You may not even have met the woman yet, but I guarantee you'll be married before the first year of your reign comes to an end. That means no more skirt chasing. You have to take this seriously. You have to really connect with someone, and I don't see that coming easily to you."

"You don't think I can connect with someone?" He seemed insulted by her insinuation.

"Relationships—*real relationships*—are hard. Love and trust and honesty are difficult to maintain. I've only been around here for a few days, but I haven't seen you interact with a single person on a sincere level. You have no real relationships, not even with your family."

"I have real relationships," he argued, but even as he spoke the words, she sensed a question in his voice.

"Name one. If something huge happened in your life, who would you run to with the news? If you had a secret, who would you confide in?"

There was an extended silence as he thought about the answer to her question. There would be a quicker response for almost anyone else she asked this question of. A mother, a brother, a best friend, a buddy from college… Gabriel had no answer. It was both sad and disconcerting. Why did he keep everyone at arm's length?

"I have plenty of friends and family. Since I've been announced as the future king, they've been coming out of the woodwork. I don't know what you're talking about."

"I'm talking about having a person in your life who you can tell anything, good or bad. Someone to confide in. I don't think Jessica or Tammy is the right answer. But I also don't think Rafe or Bella are, either. Everyone needs a person like that in their lives. I feel like there are people who would be there for you, but you won't let them in. I feel a resistance, a buffer there, even with your own family, and I don't know what it's about. What I do know is that you need to learn to let those walls down or this week will be nothing compared to the next year."

"I figured the opposite would be true," he replied at last. "When you're the king, everyone wants something from you. You can't trust anyone. Your marriage is arranged, your closest advisers jockeying for their own pet projects. I would've thought that keeping my distance would be an asset in that kind of environment."

"Maybe you're right," she admitted with a sad shrug. "I certainly would've been more prepared for the world of modeling if I'd gone in believing that everyone wanted something from me and that I couldn't trust them. But I think everyone, even a king, needs someone."

"Believe me, it's easier this way," he said. "If you don't trust anyone, they can't betray you and you'll never be disappointed."

There was an honesty in his words that she hadn't heard in anything else he'd said when they were together. That worried her. Someone, at some point, had damaged Gabriel. She knew it shouldn't be her concern, but she couldn't help wondering what had happened and how she could help.

The people of Alma—Serafia included—wanted

more from their king than Gabriel was willing to give them. He hadn't even been crowned king yet and she worried this was going to be a mistake. No amount of haircuts or fancy clothes could fix the break deep inside of him.

He had to do that himself.

Four

Two days later, Gabriel stepped onto a private jet and left the life he knew behind him. They flew overnight, his father, Rafael, sleeping in the bedroom of the plane as he and Serafia slept in fully reclining leather chairs. It was a quiet flight without a lot of conversation once they finished their dinners and dimmed the cabin lights.

Gabriel slept soundly, and when he awoke, they were thirty minutes out from landing in his new country. He'd only been there once before with Rafe on a whirlwind tour, but when he got off the plane this time, he was supposed to be their leader.

"You need to get dressed," Serafia said beside him. "Your suit is hanging up in the bathroom."

He hadn't heard her get up, but she had changed her clothes, refreshed her makeup and styled her thick, dark hair into a bun. For the next week, she was publically filling the role of his social secretary while privately coaching him through all the events. She was dressed for the part in a ladies' taupe suit. The blazer was well tailored and didn't look boxy, and the sheath dress beneath it was fitted and came down just to her knee, showcasing her long and shapely calves.

It was elegant, but Gabriel found himself longing for the clingy red silk gown from their first night together. In this outfit, she completely faded into the background. He supposed that was the idea, but he didn't like it. Serafia might not care for the spotlight, but she was born to be in it.

He went to the bathroom, getting ready and changing into the navy suit she'd hung out for him. She'd paired it with a lighter blue shirt and a plain blue tie. It was a sophisticated look, she'd argued, but it seemed boring to him. It made him want to wear crazy socks, but he wouldn't. She'd already laid out a pair of navy socks for him.

By the time he came back out, his father had emerged from the bedroom and the pilot was announcing their descent into Del Sol, the capital of Alma.

"The press will be waiting for you when we arrive. They've arranged for a carpet to be laid out and your royal guards will be there for crowd control. They've already secured the area and screened all the attendees. Your press secretary, Señor Vega, briefed everyone on appropriate questions, so things should go smoothly. I will exit the plane first and make sure everything is okay," Serafia explained. "Then Señor Montoro, and then you're last. Wait until the carpet is clear. Take your time so everyone can get their photos."

Gabriel nodded, taking in her constant stream of instructions as he had done all week. She was a font of information.

"Don't forget to smile. Wave. It should just be the press, so no need to greet anyone in the crowd. No speeches, no interviews. Just smile and wave."

The wheels of the jet touched down and suddenly everything became very real. Gabriel looked out the window. Beyond the airport, he could see the great rock hills that rose on the horizon, their gray stone peppered with evergreens. Closer to Del Sol was a smaller hill topped with some kind of ancient fortress. Climbing up the incline were whitewashed buildings clustered together with clay tile roofs.

Ahead, clear blue skies with palm trees led the way toward the beach. His last trip here with his brother had been all business, so he had no idea what kinds of beaches they had in Alma, but he prayed they were at least halfway as nice as the ones in Miami. He was already feeling pangs of homesickness.

The plane stopped and the engines turned off. The small crew unlocked and extended the staircase. Serafia gathered up her bag and her tablet. "Smile and wave," she said one last time before disappearing down the stairs.

His father followed her a moment later and then it was Gabriel's turn. His heart started pounding in his rib cage. His lungs could barely take in enough air, his chest was so tight. Once he stepped out of this plane, he was a coronation away from being *Su Majestad el Rey Don Gabriel I*. It was a terrifying prospect, but he pushed himself up out of his seat anyway.

Taking a deep breath, he stepped into the doorway.

He was momentarily blinded by the sun. He paused for a moment to adjust, a smile on his face and his arm raised in greeting. He slowly made his way down the stairs, careful not to fall and make the worst possible impression. By the time he reached the bottom, he could look out into the crowd of photographers. There were about fifty of them gathered with cameras and video crews.

To the left and right of the stairs were two large gentlemen in military suits similar to the one Serafia had recently had tailored for him. In addition to their shiny brass buttons and collections of metals, they wore earpieces with cords that disappeared under their collars. He hadn't really given the idea of his personal security much thought until now.

The men bowed, and after he nodded to them both, they walked two paces behind Gabriel as he made his way down the carpet. At the end of the path, he could see his father and Serafia waiting for him with a man he presumed was his press secretary. Serafia had an exaggerated smile like a stage mom, reminding him to smile and wave.

He was almost to the end when a man with a video crew charged to the edge of the barricade and shouted to him. "Gabriel! How do you feel about your brother's abdication? Did you know he had a child on the way?"

The bold question startled him.

"Rafe made his choice. I don't blame him for his decision." Serafia had told him he wasn't to answer questions, but he was thrown off guard with a film crew pointing the camera right in his face.

"What about the child?" the man pressed.

He felt a protectiveness build up inside him, his fists

curling tight at his side. "I was unaware of the serious-ness of his relationship with Ms. Fielding, but the mat-ter of their child is their business, and I must insist that you respect their privacy."

"Have you chosen a queen yet?" Another reporter shouted before he could take another step. From there, it was a rapid fire he couldn't escape.

"Will she be a citizen of Alma or a member of a Eu-ropean royal family to strengthen trade agreements?"

"Did you leave a lover behind in America?"

Gabriel felt his throat close. He didn't know how to even begin addressing these questions, but he was certain his required smile had faded.

"Please!" Serafia shouted, stepping in front of him and holding her hands up to the camera. "He's been in Del Sol for five minutes. Let's allow Don Gabriel to get settled in and perhaps coroneted before we start wor-rying about the line of succession, shall we?"

She took his arm and with a forceful tug, led him down the rug and inside the terminal. From there, se-curity ushered them quickly out a side door to a black SUV with Alma's flag flying on each corner of the hood.

The door had barely shut before the convoy was on the road. The inside of the vehicle was quiet. He was stunned by the turn of events. Serafia was stiff be-side him.

"What the hell was that?" his father finally asked.

"I didn't realize—" Gabriel began to defend himself to his father, but he realized he was looking at Serafia with eye daggers.

"You said there were to be no questions," Rafael snapped. "Why wasn't the press properly briefed?"

"They were," she argued, her spine lengthening in defiance. "Hector assured me that they were told Gabriel wasn't answering questions, but to tell them they can't ask is suppression of free press. No matter what they're told, reporters will ask questions in the hopes they can catch someone off guard and get an answer that will provide a juicy headline."

"Unacceptable."

Serafia sighed angrily. "I can assure you that I will work with Hector to have the offending reporters identified and will see to it that their press privileges are suspended."

"Gabriel should've been briefed. If you knew the press might push him for questions, he should've been better prepared. That's your job."

"I'm an image consultant, not his press secretary. What kind of briefing does he need to walk down a rug and wave? I suggest that when we arrive at the palace, we arrange to meet with Hector immediately. He'll need to be able to handle those sorts of things better in the future. There are more public appearances this week. We can't risk that happening again. I'm sorry that—"

"Stop," Gabriel said. He'd grown angrier with every apologetic word out of her mouth. There was no reason for her to ask for forgiveness. "You've done nothing wrong, Serafia. I apologize for my father's harsh, inappropriate tone. I should've anticipated they would ask questions like that. I will be more prepared next time. End of discussion. For now, let's just focus on getting settled in and prepared for our next event."

His father's sharp gaze raked over him as he spoke, the older man's tan Mediterranean complexion mottled with red. He was clearly angry his son had shut him down, but that was too bad. The balance of power had shifted in the family. The moment Gabriel stepped off that plane, he was in charge. They weren't in Miami anymore where his father ruled over the family with an iron fist.

They were in Alma now and Gabriel was going to be the king. His father had ruined his chance to be the boss when he divorced Gabriel's mother without an annulment, so he'd better get used to the way things were going to be now. Gabriel was no longer the useless middle son who could be berated or ignored.

Gabriel was going to be king.

"It's beautiful," Serafia said as they entered the main room of the palace.

El Castillo del Arena was the official royal residence in Del Sol. Looking like a giant sandcastle, hence its name, it sat on a fortified wall overlooking the bay. The early Arabian influences on the architecture were evident everywhere you looked, from the arches to the intricate mosaic tile work. The inner courtyards had gardens that made a cool escape from the sun with lush trees, fountains and blooming flowers in every direction.

Clearly it wasn't as grand a palace as it had once been: the Persian rugs had threadbare corners and the upholstery on the furniture was worn and dirty. Seventy years in the hands of a dictatorship had made their mark, but it still had the grand design and details of its former glory. It wouldn't take long to restore the palace.

Few people had been allowed in under the Tanta-berras. It was a pity. The grand rooms with the arched

ceilings were begging for a royal event with all the elite
of Alma in attendance.

From the expression on his face, Gabriel wasn't
as impressed. Since the heated discussion in the car,
he'd been quiet. She thought that when Señor Montoro
skipped the tour and asked to be shown to his rooms
so he could nap Gabriel would perk up, but he didn't.
Now he silently took it all in as they followed his personal steward, Ernesto, on a tour through the palace.

"These are the king's private chambers," Ernesto
said as he opened the double doors to reveal the expansive room.

There was a king-size bed in the center of the room
with a massive four-poster frame. It was draped in
red fabric with a dozen red and gold pillows scattered
across the bed. Large tapestries hung on the walls, and
a Moroccan rug covered the stone floors.

"Your bath and closet are through those doors," Ernesto continued.

She watched as Gabriel looked around, a slightly
pained expression on his face. "It's awfully dark in
here," he complained. "It's like a cave or an underground cellar. Are there only those two windows?"

Ernesto looked at the two arched windows crafted
of stained glass and nodded. "Yes, Your Majesty."

She watched Gabriel tense at the use of the formal
title. "I'm not king yet, Ernesto. You can just call me
Gabriel."

The man's eyes grew wide. "I would rather not, Your
Grace. You're still the crown prince."

"I suppose." Gabriel sighed and fixed his gaze on
a set of double doors on the other side of the room.
"Where do those doors go to?"

Ernesto, lean and dark-complexioned, moved quickly to the doors and opened them. "Through here are the queen's rooms. And beyond it are chambers for her ladies-in-waiting, although the rooms may be better suited in these times as an office or a nursery. The rooms haven't really been used since your great-grandmother, Queen Anna Maria, fled Alma."

Gabriel frowned. "The queen doesn't share a room with the king?"

"She may. Traditionally, having her own space allowed her to pursue more feminine activities with her ladies such as sewing or reading without interfering with the running of the state."

"It's like I've gone back in time," Gabriel grumbled, and ran his fingers through his hair in exasperation.

"The staff is still working on restoring and modernizing the palace. Perhaps Your Majesty would prefer to spend some time prior to the coronation at Playa del Onda. It's a more modern estate, built for the royal family to vacation at the beach in the summers. It's lovely, with floor-to-ceiling windows that overlook the sea and bright, open rooms."

For the first time since they'd arrived, Serafia noticed Gabriel perk up. "How far is it from here?"

"It's about an hour's drive along the coastal highway, but you won't mind a minute of it. The views are exquisite. I can call ahead to the staff there and let them know you'll be coming if you'd like."

Gabriel considered his options for a moment and finally turned to look at Serafia. "I know we'll be coming back to Del Sol for a lot of activities this week, but I think I'd like to stay out there while I can. Care to continue our work at the beach?" he asked.

She nodded. The location wasn't important to her, but she could tell it mattered to him. He seemed to have a tense, almost claustrophobic reaction to his own quarters, despite the room being massive in scale with tall, arched ceilings. If he could relax, he would absorb more information. She could accommodate the extended drive times in their schedule.

"Then let's do that. My father will be staying here, but Señorita Espina and I will be going to Playa del Onda. We'll be staying there for the next week. I'll return as we start preparing for the coronation."

"Very good. I'll arrange for your transportation."

"Ernesto?"

The steward paused. "Yes, Your Majesty?"

"See if you can arrange for a convertible with a GPS. I'd like to drive myself to the compound and enjoy the sun and sea air on the way."

"Drive yourself?" Ernesto seemed stumped for a moment, but then immediately shook off his concerns. It wasn't his place to question the king's requests. "Yes, Your Grace." He turned and disappeared down the hallway.

"They're not going to know what to do with a king like you," Serafia said.

"Me, neither," Gabriel noted dryly. "But maybe if we spend a couple days at the beach, we can all be better prepared for my official return to the palace."

They walked out of the king's chambers and down the winding staircase to the main hall. Within minutes, they were greeted by the royal guard, who reported that they already had a car waiting for him outside. They would be following in the black SUV that brought him there.

Gabriel didn't argue. Instead they walked out into the courtyard. A cherry-red Peugeot convertible was parked there. "Whose car is this?" he asked as an attendant opened the door for Serafia to get in.

"It is Señor Ernesto's car, Your Majesty."

"What will he drive while I have it?"

"One of the royal fleet." The attendant pointed to an area with several vehicles parked there. "He is happy to let you borrow it. The address of the beach compound is already entered in the system, Your Majesty."

Gabriel took the keys, slipped out of his suit coat and got in beside her. He waited until the guard had assembled in the SUV behind them; then he started the car and they headed toward the gates.

Once they slipped beyond the fortress walls, Serafia noticed Gabriel's posture relax. It was as if a weight had been lifted from his shoulders. She couldn't help feeling the same way. Ernesto had been right: the view was amazing. Once they escaped Del Sol and started climbing up the mountain, everything changed. The winding coastal road showcased wide vistas with bright blue skies, turquoise waters and ships along the shoreline.

With the sun warming her skin and the ocean air whipping the strands of her hair around her face, she felt herself relax for the first time since she'd left Barcelona. Although the Atlantic islands were different from her Mediterranean hacienda, it felt as if she were back there, the place where she felt the most at home, and safe.

"Are you hungry?" he asked.

"Yes." They'd had croissants and juice on the plane, but it was past lunchtime now and she was starving.

Gabriel nodded. A mile up the road, he slowed and

pulled off at a small, hole-in-the-wall restaurant over-looking the sea. A moment later, the royal guard pulled up beside them and lowered a window.

"Is there a problem, Your Majesty?" the one with the slicked-back brown hair who was driving the SUV asked.

"I'm hungry. Have you two had lunch?"

The two guards looked at each other in confusion and the driver turned back to him. "No, we haven't."

"Is this place any good?" he asked.

"I have eaten here many times, but in my opinion, it isn't fit for the king."

Gabriel looked at her and smiled widely. "Perfect. I'm starving. Let's all grab something to eat."

The two of them waited outside with the younger blond guard as the other went inside to make sure the restaurant was secure. It wasn't big enough to house much more than a tiny kitchen and a few tables on the veranda.

When they got the all-clear, a small, slow-moving old woman greeted them as they came in and gave them their choice of tables outside. As Gabriel had insisted they eat as well, the guards took a table near the door to watch anyone coming in or out, allowing him and Serafia privacy while they dined.

The menu was limited, but the royal guard with the dark hair named Jorge recommended the *caldereta de langosta*. It was a seasonal lobster stew with tomatoes, onions, garlic and peppers, served with thin slices of bread.

They all ordered the caldereta and Serafia was not disappointed. Normally she gave great care and thought into every bite she put in her mouth, but the stew was too amazing to worry about it. The lobster was soft and buttery in texture, while spicy in flavor thanks to the peppers. The bread soaked up the broth perfectly and helped carry the large pieces of lobster to her mouth without her wearing most of it on her pale taupe suit.

"This is wonderful," she said, when she was more than halfway finished with her stew. "Thank you for stopping."

"I was getting cranky," Gabriel said. He glanced over the railing at the sparking blue sea below them. "If I can be cranky looking at a view like this, I've got to be hungry."

"I would've thought the incident this morning had more to do with it than hunger."

"This morning was nothing and my father wanted to make it into something. I have enough to worry about without him making you uncomfortable. You've gone out of your way to help me through this. You've tolerated my bad moods and my childish behavior. I think I will be a better king for what you've done, so I should be thanking you, not criticizing you."

Serafia was stunned by his thoughtful words. He seemed to be almost a different person since they'd arrived in Alma. Or at least since the moment he'd stood up to his father. He had seemed to grow taller in that moment, physically stronger even, as he sat in the vehicle. Perhaps he truly was gaining the confidence he needed to rule Alma.

"Thank you," she said. "I appreciate that. And I appreciate you standing up for me this morning. The look on your father's face when you put an end to the discussion was priceless, really."

Gabriel looked at her with a wry grin. "It was good,

wasn't it? It's the first time I've stood up to him in my whole life and I'm glad I did."

"Is he always like that?"

Gabriel sipped his sparkling water and nodded. "Nothing was ever good enough for my father, but especially me. I could never understand it growing up. I did everything right, everything he wanted me to do. I went to school where he wanted me to go, took the position at the company he wanted me to have. I let him banish me to South American Operations. After everything that happened there, I almost got the feeling he was disappointed I came back. I've never understood why."

"After everything that happened there?" Gabriel seemed to be alluding to some incident she was unaware of. "What happened?"

With a sigh, he popped the last of his bread in his mouth and shook his head. "It doesn't matter. What matters is that I learned some valuable lessons. First, that you have to be careful who you can trust. And second, that I'm a grown man who can live and do however I please. These last few years my behavior has just been written off by my family as reckless and selfish, but it's been good for me. If my father doesn't approve of me either way, I should do whatever I want to, right?"

Serafia suppressed her frown. How had she not seen how wounded he was before now? The cracks in his facade were starting to show and they made her wonder what had turned the obedient middle son into the rebellious, distant one. He didn't want to talk about it and she understood. She had dark secrets of her own, but she couldn't help wondering if his past and its effect on him might hinder his leadership in Alma.

"I never wanted to be king, but now that I'm here, I think this might work out. My father may still disagree with what I do and how, but now I don't have to listen to it any longer." Abruptly standing, he pulled some euros from his wallet and threw them down on the table to cover everyone's lunch tab. Serafia got up as well, placing her napkin on the table.

"Let's get back on the road."

Five

"You look very handsome tonight."

Serafia stood at Gabriel's side and looked over the railing at the crowd below. There was a sea of people there, all dressed in their finest tuxedos and gowns. A string quartet was in the corner, filling the large space with a soothing background melody. It was a glittering display of marble floors, towering flower arrangements and twinkling crystal chandeliers. Patrick Rowling spared no expense when it came to his home or the parties he hosted there.

They had arrived at the Rowling mansion via a side door and were escorted upstairs to wait in Patrick's library so Gabriel could make a grand entrance. To their right was an elaborate marble staircase that twisted its way into the center of the ballroom. It just begged for a king to stroll down with a regal air.

Regal was not the vibe she was getting from Gabriel. Her compliment seemed to unnerve him. He shifted uncomfortably under her scrutiny, although there was no reason for him to be nervous. The ceremonial dress had been tailored beautifully and despite his complaints, he looked noble, powerful and very appropriate for a party like this. He had come a long way in the last week and she'd felt a swell of pride in her chest when he stepped out of his bedroom in full regalia earlier.

"I still feel like Prince Charming at the ball. And from the look of the crowd here tonight, all the eligible young maidens have come to land a king for a husband."

"I did notice that," she admitted. There were a lot of young women at the party, all painted and coiffed to the max. Decked out in an array of eye-catching jewel-tone silks and satins, they were like parading peacocks among the dark tuxedos. If Serafia had to guess, she'd say that millions of dollars had been laid out tonight in the hopes that they might catch the future king's eye.

She had gone the opposite route. Her gown was a very soft pink, almost a blush color. The organza ruching wrapped around her body, dotted with tiny crystals and beads. While sedate in color, it still had a few scandalous details like a plunging V-cut neckline and a slit on the side that almost reached the top of her thigh. She wanted to look as if she belonged, but she didn't want to stand out. She wasn't here to enjoy a party; she was here to help Gabriel get through his first real event in Alma.

"It certainly looks like you have your pick of ladies here tonight."

"Do I?"

Serafia turned to look at him and was surprised to see the serious way he was looking at her. He had the same heated intensity in his eyes he'd had the day he pinned her against the armoire. What exactly did he mean by that? She couldn't possibly be his pick when there were so many younger, more attractive women in the room tonight. "I…uh…" She hesitated. "I…think you've got a lot to choose from and a long night ahead of you. Don't make a decision too quickly. Keep your options open."

Gabriel sighed and turned away to look at the crowd. "I'll try."

A man in a tuxedo approached them on the landing and bowed to Gabriel. "If Your Majesty is ready, I'll cue the musicians to announce your arrival."

"Yes, I suppose it's time."

"May I escort you downstairs, Señorita Espina?"

"Yes, thank you." She took the man's arm and turned back to Gabriel. "I'll see you downstairs after the guests have all been presented."

"You're not going down with me?"

Serafia chuckled. "This is like the arrival at the airport, but without the pushy reporters. You need to have your moment. Alone." She wouldn't make many new girlfriends tonight if she showed up on the king's arm and beat them all to the punch.

"Good luck," she said, giving him a wink before carefully descending the staircase and joining the crowd. She parted with her escort, finding a spot at the edge of the room near one of the royal guards to watch Gabriel's entrance.

The orchestra started playing Alma's national anthem. The bustling crowd immediately grew silent and everyone turned their gaze to the flag hanging from the second-floor railing. When the last note died out, Gabriel appeared at the top of the stairs looking as much like a king as a man raised to have the position.

"His Royal Highness, El Príncipe Gabriel, the future El Rey Don Gabriel the First of Alma."

The crowd applauded as he came down the stairs. The air in the room was electric with excitement. Gabriel didn't fully appreciate how important this was for the people of Alma. They were free, and his arrival was the living, breathing evidence of that freedom. People bowed and curtseyed as he passed.

"Oh my God, he's so handsome. I didn't think it was possible, but he's even more attractive than Rafe."

Serafia turned to see a young woman and her mother standing nearby. The woman was maybe twenty-three and she was in a sapphire-blue gown that looked amazing with her golden skin and flaxen hair. Her mother was an older carbon copy in a more sedate silver gown. They were both dripping with diamonds, but the twinkle in their eyes sparkled even brighter as they looked at Gabriel.

"Oh, Dita," the mother gushed. "He's perfect for you. This is your big chance tonight. You look absolutely flawless, better than any of the other girls here." She looked around the room, scanning the competition again. Her gaze lit on Serafia for only a moment, then moved on as though she were an insignificant presence. Apparently the woman didn't read *Vogue*, or she would realize she was standing beside a former supermodel.

Serafia recognized *her*, however. At the mention of her daughter's name, she realized the mother was Felicia Gomez. The Gomez family was one of the richest in Alma, although unlike the Rowlings, they were natives like the Espinas. Many of the wealthier families had fled Alma when Tantaberra came to power, but the Gomez family had stayed.

Serafia had never met them, but she had heard her mother talk about them from time to time. It was rarely flattering. She got the impression that they were fair-weather friend types who worked hard to ingratiate themselves with whoever was in power. She didn't know what they had to do to maintain their money and lands under the dictatorship, but she was certain it was a price the Espinas wouldn't have paid.

It would not surprise her mother at all to know they were here on the hunt for a rich husband. With the dictatorship dissolved, they had to put themselves in a good position with the new royal family, and what better way than to marry into it? Serafia took a step closer to listen in as Felicia continued her instructions to Dita.

"When we're introduced to the king, remember everything I've told you. You've got to make a good impression on him. Be coquettish, but not too aggressive. Make eye contact, but don't hold it for too long. Make him come to you and then you'll have him like putty in your hands. It worked on your father. It will work on him. You deserve to be queen, always remember that."

Serafia tried not to chuckle. She was certain a similar conversation was taking place all over the room. There were easily thirty bright-eyed girls here with their parents. All were after the same prize. Serafia might be the only single woman in the room who wasn't on the hunt. She had no interest in competing with a bunch of little girls for Gabriel's attention.

When Gabriel reached the bottom of the stairs, he

was greeted by his father and Patrick Rowling. They escorted him over to a raised dais on the far side of the room. They took their seats there and the crowd gathered for a receiving line. Everyone was excited for their chance to be introduced to the new king.

Serafia took advantage of the distraction to go to the empty bar. She got glasses of wine for them both, hugging the edge of the room to deliver the drink to Gabriel. As she got close, Patrick was introducing his sons, William and James, to Gabriel and his father. Will was Patrick's heir apparent to the oil and real estate empire they'd built. James, like Gabriel, was the second son, the spare heir, even though he was born only minutes after his twin brother.

Neither of the men looked particularly happy to be here tonight. Even then, they seemed more comfortable than Gabriel. He kept cycling between a stiff regal pose, a slightly slumped-over bored stance and a fidgety anxious carriage that made it obvious to Serafia that he was very uncomfortable. Perhaps a glass of wine would be enough to relax him without loosening his tongue too much.

Out of the corner of her eye, Serafia spied one of the party's many servers. The petite girl with chin-length black hair was lurking along the edge of the room, her gaze focused fully on the Rowling brothers as they greeted the king.

It took a moment, but Serafia was finally able to wave her over. As a model, she was used to towering over people, but the server was probably close to five feet tall, a little pixie of a thing with sparkling dark eyes that immediately caught Serafia's attention. On her immaculately pressed black shirt, she wore a small brass nametag that read *Catalina*.

"Yes, ma'am?"

"Would you please take this wine to Prince Gabriel?" Serafia placed the wine on her tray.

Catalina took a deep breath and nodded. "Of course," she said, immediately departing. Well trained, she waited until Will and James were escorted away, slipping over quietly to deliver the drink, then disappearing so quickly that some people might not have even seen her.

Gabriel took a heavy sip of the wine, searching Serafia out in the crowd. When his gaze lit on her, Serafia felt a chill run down her spine. Goose bumps rose across her bare arms, making her rub them self-consciously. He winked at her, and before she could prompt him to smile, he broke out his practiced grin and turned to the next family being presented.

Serafia had to admit she was pleased with the results of her work. In only a week, they had managed to smooth over his rough edges and mold him into a man fit to be royalty. As she watched him interact with the Gomez family and the young and beautiful Dita, she couldn't help the pang of jealousy inside her.

Perhaps she had done too good a job. She had polished away all the reasons she needed to stay far, far away from Gabriel Montoro.

Gabriel was exhausted. All he'd done for the last hour was get introduced to people, but he was done. He was tired of smiling, tired of greeting people. It wasn't as if he was going to be able to remember a single name once each person turned away and the next was presented.

Unfortunately there were hours left in the night. Now started the dancing and the mingling. With the formalities out of the way, people would seek him out for more casual discussions. The ladies would expect him to solicit a dance or two.

He did none of those things. Instead he sought out another glass a wine and a few bites from the buffet of canapés and fresh fruits. He was hoping to find Serafia, who had disappeared at some point, but instead his father cornered him at the baked brie.

"What do you think of William?"

William? Gabriel went through the two hundred names he'd just heard and drew a blank.

"William Rowling, Patrick's oldest son," Rafael clarified, seemingly irritated with Gabriel for dismissing the Rowlings so easily.

"Oh," Gabriel said, taking a sip of wine. He refrained from mentioning to his father that he couldn't tell the two brothers apart. That would just agitate him. "He seemed very nice. Why? Are you trying to fix me up with him? He's really not my type, Dad."

"Gabriel," Rafael said in a warning tone. "I was thinking about him and Bella."

Gabriel tried not to frown at his father. All this royalty nonsense was going to his father's head if he thought he could start arranging marriages and no one would question it. "I think Bella would have a great deal more to say on the subject than I would."

"Rowling is the most powerful businessman in Alma. Combining our families would strengthen our position here, both financially and socially. If he had a daughter I'd be shoving her under your nose, too."

"Dad, it's a marriage, not a business merger."

"Same difference. I had a similar arrangement with your mother and now our company is in the Fortune 500."

"*And* you're divorced," Gabriel added. Their mother was living happily on another continent and had been since Bella turned eighteen and she had fulfilled her obligation to Rafael and the children. That was just what Bella would want for her own marriage, Gabriel was sure. Turning from his father, he scanned the crowd again.

"Who are you looking for?" Rafael pressed.

"Serafia."

Rafael popped a shrimp into his mouth and chewed it with a sour expression. "Don't get too dependent on her, Gabriel. She's just here through the end of the week. You've got to learn to stand on your own without her."

Gabriel was taken aback by his father's words. What did he care as long as Gabriel parroted all the right words and did all the right things? "I'm not dependent on her. I simply enjoy her company and I'm finding this party tedious without her."

"Yes, well, don't get too involved on that front, either. If you're bored, I suggest you focus on the ladies here tonight. Take Dita Gomez or Mariella Sanchez for a spin around the dance floor and see if you feel differently."

"And what if I want to take Serafia for a spin around the dance floor, Father? Stop treating her like she's just an employee. The Espinas are just as important a noble family in Alma as any of these others."

His father stiffened and the red blotchiness Gabriel had seen so often lately started climbing up his neck.

"Now is not the time to discuss things like this," he hissed in a low voice. "Now is the time to mingle with your new countrymen and start your search for a suitable queen. We will talk about the Espina family later. Now go mingle!" he demanded.

Gabriel didn't bother arguing with him. If mingling meant he could get away from his father for a while, he'd do it gladly. Perhaps he'd find where Serafia was hiding in the process. With a nod, he set aside his plate and ventured out into the crowd. Every few feet he was stopped by someone and engaged in polite banter. How did he like Alma so far? Did the weather suit him? Had he had the opportunity to enjoy the beaches or any of the local culture?

He was halfway through one of these discussions when he spied Serafia over the man's shoulder. She was standing across the room chatting with a gentleman whose name he had immediately forgotten when they were introduced in the receiving line.

Gabriel had seen a lot of beautiful women tonight, but he just couldn't understand how his father could think that any of them could hold a candle to Serafia. She was breathtaking, catwalk perfection. Sure, she wasn't as rail-thin as she had been in her modeling days, but the pounds had just softened the angles and filled out the curves that her gown clung to. The pale pink of her dress was like soft rose petals scattered across her olive complexion. It was a delicate, romantic color, unlike all the bold look-at-me dresses the other women were wearing.

Serafia didn't need that for men to look at her, at least for Gabriel to look at her. He had a hard time looking anywhere else. Her silky black hair was loose tonight in shiny curls that fell over her shoulders and down her back. She wore very little jewelry—just a pair of pink sapphire studs at her ears—but between the beads of her dress and the glitter of her delicate pink lipstick, she seemed to sparkle from head to toe.

He felt his mouth go dry as he imagined her leaving a trail of glittering pink lipstick down his bare stomach. He wanted to pull her body hard against his and bury his fingers in the inky black silk of her hair. For all he cared, this party and these people could disappear. He wanted to be alone with Serafia and not for etiquette lessons or strategy discussions.

He hadn't given much thought to the man she was speaking to, but when he laid a hand on Serafia's upper arm, Gabriel felt his blood pressure spike with jealousy. Quickly excusing himself from the conversation he'd been ignoring, he moved through the room, arriving at her side in an instant.

Serafia's eyes widened at his sudden arrival. She took a step back, introducing him to the man she was speaking to. "Your Majesty, may I reintroduce you to Tomás Padillo? He owns Padillo Vineyards, where we'll be taking a tour tomorrow afternoon. I was just telling him how much you've enjoyed the Manto Negro from his winery since you arrived."

"Ah yes," Gabriel replied with a nod of recognition. He held up his glass. "Is this a vintage of yours, as well?"

"Yes, Your Majesty, that's my award-winning Chardonnay. I'm honored to have you drink it and looking forward to hosting your visit with us tomorrow."

The man seemed harmless enough; then again, Ga-

briel didn't see a ring on the man's hand. He didn't intend to leave Serafia alone with him.

"I'm looking forward to it, as well. May I steal away
Miss Espina?" he asked.

"Of course, Your Majesty."

Gabriel nodded and scooped up Serafia's arm into
his own. He led her away into a quiet corner behind
the staircase where they could talk.

"Is everything going all right?" she asked.

Gabriel nodded. "I think so. My dad is pressuring
me to mingle with the ladies, but I haven't gotten that
far yet."

Serafia sighed and patted his forearm. "You've done
your fair share of wooing ladies, Gabriel. This shouldn't
be very difficult for you."

"That was different," he argued. "Picking up a
woman at a nightclub for a little fun is nothing like
shopping for a wife. It feels more like a hunt anyway,
except I'm the fox. I'm surprised one of the hounds
hasn't ferretted me out from our hiding place by now.
Would you stay with me for a while?"

"Not while you dance!"

"Of course not. But go around with me while I mingle for a while. I think I'll be more comfortable that
way. You might remember people's names."

"Gabriel, you need to be able to—"

"Please…" he said, looking into her eyes with his
most pathetic expression.

"Okay, but you have to promise me you will ask no
fewer than two ladies to dance tonight. No moms or
grandmothers, either. Eligible, single women of marrying age. And not me, either," she seemed to add for
good measure.

"If I dance with two women who meet your criteria, would you be willing to dance with me just for fun?"

Serafia gave him a stern look, but the smile that teased at the corners of her full lips gave her away. "Maybe. But you've got to put in a good effort out there. You're looking for a queen, remember. If you don't find a good one, your father will do it for you, like poor Bella."

"You've heard about that?" Gabriel asked.

"Yes. I overheard Patrick discussing the idea of it with Will."

"How'd he take it?"

"About as well as Bella would, I expect. But my point is that you need to get out there and make that decision yourself."

"Fair enough." Offering her his arm, he led them back into the main area of the room. As they slipped through the crowd, he leaned down to whisper in her ear, "Who would you choose for me? Where should I start?"

Serafia looked thoughtfully around the room, her gaze falling on a buxom, almost chubby redhead whose fiery hair was in direct contrast to her personality. She was a shy wallflower of a girl who had barely met his gaze when they were introduced.

"Start with Helena Ruiz. Her family is in the sea-food business and they provide almost all the fresh fish and shellfish to the area and to parts of Spain and Portugal, as well. And," she added, "unlike the others, she seems to be *reluctantly* hunting for a husband. She reminds me very much of a lot of the girls I work with in my business. Choosing her first might be good for her social standing and her self-esteem."

Gabriel was pleased with Serafia's choice and her reasoning behind it. It was one of the things about her that really stuck with him. She wasn't just concerned about making over his outside, but his inside, as well. In their training sessions, they'd discussed charities he'd like to support and causes he wanted to rally behind as king. Parliament and the prime minister would draft and enforce the laws of Alma, but as king, he would have a major influence over the hearts and minds of the people. He had a platform, so he needed to be prepared to have a cause.

In such a short time, Serafia had not just made over his wardrobe. She had made over his soul. He felt like a better person, a person more deserving of a woman like her. He'd never felt that way before in his entire life. He'd always been second to Rafe, not good enough in his father's eyes. His mother had recognized the value in him, but even she couldn't sway his father's opinion.

Since he returned home from Venezuela after the kidnapping, he'd been a different man. He'd stopped seeking everyone's approval, especially his father's. With his mother traveling the world and unable to call him on it, he'd settled happily into his devil-may-care lifestyle. It had suited him well and no one had questioned the change in him. But Serafia had. She had the ability to see through all his crap, and it made him think that perhaps he could open up to her, really trust her, unlike so many others in his life.

As he left her side and approached the doe-eyed Helena, he knew Serafia had made the right choice. The bright, genuine smile on the girl's face and the pinched, jealous expressions of some of the other girls proved that much. He led her out onto the dance floor for the first official dance of the evening. Helena was nearly trembling in his arms, but he reassured her with a smile and a wink.

Serafia made him want to be a better man. She helped him become a better man. He could think of no other woman who should be at his side but her. And he would tell her that.

Tonight.

Six

"Okay," a voice announced over Serafia's shoulder. "I have met your requirements."

She turned to find Gabriel standing behind her. She'd been expecting his arrival. It had been nearly two hours since she sent him out onto the dance floor with Helena Ruiz. He had danced with her and at least five other ladies Serafina had chosen for him. Her inner spiteful streak had led her not to choose Dita as one of the dance partners. She wasn't entirely sure if it was because she knew the Gomezes were disingenuous, or if it was because the idea of him dancing and potentially falling for the statuesque beauty made her blood boil.

"You have," she said with a pleased smile. "You've more than met them. You've exceeded them. Well done, Your Majesty. Any pique your interest?"

Gabriel arched an eyebrow at her and held out his hand. "Join me on the dance floor and I'll tell you."

There were quite a few pairs dancing now, so the two of them would not stand out as much as they would have earlier. Deciding there was no harm in it—and she had promised—she took his hand and followed him out into the center of the dance floor.

Gabriel slipped his arm around her waist and cupped her hand with his own. For the first twenty seconds or so of the dance, she found she could hardly breathe. Her bare skin sizzled where they touched, and her heart was racing in her chest. Fortunately Gabriel was a strong lead and she didn't have to think too much about her feet. She simply followed him across the floor and focused internally on suppressing the physical reaction she had to his touch.

"So, find any chemistry out on the dance floor?" she asked, desperate for a distraction.

"Not until now," he said, his green gaze burrowing into her own.

"Gabriel," she scolded, but he shook his head as though he wasn't having any of that.

"Don't start. I've had enough of the reasons why I can't have what I want. I don't really care. All I know is that I want you."

The power of his words struck her like a wave and she struggled to argue against it. "No, you don't."

"Are you honestly going to stand there and tell me you know my feelings better than I do?"

She shook her head, focusing her gaze on the golden ropes at his shoulder instead of the intensity in his eyes. "You might want me for tonight, for one of your one-night flings, but not for your queen."

"Do we have to decide what it will be tonight?"

If she had to decide in the moment, she would say

no. She was wrapped up in the sensation of being so close to him. Her body was rebelling against her, desiring him desperately even as she argued against the very idea of it. "You aren't in Miami anymore, Gabriel. Every eye in the room is on you tonight. This feeling for me will pass and then you can focus on making a smart decision about your future. A future without me."

"Serafia, you are beautiful. You're the most stunning woman I've ever seen in real life or on a magazine cover. You're graceful, elegant, thoughtful, smart and incredibly insightful. I don't know why you find it so hard to believe that I could want you so desperately."

Desperately? Her gaze met his, her lips parting softly in surprise. His words were said with such sincerity, but she simply didn't believe a single one. She was too aware of her own faults to do that. She'd spent too many years having every aspect of her appearance ripped apart by modeling experts, their voices far louder than any of her fans' praises. And even if he could see past all her imperfections, he didn't know how broken she was. The truth of her past would send any man running. "You don't want me, Gabriel. You want your teenage fantasy from ten years ago. That person doesn't exist anymore."

She pulled away from his grasp as the music ended and made her way through the crowd of people coming on and off the dance floor. Spying a set of French doors, she opened them and slipped outside into the large courtyard of the Rowling mansion. She kept going, following a path into the gardens. It was landscaped like the formal English gardens of Patrick's homeland, so she continued on a gravel path along a long line of neatly trimmed shrubs until she came upon a clearing and a circular fountain.

She collapsed onto the stone ledge of the fountain
and took a deep breath. She felt much calmer out here,
away from the crush of people in the ballroom, but the
sense of relief didn't last long. Not a minute later, she
heard the sound of footsteps on the gravel and spied
Gabriel coming toward her on the garden path.

He approached silently and sat on the edge of the
fountain beside her. She expected him to immediately
give her the third degree for running out on him. It
was incredibly rude, after all, and she kept forgetting
he was the king. People were probably inside talking
about her hasty departure.

But Gabriel didn't seem to be in a hurry. He seemed
to enjoy the garden as well, taking a deep breath and
gazing up at the blanket of stars overhead. She did
the same, relaxing as she tried to identify different
constellations. Looking at the stars always made her
problems seem less important, less significant. The
universe was a big place.

When he finally got around to speaking, Serafia
was ready to answer his questions. She was tired of
hiding her illness, anyway. She might as well put it all
out there, warts and all. It would likely put an end to
their pointless flirtation and she could stop torturing
herself with possibilities that didn't really exist.

"What was that all about in there? Really? Why
is it so impossible that I would want you as you are,
right now?"

"It's impossible for me to believe it because I know
how seriously messed up I am, Gabriel. The truth is
that I don't have a congenital heart defect and I didn't
spend a year having surgeries to correct it."

Gabriel frowned at her. "Well, then, what really happened to you?"

Serafia sighed and shook her head. "No one knows the truth but my family and my doctors. My parents thought it would be easier for me if we told everyone the cover story, but that was all a lie. I had a heart attack on that runway because I had slowly and systematically tried to kill myself to be beautiful. The modeling industry is so high pressure and I couldn't stand up to it. I swallowed the lies they told me along with the prescription diet pills. I barely ate. I exercised six to eight hours a day. I abused cocaine, laxatives…anything that I thought would give me an edge and help me drop those last few pounds. My quest to be thinner, to be prettier, almost made me a very attractive corpse."

She was terrified to say the words aloud, but at the same time, it felt as if a weight was lifted from her chest. "The day I collapsed on the runway, I was five foot nine and ninety-three pounds. I was nothing but a walking skeleton and I received more compliments that morning than I ever had before. After I collapsed, I knew I had to leave the modeling industry because the environment was just too toxic. I had to spend a year in rehab and inpatient therapy for anorexia. I had to be completely reprogrammed, like I'd left some kind of cult."

Gabriel didn't recoil or react to her words. He just listened until she got it all out. "Are you better now?" he asked.

That was a difficult question to answer. Like an alcoholic, the danger of falling off the wagon was always there. "I've learned to manage. I've put so much strain on my heart that my day-to-day life is a very delicate balancing act. But for the most part, yes, the worst of it is behind me."

He sat studying her face for a few minutes. "I can't believe anyone had the audacity to tell you that you were anything but flawless. I mean, you're *Serafia*— supermodel extraordinaire, catwalk goddess and record holder for most *Vogue Italia* covers."

Once again, she started to squirm under his praise. "When you say things like that, Gabriel, it's really difficult for me to listen and even harder for me to accept. I was told for so long that I was fat and ugly and would never make it in the business. Even when I made it to the top, there's always someone there to try and knock you down. The modeling industry can be so venomous. You're never thin enough, pretty enough, talented enough, and both your competition and your customers feed you those criticisms every day. You believe something after you hear it enough times. Even all these years later, after all the therapy, there's a part of me that still believes that and thinks everything you're saying is just insincere flattery."

Gabriel reached out and covered her hand with his own. It was comforting and she was thankful for it, even as it surprised her. She expected him to finally see her flaws and run, but he didn't.

"It might be flattery, Serafia, but it's true. Every word. If I have to say it each day until you finally believe it, I will. I know how hard it can be to trust someone once that faith is abused. Once it's lost, it's almost impossible to get back, but I want to help you try."

There was a pain in his expression as he spoke. The lines deepened in his forehead with his frown. She knew something had happened to him in South

America. Perhaps now, perhaps here, after she'd told her story, he might finally tell her his. "How do you know? What happened to you, Gabriel?"

With a sigh, he sat back and looked up at the sliver of a moon overhead. "I was fresh from college and my father named me VP of South American Operations. As part of my job, I had to travel to our various shipping and trade ports in Brazil, Argentina, Venezuela and Chile. Dealing with Venezuela was controversial, but my father had decided that the country had oil and needed it shipped. Why shouldn't we profit from it instead of someone else?

"I saved Caracas for my last stop and things had gone so well in the other locations that I wasn't wary any longer by the time I arrived in Venezuela. I went down there and spent a few days getting acclimated and met with the team there. One evening, my guide and translator, Raoul, offered to take me out for an authentic Venezuelan dinner. The moment we stepped outside, a van pulled up by the curb. Raoul hit me on the back of the head with something and I blacked out. The next thing I knew, I was lying on a stinky, lumpy mattress in a cold, dark room with no windows. My wrists and ankles were tied with thick rope."

Serafia could barely believe what she was being told. How had she never heard about this before? She wanted to ask, but she didn't dare interrupt.

"When my captor finally showed up a few hours later, he told me that I was being held for ransom and as soon as my family paid them, I'd be released."

"Did they pay them?" she asked.

He avoided her gaze, swallowing hard before he spoke. "No. I was in that underground room in virtual darkness for over a week. Every day the guy would come down and bring me a jug of water and some food, but that was it. After about the sixth day alone with my thoughts, and with constant taunts from my captor that my family hadn't paid the ransom yet and must not care if I lived or died, I came to the conclusion that if I wanted out of this place, I'd have to save myself. And I decided that when I did, I was going to live the life I wanted from that moment on."

"You escaped?" Serafia asked, near breathless with suspense.

"My rusty metal bed frame was my savior. I used it to slowly cut through my bindings. It took almost all day to do it. When my captor opened the door to bring my evening meal, I was waiting for him. I leaped on him, beating his head against the concrete floor until he stopped fighting me. Once I was sure he was unconscious, I took his gun and keys, locking him in the room. It turned out he was my only guard, so I literally went up the stairs and walked out onto the busy streets of Caracas. I made my way to the US embassy, told them what had happened and I was back in Miami by sunrise."

Serafia was nearly speechless. "Did they ever catch the people responsible?"

"Raoul was arrested for his part in the conspiracy, but he was just a facilitator paid a flat fee for delivering me at a special place and time. They found my captor still locked in the room where they kept me. Anyone else who was involved got away with it. But really, in the end, I wasn't angry with them. I was angry with my family. They knew what could happen if they sent me down there."

"What did they say when you showed up at home?"

Gabriel stiffened beside her and shrugged. "They welcomed me home and then tried to pretend it never happened. But I could never forget."

It was a horrible story to hear, but suddenly so much of Gabriel's personality suddenly made sense to her. He never got close to anyone and got a lot of grief from his family for being superficial. Even Serafia had been guilty of judging him, thinking he cared more about partying than worrying about anything serious. She'd accused him of being reckless, but when they were both faced with death, they reacted differently. She became supercautious, nearly afraid to live life for fear of losing it for good. He had done the opposite: living every moment to the fullest in case it was his last. Who was she to judge him?

Serafia reached out and took his hand. She felt a surge of emotion when they touched. When she looked at him, for the first time she was able to see the sadness in his green eyes, the wariness behind the bright smile. The bad boy facade kept people away and she had fallen for it. She didn't want to keep him at arm's length any longer.

Gabriel gripped her hand in his, letting his thumb brush across her skin. It sent a shiver of awareness down her spine, urging her to lean in closer to him.

"I know that's a lot of information to process," he said. "I didn't tell it to you so you'd feel bad for me. I told you because I wanted you to understand that we're coming from a similar place. No one is perfect. We're all messed up somehow. But it's how we deal with it that matters. I'm an expert at pushing people away. You're the first woman I've ever met who had made me want to try to trust someone again. Stop thinking that you don't measure up somehow, because you're wrong."

Serafia gasped at his bold words. She couldn't hold back any longer. She lunged forward, pressing her lips against his own before she lost her nerve. It had been a long time since she had trusted herself in all the various areas of her life, and romance had fallen to the bottom of the stack. What good was she to a man in the state she was in? Especially a prince? Still, she couldn't help herself. And neither could Gabriel.

He met her kiss with equal enthusiasm. He held her face in his hands, drawing her closer and drinking her in. He groaned against her lips and then let his tongue slip along hers. His touch made her insides turn molten with need and wore away the last of her self-control.

At last, Gabriel pulled away, their rapid breaths hovering between them in the night air. "Is it too early to make our exit?" he asked.

Serafia shook her head and looked into his eyes. "I think the prince can leave whenever he wants to."

It wasn't as simple to leave as Gabriel had hoped. He'd had to make the rounds, thank Patrick for his hospitality and avoid the cutting glares of his father, but within half an hour, he and Serafia were in the back of the royal limousine on their way home to Playa del Onda.

When they climbed inside, Gabriel couldn't look away from the high slit in her pink gown and how it climbed nearly to her hip as she sat. He wanted to run his hands over that bare skin. His palms tingled with the need to reach for her, but there was a forty-five-minute drive home from the Rowling Estate.

Eyeballing the limousine's tinted partition, Gabriel called out to his driver, "We're going to need a little privacy back here, please."

"Of course, Your Majesty." In an instant, the heavily tinted glass slid up, blocking them from their driver's view and making for a more private drive home.

"What are you doing?" Serafia asked.

Gabriel turned to her, placing his hand on her knee. "I want you. Right now. I can't wait until we get back."

"We're in a car, Gabriel. The driver is right there. The royal guard are in the SUV right behind us."

"They can't see us." His hand glided higher up her leg, brushing at the sensitive skin of her inner thigh. "Whether or not the driver *hears* us is up to you."

"I don't know about this," Scrafia said, biting her full bottom lip.

Gabriel brushed his fingertips along the lacy barrier of her panties, making her gasp. "You may have reformed me, but there's still a little bad boy inside me." He stroked harder, making her stiffen and close her eyes. He leaned into her, placing a searing kiss against her neck before he whispered, "Let's both be bad tonight."

He gripped one strap of her gown, easing it down her shoulder, and then dipped his head to taste her flesh, nibbling on the column of her throat, the hollow behind her ear and the round of her shoulder. He slipped one hand behind her, finding the zipper of her gown and tugging it down enough to allow her gown to slip farther and expose the round globes of her large breasts.

They were more glorious than he'd ever imagined after seeing her in bikinis and skimpy gowns on magazine covers. "So beautiful," he murmured as his gaze devoured her. They were full and heavy, tipped with tight mocha nipples that he immediately covered with his hands and then his mouth.

Serafia bit her lip hard to keep from crying out as his tongue flicked across her skin. He teased her flesh, and then sucked hard at her breast. The hand he'd kept beneath her gown continued to stroke her, finally slipping under the lacy edge of her panties to feel the moist heat of her desire hiding beneath it.

"Gabriel!" she exclaimed in a hoarse whisper.

"Just lie back and enjoy it," he replied, turning with her as she leaned back across the seat to rest on her elbows. When she shifted her hips, he was better able to slide her gown out of the way and part her thighs. He stopped touching her only long enough to slip off her panties.

When he returned, he leaned down, parted her flesh and stroked her with his tongue. Serafia squirmed and writhed against him, but he didn't let up. He wrapped his arms around her thighs to hold her steady as he teased at her sensitive flesh again and again. Gabriel waited until he had her hovering on the edge; then he slipped one finger inside her. It sent her tumbling over, gasping and whimpering as quietly as she could manage while her release rocked through her.

When at last her body stilled except for her rapid breaths, Gabriel pulled away. While she recovered, he unbuttoned his suit pants and tugged them down. Reaching into his back pocket, he pulled a condom from his wallet and slipped it over the length of him. When he turned back to Serafia, she was watching him with a twinkle of deviousness in her dark eyes.

He reached for her and tugged her into his lap, her thighs straddling him as the limousine raced down the highway. Gabriel gripped her waist as she eased down and pushed him inside her. He gritted his teeth and pressed desperate fingertips into her flesh as he fought for control. She felt amazing. When he was buried fully inside her, he held her still for a moment, then reached for her face. He pulled her forward and captured her lips with his own.

As his tongue slipped inside her mouth and stroked her, he started moving slowly beneath her. Pushing the pink organza of her gown out of the way, he gripped the curve of her rear to guide her hips. At first, their movements were deliciously slow, and he savored every pang of pleasure. As the intensity built, they moved more frantically. Serafia grasped his shoulders and threw her head back, a silent cry in her throat.

"Let go for me," Gabriel pressed. "I want to watch it happen. You're so beautiful when you come undone."

She found her release again. This time, he held her close, not just watching, but feeling the pleasurable tremors running through her body and experiencing them with her. Her inner muscles tightened around him, coaxing his own release. As she collapsed against him, he wrapped his arms around her waist and thrust into her one last time. He buried his face in her neck, growling his climax against her flushed skin.

They sat together, not moving for several minutes.

In the stillness, Gabriel was finally able to mentally catch up with everything that had happened in the last few hours.

The moment he had stepped out into the garden after her, he knew things would be different. He wasn't going to let her keep pulling away from him, and if opening up to her about his own past was what it took, he was willing to do it. She…inspired him in a way no other woman had. It wasn't just an attraction; it was more. She didn't want anything from him. Unlike the sharks circling around the Rowling ballroom, Serafia didn't need his money and she certainly didn't want to share his spotlight. He felt that she was someone he could trust, especially after she shared her own story with him. Her past was different from his but he could tell that it had scarred her in a similar way. The difference was that he didn't trust others and she didn't trust herself. But she should. And he wanted to help her with that.

It made her ever more attractive to him, if that was possible. She wasn't just the supermodel from his teenage fantasies. She was so much more. He just had to convince her of that.

"The car is slowing down," Serafia noted. She climbed from his lap and quickly started pulling herself back together.

Gabriel turned and looked out the window. They were approaching the gate to the compound. "We're home. Time to get dressed so we can go inside and I can take it all off you again."

Serafia tugged the top of her dress back up over her shoulders and looked at him. "Really?"

How silly she was to doubt him on that point. "Oh yes," Gabriel said in a tone as serious as he was capable of. "That was just to hold me over until we got home."

Seven

Serafia woke up the next morning with a small smile on her lips. Opening her eyes, she spied Gabriel's broad shoulders as he slept beside her. She rolled onto her back with a yawn and reached for her phone to check the time. It was eight-thirty, practically midday for her. She wasn't surprised, considering that Gabriel hadn't let her sleep until after three.

Flinging back the sheets, she gently slipped out of the bed so she wouldn't wake Gabriel. She snatched up a blanket off the foot of the bed, wrapped it around her naked body and walked toward the wall of French doors that led from the master bedroom onto a secluded patio that overlooked the sea.

She stepped out onto the balcony, pulling the door shut behind her. The sun was bright, warming her skin as she took in the remarkable view.

Playa del Onda was built on a sheer cliff overlooking the sea. It was perched at the apex of a crescent-shaped bay lined with sailboats and beaches that would hopefully draw tourists now that the Tantaberras had fallen. The water was an enchanting mix of blues and greens that begged you to dip a toe into it. It reminded her of her hacienda in Barcelona. Her view overlooked the Mediterranean, but the feelings it inspired in her were the same. Peacefulness. The ability to breathe. Relaxation.

She wanted to take a mug of coffee and sit out here the rest of the morning, but that just wasn't possible. The house was crawling with guards and servants. She couldn't stroll into the kitchen wearing a blanket and slip back into the prince's suite without someone noticing. Not that it was necessarily a secret to those who'd traveled back to the beach house with them last night, but she thought it was inappropriate to flaunt it.

As it was, she needed to get down the hall to her own room. Going back inside, she checked to see that Gabriel was still asleep. She had worked wonders with his transformation, but bless him, he was still a night owl.

She retrieved her gown from the floor and slipped it back on, and then slowly opened the door of his bedroom, glancing both ways down the hall to see if anyone was there. The coast was clear. She slipped out, pulling the door closed. She had taken about three steps toward her room when she heard something behind her.

"Good morning, Señorita Espina."

She turned to find the houseman, Luca, standing behind her. "Good morning, Luca," she said, self-consciously smoothing her hand over her tousled hair and trying to downplay how overdressed she was for the early morning hours.

His dark gaze traveled over her quickly, a twinkle of amusement in his eyes, but he didn't mention her appearance. "Is His Majesty still sleeping?" he asked.

"Yes, he is. But he should be getting up soon. Please wake him by ten if he hasn't roused by then."

"As you wish."

Serafia started to turn back toward her room, and then she stopped. "Please don't mention this to anyone," she said.

Luca shook his head. "Of course not, señorita. The affairs of the prince are no one's concern but the prince's. But…" He hesitated. "You should know your involvement with the prince is no secret."

Serafia looked up at him with eyes wide with panic. "What does that mean?"

He unfolded the Alma newspaper he'd been clutching in his hand and held it up for her to read. On the front page, just below the article about Gabriel's big introduction at the Rowling party, was a headline that read *"The Future Queen?"* Another article followed, speculating about a romance brewing between her and Gabriel. A grainy black-and-white photo of them kissing by the fountain accompanied the story.

With a sigh, she closed her eyes. She felt foolish for thinking she could have one moment of privacy. "Thank you for showing me this, Luca. May I take it to my room and read it?"

He folded the paper and handed it to her. "Of course."

Serafia tucked it under her arm. "Please don't mention it to the prince until I have a chance to read the article. I'll discuss it with him at breakfast."

"As you wish. I'll have Marta start preparing it."

Luca disappeared down the hallway, leaving Serafia with the newspaper clutched against her. Before anyone else saw her, she dashed down the hallway to her own room.

Throwing the paper onto the bed, she headed straight for the shower. As the steaming hot water pounded her sore muscles and washed away Gabriel's scent from her skin, her mind started to race with the implications of the article. From what little she'd read, the tone didn't seem negative. The prince and his quest for a bride would be front page news no matter who he was seen with. But that didn't do much to calm her anxiety.

She should've known better than to think that someone hadn't noticed their departure from the ballroom and followed them outside. She hadn't noticed anyone there, but with the walls of hedges and arborvitae columns, there were plenty of places to hide and spy on their painfully private moments together.

Hopefully whoever took their picture hadn't been able to hear their conversation over the sound of the nearby fountain. The photo was one thing, but she didn't want the revelations about her departure from modeling to taint Gabriel somehow.

Stepping from the shower, Serafia wrapped herself in a fluffy white towel and started combing through the thick and easily tangled strands of her hair. She rushed through the rest of her morning routine. Trying to maintain a bit of professionalism, she put her hair up in a tight bun and dressed in a dark plum pantsuit. They had another official event to attend this afternoon, so she might as well get ready and put her consultant hat back on.

After she slipped on her shoes, she reached for the paper and read through both articles on Gabriel. The first, about his introduction at the Rowling party, was extremely positive. The consensus was that he was well received and those in attendance were pleased to have such a fine man to be their future king.

The second article, about her, wasn't really bad, either. It discussed the various ladies he had danced with that night, highlighting Helena Ruiz as his first choice and Serafia as his last. Of course, there was the photo of them kissing, and then a lot of speculation about whether or not she was really his social secretary, or if it was a cover for their relationship. If they were dating, was it serious? Might she be their new queen? The few people they interviewed for the article seemed to think she'd make a good candidate for queen of Alma and would make a charming match for Gabriel.

It wasn't a horrible write-up, but she really wished she could have avoided the papers. How could he turn around and select one of the other women in Alma after this? No one wanted to be second choice and really, she wasn't in the running to be queen, despite what they might think.

Or was she?

Gabriel seemed as serious about her as he had been about anything they'd discussed so far. He'd swept her off her feet and for once, she'd gone with it and had an amazing night. She hadn't entertained second thoughts about it, but now anxiety started pooling in her stomach. She wasn't opposed to being his lover, but queen? She wasn't sure she could handle that. The only people more famous in Europe than models were the royal families. The United Kingdom's Princess Kate couldn't wear an unflattering dress or have a bad hair day without it being in the papers and commented on. Every time Prince Harry was seen with a woman, the rumors would fly.

Serafia knew what it was like. In her modeling days, it wasn't enough for everyone to critique her appearance, and they did. Her whole life was public. The cameras showed up on dates, on vacations, while she was trying to spend a day with her family. If she was dating anyone famous, the magnifying glass tripled along with the coverage. It was incredibly difficult to maintain a relationship under the microscope, much less a shred of self-esteem.

It had nearly killed her to do it, but Serafia had escaped the spotlight. Gabriel's queen would be subject to the same kind of scrutiny. The private would become painfully public, with every aspect of her life exposed. She had no intention of ever going back in front of the cameras.

Even for Gabriel. Even for the chance to be queen. She would be much happier in Barcelona, living a quiet, unexciting life. Passionless, yes, but private.

With a sigh, she folded up the paper and headed out to breakfast. By the time she reached the dining hall, Gabriel was dressed and waiting for her there. Without her standing by the closet, laying out his clothes, he'd opted for a pair of jeans and a clingy green T-shirt that matched his eyes. His hair was still wet and slicked back, his cheeks still slightly pink from his shave. He was sipping a cup of coffee and thumbing through emails on his smart phone.

"Good morning," she said as she entered the room.

She had her tablet in one hand and the newspaper in the other.

Gabriel smiled wide when he looked up at her. There was a wicked light in his eyes. "Good morning."

Serafia took a seat at the table across from him, holding off their discussion as Marta poured her a cup of coffee and returned to the kitchen to bring out their breakfast. They were three bites into their *tortilla de patatas* before she spoke about it.

"Apparently," she began, "we were not the only people out in the garden last night. Our kiss made the front page of the newspaper." She laid the paper out on the table for Gabriel to look at it.

He picked it up, reading over the article as he chewed his eggs, a thoughtful expression on his face. "I'm not surprised," he said at last, dropping the paper on the table and returning to his breakfast. He didn't seem remotely concerned.

"It doesn't bother you?" she asked.

"This isn't my first romance documented in a gossip column. Nor is it yours, I'd wager. There's nothing inflammatory about it, so why should I care? You're not a dark secret I'm trying to hide."

"The press scrutiny will be higher now. They'll question every moment we're together. We'll need to meet with your press secretary, Hector, to discuss how to handle it."

"I know how we'll handle it," he said, sipping his orange juice. "The palace will not comment on the personal life of the prince. Period. If and when I select a queen, I will announce it through the proper channels, not through some gossip column. They can speculate all they like. It doesn't concern me."

Serafia sat back in her chair. She was near speechless. That was the most tactful and diplomatic thing he could've said on the subject. Maybe her lessons were finally sinking in. "That is an excellent answer. I'll make sure Hector knows that's the official position of the palace."

After a few minutes of silent eating, Gabriel put down his fork and looked at her. "What do you think about the article? You seemed to be more concerned about it than I am. Am I missing something?"

"No, it's not the content of the article itself, so much as being in it. I've lived happily out of the spotlight for years," she explained. "Finding myself back in the papers was...unnerving to say the least."

"Do you regret last night?" he asked.

Serafia's gaze lifted to meet his. "No. But I regret not being smarter about it."

Gabriel nodded and speared a bite of tortilla with his fork. "Good. Then we can do it again."

Lord, but Gabriel was hot. He would've been much more comfortable in the jeans and T-shirt he'd started the day in, but Serafia had made him change before they left Playa del Onda. Did Serafia give no thought when she selected his wardrobe that he would be touring the countryside of Alma in July? The vineyards were beautiful, and he really was interested in everything Tomás was telling him, but it was hard to focus when he could feel his back sweating under his suit coat.

As they walked through the arbors, he turned to look at Serafia. She had her hair up in a bun off her neck. She was wearing a wide-brimmed hat and a linen shift dress in a light green that looked infinitely cooler than his own suit.

"I'm dying here," he whispered, leaning into Serafia's ear. "I'm no good to anyone if I melt into a puddle."

"We're going inside in a minute."

Gabriel sighed. "We better be or I'm going to look terrible if the press take any more photos." There was a small group invited to the vineyard today. They'd taken some shots as he arrived and as they toured the fields and sampled grapes from the vines, but they had given him some space after that. They were probably hot, too, and waiting for the group to return to the air-conditioned comfort of the building.

"Such a warm day!" Tomás declared. "Let's head inside. I'll give you a tour of the wine cave, and then we'll get to the good part and sample my wares."

Gabriel's ears perked up at the mention of a wine cellar. He was happy to go inside, but that didn't sound like a place he was interested in visiting. "Did he say 'cave'?" he asked as they trekked back up the hill to the villa.

Serafia frowned at him. "Yes. Why?"

"I don't like going underground."

"I'm sure it will be fine. Just relax," she insisted. "We really need a nice, uneventful visit today."

Gabriel snorted. She was optimistic to a fault. "Do you actually think that's ever going to happen with me as the king?"

She tipped her head up to look at him from under the wide brim of her white-and-green hat. Her nose wrinkled delicately as she said, "Probably not, but I'll keep striving for it. Before long, I'll be turning you over to your staff and going home. I hope they're prepared."

They finally reached the top of the hill and stepped through the large doors of the warehouse. Inside, they were greeted by a servant with a tray of sparkling water and a bowl with cool towels.

"Please, take a minute to cool off," Tomás said. "Have you enjoyed the tour so far?"

"It's been lovely, Tomás. There's no doubt that this is the finest vineyard in Alma," Serafia said, sipping her water.

She must not have trusted Gabriel to say the right thing. "It's a beautiful property," he chimed in. "How many acres do you have here?"

"About two hundred. It's been in my family for ten generations."

"You withstood all the political upheaval?"

Gabriel felt Serafia tense beside him. He supposed it was impolite to ask the residents of Alma how they managed to cope with the dictatorship, but he was curious. Some fled, but most made the best of it somehow.

"My great-grandfather refused to abandon his family's home. It was that simple. To survive, we supplied our finest wines to the Tantaberras and were forced to pay their heavy commercial taxes, but we survived better than others. We had a commodity he wanted."

Lucky. Gabriel sipped the last of his water and after dabbing his neck and forehead, returned the cloth to the bowl. "And now?"

Tomás smiled brightly. "Much better, Your Grace. Now we are finally able to export our wines to Europe and America. Before, we were restricted by heavy trade embargos that punished us more than the dictatorship. The free trade of the last few months has had a huge impact on our sales and profits. We were able to hire more staff and plant more grapes this year than ever before. We are prospering."

Gabriel smiled. He had nothing to do with the changes, but he was happy to see them. Serafia had impressed upon him how hard it had been on his people since the Montoros left. He was glad to see the course reverse so quickly with the Tantaberras gone.

"Are we ready to continue?"

Gabriel was not, but he followed behind Tomás, anyway. A few of the journalists joined them as they walked through the warehouse to a heavy oak door. Tomás went down first with a few others, leaving Gabriel standing at the top of the stairs with a sense of dread pooling in his stomach. His hands clutched the railing, but his feet refused to take another step.

"Go!" Serafia urged him from behind.

He could see Tomás standing at the bottom of the stairs waiting for him with a few reporters. The light was dim and the air cool. Their host had an expectant look on his face as he stood there waiting for Gabriel to follow.

Serafia nudged him in the back with her knee and he took a few steps down without really wanting to. It was only two more steps to the bottom, so he forced himself to go the rest of the way down. At the very least he needed to keep going so that the ladder would be clear for his escape. Right now Serafia, a vineyard assistant and a few other reporters were behind him.

Gabriel took a labored breath and looked around him. The room was bigger than he'd expected. The long corridor with its arched ceiling stretched on for quite a distance. Dim gold lights were spaced out down the hall, providing enough light to see the hundreds of barrels stored there.

The air was also fresher than he'd anticipated. He looked up, spying air vents that led to some type of ventilation system. At least the room didn't smell of stale bread and mildew. But it didn't need to. Gabriel's brain easily conjured those smells. Dank, musty air filled his lungs, tainted with the stench of his own waste and leftover food that was rotting in the corner of his prison.

"This is my pride and joy," Tomás said, taking a few steps down the rows of barrels. "This is a natural cave my family found on the property. It was perfect for storing our wine barrels, so we didn't have to build a separate cellar. My great-grandfather added the electrical lighting and ventilation system so we can maintain the perfect temperature and humidity for the wine."

He continued to talk, but Gabriel couldn't hear him. All he could hear was his own heartbeat pounding in his ears. There were no windows, no natural light. He hated that. He couldn't even stand his room at the palace with the dim light and cavelike conditions.

It was all too much. He could feel the walls start to close in on him. He could feel the rope chafing his ankles. Beads of perspiration that had nothing to do with heat formed on his brow and on his palms. He rubbed his hands absently against the fabric of his light gray suit, but it didn't help. They were starting to tremble.

"We have nearly five hundred barrels—"

"I have to go!" Gabriel announced, interrupting Tomás and pushing through the crowd to reach the staircase. He ignored the commotion around him, taking the steps two at a time until he reached the ground floor.

There, he could finally take a breath. Bending over, he clasped his knees and closed his eyes. He breathed slowly, willing his heart rate to drop and his muscles to unwind. He stood upright and turned when he heard the stampede of footsteps coming up the steps behind him.

"Your Majesty, are you well?" Tomás approached him, placing a cautious hand on his shoulder.

Gabriel raised his arm to dismiss his concerns. "I'm fine. I'm sorry about that. I don't do well in closed in spaces."

"I wish I had known. I would never have taken you down there. Señorita Espina didn't mention it."

"She didn't know." Not really. He'd explained about his kidnapping the night before, but he hadn't expressed how much things like small spaces or wrist watches bothered him as a result. He didn't like talking about it. To him, it felt like a weakness. Kings weren't supposed to have panic attacks. He didn't mind being flawed, but he hated for anyone, and especially Serafia, to think of him as weak.

"Gabriel, are you okay?" Serafia asked, coming to his side with concern pinching her brow.

"I just needed some air. Sorry, everyone, the heat must've gotten to me," he said more loudly to the crowd that followed him.

"I think what you need is a seat on the veranda with some wine and food to reinforce you," Tomás suggested.

They followed the crowd into the villa, but before they entered, Serafia tugged at his jacket and held him back. "What was all that about?" she asked once they were alone.

As much as he hated to tell her, he needed to. He couldn't have another incident like this. "I've developed a sort of claustrophobia since my kidnapping. I can't take small or dark spaces, especially underground ones like the room where I was kept. I have panic attacks. It's the same with watches. I can't bear the feel of things against my wrists."

Serafia sighed and brought her hand to his cheek. "Why didn't you tell me?"

Gabriel covered her hand with his own and pulled it down to his chest. When he looked into her dark brown eyes, he felt overcome with the urge to tell her whatever she wanted. He wanted to be honest with someone for the first time since he came home from Venezuela. Serafia was the one person he could trust with his secrets.

"Because I've never told anyone."

Eight

Serafia got up early the next morning, slipping from Gabriel's bed to get ready. An hour later she returned and started sifting through his clothes for the perfect outfit.

"It's seven-thirty," he groaned as he sat up in bed. His hair was tousled and as the sheets pooled around his waist, Serafia couldn't help stealing a glance at the hard muscles she'd become accustomed to touching each night. "Why are you up so early clinking wooden hangers together?"

With a sigh, she turned back to the closet. "I'm trying to figure out what you should wear today for the parade."

"I'm going to be in a parade?"

It was becoming clear to her that in the early days of working together, Gabriel had paid very little attention to what she'd said. The prime minister's office had arranged for a full week of activities and Gabriel had been briefed on them in detail while they were still in Miami. And yet each day was like a surprise for him.

After the incident at the vineyard, Serafia was afraid to know if Gabriel had a problem with parades, too. She didn't dare ask. "Yes. As we discussed in Miami," she emphasized, "they're holding a welcome parade for you this morning that will go through the capital of Del Sol."

"Are there going to be marching bands and floats or something?"

"No, it's not really that kind of parade." She pulled out a gray pin-striped suit coat. It would be too hot for his ceremonial attire and that was better saved for the coronation parade, anyway. A nice suit would be just right, she thought. Eyeing the ties, she pondered which would look best. She knew Gabriel would be more inclined to skip the tie, but that wouldn't look right. She frowned at the closet. The more she got to know Gabriel, the more she realized she was trying to force him into a box he didn't really fit in, but he was still royalty and needed to dress appropriately.

"People are just going to stand out on the sidewalk and wait for me to come by and wave? Like the pope?"

Serafia looked at him with exasperation and planted her hands on her hips. "You're going to be the king! Yes. People want to see you, even if it's just for a moment as you drive by and wave. It won't be as big as your formal coronation parade, but it gives everyone in Alma the chance to come and see you, not just the press or the rich people at Patrick Rowling's party."

"For their sake, I hope there are at least vendors out

there selling some good street food," he muttered as he climbed out of bed.

"Get in the shower," Serafia said, laying the suit out across the bed.

Gabriel came up behind her and pulled her into his arms, crushing her back against his bare body. "Wanna get in there with me?" his low voice grumbled into her ear.

Serafia felt a thrill rush through her body, but she fought the reaction. They didn't have time for this now, as much as she'd like to indulge. There were thousands of people already lining the streets in the hopes of getting a good spot to see Gabriel. She turned in his arms and kissed him, then quickly pulled away. "Sorry, but you're going it alone today," she said. "We leave in less than an hour."

She was amazed they were able to keep to their schedule, but everything went to plan. They rendezvoused with the rest of the motorcade a few miles away from the advertised route. Gabriel was transferred to a convertible where he could sit on the top of the backseats and wave to the crowd. Royal guards and Del Sol police would be driving ahead of his car and behind, with guards running alongside them.

"Remember," Serafia said as he got settled in the back of the car. "Smile, wave, be sure to turn to look at both sides of the street. People are excited to see you. Be excited to see them, too, and you'll win the hearts of your people. I'll see you at the end of the route."

"I thought you might ride with me."

Serafia shook her head. "You're Prince Gabriel, soon to be King Gabriel. As far as anyone else knows, I'm your social secretary. Social secretaries wouldn't ride along on something like this. We don't need to give the newspapers any more material to put into their gossip columns. So no, I'm not going with you. You'll do fine."

Ignoring nearly everything she'd just said, he leaned in and gave her a kiss in front of fifty witnesses. Hopefully none of them had cameras. "See you on the flip side," he said.

Serafia shook her head and climbed into another car that was driving ahead to ensure that the route was clear and to secure the end rendezvous location.

Looking out the window, she was impressed by how many people were lining the streets. Thousands of people from all over, young and old alike, had come to the capital to see Gabriel. Some held signs of welcome; others had white carnations, the official flower of Alma, to throw into the street in front of Gabriel's car. Their faces lit up with excitement and anticipation as they saw Serafia's official palace vehicle drive down the road, indicating that the new king would soon follow.

They needed a reason to smile. The Tantaberras had ruled over these people with an iron fist for too long. They deserved freedom and hope, and she sincerely believed that Gabriel could be the one to bring it to them. He wasn't the most traditional choice for a king, but he was a good man. He was caring and thoughtful. There might be a rocky start, but she could tell these people were desperate for the excitement of a new king, a new queen and the kind of royal baby countdown that the British had recently enjoyed.

Serafia spied a different sign as they neared the end of the route. A little girl was holding up a board with Gabriel's picture and her own. Across the top and bottom in blue glitter it read "We need a fairy tale romance! King Gabriel & Queen Serafia forever!"

A few feet down, another declared "We have our king, please choose Serafia as our queen!" This one was held by an older woman. A third declared "Unite the Montoros & the Espinas at last!"

Serafia sat back in her seat in surprise. Although she preferred to avoid the press in general, the tone of the earlier article about her and Gabriel had been positive. The crowd here today seemed to corroborate that. They had their king and now they wanted their fairy tale. But her? Serafia didn't need to be anyone's queen. She was done with the spotlight.

The only hitch was her growing feelings for Gabriel. She'd never planned them. If she was honest, she hadn't wanted to have feelings for him at all. And yet, over the last two weeks, he had charmed his way into her heart. She wasn't in love, but she was closer than she'd been in a very long time. Her time with Gabriel was coming to an end. Soon he would be on his own, transitioning into his role as king. Serafia planned to return to Barcelona when it was over.

But as the time ticked away, she felt herself dreading that day. What was her alternative? To stay? To let her relationship with Gabriel grow into something real? That would give the people of Alma what they wanted, but it came at too high a price. Serafia didn't want to be queen. She was done with the criticism and the magnifying glass examining her every decision and action.

The car stopped at a park and she got out, waiting with a small crew of guards and Hector Vega, who was speaking to some journalists. She found a spot in the shade where she could lean against one of the vehicles and wait for the royal motorcade. It wasn't in sight yet, so she glanced down to pull out her tablet to make some notes.

"Serafia?"

She looked up at the sound of a woman's voice and noticed Felicia Gomez and her daughter crossing the street to speak with her. The older woman had traded her ball gown for a more casual blouse and slacks, but she was wearing almost as many diamonds. She was smiling as much as her Botox would allow, but there wasn't much sincerity in the look. Dita was wearing a sundress and a fresh-faced look guaranteed to turn Gabriel's head.

Serafia swallowed her negative observations and tried to smile with more warmth than she had. "Señora Gomez, Dita. Good morning. How are you?"

"I'm well," Felicia replied, coming to stand beside her. "We came down in the hopes we'd get a chance to speak with the prince after the parade. We didn't get a lot of time at the Rowling party."

Felicia's tone was pointed, as though Serafia were the one responsible for that fact. In a way she was, she supposed. Serafia didn't want the crown, but she really didn't want the spoiled Dita to have it, either.

Instead of responding, Serafia just smiled and turned to look down the street. She could see the motorcycle cops leading the motorcade. "Here's your opportunity," she said.

Within a few minutes, all the vehicles had pulled into the park. Gabriel leaped out of the back of the convertible with athletic grace. He shook the hands of his driver and the guards who were running along with him, and then made his way over to Serafia. He was smiling as he looked at her, barely paying any attention to the Gomez women standing beside her.

"I'm starving," he said. "All that waving and smiling has worked up a hellacious appetite. I caught a whiff of something delicious on the parade route. I think it was coming from this little tapas place. I tried to remember the landmarks and I'm determined to track it down for lunch."

"That's fine, we're almost done here."

"What else do I have to do?" he asked.

Serafia shifted her gaze toward the two expectant women beside her without turning her head. Gabriel followed the movement and put on his practiced smile when he noticed who it was. She'd taught him well, it seemed. "Señora and Señorita Gomez have been waiting for you."

"Your Grace," Felicia said as both she and Dita gave a brief curtsey. "We'd hoped to have a moment of your time after the parade. The party had simply too many people for us to have a proper conversation."

That translated to: *You didn't spend enough time with my daughter and if she's going to be queen, she needs time to work her charms on you.*

"Are you hungry?" he asked.

Felicia seemed a little taken aback. "Hungry, Your Grace?"

"I was just telling Señorita Espina that I spied the most delicious-smelling tapas restaurant. It looks like a hole in the wall, but I'm anxious to try it. Would you care to join us?"

Serafia could see the conflict in Felicia's eyes. The Gomez family wasn't one to be seen at a run-down tapas restaurant. Serafia fought to hold in a twitter of laughter as she watched the older woman choose between two unpleasant fates—dining with commoners and being turned away by the prince once again. There was a pained expression on her face as she finally responded.

"That is very kind of Your Grace. We have already eaten, unfortunately. But perhaps you would give us the honor of hosting you at our home for dinner sometime soon."

"That's a very kind offer. I'll see when I can take you up on it. It was good to see you both again. Señora Gomez. Señorita Gomez," he said, tipping his head to each in turn. "Have a lovely afternoon."

At that, he smiled and put his arm around Serafia's shoulder. Together, they made their way from the disgruntled Gomez women over to his private car to track down some tasty tapas.

Serafia waited until the car door was shut and the tinted windows blocked them from sight, and then burst out laughing. "Did you see the look on her face when you invited her to go get some lunch? I nearly dislocated a rib trying not to laugh."

"Did I handle it okay?"

"You did very well. It isn't your fault she won't stoop to the level of an average person. She isn't going to give up, though. She wants you to marry Dita and she'll keep trying until you do."

Gabriel looked at her in a way that made her bones turn to melted butter. "She can *try*," he said. "But I'll be the one with the crown on my head. I make the decisions when it comes to who I date and who I'll marry."

Serafia felt her heart stutter in her chest as he spoke the words, looking intently at her. She knew in that moment that she needed to be very, very careful if she didn't want the crown of Alma on her head, as well.

The following morning, Gabriel decided he wanted to take his breakfast out on the patio overlooking the sea. The weather was beautiful, the skies were blue and the fresh sea air reminded him of home.

Sitting in the shade of the veranda, he sipped the coffee Luca brought him and watched a sailboat slip across the bay. How long had it been since he'd gone sailing? Too long. Once this coronation business was over and he could settle into being king, he intended to remedy that.

He could just picture Serafia standing on the deck, clutching the railing and watching the water as they cut through the waves. He imagined her wearing nothing but a pair of linen shorts hugging the curve of her rear and a bikini top tied around her neck. Her golden skin would darken in the sun, her long dark hair blowing in the sea breeze.

That sounded like heaven. It made him wonder if there was already a boat in the possession of the royal family. If there was, he'd ensure that they took it out for a spin as soon as possible.

As he took another sip, Luca appeared in the doorway. "Luca, do you know if we have a boat?"

"A boat, Your Grace?"

"Yes. We have a beach house. Do we have a boat?"

"Yes, there is a sailboat at the marina. The youngest Tantaberra was an avid sailor."

At the marina. Perhaps they could go out sooner than later. When he looked back at Luca, he realized he had the Alma newspaper in his hand. "Is that today's paper?" he asked.

Judging by the concerned expression on Luca's face, the latest royal coverage was not as positive as he'd hoped. He imagined the press had had a field day ragging on him about that panic attack at the vineyard. It wasn't the most kingly thing he'd done this week. He'd thought the parade went alright, though.

Gabriel frowned as he looked at Luca. "That good, eh? Should I go ahead and call Hector?"

"Señor Vega already knows, Your Grace. Ernesto called a moment ago to let me know that Señor Vega was already on his way here to speak with you."

Great. Gabriel would much rather use his spare time to get acquainted with every square inch of Serafia's body, but instead he would be discussing damage-control strategies with his high-strung press secretary. He had only met Hector a few times, and that was enough. The man consumed entirely too much caffeine. At least, Gabriel hoped he did. If the man was naturally that spun-up, he felt bad for the mother who'd had to chase him around as a toddler.

Hector made him anxious. Serafia made him calm. He knew exactly who he preferred to work with. He had to convince her to stay beyond the end of the week, be it as a paid employee or as his girlfriend.

"Let me see the damage before he gets here," Gabriel said, reaching out for the paper. "It must be bad if Hector immediately hopped in his car."

Gabriel glanced at the headlines, expecting the story to be about him, but instead he found a scathing story about the Espina family. He looked up at Luca. "Have you told Miss Espina about this, yet?"

"No, sir, but she should be down for breakfast momentarily. Would you like me to warn her?"

"No, I'll tell her."

Maybe they could have a game plan before Hector arrived and started spinning.

Turning back to the article, he started reading it in depth. Apparently, back when the coup took place in the 1940s, there were rumors about the loyalty of the Espina family. He hadn't heard that before. Surely if there had been any legitimacy to that claim, their families wouldn't have vacationed together and his father wouldn't have allowed Serafia to work with him these past few weeks.

Of course, his father had been quite curt where Serafia was concerned. He'd alluded to her family being unsuitable somehow, but Gabriel hadn't had a moment alone with his father to press him on that point. He was sure it was nothing to do with Serafia herself. Gabriel had chalked up his father's bad mood to jealousy. That was the most likely reason for his behavior since they arrived in Alma.

"Good morning." Serafia slipped out onto the patio in a pair of black capris and a sleeveless top. Her dark hair was swept up into a ponytail and she was wearing bejeweled sandals instead of dress pumps. They didn't have any official events on the calendar today, so she had apparently dressed for a more casual afternoon by the sea.

"Hector is on his way," he replied, not mincing words.

Serafia's smile faded and she slipped down into the other chair. "What happened?"

"Apparently the newspaper headlines have gone from speculating about your role as future queen to

speculating about your family's role in the overthrow
of the Montoros."

Serafia's eyebrows drew together in concern as she
reached for the paper. "What are they talking about?"
Her gaze flicked over the paper. "This is ridiculous.
Our families aren't enemies and we most certainly
didn't have anything do with the coup. Have they forgotten that the Espinas were driven from Alma, too?
They lived in Switzerland for years until the dictatorship fell in Spain. I was born in Madrid just a few years
after they left Switzerland."

Gabriel shrugged. "I am deficient in Alman history. We should probably fix that. I didn't even have
a clue our families had been rivals for the throne at
one point."

"That was over a hundred years ago. How is that
even relevant to what's going on now?"

"It has everything to do with what's happening
now," Hector Vega said, appearing in the doorway and
butting into their conversation. He, too, had the newspaper under his arm. "Your family had the crown stolen
away from them two hundred years ago. The Espinas
and Montoros fought for years to seize control of these
islands. The Montoros ended up winning and eventually the families did reconcile. They even planned to
marry and combine the bloodlines.

"But," he continued ominously, "Rafael the First
broke off his engagement with Rosa Espina to marry
Anna Maria. There were more than a few hurt feelings
about that and plenty of rumors went around during
the time of the coup about the Espinas' involvement.
Your whole family vanished from Alma right before
everything fell apart. Some see that as suspicious."

"And now?" Serafia pressed. "I think my family has gotten over the embarrassment of a broken engagement during the last seventy years. There is no reason to suspect us of anything."

"Isn't there? With the Tantaberras gone and the Montoros returning to Alma, your family is closer to reclaiming their throne than ever before," Hector explained.

"How?" Gabriel asked. "By marrying me? That plan only works if I'm on board with it."

Hector shrugged. "That's one way to do it." He moved out onto the veranda with them, but instead of taking a chair, he started pacing back and forth across the terra-cotta tiles of the patio. "Another way is to remove the Montoros entirely. If the Montoros and the Salazars were scandalized or discredited, Senorita Espina's family would be the next in line."

Gabriel had no idea that was the case, and judging by the surprised drop of Serafia's jaw, she didn't know it, either. "But there are several of us in line. They'd have to discredit us all, not just me."

"There are fewer of you than you think. Your father and brother have already been put aside. That just leaves you, Bella and Juan Carlos. Don't think it can't be done."

"There is no way that Juan Carlos can be discredited by scandal," Gabriel insisted. "He's annoyingly perfect."

"It doesn't matter," Hector said. "That article insinuates that Serafia was deliberately planted within the royal family to undermine you from the inside."

"She's here to help me!" Gabriel shouted. He was

irritated that this stupidity had ruined a perfectly beautiful morning.

"Is she?" Hector stopped moving just long enough to look over Serafia with suspicion.

"Of course I am. How dare you suggest otherwise?" Serafia flushed bright red beneath her tanned glow.

Hector raised his hands in defeat. "Fine. Fine. But the accusations are out there. We have to figure out how we're going to address them."

"They're ridiculous," Gabriel said. "I don't even want to address the rumors. At least not yet. It could all blow over if we treat it like the unfounded gossip it is."

Hector nodded and stopped pacing long enough to take notes in the small notebook he had tucked into his breast pocket.

"I just don't understand," Serafia said. "The press was so positive toward our relationship just a day ago. What changed so quickly?"

Hector put his notebook away and turned to look out at the sea, his fingers tapping anxiously on the railing. "My guess would be that someone leaked the story to discredit Serafia."

"Why?" Gabriel asked. "What could she have done to anger someone so quickly?"

Hector's gaze ran over Serafia with his lips pressed together tightly. "She didn't do anything. My guess is that it was your doing. You rejected the daughters of all the wealthiest families at the Rowling party."

Gabriel rolled his eyes. "Even if I hadn't left that night with Serafia—which really means nothing, since she's staying here with me for work—only one woman can be chosen as queen. There were easily twenty or thirty girls there that night. How could I possibly choose without offending *someone*?"

"It bet it was Felicia Gomez," Serafia said, speaking up. "Yesterday's incident just compounded their irritation over the party. The Gomez family doesn't like to lose and as I recall, you didn't even dance with Dita that night. I imagine Felicia would see that as a major snub. Combine that with yesterday after the parade… I'm sure they ran right to the press after we left. She can't take it out on you, as king, so she focused her ire on their main competition—me."

Gabriel muffled a snort and shook his head. "They wouldn't go to this much trouble if they knew the truth."

"What's the truth?" Serafia asked.

Gabriel looked into her dark eyes with a serious expression. "They're hardly your competition."

Nine

"How, exactly, did you come up with a boat?" Serafia asked as she turned to Gabriel.

Gabriel looked up from the wheel of the yacht and grinned. After a morning of unpleasantness with Hector, he'd had Luca arrange for the boat to go out. He needed to escape, to think, and there was nothing better than the sea for that.

Marta had packed them a picnic basket so they could dine on the water. The sea was calm and the breeze was just strong enough to fill the sails and keep them from getting too hot. "Turns out it's mine," he said. "Or at least it is now. I thought it was a good day to be out on the water."

"To escape the press?" she asked.

He chuckled and shook his head. "That's just a bonus. Mainly I wanted to see you in a bikini."

Serafia smiled and held out her arms to display her mostly bare curves. She was wearing a bright blue-and-pink paisley bikini top with a pair of tiny denim shorts that made her legs look as if they went on for miles. He ached to touch them, but he needed to steer the boat.

"You got your wish," she declared.

"Indeed I did." The reality standing in front of him was even better than he'd imagined this morning.

"If they know we're out here, the paparazzi will follow us, you know."

"Then they'll get an eyeful and the pictures will leave no doubts that their seedy story made no impact on my opinion of you."

He focused on steering the boat out of the sheltered bay and into open water as she laid a beach towel down on the polished wooden deck. She slipped out of the tiny shorts and went about rubbing sunblock all over her golden skin.

Thank goodness there weren't many ships out on the water today. His eyes were so glued to her that he could've run aground or rammed another boat. He couldn't wait to find a good place to stop so he could join her on the deck.

Serafia glanced up at him and smiled. She looked beautiful and carefree for once; she'd even left her tablet behind today. Not at all like someone scheming her way into his life, he thought, as the events from the morning intruded on his admiration of her. The whole thing was just absurd. Their families might have had animosity a hundred years ago, but that wasn't the case now. The people involved in that were long dead. It didn't have a thing to do with him or Serafia.

The idea that she had been "planted" in his inner

circle to undermine him made his hands curl into fists at his side. Serafia hadn't been *planted* anywhere. He had hired her. She hadn't even suggested the idea; in fact, she'd been very reluctant to take the job. If she was here to lure him into bed, she'd certainly made it difficult. He'd worked harder on her seduction than he had in a long time.

As much as he wanted to just laugh off the story, he couldn't. It made him too angry. He wouldn't tolerate such ugly speculation, especially about Serafia or her family. He'd quietly tasked Hector with tracking down the author of the article and seeing if the source could be identified. If the Gomez family really was behind this story, they'd regret it. If they thought his snubbing Dita at the dance was a huge deal, they'd better be prepared to be shut out of his court entirely. Gabriel was able to carry grudges for a very long time. He wouldn't quickly forget about the people who tried to undermine his faith in the one person he trusted.

Everyone had seen that article. Not long after Hector left, Gabriel's father had called from Del Sol. Rafael was agitated about the whole thing, repeating what he'd said at the Rowling party about the Espinas. Since this time they weren't in public where they could be overheard, Gabriel had pushed his father for more information. Arturo Espina was one of his father's best friends. How could he turn around and be suspicious of the family?

Rafael insisted it wasn't the truth that was the problem. It was seventy years of rumors that would taint his relationship with her. If he were to go as far as to make Serafia his queen, they would forever be dogged by those same ugly stories. Everyone had seen this ar-

ticle and it was just the beginning. Rafael insisted he
was just trying to help Gabriel avoid all that. Being
king was hard enough, he reasoned, without adding
unnecessary complications.

If staying away from Serafia was the only way to
save his reign from rumors, innuendo and scandal, too
bad. He wasn't going to let something like this drive a
wedge between them.

"It's so beautiful out here," Serafia declared, pulling him from his dark thoughts.

It was beautiful. The water was an amazing mix of
blues and greens; the sky was perfectly clear. Looking
back to the shore, you could see the coastline dotted
with marinas and tiny homes hanging on the side of
the cliffs. He couldn't imagine a more amazing place
to rule over.

Before too long, he would be king of this beautiful
country.

From the moment he found out, he had fought the
news. He'd made a bold decision to take control of his
own life after his abduction, and yet somehow fate had
taken away his free will once again. Most people would
probably jump at the chance to be in his shoes, but all
Gabriel had been able to see were all the reasons why
he was a bad choice.

But now that he was here with Serafia at his side, it
seemed as though things might work out. The people
were welcoming and friendly. The land was beautiful and full of natural resources that would help the
country bounce back from oppression. Prime Minister Rivera was a smart man and a good leader, taking
the reins on the important decisions for the management of the country. The press were the press, but once

he chose a queen and married, hopefully they would settle down.

Gabriel was told that he would soon sit down with his council of advisers, a group of staffers that included Hector and others. He was certain they would have lots of opinions about whom he should choose for his queen. There were geopolitical implications that even he didn't fully understand. Marrying a Spanish or Portuguese princess would be smart. Securing trade by marrying a Danish princess wouldn't hurt, either. Then there were the local wealthy citizens whose support was so important to the success of the new monarchy.

But factoring in all those things would mean he was following his head, not his heart. Gabriel wasn't exactly known for making the smart choices where women were concerned. When it came to Serafia, none of those other things mattered. The minute he saw her out on the patio in Miami, he'd wanted her. And the more he'd had of her, the more he'd wanted. He wasn't just flattering her when he told her the other women in Alma were no competition. It was the truth.

Serafia was smart, beautiful, honest, caring...everything a good queen should be. She was from an important Alman family—one with blood ties to the throne if that article could be believed. He saw more than one sign at the parade declaring the people's support for her as queen. She was a good choice on paper and a great choice in his heart.

He wasn't in love with Serafia. Not yet. But he could see the potential there. In any other scenario, he would've anticipated months or years together before they discussed love and marriage, but as king, he saw this as an entirely different animal. He was expected to make a choice and move forward. With Serafia, he had no fears that their marriage would be a stiff, arranged situation with an awkward honeymoon night. It could be the best of both worlds if they played their cards right.

He just had to get her to stay past the end of the week. If he could do that, then maybe, just maybe, she would agree to be his queen someday soon.

"This looks like a good spot. Drop the stupid anchor and get over here. I'm lonely."

Gabriel checked the depth sounder for a good location. They seemed to be in an area with a fairly level depth. He lowered and secured the two sails, slowing the boat. It took a few minutes to get the anchor lowered and set, but the boat finally came to a full stop.

He turned off any unnecessary equipment and made his way over to where Serafia was lying out. She was on her back, her inky black hair spilling across the sandy blond wood of the deck. She had her wide, dark sunglasses on, but the smile curling her lips indicated she was watching him as he admired her.

Gabriel dropped down onto the deck beside her. He slipped out of his shoes and pulled his polo shirt over his head, leaving on his swimming trunks.

Serafia sat up, grabbing her bottle of sunscreen and applying some to his back. He closed his eyes and enjoyed the feel of her hands gliding across his bare skin. After she finished his back and arms, she placed a playful dab on his nose and cheeks. "There you go."

He rubbed the last of the sunscreen into his face. "Thanks. Are you hungry?"

"Yes," she said. "After everything this morning, I couldn't stomach any breakfast."

Gabriel reached for the picnic basket and set it closer to them on the blanket. Opening it, they uncovered a container filled with assorted slices of aged Manchego and Cabrales cheeses, and cured meats like *jamón ibérico* and *cecina de León*. Smaller containers revealed olives, grapes and cherry tomatoes dressed in olive oil and sherry vinegar. A jar of quince jam, a couple fresh, sliced baguettes and a bottle of Spanish Cava rounded out the meal. His stomach started growling at the sight of it.

Serafia started unpacking the cartons, laying out the plates and utensils Marta had also included. "Ooh," she said, lifting out a package wrapped in foil. "This smells like cinnamon and sugar." She unwrapped a corner to peer inside. "Looks like fruit empanadas for dessert."

"Perfect," Gabriel said.

They scooped various items onto their plates and dug into their meals. They took their time enjoying every bite in the slow European fashion he was becoming accustomed to. In America, eating was like a pit stop in a race—to quickly refuel and get back on the track. Now, he took the time to savor the food, to really taste it while enjoying his company. He sliced bread while Serafia slathered it with jam. She fed him olives and kissed the olive oil from his lips. By the time the jars were nearly empty, they were both full and happy, lying on the deck together and gazing up at the brilliant blue sky.

Gabriel reached out beside him and felt for Serafia's hand. He wrapped his fingers through hers and felt a sense of calm and peace come over him. He didn't know what he would've done without her these last few days. In that short time, she had become such a necessary fixture in his life. He couldn't imagine her going back to Barcelona. He wanted her here by his side, holding his hand just as she was now.

"Serafia?" he asked, his voice quiet and serious.

"Yes?"

"Would you…consider staying here in Alma? With me?"

She turned to him and studied his face with her dark eyes. "You're going to be fine, Gabriel. You've improved so much. You're not going to need my help any longer."

Gabriel rolled onto his side. "I don't want you here for your help. I'm not interested in you being my employee, I want you to be my girlfriend."

Her eyes grew wide as he spoke, her teeth drawing in her bottom lip while she considered his offer. Not exactly the enthusiastic response he was hoping for.

"You don't want to stay," he noted.

Serafia sat up, pulling her hand away from his to wrap her arms around her knees. "I do and I don't. I have a life in Barcelona, Gabriel. A quiet, easy life that I love. Giving that up to come here and be with you is a big decision. Being the king's girlfriend is no quiet, easy life. I don't know if I'm ready."

Gabriel sat up beside her and put a comforting hand on her shoulder. He knew he was asking a lot of her, but he couldn't bear the idea of living in Alma without her. "You don't have to decide right now. Just think on it."

She looked at him with relief in her eyes. "Okay, I will."

* * *

After a day at sea, they'd returned to the house and taken naps. They decided to dine al fresco on the patio outside his bedroom. It was just sunset as they reconvened with glasses of wine to watch the sun sink into the sea. The sky was an amazing mix of purples, oranges and reds, all overtaken by inky blackness as the night finally fell upon Alma.

It was beautifully peaceful, but Serafia felt anything but. Despite the surroundings, the wine and the company, she couldn't get Gabriel's offer out of her mind. To stay in Alma, to be his girlfriend publically...that would change her entire life. She wasn't sure she was ready for that, even though her feelings for him grew every day.

The king didn't have a girlfriend. At least not for long. Unless something went wrong pretty quickly, being his girlfriend would mean soon being his fiancée, and then his queen. That meant she would never return home to her quiet life in Barcelona.

But was that life becoming too quiet? Had she been hiding there instead of living?

The questions still plagued her as they finished the last of the roasted chicken Marta had made for dinner. She felt pleasantly full as she eased back in her chair, a sensation she wasn't used to. She might be comfortable hiding from the world in her hacienda, but she wasn't living her life and she wasn't really getting better. She was managing her disease, controlling it almost to the point that she'd once let it control her. But in Alma, with Gabriel, the dark thoughts hadn't once crept into her mind. He was good for her. And she was good for him.

Maybe coming here was the right choice. Her heart certainly wanted to stay.

She didn't have to decide now, she reflected, and the thought soothed her nerves. To distract herself, she decided now was the right time to give Gabriel his gift. "I got you something."

Gabriel looked at her in surprise and set down his glass of wine. "Really? You didn't have to do that."

"I know. But I did it, anyway." Serafia got up and went to her room, returning a moment later with a small black box.

Gabriel accepted it and flipped open the hinged lid. She watched his face light up as he saw what was inside. "Wow!" He scooped the gift out of the box, setting it aside so he could admire his gift with both hands. "A pocket watch! That's great. Thank you."

Gabriel leaned in to give her a thank-you kiss before returning to admiring his gift. The pocket watch was a Patek Philippe, crafted with eighteen-karat yellow gold. It cost more than a nice BMW, but Serafia didn't care. She wanted to buy him something nice that she knew he didn't have. "I told you in Miami that I would find a way to get around your watch issue."

"And you've done a splendid job. It's beautiful."

"It comes with a chain so you can attach it inside your suit coat."

He nodded, running his fingertip along the shiny curve of the glass. Closing the box, he put it on the table and stood up. He approached her slowly, wrapping his arms around her waist and tugging her tight against him. "Thank you. That was an amazingly thoughtful gift."

Serafia smiled, pleased that he liked it. When she

bought it, she wasn't sure if he would see it as a further criticism of his time-management issues or if he would feel it was too old-fashioned for him. She'd known it was perfect the moment she saw it, and she was pleased to finally know that he agreed.

"I feel like I need to get you something now," he said.

"Not at all," she insisted. "After our discussions about watches earlier and realizing why you disliked them so much, I knew this was something I wanted to do for you. There's no need to reciprocate."

He stared at her lips as she spoke, but shook his head ever so slightly when she was finished. "I'll do what I like," he insisted. "If that means buying you something beautiful and sparkly, I will. If that means taking you into that bedroom and making love to you until you're hoarse, I will."

"Sounds like a challenge," she said.

When his lips met hers, the worries in her mind faded away. Serafia wrapped her arms around his neck and melted into him. The roar of the waves below was the only sound except for the pounding of her heart.

After a moment, he started backing them into the bedroom. Their lips were still pressed together as they moved across the tile to the king-size bed against the far wall. Serafia clung to him, losing herself in touching and tasting Gabriel. No matter what happened each day, she knew it was okay because she knew he would help her forget all her worries each night.

When her calves met with the bed, they stopped. Serafia tugged at his shirt, pulling it up and over his head. She ran her fingertips across his bare chest and scattered soft kisses along his collarbone. His skin was warm from a day in the sun and scented with the hand-made soaps they kept in the bathrooms here.

She felt Gabriel's fingertips on her outer thighs, slowly gathering up the fabric of her dress. Before he could pull it any higher, she turned them around so that his back was to the bed. Then she shoved, thrusting him onto the mattress, where he sprawled out and bounced.

"Are we playing rough tonight?" he asked with a laugh.

Serafia shook her head and took a few steps backward. "I just wanted you to sit back and enjoy the view."

Pushing aside her self-consciousness, she let the straps of her sundress fall from her shoulders, the soft cotton dress pooling at her feet. She coyly turned her back to him, unfastening her bra and letting it drop to the floor. With a sly glance over her shoulder at him, she slipped her thumbs beneath her cheeky lace panties and slid them down her legs. Completely nude, she turned back to face him.

Gabriel watched from the bed with a glint of appreciation in his eyes. He really, truly thought she was beautiful, and knowing this made her feel beautiful. She lifted her arms to brush the cascading waves of her hair over her shoulders, displaying her breasts and narrow waist. He swallowed hard as he watched her, his jaw tightening.

"Come here," he said.

Serafia took her time, despite his royal command. She sauntered over to the bed, crawling across the coverlet on all fours until she was hovering between his thighs. She reached for the fly of his jeans, but the moment she was within Gabriel's reach, he lunged for her.

Before she knew quite what had happened, she was on her back and the weight of Gabriel's body was pressing her into the soft mattress.

He kissed her, his mouth hard and demanding against her own. His fingertips pressed into her, just as hard. She gasped for air when he pulled away to taste her throat. His teeth grazed her delicate skin, almost as though he wanted to mark her, claim her as his own.

She wanted to be his. His alone. At least for tonight. She could feel his desire against her bare thigh, the rough denim keeping them apart. She reached between them, slipping her hand beneath his waistband to grip the length of him. He growled against her throat, leaning into her for a moment, and then reluctantly pulling away before she wore out the last of his self-control.

Slipping off the edge of the bed, he removed the last of his clothes, sheathed himself in latex and returned to his home between her thighs. Without saying a word, he drove into her, stretching her body to its limit. She cried out and clung to his back, her fingernails pressing crescents into his skin.

Their lovemaking was more frantic tonight, more passionate and intense. She wasn't sure if it was the end of their relationship looming that pushed them to a frenzy, but she happily went along for the ride. Nothing else mattered as he drove into her again and again. All she could do was give in to the pleasure, live in the moment and not let the future intrude on their night together. It wasn't hard. Within minutes he had her gasping and on the verge of unraveling.

That was when he stopped moving entirely.

Her eyes flew open, her breath ragged. "Is something wrong?" she asked.

"Stay with me," he demanded.

She wanted to. She wanted to give him her body, her heart and her soul. In that moment, she knew she already had. Despite her hesitation, despite her worries, she had fallen in love with Gabriel Montoro, future king of Alma. But was she good for him? Would she be the queen the country needed?

Those critical articles were just the first of many she was sure would surface. Rumors about her family wouldn't disappear overnight. She didn't want to bring scandal to the new monarchy. It was too new, too fragile. She couldn't risk that, even for love.

She also couldn't risk herself. Would she slip back into her old habits with the eyes of an entire country on her? It was a dangerous prospect.

But when he looked at her like that, his green eyes pleading with her, how could she say no? She wanted to stay. She wanted to be with him, to help him on his new journey. If that meant she might someday be queen and take on all the pressures and joys that entailed...so be it.

"Yes," she whispered into the darkness before she could change her mind.

Gabriel thrust hard into her and she was lost. The waves of emotions and pleasure collided inside her, making her cry out desperately. She repeated her answer again and again, encouraging him and confirming to herself that she truly meant it. She loved him and she was going to stay.

His release came quickly after hers. He groaned loud against her throat, surging into her one last time as he came undone. Serafia held him, cradling his hips between her thighs until it was over.

When he'd finally stilled, she heard him whisper almost undetectably in her ear, "Thank you."

He was grateful that she'd agreed to stay. She just hoped that would still be the case in the upcoming weeks.

Ten

Serafia should've woken up on cloud nine. She was in love, she'd agreed to stay in Alma with Gabriel and everything was perfect. And yet there was a cloud hanging over her head. It was as though she couldn't let herself breathe, couldn't let herself believe that this was really going to work between them, until after today.

Today was the last hurdle before the coronation. After today's public appearance, Gabriel would have met all the initial requirements and could settle quietly into his life at Alma while the preparation for the coronation took place. She didn't anticipate any problems today. All they had to do was make it through the tour of one of Patrick Rowling's oil platforms off the coast, but for some reason, she woke up anxious.

They got on the road after breakfast, driving the hour back into Del Sol, where they would take a helicopter out to sea. Helicopters. Better safe than sorry, she decided to get his opinion on it during their drive to the capital.

"Are you okay with helicopters?" Serafia asked.

Gabriel straightened his tie and nodded. "Helicopters are fine. The weather seems pretty calm today, so it shouldn't be a bumpy ride."

"Good." She sighed with relief. That was one less worry. "The only other option to get out there is to take a boat and get lifted by crane onto the platform while you cling to a rope and metal cage called a Billy Pugh. I wasn't looking forward to that at all."

Gabriel smiled. "That actually sounds pretty cool."

"You're the rebellious one," she said. "I'm interested in staying alive."

"Fair enough. How far out is the oil platform?"

Serafia looked down at her tablet as their car approached the heliport. "The one we're going to is about twelve kilometers off the coast. It's the newest one they've constructed and Patrick is very eager to show off his new toy."

Gabriel frowned. "I'm sure he is."

"What's that face about?"

"I'm not sure how I feel about the Rowlings yet. At least Patrick. He seems a little showy, a little too cocky for my taste. His sons seem nice enough, although I can't wait to see the look on Bella's face when she's introduced to the guy Dad wants her to marry. If there aren't instant fireworks between them, she just might kill our father in his sleep. We might need her to stay at the beach house when she gets here."

"I wouldn't worry too much about Patrick or Bella today. I'm sure the trip will be fine and you'll be off the hook for a while until the coronation. Today, we'll be flying over with Prime Minister Rivera. He asked to join us on the tour."

"What about Hector?"

"Apparently he doesn't do helicopters, but he's briefed everyone and he'll be meeting with you afterward to go over how it went with Rivera."

"That's fine. I've only had one short meeting with the prime minister, so it's probably a good idea to have some more face time. I don't think we'll get much talking done in the helicopter, though. Aren't they loud?"

Serafia had never been in one, but she'd heard they were. "Yes. I'm pretty sure you won't be conducting any business in the helicopter."

He nodded and relaxed back into the seat. "Good. I'm not sure I'm ready for any hard-core discussions. Is the helicopter large enough for the royal guard, as well? That's quite a few of us to fit into one."

Serafia shook her head. "They've already got a crew of guards there at the rig. They cleared the platform this morning and are standing by for your arrival. All the details have been taken care of," she assured him. Turning to glance out the window, she realized they were at their destination. "And here we are."

They climbed from the car at the heliport and made their way over to the helicopter waiting for them. The prime minister was already there, rushing over to shake Gabriel's hand. Then as a group, they climbed into the helicopter and headed out to sea.

Serafia was glad Gabriel was okay with helicopters. She wasn't exactly thrilled with the idea, so it was good that at least one of them wasn't freaking out. When the engine started, she put on the ear protection and closed her eyes. The liftoff sent her stomach into her throat, but after a few minutes the movement was steady. Thankfully it wouldn't take long to get out there, so she took some deep breaths and tried not to think about where she was.

A thump startled her, and she opened her eyes in panic only to realize they'd already landed on the oil platform. Thank goodness. Everyone climbed out and Patrick came to greet them. With him, he had the lead rig operator, his son William and a few members of Patrick's management team who always seemed to be following him around. This, in addition to a large contingent of press, as always. They'd come out earlier on the boat. Once everyone was fitted with hard hats, the tour began.

With all the cameras so near today, Serafia decided to take a step back from Gabriel. There was no need to stir any more rumors or give any of them a reason to write another scathing article about her family or their romance. He didn't seem to notice she was gone. With everything going on, he surged ahead, carried by the crowd with Rivera and Patrick Rowling at his side.

Serafia trailed the group as they walked around the open decks of the platform, admiring the massive drill and other equipment. She couldn't hear what Patrick and the others were saying, but she didn't mind. She wasn't really that interested.

After that, they went inside to tour the employee quarters and cafeteria, the offices and the control room. It was a tight fit for the men who lived on the rig up to two weeks at a stretch.

The day was going fairly well, so far. She'd begun to think she'd been anxious for no reason.

It wasn't until they went back outside and started climbing down a set of metal stairs that went below the platform that Serafia started to feel the niggling of worry in the back of her mind. The only thing below the platform were the emergency evacuation boats, some maintenance equipment and the underwater exploration pod they used for maintenance.

Oh God. Her heart very nearly leaped out of her chest and into her throat when she realized what was about to happen.

The submarine.

She'd forgotten all about it. It had always been a part of the plan. They were to tour the oil rig, and then their exploration pod, which was essentially a small, four-man submarine, would take Gabriel under the surface to see the rig at work. It was a harmless photo op, and when she was given the original itinerary, she hadn't thought a thing about it. Gabriel certainly hadn't mentioned having a problem with it when they discussed the agenda back in Miami.

Since then, she'd learned about Gabriel's issues with small, dark spaces, but so much had happened that the submarine had slipped her mind.

That had to be where they were going. Unfortunately there were twenty people between Gabriel and her on the narrow deck and staircase. He was below the platform and she was stuck above it at the very back of the pack. She was unable to get close enough to warn him before it was too late.

She rushed to the metal railing, peering over the side at the party below. They were still walking around while Patrick pointed out one thing or another, but she could see the open hatch of the exploration pod a few yards in front of them.

"Gabriel!" she shouted, but no one but a few of the reporters and crew members turned to look at her. The sounds of the ocean and the operating rig easily drowned out everything. Everything but the expression on his face.

Serafia knew the instant that he realized where they were going. He stiffened, his jaw tightening. His hands curled into fists at his side. Everyone around him continued to talk and laugh, but he wasn't participating in the discussion. He was loosening his tie, looking around for another option to escape, short of leaping into the ocean and swimming back to the mainland.

Patrick Rowling and the prime minister were the first to crawl inside the exploration pod. Gabriel stood there at the entrance for several moments, looking into the small space. He was white as a sheet and he gripped the railing with white-knuckled intensity. She could tell the others were trying to encourage him, but he likely couldn't hear anything they said if he was having a full-blown panic attack.

Then he shook his head. Backing up, he nearly ran into someone else, then turned and pushed his way through the crowd back to the stairs. Serafia could barely make out the sounds of shouts and words of concern. Patrick climbed back out of the submarine, calling toward Gabriel, but he didn't stop. He leaped up the stairs, finally colliding with Serafia as he reached the top.

He looked at her, but his eyes were wild with panic. It seemed almost as if he didn't really see her at all.

"I'm so sorry, Gabriel. I forgot all about the submarine. I would've warned you if I remembered."

He looked at her, his expression hardening. There was venom in his gaze, a place where she'd only ever seen attraction and humor. She reached out for his arm, but he shoved it aside and took a step back.

"It's not a big deal," she reassured him. "They can go on ahead without you. I'm sure you're not the only person who doesn't fancy the idea of a ride in that thing."

The look on his face made it clear that he didn't agree. It was a big deal, at least to him. Without saying a word, he turned and took off down the metal-grated walkway toward the helipad.

"Gabriel, stop! Wait!" she shouted as she pursued him, but he kept on going. She finally gave up just as she was overtaken by the press. They pushed her aside as they chased Gabriel, but before they could reach him, she spied the helicopter rising over the top of the rig.

With nothing else she could do, Serafia stood and watched the helicopter disappear into the horizon. Once it was gone, all she could see, all she could think of, was the look of utter betrayal on his face. He blamed her for this. And maybe he should. She'd made a very big error today.

"What happened?" The prime minister stopped beside her, his brow pinched in confusion. "Is the prince okay? He looked quite ill."

"I don't know," Serafia said. She wasn't going to be the one to tell him, and any of the surrounding reporters, that Gabriel was claustrophobic. That would make it seem as if she was deliberately trying to undermine him. He should've been the one to say it. All it would've taken was a polite pass and he could've avoided it. Instead, he'd run like he'd been ambushed.

A sinking feeling settled into Serafia's stomach at the thought. Was that what Gabriel believed she was doing? This was just one oversight, but when added to the string of other problems they'd had over the last week, did it add up to the appearance of sabotage? He couldn't possibly believe she'd do that to him. He hadn't given that newspaper article a second thought.

Or had he?

Serafia feared he'd begun to suspect her. That look had said everything. Serafia had ruined it. She hadn't meant to, but she'd ruined her relationship with Gabriel before it ever started.

Even though Gabriel had his driver take him back to Playa del Onda right away, he was discouraged to find Hector already waiting for him there. Judging by his press secretary's dour expression, the news of the incident on the oil rig had beaten Gabriel home. He just wanted to take off his tie, pour a glass of scotch and relax, but Hector was the hitch in that plan.

"Where's Serafia?" he asked as Gabriel blew past him.

"I don't know. I left her at the oil platform."

Hector made a thoughtful noise and followed him into the den. Gabriel poured a drink and ripped off his tie before collapsing onto the couch. "Why?"

"Well, I wanted to speak to you privately about those rumors. I'm concerned that the Espinas may be trying to undermine your coronation."

Gabriel was tired of hearing about this. "We've discussed this already."

"Yes, but that was before the prime minister called and briefed me about what happened today. He was concerned about you. He'd heard about the incident at the winery, as well."

Great. Now they were talking about him and his issues behind his back. "I don't do well in small spaces," Gabriel explained. "When I start having a panic attack, I have a very aggressive flight response. I overreact, I'm aware of that, but in the moment, I just have to get away from the situation. All the pressure I'm under to be poised and perfect every moment is just making it that much worse because I try to fight my way through it and it doesn't work. Then I feel like a fool."

Hector listened carefully. "I'll make certain we don't have these issues in the future. In exchange, I ask that you speak up when you're uncomfortable so we don't make a bigger scene out of it. Does Serafia know about your claustrophobia?"

"Yes." She didn't know until after the winery incident, but she knew today.

"I see. Your Majesty, my concern is about why these situations keep popping up. Rivera said he asked Patrick Rowling about the submarine and said that it had been Serafia's idea. I understand that you two are… whatever you are. But you really need to put your feelings for her aside and consider the possibility that all these unfortunate incidents are actually carefully orchestrated by the Espina family."

Gabriel dropped his face into his hand. He'd had a horrible day and he didn't really want to face this right now. "I'll take care of it," he said.

"Your Majesty, I—"

"I said, I'll take care of it!" Gabriel shouted. Suddenly his overwhelming apprehension had morphed into anger. He knew he shouldn't direct it at Hector, but he didn't care. He would kill the messenger because he didn't know what else to do.

"Very good, Your Grace. Thank you for your time." Hector gave a curt bow and left the room.

Gabriel watched Hector leave, the questions and anxiety spinning in his mind. Unable to sit still, he headed out to the veranda to await Serafia's return to the compound. The longer he waited, the more his blood began to heat in his veins. He had been upset at the oil platform, but after his discussion with Hector, every minute that ticked by tipped his emotions over into pure anger.

If he was right, this was the ultimate betrayal. Serafia would've known exactly what she was doing. She knew he couldn't stand small, confined spaces. How could she schedule him for what amounted to a miniature submarine ride under an oil platform? Even people who hadn't been through the kind of experience he'd had would balk at that. And yet, he felt this pressure as the future king to do it. He had to be strong; he couldn't show weakness. His father expected it. His country expected it. And all it did was backfire on him and make him look like more of a coward when he fled.

The situation had snuck up on him. They were walking around the lower level and the next thing he knew, he was confronted with his personal nightmare. As he'd looked down into the small round hatch at the metal ladder that would take him into a space too cramped for more than four full-grown men, he felt himself launch into a full-blown panic attack.

This wasn't like the incident at the vineyard. There, the room was dark and underground, but he could escape any time he chose, and did. The minute Gabriel climbed down that ladder, and the hatch was sealed, he would be trapped. His lungs had seized up as if a vise was crushing his rib cage. His heart had been racing so quickly he could barely tell the rhythm of one beat from the next. He'd been sweating, wheezing and damn near on the verge of crying while Patrick Rowling and the prime minister tried to coax him on board.

No way. He didn't care if he offended the richest man in Alma. He wasn't about to have that image on him on television, blasted around the internet and on the front page of every paper. New King of Alma Cries Like a Baby When Forced Into a Submarine! They might as well send a stamped invitation for the Tantaberra family to come back and take over again. It was better to leave before it got worse.

It was bad enough everyone had witnessed his behavior. The Rowlings, the press and even the prime minister were all standing by as he'd completely flipped out, shoved people aside to escape and run across the platform to the helicopter pad as if he were on fire. It must have been a sight to see…his guards chasing after him, people shouting at him to come back, the press recording every moment of it… *The Runaway King.* Now, there was a nickname for his upcoming illustrious reign.

He hadn't registered much in the moment. Gabriel had only been motivated by a driving need to get away from that submarine, off the platform and onto dry land with sunshine on his face as soon as possible. But he could hear Serafia as she'd tried to comfort him. He'd registered the panic and worry on her face as she rushed toward him, but he wasn't slowing down for her or anyone else. Besides, it had been too late. The damage was already done.

Of course, that might have been part of her plan, right? The article had insinuated that the Espina family was determined to gain the throne back one way or another. If not through seduction, perhaps through scandal and humiliation. Serafia had been throwing grenades at him since he arrived. The watch, the debacle at the airport, the vineyard and now the oil platform... Even the supposedly successful party at Rowling's house had proven controversial when he snubbed the Gomez girl at Serafia's suggestion.

He'd paid her to help this week go smoothly, to prepare him for any eventuality as king, and it had started to seem more as if she was deliberately setting him up to fail.

He heard the sound of his bedroom door open. After taking a large sip of his scotch, he set the mostly empty glass down. The amber liquid burned in his stomach, just as his anger shot hot through his veins.

Finally Serafia stepped through the open doorway, looking as worn and ragged as if she'd jogged all the way back from the oil platform. Her shirt was untucked and wrinkled. There was a run in her stocking, and her heels were scuffed. Her hair had been up in a bun, but now it was half up, half down in a silky black mess. She was flushed, with bloodshot eyes and dried tear tracks down her cheeks. It made him wonder how long it had taken her to put together this look and assume the role of the innocent in all this. Maybe that was why it took forever for her to get here.

"I'm so sorry, Gabriel. I didn't—"

"Just stop!" he shouted more forcefully than he intended. The anger that had simmered inside him was approaching a full boil now that he was face-to-face with her again. "Don't tell me you didn't know about this, because I know that's a lie." He gestured to the white sheet of paper on the table in front of him. "I found the schedule you gave me back in Miami for this week. This event was on there. Patrick Rowling said you actually suggested it. You knew all this time what we were building up to."

Serafia crossed her arms over her chest in a defensive posture. "In Miami, I didn't know anything about your abduction. Yes, it was my suggestion because I thought it would be an interesting activity for you. When we reviewed your schedule for the visit, I mentioned it and you said nothing. You just tuned me out half the time. I'm surprised you even had the schedule anymore."

"And after you knew about what happened to me in Venezuela? After the incident at the vineyard? Did it not occur to you then that these plans for the visit to the oil platform might be a bad idea?"

"I'd forgotten," she said, tears forming in her eyes again. "With everything that has happened over the past week, I forgot all about the submarine. It slipped my mind and by the time I remembered, it was too late. We were separated by the crowd and I couldn't warn you without making a scene. I was trying to warn you before they got to that part of the tour."

Gabriel stood up, his dark gaze searching her face

for signs of the treachery he knew was there. Hector had helped him cast her under a shadow of suspicion he couldn't shake. She'd been hiding her secret agenda beneath a disguise of coy smiles and stiff, respectable suits, but it was there nonetheless. And he'd fallen for it.

"And you showed up to warn me at the perfect time," he replied with bitterness in his voice. "Late enough for me to embarrass myself and undermine my future as king, but not so late as to convince me that it was deliberate just in case the ploy didn't work and you might still end up queen."

A strange combination of emotions danced across Serafia's face, ending in a look of exasperation. "I don't want to be queen. I never have and you know why!"

If she really didn't want to be queen, that only left one option. "Just wanting to stay close enough to ruin me and my family, then?"

Serafia threw her arms up, spinning in a circle before facing him with her index finger held up. "One incident. *One*. And suddenly those newspaper accusations you dismissed are gospel? Do you have no faith in me at all?"

"I did. For some stupid reason, I pushed aside all my suspicions and allowed myself to trust you more than I've trusted anyone in years. Even when that article came out, I dismissed it as nasty gossip or old news from another time and place. I couldn't believe that you could be using me to get to the throne."

"Because I'm not," she insisted.

Gabriel just shook his head sadly. "You're just as bad as the Gomez family. You know what? You're even worse. At least they're transparent about their ambitions. You and your family just sidle up to us like friends, then pervert the entire relationship to suit your own purposes."

"Gabriel, you said yourself that that story was nonsense. I didn't get planted with you. You hired me."

That was the detail that had bothered him, but the longer he sat on the patio, the more he'd begun to wonder if that was really true. "What *were* you doing in Miami, Serafia? I hadn't seen you in years, and then all of a sudden, you fly all the way to Miami from Barcelona for my going-away party? You could've just waited to see me in Alma if you were that interested in congratulating me, and saved yourself a fortune in time and money."

Serafia stiffened, her eyebrows drawing together into a frown. "I was in the States for another project and my father asked me to attend on behalf of the family."

"What project?" he pressed. "Who were you working for?"

Serafia started to stutter over her words, as though she was failing to come up with an adequate lie when she was put on the spot. "I—it w-was for a confidential client. I can't tell you who it was."

"A confidential client? Of course it was." Gabriel tried not to take it personally that she thought he was so stupid. "You may not have been a plant, but you were a tempting little worm dangling on a hook right in front of me. I snatched you up just as surely as you'd weaseled your way into my inner circle on your own. You pretended to help me be a better king, building up my confidence in and out of bed, while slowly undermining every inch of progress I've made along the way."

Serafia looked at him with hurt reflecting in her

dark eyes. "Is that all you think of the two of us? Of what we have together?"

"I didn't at first, but now I see how wrong I was. I can see it must have been really difficult for you."

She narrowed her gaze at him, her tears fading. "What must be?"

Gabriel swallowed hard and spat out the words he'd been holding in all day. "Trying to screw me in two different ways at once."

Serafia gasped and raised her hand to cover her mouth. She stumbled back on her heels until her back collided with the doorframe. "You're a bastard, Gabriel."

"Maybe," he said thoughtfully. "But it's people like you who made me this way."

"I quit!" she shouted, disappearing into the house.

"Fine. Quit!" he yelled back at her. "I was just going to fire you, anyway."

He heard her bedroom door slam shut down the hallway. With her gone, the anger that had boiled over suddenly drained out of him. He slumped back into his chair and dropped his head into his hands.

It didn't matter whether she quit or he fired her. In the end, the damage was done and she would soon be gone.

Eleven

Harder. Faster. Keep pushing.

It didn't matter if Serafia's lungs were burning or that her leg muscles felt as if they could rip from her bones at any second. She had to keep going.

Just when she hit the point where she couldn't take any more, she reached out for the console and dropped the speed on the treadmill by half a mile. Giving herself only a minute or two to recover, she then increased it by a whole mile. Her sneakers pounded hard against the rotating belt, which was reaching speeds she could barely maintain in the past.

But she had to now. She had to keep running or everything would catch up with her. It wasn't until she could feel her heart pounding like Thor's hammer against her breast that she realized she'd taken this too far. She reached out and pounded the emergency stop button, slamming into the console and draping her broken body over it. The air rushing from her lungs blazed like fire, her heart feeling as if it was about to burst. She'd run for miles today. Hours. Longer and harder than her doctor-appointed forty-five-minute daily limit.

And yet the moment she looked up, the world around her was just the same. The same heartache. The same confusion. The same anger at herself and at Gabriel. All she'd managed to do was pull a hamstring and sweat through her clothes.

She gripped her bottle of water and stepped down onto the tile floor with gelatinous, quivering legs. Unable to go much farther, she opened the door to her garden courtyard. The cold water and ocean breeze weren't enough to soothe her overheated body, so she set down her bottle and approached her swimming pool. Without stopping to take off her shoes, she stepped off the edge, plunging herself into the cool turquoise depths.

Rising to the surface, she pushed her hair out of her face and took a deep breath. She felt a million times better. Her heart slowed and her body temperature was jerked back from the point of disaster.

And yet she was still at a loss over what to do with herself. She had returned home to Barcelona in disgrace. Her last-minute flight had delivered her home late in the night; she hadn't even told her family or staff that she was returning. All she knew was that she had to get out of Alma that instant. She would work the rest out later.

Once she'd escaped…she didn't know what to do. She had no jobs lined up for several weeks. She'd cleared her calendar when she took the Montoro job because she wasn't sure how long it would truly take. The first few days in Miami had been excruciating and she'd wondered if two weeks would be enough.

Two weeks were more than enough, at least for her. And while she was relieved to be home, returned to the sanctuary she'd built for herself here, something felt off. She'd wandered through the empty halls, sat on the balcony overlooking the sea, lay in bed staring at the ceiling…the thought of Gabriel crept into everything she did.

Serafia swam to the edge of the pool and crossed her arms along the stone, lifting her torso up out of the water. She dropped her head onto her forearms and fought the tears that had taunted her the last few days. As hard as she'd resisted falling for the rebellious prince, it had happened, anyway. Even with the threat of returning to the spotlight, the potential for becoming queen and all the responsibilities that held, she couldn't help herself.

And then he turned on her. How could he think she would do something like that on purpose? The minute she realized where they were headed, the panic had been nearly overwhelming. And then when he'd looked at her with the betrayal reflecting in his eyes, she felt her heart break. He was so used to people using and abusing his trust that he refused to see that wasn't what she was doing.

Perhaps she should have stayed in Alma and fought to clear her name. Running away made her look guilty, but she just couldn't stay there. Her family might have been from Alma decades ago, but she was born and raised in Spain and that was where she needed to be.

She just needed to get her life back on track. The

dramas of Alma would fade, Gabriel would choose his queen and she would go on with her life, such as it was.

At least that was what she told herself.

The French doors to the courtyard opened behind her, and Serafia's housekeeper stepped out with a tray. "I have your lunch ready, señorita."

Serafia swam back to the shallow end of the pool to greet her. She wasn't remotely interested in food with the way she felt, but it would hurt her housekeeper's feelings if she didn't pretend otherwise. "Thank you, Esperanza. Please leave it on the patio table."

Esperanza did as she asked, hesitating a moment by the edge of the pool with a towel in her hands. She seemed worried, her wrinkled face pinched into an expression of concern. "Are you going to eat it?"

Serafia frowned and climbed up the steps. "What do you mean?"

"You barely touched your breakfast, just picking at the fruit. I found most of last night's dinner plate scraped into the trash so I wouldn't see it. I have all your favorite snacks and drinks in the house since your return and I haven't had to restock a single thing."

Serafia snatched the towel from the housekeeper's hands, the past anxiety of being caught in the act rushing back to her. "That's none of your business. I pay you to cook my meals, not monitor them like my mother."

The hurt expression on the older woman's face made her feel instantly guilty for snapping at her. Esperanza was the sweetest woman she knew and she didn't deserve that kind of treatment. "I'm sorry. I shouldn't have said that. Forgive me." Serafia slipped down into the patio chair and buried her face in her towel.

"It's nothing. When I don't eat, I get grumpy, too," Esperanza offered with a small smile. She was a plump older woman with a perpetually pleasant disposition. Probably because she got to eat and wasn't eternally stressing out about how she looked. "But I worry about you, señorita, and so do your parents."

Serafia's head snapped up. "They've called?"

"*Sí*, but you were out walking on the beach. They asked me not to tell you. They seemed very interested in your eating habits, which is why I noticed the change. They said if you started visibly losing weight, I should call them straightaway."

Great. Her parents were having her own employee spy on her. They must really be concerned. Serafia sighed and sat back in her chair. They probably were right to be. In the last few days since returning from Alma, she'd already lost five pounds that she shouldn't have. She was at the low end of the range her doctors had provided her. If she got back into the red zone, she risked another round of inpatient treatment, and she didn't want to do that.

Damn it.

"Thank you for caring about me, Esperanza." Serafia eyed the tray of food she brought her. There was a large green salad with diced chicken, a platter with a hard-boiled egg, slices of cheese and bread and a carafe of vinaigrette. Ever hopeful, Esperanza had even included two of her famous cinnamon-sugar cookies. All in all, it was a healthy, balanced lunch with plenty of vegetables, proteins and whole grains. The kind Serafia asked her to make most days.

And yet she had a hard time stopping her brain from mentally obsessing over how many calories were sitting there. If she only ate the greens and the chicken with no dressing, it wouldn't be too bad. Maybe one piece of cheese, but definitely no bread. They were the same compulsive thoughts that she'd once allowed to take over her life. She'd battled this demon for a long time. A part of her had hoped that she'd beaten it for good, but one emotional blow had sent her spiraling back into her old bad habits.

Habits that had almost killed her.

"It looks wonderful," she said. "I promise to eat every bite. Are there any more cookies?"

"There are!" Esperanza said, her face brightening.

"I'll take some of those this afternoon after my siesta."

"Muy bien!" Esperanza shuffled back into the house, leaving Serafia alone on the patio.

She knew she should change out of her wet workout clothes, but she didn't care. She knew that she needed to eat. Now. Voices in her head be damned.

She started with one of the cookies for good measure. It dropped into her empty stomach like lead, reminding her to take it slow. Her doctors had warned her about starving herself, then binging. That was another, all new, dangerous path she was determined not to take.

Nibbling on the cheese and bread, she started to feel better. She knew that her body paid a high toll for her anorexia. As she was driven to exercise and ignore all the food she could, it made her feel terrible. Even this small amount of food made the difference. Picking up her fork and pouring some of the vinaigrette over the salad, she speared a bite and chewed it thoughtfully.

All this was in marked contrast to the way she'd felt in Alma. For some reason, her past worries had slipped away as she focused on preparing Gabriel to be king. Perhaps it was because he thought she was so beautiful, even with the extra pounds she resented. He worshipped every inch of her body in bed, never once stopping to criticize or comment on her flaws. That made her feel beautiful. When they ate together, it was a fun, enjoyable experience. She was too distracted by the good food and even better company to worry about the calories. There were a few days in Alma where she'd even forgotten to exercise. Before that, she hadn't missed a day of exercise in years. When she was with Gabriel, she'd been able to stop fighting with her disease and simply *live*.

She had been doing so well, and the minute it was yanked away from her, the negative thoughts came rushing back in. She couldn't do this. If there was one thing she'd learned in the years since her heart attack, it was that she loved herself too much to keep hurting herself.

Reaching for a slice of bread with cheese, she took a large bite, then another, and another, until her lunch was very nearly gone.

She couldn't allow loving Gabriel to undo all the progress she'd made.

The report on Gabriel's lap told him what he already knew in his heart, but somehow, seeing the words in black-and-white made him feel that much more like the ass he was.

Hector had done as he'd asked. His people in the press office had reached out to the author of the scathing article on the Espinas. It hadn't taken much pressure for him to reveal that he'd been approached by Feli-

cia Gomez. He admitted that while the historical por-
tions of the article were researched and fact-checked,
the insinuations of Serafia's nefarious intentions were
purely speculation based on Felicia's suggestions. It
didn't mean that her family didn't help overthrow the
Montoros, but in the end, that really didn't matter anymore. All that mattered was that Serafia was innocent
of all those charges.

He knew it. He knew it when he'd read the article
the first time and he knew it when he'd thrown accusations at Serafia and watched her heart break right
before his eyes. He'd been humiliated. Angry. He'd
lashed out at her because he'd allowed his own fears
to rule his life and publically embarrass him. It was
easier to blame her in the moment than face the fact
that he'd done this to himself.

Gabriel felt awful about the whole thing. Serafia had
been the only person in his life he thought he could
trust, and yet he'd turned around and abused her trust
of him at the first provocation. It made him feel sick.

He needed to do something to fix this. Right now.

Looking up from his report, he spied Luca walking
down the hallway past his office. "Luca, can you find
out if the Montoro jet is still in Alına?"

Luca nodded and disappeared down the hallway.

Gabriel took a deep breath and resolved himself to
his sudden decision. He didn't entirely have his plan
together, but he knew he needed to get out of Alma to
make this happen. That meant getting on a plane. Serafia had returned to Barcelona. He was certain she
wouldn't answer his calls if he tried, and anyway, he
knew in his heart that they needed to have a conversation in person. The only catch would be whether or

not the jet was here. His father had sent for Bella to come to Alma. Gabriel wasn't sure what day that was happening, but if the jet was with her in Miami, he'd have to find another way to get to Serafia. Could a prince fly coach?

He didn't care if he was crammed in a middle seat at the back of the plane, he had to get to her. Saying he was sorry wasn't enough. He needed to follow that up with how he felt about her. It had taken losing her for him to get in touch with how he truly felt. There was nothing quite like waking up and realizing he was in love and he'd just ruined everything.

But maybe, just maybe, apologizing and confessing his love for her would be enough for Serafia to forgive his snap judgments.

Luca appeared in the doorway, an odd expression on his face.

"Where's the jet?" Gabriel asked.

"It's still at the airport in Del Sol, Your Grace."

He breathed a sigh of relief. "Good. Tell them I want to go to Barcelona as soon as possible. I need a car to meet me at the airport and I need someone to track down Serafia's home address. I have no idea where she lives."

"Yes, Your Grace. I will see to all that. But first, you have…a visitor."

Gabriel could feel his own face taking on Luca's pinched, confused expression. "A visitor?" Could people just stroll up to the royal beach compound and knock on the door to join him for tea?

"Yes. It's an old woman from Del Sol. She told the guards at the gate that she took a taxi out here to speak with you. She said it's very important."

Gabriel was certain that everything people wanted to say to the king was very important, but he was at a loss. He wanted to pack his bag and be in Barcelona before dinnertime. Certainly this could wait…

"She says it's about Serafia."

Gabriel stiffened. That changed everything. "Have her escorted into the parlor. Tell Marta to bring some tea and those almond cookies if we have any left. That will give us some time to make the arrangements before I leave."

Luca nodded and went off to fulfill his wishes. Gabriel returned to his closet to pick a suit coat. He'd been dressing himself for the last few days and if he was honest with himself, he wasn't doing a very good job. He knew that Serafia would want him to wear a jacket to greet a guest, especially an elderly one with more conservative ideas about the monarchy. He selected a black suit coat that went with the gray shirt he was already wearing. He knew he should add a tie, but he just couldn't do it. He was in his own home; certainly he could get away with being a little more casual there.

By the time he reached the parlor, all his instructions had been executed beautifully. Marta had placed a tray of lovely treats on the coffee table and was pouring two cups of tea. Seated on the couch was a tiny woman. Perhaps the smallest he'd ever seen, withered and hunched over with age. She was at least eighty, the life shriveling out of her just as the sun had seemed to tan her skin to near leather. Her hair was silver and pulled back into a neat bun. She looked like everyone's *abuela*.

"Presenting His Majesty, Prince Gabriel!" one of

the guards lining the wall announced as he entered the room.

The old woman reached for her cane to stand and curtsey properly, but Gabriel couldn't bear for her to go to that much trouble just for him. "Please, stay seated," he insisted.

The woman relaxed back into her seat with a look of relief on her face. "*Gracias*, Don Gabriel."

He sat down opposite her, offering the woman sugar or cream for her tea. "What can I do for you, señora?"

She took a sip of tea, and then set it down on the china dish with a shaky hand. "Thank you for taking the time to see me today. I know you are very busy. My name is Conchita Ortega. In 1946 when the coup happened, I was just fifteen years old and working as a servant in the Espina household. I have seen what was published in the papers over the last week or so, and now I have heard that Señorita Espina has left Alma."

"Señorita Espina was only working for me for a few weeks. She was always supposed to return home."

The older woman narrowed her gaze at him. "I understand, Your Grace, but I also understand and know *amor* when I see it. I know in my heart you were a couple in love and those vicious lies have ruined it. I had to speak up so you would know the truth."

Gabriel listened carefully, his interest in what the woman had to say growing with each additional word she spoke. Even though he didn't hold the past of her family against Serafia, it would help to know the truth of what really had happened back then. This woman might be one of the only people left alive who knew the whole story. "Please," he replied. "I'd love for you to tell me what you know."

She nodded and relaxed back in her seat with a cookie in her hand. She took a bite and chewed slowly, torturing Gabriel by delaying her story. "By the time everything fell apart," she began, "the hurt feelings about the broken engagement between Rafael the First and Rosa Espina were nearly a decade in the past. Rafael had married Anna Maria, Rosa had married another fine gentleman and the young Prince Rafael the Second, your grandfather, was seven years old. All had turned out for the best. The Espina family would not, and did not, conspire against the Montoros during the coup. In fact, they were your family's closest confidantes."

"How do you know?"

"At fifteen, I was like a little mouse, moving quiet and unseen through the house. I was privy to many discussions with no one giving any thought to my presence. I was serving tea when Queen Anna Maria came to the Espina Estate in secret. She'd come to ask your family to help them. Alma had weathered the Second World War, but they feared the worst was yet to come for them. Tantaberra was growing in power, staging large demonstrations and causing unrest all over Alma. The royal family was worried that they were losing hold of the country.

"The queen asked the Espinas to help them protect Alma's historical treasures by smuggling them out of the country before things got worse. The Montoros had to stay as long as they could to appear strong against their opposition, but they feared that when they did leave, they'd have to leave everything behind. The queen couldn't bear for such important things to be lost, so they arranged for the Espinas to move to Swit-

zerland and take the country's most important historical artifacts with them."

Serafia had mentioned that her family lived in Switzerland before moving to Spain. The article had said
the family fled before the coup, which was interpreted
as suspicious at the time. "What kind of things?" he
asked.

"The royal jewels and stores of gold, an oil portrait
of the first king of Alma, handwritten historical re-
cords of the royal family...everything that would be
considered irreplaceable."

"Were they successful in smuggling everything out?"
he asked.

"Yes. I helped load the ship myself. They sailed
from Alma with all of their things and a secret cargo of
Alman treasure. They traveled down the Rhine River
to Switzerland, arriving just weeks before everything
fell apart. Your family was not so lucky. They fled to
America with nothing, leaving everything else behind
for Tantaberra to claim as his own."

"What about you?"

"I had the option to go with the Espinas, but I
couldn't leave my family behind. I stayed. But I'm
glad I did so I could be here to tell you the truth. The
Espinas are not traitors. They're heroes, but no one
knows the truth."

"Why doesn't anyone know about this? Not even
my father has mentioned it."

"It is likely he does not know. The queen orchestrated everything and may not have told anyone in
the family so they could not be tortured for the information. It was a closely guarded secret and everyone
was instructed not to speak of it while the Tantaber-

ras were still in power. At the time, they had ties with
Franco in Spain and they feared that if anyone knew
the truth, their network would seek out the Espinas and
retaliate. They were instructed not to breathe a word
to anyone until the royal family was restored officially
to the throne again."

"Do you think the family still has the treasures after
all these years?"

"I have no doubt of it. I ask you to reach out to Señor
Espina in Madrid. He can tell you the truth. After all
these years, I'm sure he will be happy to return the
royal treasure to where it belongs after the coronation."

Gabriel was stunned by the entire conversation. Apparently this information had not been passed down
through the generations the way it should've been. But
as they finished their tea, a plan started to form in his
mind. He arranged for a car to take Señora Ortega
home and finalized the preparations for his flight. Instead of going to Barcelona, he decided a visit to Madrid to see Serafia's father was in order. If her family
had his country's treasures, they needed to be restored
to the people. Once he knew for certain the story was
true, he intended for the whole country to know the
truth about the Espinas. They deserved a parade in
their honor, and all the vicious rumors to be put to bed
once and for all.

And while he was there...he wanted to ask Señor
Espina for his daughter's hand in marriage.

Twelve

It was a quick flight to Madrid, but still too long in Gabriel's eyes. The car that picked him up at the airport rushed him through the streets of the city to the Espina residence. Now all he had to do was face Serafia's father and accept his punishment for hurting her.

Arturo Espina opened the front door and glared at Gabriel. He had been expecting a less than warm reception. Serafia had no doubt told her family how horribly he'd treated her. He was on a journey to make amends not only with Serafia, but also with her parents. If what Señora Ortega said was true, things needed to be made right with the Espinas. By keeping Queen Anna Maria's secret so diligently, they'd lived in the shadow of suspicion and rumors for too long. And Gabriel had a long path to redemption where Serafia was concerned. The pain would start here, now, but it had to start somewhere.

"Señor Espina," he said, hoping his smile didn't give away how nervous he was. "Hello."

The older man glanced over Gabriel's shoulder at the royal guard hovering nearby. The irritation suddenly faded and was replaced with a respectful bow. "Prince Gabriel. To what do we owe the honor of your presence?"

"Please," Gabriel said. "You bandaged my skinned knee once. Let's drop the formalities. I'm not here as prince. I'm here about Serafia."

Arturo nodded and took a step back to allow him inside. The guard remained outside the door at Gabriel's request. Arturo led him through the large mansion to an inner courtyard landscaped with trees and a sparkling tile fountain. "Please, have a seat," he said. "May I offer you a drink? Something to eat?"

Gabriel shook his head. "No, thank you."

"I'm surprised to see you here, Gabriel. Serafia hasn't mentioned what happened in Alma, but considering how she rushed home, I'm assuming things did not end well. What I've read in the Alma newspapers has been disheartening, to say the least."

"I know, and what I'm really here to do is apologize. And maybe, if my apology is accepted, I'd like some information only you can give me."

Arturo sat down across from him and waited for the questions to come.

"First, I want to apologize for the way I've handled all this. Regardless of the truth, I behaved poorly, lashing out at Serafia, and I'm ashamed of that. Your family, and specifically your daughter, never gave me any reason to doubt your loyalty."

"You are not the first to be suspicious of our family over the years."

"I had never heard any of those stories before," Gabriel explained. "The papers have had some terrible things to say about your family. I grew up in America in a household that very rarely, if ever, discussed Alma and what happened. Our families have always been friends, so I was blindsided by those stories. I feel like a fool, but I allowed those articles to taint my feelings for your family and for your daughter. I shouldn't have let that happen, but I was upset with myself and took it out on her."

"I read about what happened at the oil rig. Am I wrong in thinking that was related to your abduction?"

Gabriel looked Arturo in the eye. "It was. I wasn't sure how many people knew about it. My father wanted to keep it all pretty quiet."

"He called me while it was happening and asked for advice. Rafael was torn up about the whole thing and how it was taking so long to bring you home. Rafael was so frustrated—he felt helpless for the first time in his life. When you showed back up in Miami, I think he was embarrassed about how it was all handled and never wanted to talk about it again. He thought you would blame him for everything, so he wanted to forget about it all."

"I didn't blame him," Gabriel said. "But I've always felt like I was a disappointment to him, somehow. I tried to hide my claustrophobia because I thought he'd see it as another weakness."

"No one—your father included—would hold something like that against you. You went through a terrible experience. He probably thought that putting it behind you would help. We did that with Serafia and I've never been certain it was the right course. But as parents, you do what you can to protect your children."

Gabriel sighed. He'd come here for answers about the Espina family and ended up with more than he'd expected. "Thank you for telling me that. I've never really been able to get past what happened. I don't do well in small spaces since my kidnapping, and I blamed Serafia for not warning me ahead of time about what was in store on the oil rig. It wasn't her fault. I ruined everything with her, and then I find out that all those rumors that poisoned my mind weren't even true."

"Do you mean the rumors about the Espinas helping Tantaberra depose your family?" Arturo asked. His tone was flat, as though he'd had to hear these slanderous charges his whole life.

"Yes. An old woman who worked for your family back then came to the house today and explained the truth about how the Espinas safeguarded the royal treasure. At least, I hope it's the truth."

Arturo nodded. "We've had to keep quiet about our family's role in all this for decades, ignoring the rumors so we didn't risk anyone finding out the truth. I don't think any of them believed the dictatorship would last as long as it has. We feared that the Tantaberras would come after us if they knew what we were hiding, or worse, come after your family if they had any knowledge of it. Even after all this time, we had to deliberately keep it from you and others in your family."

"I can't imagine that burden."

"I think it was worth it. I heard that Tantaberra was furious when he took the palace and all the gold and jewels he'd coveted were gone."

Gabriel had never given much thought to his great-grandmother, Anna Maria, but in that moment, he admired her fire. He wished he could've seen the dictator's face when he realized that the Montoros had outsmarted him. "That means your family still has it?"

Arturo stood. "Wait here. I'll be right back." He disappeared down a hallway and returned a few minutes later with something in his hand. When he sat down again, he placed two small items on the table. One, a gold coin, and the other, a diamond and ruby ring. "This is just a small part of what my family has protected for seventy years."

Gabriel reached out and picked up the coin. It was a coin minted in Alma in the 1800s. "You keep it here?"

"No. I've always kept a few tiny items in my safe for a moment like this, but the rest is in a vault in Switzerland. We were to keep it until the coronation took place, to ensure it was official, and then it can all be restored to the palace. I've always hoped to see this day happen. It's been a weight on my shoulders since my father told me the truth."

Returning the coin, Gabriel examined the ruby ring and felt a touch of sadness come over him. It was so beautiful, with a dark red oval ruby that had to be nearly four carats. It was surrounded by a ring of tiny diamonds and flanked on each side by a pear-shaped diamond. The setting was a mix of platinum and gold filigree. It was more beautiful than any ring had a right to be. He was incredibly grateful the Espinas had hidden it away from the Tantaberras, yet sad that no one had enjoyed the ring for all these years. This ring was meant to be on the hand of a queen—a woman like Serafia.

"I've betrayed the family that I should've trusted above all others. I'm so sorry. I can't apologize enough. I want to see to it that the truth gets out. When the treasure is restored, I want it put on display in Alma's national museum so that everyone will know how the Espinas safeguarded it all these years, and put an end to the rumors once and for all."

"That would be wonderful," Arturo said. "I would like to move back to Alma one day. My father was born there. I grew up in Switzerland, but I've always dreamed of going back to where my people belonged."

Looking down at the ring, Gabriel was reminded of the other reason he'd come here today. The truth was nice, but even if the old woman's story was just a fabrication, his first priority was getting Serafia to forgive—and marry—him. He put the ring back on the table and looked at Arturo.

"I also came here today because I want Serafia in my life," he said. "I...I love her. I want her to be my queen. Do you think she'll ever be able to forgive me for the way I've treated her?"

Arturo sat back in his seat and looked at him with a serious expression. "I don't know. She's taken this very hard. Her mother and I have been worried about her."

Gabriel's gaze met his. "Worried?"

"Did she tell you about her illness?" Arturo asked.

"The anorexia? Yes, but she said that was behind her."

"We'd hoped so," Arturo explained, "but her doctors had warned us that patients are never fully cured of this disease. Stress, especially emotional upheaval, can send her spiraling back into her bad habits. Her housekeeper has told us that she is hardly eating. That she does nothing but exercise and sleep since she returned to Barcelona. There have been a few times where she's fallen into this slump before, but she's righted herself before it went too far. I'm hoping that you can help pull her out of it."

Gabriel sensed the worry and fear in Arturo's voice and felt even more miserable than he had before. He knew how much Serafia struggled with her image and how hard she'd worked to overcome her illness. She'd done so well when they were together that he never would've known about the anorexia if she hadn't told him the truth. If he'd sent her into such an emotional state that she fell prey to it again—if she got hurt because of it—he'd never forgive himself.

"I'm flying directly to Barcelona from here. I'll do everything I can to make things right, I promise. Even if she doesn't want me, even if she won't forgive me, I won't leave until I'm certain she's safe."

Arturo watched him as he spoke, and then nodded. "You said earlier that you wanted my daughter to be your queen. You're serious about this?"

Gabriel swallowed hard. "Yes, sir. With your permission, I'd like to ask Serafia to be my wife. I know that under the circumstances, the public role will not be an easy one for her, but I love her too much to let her out of my life. I don't think I could choose a better woman to help me make Alma that great country it once was."

Arturo nodded. "You are good for her, I know it. I've watched you two on the news together. She looks happier with you than she has been in years. You make sure she stays that way and you have my blessing."

"Yes. Of course. I only want Serafia to be happy. Thank you, Señor Espina."

Serafia's father finally smiled for the first time since Gabriel had arrived, and he felt a weight lifted from his chest.

"Do you have a ring for her?" the older man asked.

Gabriel was embarrassed to admit that he didn't. "I rushed here to see you without thinking all of it through. I don't have anything for her yet."

Arturo reached out and picked up the ruby ring from the table. "This is the wedding ring of Rafael the First's mother, Queen Josefina. If you truly love my daughter and want her to be queen, this is the ring you should give her."

Gabriel took the ring from the man who might soon be his father-in-law and shook his hand. "Thank you, sir. It's perfect."

"Good job," Esperanza said as she took away Serafia's mostly empty dinner plate.

Serafia chuckled. "Does this mean I get the tiramisu you promised me?"

"Of course."

Esperanza disappeared inside, leaving her alone on her patio, watching the sun set. It seemed like only yesterday that she was doing the same with Gabriel, only overlooking the Atlantic instead of the Mediterranean. The moment had been romantic and full of promise.

And now here she was, alone. What a difference a few days could make.

But she wasn't going to dwell on it. She'd had her moment to mope, and now it was time for her to figure out what she wanted to do with her life. Being with Gabriel had helped her realize that she was hiding here in Barcelona. She got out, she worked, but she hadn't really allowed herself to have the full life she deserved. That was over. She was determined that from this point forward, she was going to live her life to the fullest.

"Señorita?" Esperanza was at the door again.

"Yes?" Serafia said as she turned and froze in place. Standing tall behind her tiny housekeeper was Gabriel. He was looking incredibly handsome in a gray shirt and a black suit coat. Without a tie, of course.

She felt her heart skip a beat in her chest when she saw him. Every nerve awakened as her body realized he was so close. She tightened her hands around the arms of her chair to fight her unwanted reaction to him. He was a bastard. He said terrible things to her. She absolutely should not react to him like this. And yet she couldn't help it. He might be a bastard, but she still loved him. She still hadn't managed to convince her heart differently.

Taking a deep breath, she wished away her attraction and tried to focus on more important things, like what had brought him all the way to her doorstep.

Esperanza looked a little stunned. Serafia imagined that opening the door and finding a prince standing there was not exactly what the older woman had anticipated when the bell rang. "Prince Gabriel is here to see you. He would not wait outside."

"I didn't want to give you the chance to turn me away," he said, with a sheepish smile that seemed to acknowledge he was the guilty party.

"Smart move," Serafia noted in a sharp tone. He *was* the guilty party and she wanted to make sure he got his punishment. "Esperanza, could you please bring out a bottle of merlot and two glasses, please?" She wasn't sure how this conversation was going to go, but drinking certainly wouldn't hurt matters. At the very least it would help her relax. She was drawn tight as a drum.

Esperanza disappeared into the house and Gabriel joined Serafia outside. He took a seat in the chair beside her and looked out at the sea as she had been doing earlier.

"You have a beautiful home," he said.

"Thank you."

He turned back to look at her, his concerned gaze taking in every inch of her, but not in the hungry way she was used to. He seemed to be cataloguing her somehow. "How are you?" he asked.

Not once in the weeks they'd spent together had he asked her that question. Now she knew it was probably her parents' doing. They'd started calling each day, never directly asking if she was eating, but hinting around the subject, not knowing Esperanza had already ratted them out. She frowned at him. "Did my family send you down here to check on me?"

"What?" He looked startled. "No. I came here on my own, but I made a stop in Madrid on the way. Your father mentioned they were concerned about you."

"They usually are," she said. "That's why I opted to move to Barcelona and give myself some breathing room. They're very overprotective of me."

"They just want to make sure you're happy and healthy. As do I."

"Is that why you've come?" she snapped. "To make sure you didn't break my heart too badly?"

"No," he said with a grave seriousness in his voice. "I came to apologize."

"It's not necessary," she said.

"Yes, it is. I lashed out at you and it wasn't your fault. I let my own fears get the best of me, then used the most convenient excuse I could find to push you away. It was the dumbest thing I've ever done, and that's saying a lot after the antics I've gotten into the last few years. I've relived that moment in my head over and over, wishing I'd handled everything differently. I was a fool and it cost me the woman I love."

Serafia gasped at his words, but before she could respond, Esperanza returned with the wine. The interruption allowed Serafia a minute to think about his words and consider what her response should be. He loved her. She wanted to tell him that she loved him, too, but she was wary of giving away too much. He'd hurt her, abused her trust. She wasn't just going to take him back because he decided he was in love and that made everything better.

When Esperanza went back into the house, he picked up where he'd left off. "I never believed those stories about your family, and now that I know the truth, I'm going to see to it that those rumors are put to bed for good. The Espinas are heroes and I want everyone to know it."

"Heroes?" Serafia frowned. What was he talking about?

"Your family protected the royal treasure from the Tantaberras. That's why they left before the coup. Your father and I are going to work to have the treasure restored and put on display after the coronation. Without your family's help, the Tantaberras would've used up and destroyed our country's history."

Serafia had never heard any of this before, but she didn't doubt the truth of it. Her father had made more than a few mysterious trips to Switzerland over the years. At the same time, the truth didn't make everything okay, either. "So now that you know I don't come from a line of traitors, you've decided you can love me?"

"No. Stop jumping to these horrible conclusions. I'm happy I found out the truth, but no, that's got nothing to do with why I'm here. I had one foot out the door to come see you when all this fell into my lap. But in the end, none of it has to do with us. That's all in the past. What I'm interested in is you and me and the future."

Serafia's breath caught in her throat. She reached a shaky hand out for her wine, hoping it would steady her, but all she could do was hold the glass as he continued to speak.

"I love you, Serafia, with all my heart and all my soul. I am a fool and I don't deserve your love in return, but if someday I could earn it back, I would be the happiest man in the world." Gabriel reached out and took her hand and she was too stunned to pull away.

"I don't just love you. I don't just want you to come back to Alma. I went to Madrid because I wanted to ask your father for his blessing to marry you. I want you to be my queen."

Gabriel slipped out of his chair and onto one knee. Serafia sat stunned as she watched him reach into his inner breast pocket. She saw a momentary flash of gold and realized he was wearing the pocket watch she gave him, but then he pulled out a small ring box and her thoughts completely disintegrated into incoherence.

"I don't know if I'm the right man to be king. But fate has put the crown in my hands and because of you, I feel like I'm closer than I could ever be to the kind of man my people deserve. With you by my side as queen, all my doubts are gone. We can restore Alma to its former glory together. I don't think Alma could ask for a better queen and I couldn't ask for a smarter, more beautiful, graceful and caring bride. Would you do me the honor of being my wife?"

Gabriel opened the box and stunned her with an amazing bloodred ruby with diamonds. It was unlike any ring she'd ever seen before. It was the kind of ring that was fit for royalty.

"This ring belonged to my great-great-grandmother, Queen Josefina. It was her wedding ring and part of the treasure entrusted to your family to protect. Your father returned it to me today. He told me that it belonged on your finger and I quite agree."

Serafia let him slip the ring onto her finger. She couldn't take her eyes off it and couldn't stop thinking about everything it represented. He loved her. He wanted to marry her. He wanted her to be his queen. In that moment, all her doubts and hesitations about being in the spotlight disappeared. Before, she had been there alone. If Gabriel was by her side, it would okay. She couldn't believe how quickly everything in her life had changed.

"Serafia?"

She tore her gaze away from the ring to look at Gabriel. He looked a little confused and a little anxious as he watched her. "Yes?"

"I, uh, asked you a question. Would you like to answer it so I can stop freaking out?"

Serafia smiled, feeling quite silly for missing the critical step in the proposal process. "Yes, Gabriel, I will marry you."

He grinned wide, opening his arms to catch her just as she propelled herself at him. Her lips met his with an enthusiasm she couldn't contain. Just an hour ago, she thought she might never be in his arms again. And here she was…his fiancée. There was a sudden lightness in her heart and she felt as though she had to cling to Gabriel so she wouldn't float away.

"I love you, Serafia," he whispered against her lips.

"I love you, too, Gabriel," she answered, happy to finally say those words out loud.

Gabriel stood up, pulling her up with him. "The coronation is over a month away. I don't want to wait that long to marry you."

She knew exactly how he felt. She would happily elope if she thought they would get away with it. Unfortunately the people of Alma would want their royal wedding. As would her mother. There was no avoiding that. "How quickly do you think we can pull off a wedding?"

"Well," Gabriel said thoughtfully, "my brother's wedding is already in the works. He abdicated, but he's still prince, so father insisted he and Emily have their ceremony in Alma. That's only a few weeks away. What would you say to a double wedding?"

"A double wedding?"

"Why not? They've already got the plans in place. All the same people will be coming. Why can't we have one giant celebration and both marry at the same time?"

Serafia looked at her handsome fiancé thoughtfully. He was not a woman. He didn't understand what kinds of expectations went into a wedding. Serafia might not mind a double wedding, but Emily certainly might.

"How about this…?" she proposed. "You talk to Rafe and Emily about it. If they are both fine with it, then I'm okay with it, too."

Gabriel grinned wide. "I'm sure they will be, but I'll check. And then you'll be Mrs. Gabriel Montoro, soon to be *Su Majestad la Reina Serafia de Alma*. Are you ready for that?"

Serafia wrapped her arms around his neck and nodded. "I think so, although I'm sure that being queen will be the easy part."

Gabriel arched one brow curiously at her. "What's going to be the hard part?"

She climbed to her bare toes and planted a kiss on his full lips. "Keeping the king out of trouble."

* * * * *